"Are the *kinder*

Uncomfortable with his small intrusion into her family, Carolyn said, "Kevin had a bad dream and woke us up."

"Because of the rain?"

"It's possible."

"Rebuilding a building is easy. Rebuilding one's sense of security isn't."

"That sounds like the voice of experience."

Michael sighed. "My parents died when I was young, and both my twin brother and I had to learn not to expect something horrible was going to happen without warning."

"I'm sorry. I should have asked more about you and the other volunteers. I've been wrapped up in my own tragedy."

"At times like this, nobody expects you to be thinking of anything but getting a roof over your *kinder*'s heads."

He didn't reach out to touch her, but she was aware of every inch of him so close to her. His quiet strength had awed her from the beginning. As she'd come to know him better, his fundamental decency had impressed her more. He was a man she believed she could trust.

She shoved that thought aside. Trusting any man would be the worst thing she could do.

Jo Ann Brown has always loved stories with happily-ever-after endings. A former military officer, she is thrilled to have the chance to write stories about people falling in love. She is also a photographer and travels with her husband of more than thirty years to places where she can snap pictures. They have three children and live in Florida. Drop her a note at joannbrownbooks.com.

With over seventy books published and millions in print, **Lenora Worth** writes award-winning romance and romantic suspense. Three of her books finaled in the ACFW Carol Awards, and her Love Inspired Suspense novel *Body of Evidence* became a *New York Times* bestseller. Her novella in *Mistletoe Kisses* made her a *USA TODAY* bestselling author. Lenora goes on adventures with her retired husband, Don, and enjoys reading, baking and shopping…especially shoe shopping.

JO ANN BROWN

An Amish Christmas Promise

&

New York Times Bestselling Author

LENORA WORTH

Amish Christmas Hideaway

LOVE INSPIRED
INSPIRATIONAL ROMANCE

LOVE INSPIRED®
INSPIRATIONAL ROMANCE

Recycling programs
for this product may
not exist in your area.

ISBN-13: 978-1-335-21900-8

An Amish Christmas Promise and Amish Christmas Hideaway

Copyright © 2020 by Harlequin Books S.A.

An Amish Christmas Promise
First published in 2019. This edition published in 2020.
Copyright © 2019 by Jo Ann Ferguson

Amish Christmas Hideaway
First published in 2019. This edition published in 2020.
Copyright © 2019 by Lenora H. Nazworth

This edition published by arrangement with Harlequin Books S.A.

For questions and comments about the quality of this book,
please contact us at CustomerService@Harlequin.com.

Harlequin Enterprises ULC
22 Adelaide St. West, 40th Floor
Toronto, Ontario M5H 4E3, Canada
www.Harlequin.com

Printed in U.S.A.

CONTENTS

AN AMISH
CHRISTMAS PROMISE

Jo Ann Brown

For Amanda,
who keeps us looking good

Bear ye one another's burdens,
and so fulfil the law of Christ.
For if a man think himself to be something,
when he is nothing, he deceiveth himself.
But let every man prove his own work,
and then shall he have rejoicing in himself alone,
and not in another.
For every man shall bear his own burden.
—*Galatians* 6:2–5

Chapter One

Evergreen Corners, Vermont

The bus slowed with a rumble of its diesel engine.

Michael Miller opened his eyes. A crick in his neck warned him that he'd fallen asleep in a weird position. The last time he'd ridden a bus was when he caught one to the train station in Lancaster, Pennsylvania. Then he'd traveled with his twin brother and Gabriel's *bopplin* to their new farm in Harmony Creek Hollow in northern New York.

Now he was on a bus on a late October day because he needed time away, time with peace and quiet, to figure out the answer to one vital question: Should he remain in their Amish community, or was the future he wanted beyond a plain life?

Today Michael was in Vermont, on his way to Evergreen Corners. The small village was at the epicenter of powerful flash floods that had accompanied Hurricane Kevin when the massive storm stalled over the eastern slopes of the Green Mountains last week.

The bus hit another pothole in the dirt on what once

had been a paved road. He was shocked to discover the other lane had been washed away. The road, a major north–south conduit in the state, was barely wider than the bus's wheels. He didn't see any cars anywhere, just a couple of trucks with what looked like a town seal on their doors. They were parked near a building where all the windows and doors were missing.

His stomach tightened. Had those vehicles been commandeered as ambulances? Were the people working there looking for victims?

The stories coming out of Vermont had warned that the situation was dismal. Whole sections of towns like Evergreen Corners had been washed away by torrents surging along what had been babbling brooks. People left with no place to live, all their possessions gone or covered with thick mud. Trees torn from the banks. Rocks—both giant boulders and tons of gravel—swept beneath bridges and damming the streams, forcing the water even higher.

Michael could see the road—or what there was left of it—followed a twisting stream between two steep mountains. The job of rebuilding was going to be bigger than he'd imagined when he'd stepped forward to offer his skills as a carpenter.

How much could he and the other fifteen volunteers on the bus do in the next three months? Where did they begin?

And what had made him think he'd find a chance to think about the future *here*?

God, I trust You know where I should be. Help me see.

The bus jerked to a stop, and the driver opened the door. "Here we are!"

A pungent odor oozed into the bus. It was a disgusting mix of mud and gasoline and the fuel oil that had been washed out of household storage tanks. Michael gasped, choking on the reek.

When a mask was held out to him, he took it from his friend, Benjamin Kuhns, who was sitting beside him, but didn't put it on. Like Michael, Benjamin had volunteered when a representative of Amish Helping Hands had come two days ago to Harmony Creek Hollow. Amish Helping Hands worked with other plain organizations to help after natural disasters. Benjamin announcing that he wanted to come, too, had been a surprise, because he'd been focused for the past year on working with his older brother, Menno, in getting their sawmill running. Business had been growing well, and Michael wondered if Benjamin was seeking something to help him grasp onto his future, too.

"Watch where you step," shouted the bus driver before he went out.

Michael stood and grabbed his small bag off the shelf over his head, stuffing the mask into a pocket. He noticed a few people on the bus had donned theirs.

His larger bag, where he'd packed the tools he expected he'd need, was stored under the bus. Nobody spoke as they filed out, and he knew he wasn't the only person overwhelmed by the destruction.

As his feet touched the muddy ground, he heard, "Look out!"

He wasn't sure whether to duck, jump aside or climb back on the bus. Looking around, he saw a slender blonde barreling toward him, arms outstretched.

Squawking was the only warning he got before a small brown chicken ran into him, bounced backward, turned and kept weaving through the crowd of volunteers moving to get their luggage from beneath the bus. The chicken let out another terrified screech before vanishing through a forest of legs and duffels.

The woman halted before she ran into him, too. Putting out her hands, she stopped two *kinder* from colliding with him. The force of their forward motion drove her a step closer, and he dropped his bag to the ground and caught her by the shoulders before she tumbled over the toes of his weather-beaten work boots. He was astounded that though her dress was a plain style, the fabric was a bright pink-and-green plaid.

"Are you okay?" Michael asked.

She nodded and looked at him with earth-brown eyes that seemed the perfect complement to her pale hair. She was so short her head hardly reached his shoulder. Her features were delicate. Thanking him, she turned to the *kinder*.

He hadn't expected the simple act of gazing into her pretty eyes to hit him like the recoil of a mishandled nail gun. Was she plain, or dressed simply because she was cleaning up the mess left by the flood?

He glanced at the *kinder* who'd been chasing her and the chicken. The boy appeared to be around six or seven years old. He had light brown hair, freckles and blue-gray eyes. Along with jeans and sneakers, he wore a T-shirt stained with what looked like peanut butter and jelly. Beside him, and wearing almost identical clothing, though without the stains, the little girl had hair the same soft honey-blond as the woman's. Like the boy, she had freckles, but her eyes were dark. When she grinned at him, she revealed she'd lost her two front teeth.

He couldn't keep from smiling. The *kind* was adorable, and he could imagine how she'd be twisting boys' hearts around her finger in a few years.

Just as Adah Burcky had with every guy who'd glanced her way. What a *dummkopf* he'd been to think he was the sole recipient of her kisses and flirtatious glances! He could hear her laugh when she'd walked away with another man. There had been a hint of triumph in it, as if she took delight in keeping track of the hearts she broke...including his.

What had brought Adah to mind? He'd come to Evergreen Corners to decide what he wanted to do with his future, not to focus on the past. For too long, he'd been drifting, following his twin brother to their new home, a place where he wasn't sure he belonged. Was his life among the plain folk, or was the route God had mapped for him meant to take him somewhere else? He had three months to figure that out.

"She's getting away," the boy insisted in an ever-louder voice, breaking into Michael's thoughts. "We've got to catch her before she gets hit by a car."

"There aren't a lot of cars on the road," the woman replied, ruffling his hair in an attempt to calm him.

"But there are buses." The boy flung out a hand toward the one that had brought Michael to Evergreen Corners. "See?"

Michael wasn't the only one trying to stifle a grin as the woman said, "We'll pray she'll be fine, Kevin. Place her in God's hands and trust He knows what's best."

Though he thought the boy would protest, the *kind* nodded. "Like you placed us in God's hands when the brook rose."

She nodded, but her serene facade splintered for a

second. By the time she'd turned to Michael, it was again in place, and he wondered if he'd imagined the shadows in her eyes.

"I'm so sorry," she said. "We've been chasing Henrietta for the past fifteen minutes." She gave him a wry smile. "Not an original name for a chicken, but the kids chose our flock's names."

"She went that way." He pointed down the hill where a shallow brook rippled in the late-afternoon sunshine.

"She's headed toward our place, so maybe she'll turn up in what's left of our yard if she gets hungry enough." She wiped her forearm against her forehead and readjusted the black kerchief she wore over her honey-blond hair that was, he noticed for the first time, pulled into a tight bun at her nape.

"So your house is okay?" Michael asked.

She bit her lip before standing straighter. "No. Our house is gone."

He was shocked that anyone who'd lost their home could smile as she had. Could he have faced the situation with such aplomb and the *gut* spirits she did? That was a question he hoped he'd never have to answer.

Carolyn Wiebe knew she'd astounded the handsome dark-haired man who'd stepped off the bus. What had he expected her to do? Rage against the whims of nature? The storm that decimated everything she'd worked for during the past four years had been a mindless beast whose winds tore up the valley before sending water barreling down it. Be angry at God? How could she, when He'd spared their lives and everyone else's in Evergreen Corners? That hadn't been the situation in other towns, or so rumor whispered. No one could be sure of anything, but she'd heard of five deaths. People swept away as she and her children could have been. She'd made a promise to look after them forever, and she wasn't going to let a tempest change that.

Scanning the group from the bus, she dared to take a deep breath. She didn't see any sign of Leland Reber. There were other brown-haired men, but not the formerly plain man who'd married her late sister and had two youngsters with her. Though she hadn't seen his photo in over four years, she was sure she'd recognize him whether he dressed like her *Englisch* neighbors or in plain clothing. He had a square jaw with a cleft in his chin, which her sister Regina had found appealing…until the beatings started within weeks of their marriage.

For four years, Carolyn had managed to push Leland out of her mind while she focused on raising the children her sister had entrusted to her, children who called her Mommy. Then a neighbor had told her about hearing how Carolyn and the kids had been shown on national television news when reporters had appeared the day after the flood. If so, Leland, who'd embraced an *Englisch* life, most especially television and alcohol, could have learned where they were.

Carolyn's first thought had been to flee as they had when she'd left her beloved plain community in Indiana. She realized doing that was impossible when the roads were open only to authorized vehicles. Her car had been swept away in the flood and hadn't been found so she couldn't take Kevin and Rose Anne anywhere.

Her one consolation was Leland should have as much trouble getting to Evergreen Corners. The one way he could gain entry was to pretend to volunteer and get a ride with one of the disaster services. So she asked about vehicles bringing volunteers into Evergreen Corners, and she'd devised an excuse to be nearby when the newcomers had stepped off the bus. Today, Henrietta had provided her with one. She couldn't chance Leland sneaking into town and finding her and his son and daughter.

"Do you know where we're supposed to go, Mrs.—?" asked the man who'd been accosted by Henrietta.

He wasn't classically handsome. His straight nose was prominent, but his other features, especially his kind eyes, drew her attention away from it. Sharp cheekbones and a firm jaw suggested he wasn't someone to dismiss. In the sunlight that had shone every day after the hurricane, red accents glistened in the brown hair beneath his straw hat. The breadth of the black strap on his hat as well as his accent told her that he must be from Pennsylvania.

She warned herself to be cautious. Though Leland wasn't plain, he had many friends who were. Could he have sent one to look for her?

Stop being paranoid, she scolded herself. She wasn't worried for herself, but for her niece and nephew.

"I'm Carolyn Wiebe." She spoke the name without hesitation. She'd given it to herself after leaving Indiana, and she didn't correct his assumption she was married. Even in her thoughts, she sometimes forgot her real name was Cora Hilty. She was glad neither of the children recalled the surname they'd been given at birth. "This is Rose Anne, and that is Kevin."

"Kevin? Like Hurricane Kevin?"

"Appropriate for a five-year-old boy, don't you think?" She laughed at the surprise on the man's face.

She didn't want to tell him that, with her emotions so raw, she had two choices: laugh or cry. During the day, she laughed. At night when everyone else was asleep, she gave in to tears at the thought of how the flood had taken her home and livelihood. With her kitchen gone, she could no longer bake pies and cookies for the diner in town as well as a trio of tourist farms not far out of town.

And laughing kept her from having to respond to the man's amazement when she said Kevin was five. She'd heard comments about how big he was for his age and how advanced he was. She'd brushed them aside, not wanting to admit the truth. Kevin was almost eighteen months older. She'd changed his age, as well as his sister's, to make it harder for Leland to locate these two sweet children. Assuming he was looking for them—and she had to— he would search for a nearly seven-year-old boy and a girl who'd had her fifth birthday. As far as the residents of Evergreen Corners knew, Rose Anne was four. More than one person had commented on how early she was losing her teeth, but that was always followed by a comment about how every kid was different.

"I'm Michael Miller," the man replied with a wink at Kevin. "They told us to report to a check-in center at the school. Can you point us in the right direction?"

"I'm heading that way. It's easier to show you than tell you." Her voice caught, but she rushed on, "Almost all the familiar landmarks are gone."

He nodded, and she saw his sympathy before he picked up the bag he'd dropped when she'd nearly run into him. His large duffel bag was set with others on a narrow patch of grass that had somehow not been washed away.

"We appreciate that, Mrs.—"

"Carolyn will do." She wasn't going to explain that her neighbors assumed she was a widow. Guilt tore at her each time she thought of the lies she had woven like a cocoon to protect Kevin and Rose Anne. "We're not big on formality."

After he'd introduced her to Benjamin Kuhns and James Streicher, two men who'd traveled with him from an Amish settlement across the New York line, she motioned for the trio to follow her and the *kinder.*

Children! She needed to say "children" not *kinder.*

She must remember not to use *Deitsch.* Or act as if she understood it. She hadn't realized how much she'd missed hearing the Amish spoken language until these plain men began using it. But she had to seem as ignorant of it as her neighbors. Revealing she understood the language was one of the clues that, if repeated beyond the village, could draw Leland's attention to Evergreen Corners.

Holding Rose Anne's hand to stop the curious little girl from peering over the broken edge of the road, Carolyn made sure Kevin and the men were following her as she walked along the street toward the single intersection in the village. Nothing appeared as it had a week ago. Wide swaths of ground had been wiped clean by the rushing waters, and teetering buildings looked as if a faint breeze would send them crashing onto the sidewalks.

Michael moved to walk alongside her and Rose Anne as they passed ruined buildings. She heard Kevin regaling the other two men with tales of trying to recover their ten missing chickens.

"Do you think they survived?" Michael asked. "The chickens, I mean."

"We've seen most of them around the village. I opened the fence around the chicken coop before we evacuated." She pushed from her mind images of the horrifying moments when she and the children had struggled to escape the maddened waters.

She couldn't keep them from filling her nightmares, but she didn't intend to let those memories taint her waking hours. If they did, she might get distracted and fail to discover Leland had found them until it was too late. She couldn't take the chance he'd abduct Kevin and Rose Anne as he'd tried to before her sister died.

"And now everything is gone?" Michael asked, drawing her back from the abyss of her fears.

"Not everything."

"What's left?" he asked.

"Anything more than twenty-five feet above the brook survived, though several buildings were flooded a couple of feet into the first floor. The school, where we're headed, is the closest building to the brook that wasn't damaged at all."

He looked along the road running east and west through the village. "You're talking about more than five hundred feet away from the stream's banks."

"Uh-huh." She'd started to say *ja*, but halted herself. "Look at the mountains. They make this valley into a funnel, and the water kept rising and rising. We lost two restaurants and three shops as well as parts of the town hall, the fire station, the library, the elementary school, a building supply store. Also some historic buildings like the old gristmill that used to sit next to the brook. And, of course, a lot of houses, including a couple that had been here from when the town was founded in 1750. Many of the records were saved from the town hall, and, thankfully, the local newspaper had stored its back issues from the nineteenth century in the library, because their building washed away."

"What about the library books?" asked Benjamin. "Were the books saved?"

"A lot of them were lost. The cellar and first floor of the library were flooded, and many of the ones out on loan were washed away."

The men exchanged glances, but she looked at Kevin and Rose Anne. She was glad they were talking to each other and paying no attention to the adults' conversation. Her arms ached as she remembered holding them and trying to comfort them after their escape from the flood. They'd been upset about losing their home, but having the library flooded had distressed them even more. They'd loved going there and borrowing books or listening to one read aloud to them.

"Though the books have gone swimming," Rose Anne, ever the diplomat, had said, as tears had welled in her eyes, "Jenna will tell us stories. She's nice, and she has lots and lots of the goriest stories."

Carolyn had translated Rose Anne's mangling of the language as she did each time Rose Anne came up with a new "version" of a word. She'd guessed the little girl meant *glorious* rather than *goriest*, but she hadn't wanted to take the time to ask. Instead, she'd offered the little girl what solace she could. However, after talking with her good friend Jenna Sommers, the village's librarian and the foster mother of a six-year-old little girl whom Rose Anne adored, Carolyn knew it would be many months—maybe even a year or two—before the library was operational again. First, people needed homes, and the roads had to be repaired and made safe.

And the children needed to be kept safe, too. Her sister had won full custody of the two children in the wake of her separation from Leland. He'd fought to keep them. Not because he wanted them. They would have been in the way of his rough life of drinking and drugs. He'd fought because he hadn't wanted his wife to have a single moment of joy. It hadn't been enough he'd left Regina with bruises and broken bones each time he bothered to come home. At last, her sister had agreed to let Carolyn help her escape the abuse. Regina had been free of her abusive husband for almost three months before she became ill and died two days later from what the *doktors* had said was a vicious strain of pneumonia.

"Wow," murmured one of the men behind her as they reached the main intersection where a concrete bridge's pilings were lost in a jungle of debris and branches. "Is there another bridge into town?"

"Not now. There was a covered bridge."

"Was it destroyed?" Michael asked.

"Half of it was except for a couple of deck boards. The other half's wobbly. From what I've heard, engineers will come next week to see what, if anything, can be salvaged."

"So the road we traveled in on the bus is the only way in or out?"

"For now." She didn't add it might be several months or longer before the lost and damaged bridges were repaired.

She led the men to higher ground. She listened as they spoke in hushed *Deitsch* about how difficult it would be to get supplies in for rebuilding. It was hard not to smile with relief while she listened to their practical suggestions. How splendid it was to have these down-to-earth men in Evergreen Corners! Instead of talking about paperwork and bureaucracy, they planned to get to work.

Hurrying up the street, Carolyn saw two of her chickens perched in a nearby tree. She was glad neither child noticed. Both were too busy asking the newcomers a barrage of questions.

The parking lot in front of the high school held news vans with their satellite dishes, so she cut across the lawn to avoid the curiosity of reporters looking for a few more stories before they headed to the next crisis. She nodded her thanks to Michael when he opened the door for her and the children but didn't slow while she strode along the hall that should have been filled with teenagers.

The temporary town hall was in the school's gym. She'd already heard grumbling from the students that the school had survived when so many other buildings hadn't. By the end of next week when school was scheduled to restart, she guessed most of them would be glad to be done with the drudgery of digging in the mud and get back to their books. Kevin and Rose Anne were growing more restless each day, and only the hunt for their chickens kept them from whining about it.

Voices reached out past the gym's open doors, and Carolyn said, "This is where volunteers are supposed to sign in. They'll get you a place to stay and your assignments." She flushed, realizing what she should have said from the beginning. "Thank you for coming to help us."

"More volunteers?" A man wearing a loosened tie and a cheerful smile came out of the gym, carrying a clipboard. Tony Whittaker was the mayor's husband. Asking their names, he pulled out a pen to check their names off. "Michael Miller, did you say?"

"Ja," Michael replied.

Tony's smile became more genuine. "I'm glad you and Carolyn have met already."

"Really?" she inquired at the same time Michael asked, "Why?"

"You, Michael, have been assigned to the team building Carolyn and her children a new home." He chuckled. "Hope you've made a good impression on each other, because you're going to be spending a lot of time together for the next three months."

Chapter Two

Carolyn woke to the cramped space in what once had been—and would again be—stables. The barn, along a ridge overlooking the village, was owned by Merritt Aiken, who had moved to Evergreen Corners after retiring from some fancy job in California.

The stables had become a temporary home for five families who'd been left homeless in the flood. Her cot, along with the two smaller ones the children used, left little room for any possessions in their cramped space in two stalls. They had only a few changes of clothing, donated by kind members of the Mennonite congregation.

Carolyn had been able to rescue Hopper, the toy rabbit Rose Anne had slept with since she was born. Somehow in the craziness of escaping the flood, she'd grabbed the wrong thing from Kevin's bed. Instead of his beloved Tippy, a battered dog who'd lost most of his stuffing years ago, she'd taken an afghan. Kevin had told her it was okay.

"I'm too big for a stuffed toy anyhow," he'd said.

She'd guessed he was trying to spare her feelings. That had been confirmed when the children were offered new stuffed toys. Kevin had thanked the volunteers and taken a bear, but it had been left on the floor by his cot. She'd caught sight of the stains of tears on his face after he'd fallen asleep and known he ached for his special toy.

It was too great a burden for a little boy to bear. The weight of everything they'd lost pressed down on her. It was difficult to act as if everything could be made right again. All she had from a week ago was the heart-shaped locket that had belonged to her sister and contained baby pictures of the children. It had taken her almost a month to get accustomed to wearing the necklace without feeling she was doing something wrong. A proper plain woman didn't wear jewelry, but she hoped God would understand she was fulfilling her sister's dying wish to keep the children close to her heart.

She clenched the gold locket as she savored the familiar scents of the barn. The dried hay and oats that had been a treat for the horses consigned to a meadow out back were a wonderful break from the odors closer to the brook. She let herself pretend she was a child again and had fallen asleep in her family's barn on a hot summer afternoon.

But she wasn't in that innocent time. She and the children were homeless, and she feared Leland would care enough about Kevin and Rose Anne to come to Vermont.

Assuming they'd been on the news, and he'd seen the report. Maybe he'd missed it.

Help me keep these children safe, she prayed.

The image of Michael Miller flashed through her mind, startling her. Why had she thought of him when she imagined being safe? It must be, she reassured herself, that he represented the Amish life she'd given up. Or maybe it was because he was going to be rebuilding their house. She shouldn't be envisioning his strong shoulders and easy smile, which had made her feel that everything was going to be okay simply because he was there.

She pushed herself up to sit. Was she out of her mind? Her sister and *mamm* had been enticed by good looks and charming talk, and both had suffered for it. Though *Daed* had never struck *Mamm*, at least as far as Carolyn knew, he'd berated her whenever something went wrong. Even if it'd been his fault. That abuse had continued until his death and had worn her mother down until she died the year before Carolyn left Indiana.

Carolyn heard the children shifting as they woke. She dressed and hushed Kevin as she helped him and his sister get ready for the day care center at the Mennonite meetinghouse's community center. The children had been going there while she helped prepare breakfast for the displaced and the volunteers.

After they'd made their beds and folded their nightclothes on top of the blankets, she held her finger to her lips as she led the way out of the barn.

Some of the people in the large barn were still asleep. With worries about when they'd have a home or a job to return to, many found it impossible to sleep through the night. She'd woken often during the long nights and heard people pacing or talking in anxious whispers. But, just as she did, the resilient Vermonters kept on their cheerful faces during the day.

Kissing the children and getting kisses in return, Carolyn watched as they joined the others at the low tables where they'd be served breakfast soon. She wasn't surprised Rose Anne chose a seat right next to Taylor, the librarian's foster daughter. Rose Anne and Taylor whispered in delight at seeing each other. Her niece had asked to have her hair done like Taylor's pom-pom pigtails, but Rose Anne's hair was too straight.

Carolyn waved to the women and one lone elderly man working at the day care center that morning.

Jenna Sommers, whose hair was as black as her foster daughter's, wove through the tables toward her, motioning for Carolyn to wait. More than one child halted the town's librarian and asked when she was going to read to them. Assuring them she would if they ate their breakfast, she was smiling as she reached the door where Carolyn stood, trying not to look impatient to get to work.

"Good morning, Carolyn," Jenna said in her sweet voice, which could alter to a growl when she read a book with a big dog or a giant in it. "I hear the team has arrived who is building you a new house."

"That's what Tony told me yesterday." Carolyn shifted uneasily, overwhelmed with the generosity. And how the thought of spending time with Michael Miller accelerated her heart rate. "There are other people who need a home as much as we do."

"I don't know what the policies are for this new group, but I've heard the MDS helps the elderly and single mothers first."

Carolyn had learned MDS stood for the Mennonite Disaster Service. The organization, which was celebrating its seventieth anniversary, had already sent people to evaluate where their volunteers could best be used, and she had sat through an uncomfortable interview. She was grateful people wanted to help her and the children. Having the community pitch in after a tragedy was what she'd been accustomed to while growing up. She was accustomed to such generosity.

What bothered her was that she wasn't a single mother. She was a single aunt.

Rubbing sleep from his eyes, Michael followed his friends into the long, low building attached to the simple white meetinghouse. The Mennonite chapel had no tower or steeple, and the windows were clear glass. He was curious about what the sanctuary looked like, but his destination, as his rumbling stomach reminded him, was breakfast in what the locals called the community center.

Rows of tables in every possible shape and size had been pushed together to allow for the most seating. Chairs and benches flanked them. Upholstered chairs were placed next to lawn chairs with plastic webbing. He wondered if every house in the village had emptied its chairs and tables into the space.

Many were filled with people intent on eating. He could understand because the aromas of eggs, bacon and toast coming from the kitchen were enticing.

As enticing as…

He halted the thought before it could form, but it wasn't easy when he noticed Carolyn Wiebe smiling at a man and a woman who were selecting generous portions of food at the window between the dining area and what looked like a well-stocked commercial kitchen. Her dark eyes sparkled like stars in a night sky, and her smile was warmer than the air billowing out of the kitchen. He found himself wishing she'd look his way.

"Over here?" asked James before Michael could wonder why he was acting like a teenage boy at his first youth singing.

Looking at where his friend was gesturing, Michael wasn't surprised none of James's brothers were seated nearby. James hadn't said anything, but it was clear he was annoyed with his three older brothers who'd swooped down from their homes in Ontario and insisted James join them in volunteering. He'd heard James had moved to Harmony Creek Hollow to get away from his family, though James had been happy when his younger sister had moved in with him earlier and now taught at the settlement's school.

Michael pushed thoughts of James's family from his head as he walked with his two friends to a round table between two rectangular ones. The three chairs on one side would work for them. He nodded to an older couple who sat on the other side before setting his hat on the table.

"The sweet rolls are fine this morning," the white-haired man said. "You'll want to check them out, but you may want to be careful." He winked and grinned before digging into his breakfast again.

Michael wasn't sure why the man had winked until he went to the serving window and saw Carolyn was handing out cinnamon rolls topped with nuts and raisins to each person who walked by. When she noticed him, she greeted him with the same smile she'd offered each person ahead of him.

"Gute mariye," he said, then said, "Good morning."

She laughed. "You don't need to translate. Anyone could guess what you were saying. After all, it didn't sound like you were asking for a second roll."

"Can we have two?" asked Benjamin from behind him.

"The rule is take all you want," she said with a smile, "but eat all you take."

Benjamin took a half step back and spooned more scrambled eggs onto his plate. When James arched a brow, he said, "Hey, I'm a growing boy."

"I'll have two rolls please, Carolyn," Michael said.

"Just remember the rules." Her smile became sassy, and he saw the resemblance between her and her son.

He couldn't keep from smiling back as their gazes met and held.

A nudge against his back broke the link between them, and Michael wasn't sure how long he'd stood there savoring her smile. He grabbed flatware rolled into a paper napkin before striding to the table.

"I told you to be careful," chided the old man with a grin as he stood and helped his wife gather their dishes. "Something sweet can knock a man right off his feet."

Michael hoped his friends hadn't heard the comments, but they laughed as they sat beside him. He bent over his plate for grace and watched from the corners of his eyes as James and Benjamin did the same.

Before they could tease him further, Michael began talking about the orientation session they were required to attend after breakfast. He didn't give either man a chance to change the subject, but he wondered why he'd bothered when he saw the grins they wore as they ate. He wasn't fooling anyone, not even himself. He looked forward to getting to know Carolyn better, but that's where he'd have to draw the line.

She was involved in her Mennonite congregation, and he had no idea if he intended to remain Amish.

She didn't need to have him dump his mess of a life on her when she was trying to rebuild everything that had been lost.

She was a total mess.

But so was everyone else in Evergreen Corners.

Carolyn laughed as she thought of how Gladys Whittaker, their mayor, never used to appear in public without every hair in place. Since the flood, mud on her face seemed to be the mayor's favorite fashion accessory. Elton Hershey had had stains on his pants when he gave the sermon on Sunday. Nobody had complained about their kindhearted pastor, because everyone was fighting to get rid of mud from their clothing, too.

She squatted by the brook that had changed course. There was talk that the water would be forced back into its proper channel, but it was a low priority while people needed places to live.

Washing mud off her hands, Carolyn winced as her back reminded her of the hard work she'd done. She'd joined five others cleaning out a house that had been inundated. Once they'd gotten the mud off the floors, they spent hours removing soaked drywall before mold could grow inside the walls. She'd carried the heavy pieces of wet plaster to a pile in the yard while someone else had sprayed the two-by-fours with a mold killer.

Her hands ached as well as her elbows, shoulders and back. It'd be quicker to count the muscles that *didn't* hurt. Taking care of two children and raising chickens and baking hadn't prepared her for such physical work.

Hearing the *flap-flap* sound of a helicopter, Carolyn glanced up. It was rising from the football field behind the school. She wondered what had been delivered. She hoped fresh milk. The children were complaining about the taste of powdered milk. There were a half-dozen dairy farms on the other side of the ridge, but no way to get to them. Too many roads and bridges had been destroyed, and what would have been a ten minute drive before the flood now took hours.

She stood, holding her hands against her lower back to silence the protest from her muscles. When she saw four chickens pecking at the ground, she smiled. Mr. Aiken had told them to feel free to use whatever they found in the barn. She'd seen a bucket of corn by one stall. A couple of handfuls might draw the chickens back. That would ease the children's distress.

What Kevin and Rose Anne needed was a home. Their house hadn't been big, and most of the ancient mechanicals had needed attention she didn't know how to give. She and the children had become accustomed to faucets dripping. She'd locked off the back bedroom, fearful Kevin and Rose Anne would tumble through weak boards into the cellar. Now, the cellar hole was the sole remnant of the comfortable old house.

Seeing some broken boards heaped against stones at the brook's edge, Carolyn went to pull them out of the water, one by one. If nobody else claimed them, she could use them to build a new chicken coop.

"For all I know, Father," she said as she dropped another board on top of the two she'd pulled out, "these are what's left of my old coop. But I want them to go to whoever needs them most."

A shadow slipped over her, and Carolyn looked skyward. Was it going to rain again? Panic gripped her throat, threatening to keep her from drawing another breath.

"Would you like some help?" came a deep voice.

She turned. Michael's light-blue shirt and black suspenders weren't as filthy as her dress and apron were, and she guessed he'd come from the volunteers' orientation class. The sessions were simple, but outlined who was in charge of what and when someone should seek help before making a decision. They had ended the chaos of the first two days after the flood.

"I didn't mean to startle you," he said.

"You didn't."

"Something is upsetting you. I've seen more color in fresh snow than on your face."

She let her sore shoulders relax. "Okay, you did scare me. I was deep in my thoughts."

"This is all that's left?" He looked down into the cellar hole. "There's nothing but mud."

"Everything washed away. The furnace, the water heater and the jars of fruits and vegetables I put up in August. I haven't told the children yet. I know they aren't going to be happy with grocery store canned vegetables."

He wrinkled his nose. "Sometimes it seems you can't tell the difference between the vegetables in the can and the can itself."

"You've taken a bite out of a can?"

"Of course not." He chuckled. "You don't like exaggeration, ain't so?"

She made sure her reaction to "ain't so," a common Amish term, wasn't visible. "I'm a low-key person, Michael. I prefer to keep things simple."

"And you're exhausted."

She resisted the yearning to check her reflection in the slow waters of the brook to see how bad she looked. "I guess that's obvious."

"Why wouldn't you be tired? You were up early this morning to make breakfast for us, and now you're taking care of your chickens." His eyes narrowed as his gaze settled on the stack of wood. "Have you been pulling those out on your own?"

"I thought I could use the boards to build a chicken coop."

"A *gut* idea." Without another word, he waded into the water. He stretched out and grabbed a board beyond her reach.

Tears flooded Carolyn's eyes as she watched him lift out the planks and set them with the others with an ease she couldn't have copied. She blinked them away. She must be more exhausted than she'd guessed.

Five minutes later, the wood was stacked. She thanked him, but he waved aside her gratitude before bending to wash his hands in the brook as she had.

"What do you call this stream?" he asked as he straightened and wiped his hands on the sides of his black broadfall trousers.

"Washboard Brook."

"Brook?" He shook his head, then pushed his brown hair back out of his eyes. "I never imagined anything called a brook could do all the damage this one has."

"I didn't, either. I don't think anyone did."

"You've never had a flood here before?"

"I've learned that if the snow up on the peaks melts really fast, we get some minor flooding. Puddles in yards and maybe a splash over onto the road where it's low." She flung out her hands. "Nothing like this."

"Have you considered leaving?"

She shook her head. "No."

"Not once?"

Wanting to be truthful—or at least partially because she couldn't mention Leland's name—rather than making believe she could endure anything nature could throw against the town, she said, "I've got to admit when I watched our home collapse and get sucked down into the water I wanted to run as fast as I could in any direction away from the flood."

"But you're still here."

"It's home."

"So you grew up here?"

Carolyn berated herself. She should have seen the direction their conversation could go and changed the topic before it touched on dangerous territory.

Knowing she must not appear to hesitate, she said, "No, but I've lived here for a while. For me, Evergreen Corners is home, and I hope it always will be."

That was a prayer she said every night before sleep, because if she had to leave, it would be in an attempt to escape from Leland Reber once and for all.

Chapter Three

The first project meeting for Carolyn's new house was scheduled for ten the next morning. Initially it had been set for eight, but she was signed up to serve breakfast. Some volunteers and government officials came in RVs, and they brought their own food. However, most arrived eager to work with tools and skills and not much else. Fortunately, fewer locals were depending on the community center's kitchen to provide their meals because some sections of town now had electricity again.

But the steady whir of generators hadn't decreased in the center of the village. Long orange extension cords snaked from the four in the school parking lot.

She stepped over the cords with care, holding Rose Anne on her hip. The little girl had woken with a sore throat. Though Carolyn suspected it was because she'd been yelling too much yesterday in games at the day care center, she agreed to the child's demands to stay with her. Kevin had been glad to have his friends to himself, and Rose Anne seemed to perk up as soon as they headed toward the school.

Carolyn reached to open the door, but a hand stretched

past her to grasp the handle. Seeing Michael and his two friends, she greeted them. She hadn't been sure if they'd be coming to the meeting, too, and she was glad to see the men who'd invited her and the children to share supper with them the previous night.

Rose Anne wiggled to get down as soon as Carolyn carried her into the school. The little girl threw her arms around one of Michael's legs and begged him for a piggyback ride.

"You don't have to do that," Carolyn told him.

He gave her a quick smile. Squatting, he waited for the child to lock her hands around his neck before he stood. He kept one arm against her to keep her steady as he loped a few yards along the hallway and back again.

"Go, horsey!" she called in excitement.

He set her on her feet, though she pleaded for another ride.

"One ride per customer," he said, tapping her freckled nose.

"Later?" Rose Anne persisted.

"Let's see what later brings." Carolyn put her hands on the child's shoulders and smiled her thanks to Michael. "I warned you offering rides to the kids last night was going to get you in trouble."

"*Gut* trouble, though."

"We'll see when all the children in town are asking for rides after you've put in a full day's work." She took Rose Anne by the hand and began walking toward the gym.

The three men followed her, talking in *Deitsch*. The words fell like precious rain on her ears, but she chatted with Rose Anne as if none of what they were saying made sense to her. She wasn't surprised the men were eager to get started. No plain man was accustomed to sitting in a classroom when work waited to be done. When she'd been growing up, every man she'd known had toiled from before sunrise to after dark. It didn't matter if the man was a farmer or had a job in one of the nearby factories or owned his own shop. Being idle wasn't part of the Amish lifestyle.

A woman Carolyn didn't know stood in front of the gym's closed double doors. Everything about her pose shouted she would tolerate no nonsense. When Carolyn said her name, the woman checked it on the clipboard she carried.

"Please wait out here," the woman said. "We're running about a half hour behind schedule."

"All right." Carolyn walked to the plastic chairs. Dropping into one, she lifted Rose Anne onto her lap. She should have borrowed a book from the day care center to keep the little girl entertained.

Michael sat next to her as his friends walked down the hall. Before she could ask, he said, "They're going to go look for something to do for the next half hour."

"You don't need to wait with us."

"The time will go faster if you've got someone to talk to."

Sliding Rose Anne off her lap when her niece began to wiggle, Carolyn told her to stay in sight. The little girl nodded and began to jump from one black tile to the next on the checkered floor.

"I appreciate you staying here, but it's not necessary," Carolyn said, keeping her eyes on the child who could scurry away like a rabbit running from a dog. "I'm not sure I want the time to go faster."

"Nervous?" Disbelief deepened his voice. "Why? These people are here to help you."

"It's not easy to ask others for help."

"I get that." He leaned back, crossed his arms over his chest and stretched his long legs out, much to Rose Anne's delight as she began to leap over them. "But you've got to think about your *kinder*—I mean, your children."

"They're pretty much all I think about." She wondered why it was so easy to be honest with Michael, whom she hadn't known two days ago. "I'd do anything to make sure they've got a safe place to live."

"Even deal with bureaucrats?" He reached out to steady Rose Anne when she almost tripped over his boots.

Carolyn smiled. "When you put it that way, going through this meeting isn't too much to ask, is it?"

"Only you can answer that."

"I thought I did."

His laugh resonated down the otherwise empty hall. "Do you always speak plainly?"

"No."

"I guess I should feel honored."

"I guess you should." She was about to add more, then realized the little girl was partway around a corner. Calling Rose Anne back, she said, "I shouldn't have given in to her make-believe sore throat this morning. I should have insisted she stay at day care." She crooked a finger at her niece who was edging toward the end of the hall again. "They're accustomed to having me around, especially Rose Anne. She's been going to nursery school, but it's not the same as being left at the day care center all day, every day."

"So she convinced you to let her come with you."

"She didn't have to try hard." She held out her hand, and her niece ran over to take it. "I like spending time with my Rosie Annie."

The little girl giggled as she leaned on Carolyn's knee. "I'm sweat smelling, like a rose. That's what Mommy always says."

"Maybe not always, but you do smell *sweet* today." She ruffled the child's silken hair. Rose Anne had no memories of her real mother, and Kevin seemed to have forgotten Carolyn was his aunt. She thanked God every morning and night for that, though she prayed there would come a time when she could be honest. "Last night, you were dirty. It took a while to get you clean so you smelled as sweet as a rose again." To Michael, who was grinning at how Rose Anne had called herself "sweat smelling," she added, "We're pretty much limited to a bucket of water each."

"When can I take a big-girl bath again?" Rose Anne's voice became a whine. "I miss my bath tube and my floatie fishies."

She means bathtub, Carolyn mouthed so Michael could read her lips. When he nodded his understanding, she said aloud, "I can't tell you when, but it'll be..." She didn't want to give the child a specific date because she didn't have any idea how long it would take to build their new house. And she didn't want to talk about the plastic toys Rose Anne called her floatie fishies. They had washed away with everything in the house.

Michael stood, then dropped to one knee beside her niece. That brought his eyes almost level with Rose Anne's. "I can tell you when your new house and new bathtub will be ready. It's going to be right after Christmas."

"Christmas is a loooooooong time away," Rose Anne argued.

"No, it's not. Today is October twenty-fifth, so Christmas is exactly two months away." Holding up two fingers, he lowered first one, then the other. "One-two. See? Quick like a bunny."

"That's what Mommy says. Quick like a bunny!" Rose Anne bounced with excitement. "Mr. Michael knows quick like a bunny, too."

"I know." As the little girl danced and twirled along the hall, Carolyn asked, "'Mr. Michael?'"

"One of the ladies working at supper last night called me that, and the kids started using it."

"You're good with children. Do you have any?"

"No, but my brother has year-old twins, and there are plenty of kids in our settlement." He surveyed the hall before adding, "My brother has his life set for him... as you do."

She was amazed at his wistful tone. Michael had seemed so sure of himself. Was there a tragedy in his past, too, or did he have another reason to envy his brother's choices in life?

The woman who'd stood by the gym doors came out and called, "Carolyn Wiebe? They're ready for you."

A shiver of anxiety trilled down her back, but Carolyn stood. When Rose Anne rushed to her side, she wasn't sure if the little girl was aware of her agitation or wanted a change of scenery after exploring every inch of the hall. Carolyn glanced at Michael who'd gotten up, too, and she knew she wasn't hiding her nerves from him.

But he didn't offer her trite consolation. Instead, he motioned for her to lead the way.

In the gym, four round tables with plenty of chairs had been placed between the two sets of bleachers. Mats remained under the basketball hoops. Rose Anne took off her shoes and ran to join the other children playing on them.

"The *kinder* are having *gut* fun," Michael said as the woman led them toward the most distant table.

Carolyn recognized fellow residents who'd lost their homes, and she guessed the others were volunteers like Michael and his friends. To avoid any chance of eavesdropping on their conversations, she replied, "The kids are having more fun now than we had the first night after the flood. For lots of us, those mats were our beds. We were so exhausted we would have slept on the wood floor."

"Glen," the woman with the clipboard said, "here's your client. Carolyn Wiebe."

Trying not to bristle at the woman's tone that suggested Carolyn was an unworthy charity case, she was glad when the woman walked away.

"I'm Glen Landis," said the man who was as thin as the hair across his pate. "The project director."

"We've met," Carolyn replied, pulling her tattered composure around her like a comfortable blanket. "About a year and a half ago, you came to speak at the Evergreen Corners Mennonite Meetinghouse about your experiences."

"In the recovery efforts after Hurricanes Katrina and Harvey?" He smiled as Michael's two friends jogged across the gym to join them. From his speech, she'd learned he considered rebuilding homes and communities his mission work. "Those were overwhelming experiences. I've been told you've met some of the people who'll be working on your house."

"I've met Benjamin, James and Michael." She looked at each man as she said his name. Only belatedly did she realize how foolish she'd been to speak Michael's name last. Without an excuse to shift away, her gaze lingered on him.

Michael gave her a bolstering smile, and she wished she could fling her arms around him as Rose Anne had. She hadn't realized how much she needed someone's support.

"Here comes the rest of the crew," Glen said, motioning for everyone to take a seat.

He went around the table, introducing each person. Art Kennel was the man who looked like a jolly grandfather. Jose Lopez was almost as lanky as Glen and taller. The sole woman was Trisha Lehman. She had the same no-nonsense air about her as the woman by the door, but her smile put Carolyn at ease.

After leading them in prayer to thank God for His grace in bringing them together, Glen pulled a stack of pages stapled on one side out of a briefcase by his chair. He put them in front of Carolyn.

"This is our standard house plan." He glanced around the table. "Several of you have already built one or more of these houses. If you haven't or you want to examine the plans more closely, get a copy from me after this meeting."

She stared at the simple house with a living room, kitchen, a bath and two bedrooms. It wasn't as big as her previous house, but it would be more than sufficient for what she and the children needed.

As if she'd spoken aloud, Glen said, "Carolyn, if you see things you want to have changed, now is the time to tell us."

"What sort of things?" She thought of the house the water had taken from her. That rundown house had been their home, something that couldn't be drawn on paper.

"I know you have two children, a girl and a boy. If you want a third bedroom, so each child may have their own—something I've been told by my own kids is an absolute necessity—we can add one. It's possible to get a second bathroom, but it'll depend on the amount of money raised through donors and what you can contribute."

"Definitely the extra bedroom, but one bathroom will suffice."

"That we should be able to provide within the budget we've been given." He opened a bright blue folder and wrote some notes before launching into an explanation of what each of the six pages in the plans contained.

Carolyn tried to take in the information on septic systems and wells and the required number of electric outlets and where a stackable washer and dryer could be put if she wanted to keep the coat closet by the front door and a linen cupboard in the bathroom. Her head spun with numbers and dimensions, and she was relieved when Glen reassured her they'd be revisiting the plans every day on the work site and once a week in the gym.

"The first supplies will be delivered this afternoon," he announced as he refolded the plans. "We hope to start on your house within days. It'll depend on the weather, of course."

"I understand." Looking around the table, she said,

"Thank you, everyone. Your kindness humbles me. You make me want to live *Hebrews* 13:2 'Be not forgetful to entertain strangers: for thereby some have entertained angels unawares.' My door will always be open to you." She laughed. "Once I have a door, that is."

The others joined in her laughter, and Michael took her hand under the table and squeezed it. A sense of comfort filled her at his compassion.

"Oh, one more thing," Glen said. "We've asked the press to stay away, but we hope you'll agree to a short interview, Carolyn, after we have the blessing for your new home. We've found seeing how others have worked with us leads to more people offering to volunteer. Everyone wants to be part of a happy ending to what started out as a sad story."

Carolyn stiffened. "An interview?"

"Nothing complicated. A short film to put on our website to show donors how they've helped."

Horror pulsed through every vein in her body, like the flood waters closing in around her again, only this time with fire atop of the rushing waves. She shook her head.

"Is that a problem?" asked Glen.

She pushed back her chair. "If doing an interview is a condition for your help, I can't do this."

"You don't want our help?"

Wishing she didn't have to see the shock on these kind faces, she wondered how much more appalled they'd be if she told them the truth of why she was turning down their offer. Would any of them have been able to comprehend the depth of fear stalking her in the form of Leland Reber?

"No," she whispered.

* * *

Michael came to his feet along with everyone else at the table when Carolyn stood and, taking Rose Anne by the hand as the little girl protested she needed to retrieve her shoes, started for the door. Unlike everyone else who seemed frozen in shock, he couldn't watch her throw away her future. Didn't she realize how blessed she was to know what future she wanted?

As he strode after her, he was surprised to feel a pinch of vexation. Her future was assured if she agreed to the terms set out by Amish Helping Hands' partners. She could enjoy a comfortable life with her *kinder* among her friends, neighbors and congregation. It was being handed to her, and she was turning her back on it.

How he envied her for having the chance to have the life she wanted! Nobody could offer him that, because he didn't know how he wished his future to unfurl.

He blocked Carolyn's path to the door. She started to walk around him, but he edged to the side, halting her.

"Are you out of your mind?" he asked, not caring that everyone in the gym was staring at him and Carolyn. He bent and whispered to Rose Anne to go play with the other *kinder*. As the little girl skipped across the gym, he looked at her *mamm*. "Your *kinder* can't live the rest of their lives in a barn."

"I don't want to be interviewed."

"If you're shy—" he began, though he couldn't believe that was the case. She'd been outgoing when he'd arrived.

"I don't want to be interviewed."

"Tell Glen that. I'm sure he can find someone else to talk to the reporters."

"It's not just being interviewed. I don't want anyone taking our pictures."

He frowned. "I thought the Mennonites were more liberal than we Amish are. When I first saw the news about the damage here, there were plenty of pictures of people gathered at your meetinghouse."

"I don't want it. Can't that be answer enough?"

His first inclination was to say no, but seeing how distraught she was, he relented. He couldn't help being curious why Carolyn—who'd been calm and rational yesterday—found such a simple request upsetting.

"Let me talk to Glen. You and your cute kids would provide great promotional material for them, but I'm sure he can find someone else who's willing to be the focus of the article."

She whispered her thanks, then began to apologize. When he stood near her, he was surprised how tiny she was. Her personality and heart were so big that she seemed to tower over others around her. Now she appeared broken. He wasn't sure why, but he must halt her from making a huge mistake.

"No, Carolyn. There's no need to ask for forgiveness. Not mine, anyhow, but you need to be honest with Glen and the rest of the team. They deserve to know how you feel."

She lifted her chin and drew in a deep breath. "You're right."

"It's been known to happen every once in a while." His attempt at humor gained him the faintest of smiles from her, but it was enough for him to know she'd made up her mind to negotiate for what she had to have.

When they returned to the table where the other volunteers had left Glen sitting alone, the project director had closed the blue folder.

Michael felt his stomach clench. Did that mean Glen would be shutting down work on Carolyn's house, too? Michael didn't want to believe that, but he knew little about *Englisch* ways.

Pulling out a chair, Glen motioned for Carolyn to sit. He gave Michael a pointed look over her head, but Michael decided not to take the hint and allow the two to speak alone.

"I'm sorry to distress you," Glen said in a subdued voice.

"I'm sorry I tried to storm out of here," she whispered. "I can't—I don't want to be interviewed or have the children interviewed. I understand if you can't build us a house."

Michael saw his own questions on Glen's face. Carolyn had used the word *can't*. Why couldn't she be interviewed? What was she trying to hide about herself and the *kinder*?

"Of course we're going to build your house," Glen replied. "We'd love to have you and the children be part of the information we share with possible volunteers and donors, but that's not a requirement for you. I'm sorry if I gave you that impression."

"Don't blame yourself," she said, once more with the quiet composure Michael admired. "I'm on edge. If someone says boo, I'll jump high enough to hit my head on the clouds."

Glen laughed. "We'll keep that in mind when we're ready to put the roof on your house. We wouldn't want you to go right through it the first day."

Fifteen minutes later, Michael stood in the hall with

his friends from Harmony Creek Hollow while Carolyn knelt nearby, tying Rose Anne's bright red and yellow sneakers. He spoke in *Deitsch*. Benjamin and James, peppering him with questions about why Carolyn had reacted as she had and if the project was moving forward, used the same language. He didn't want Carolyn to know they were talking about her, though he guessed she had some suspicion of that because she glanced in their direction a couple of times. He told his friends he wasn't sure what had bothered her.

"We might never know," he said.

"Women," grumbled Benjamin. "One thing I learned from my sister is it's impossible to guess what they're thinking. I've figured out it's better not to try."

James nodded. "I guess that's why we're bachelors."

Michael changed the subject to the next day when they'd start loading building materials onto a donated forklift and moving them to the construction site.

"It'll take us at least a day to get the forms set up and ready for concrete," Benjamin added.

"Do we have tarps to protect the supplies from rain and mud?"

"I saw some among the pallets of supplies." James scratched behind his ear as he mused, "There are three houses being started at the same time. I wonder if we've got enough supplies."

"Let's not look for trouble before we find it," Michael replied, clapping his friend on the shoulder.

"Thanks for coming today," Carolyn said as she walked past them. "I'm sorry for the scene I caused. Let me make it up to you. I'll have the keys for the forklift waiting for you at supper so you can get a good start in the morning. See you there."

Michael stared after her. They'd been talking in *Deitsch*. Yet, Carolyn had spoken about the forklift as if she'd understood everything they'd said.

How was that possible?

Looking at his friends, he saw the same consternation on their faces.

"*Deitsch* isn't so different from German," James said. "If she's fluent in German, she'd get the gist of our conversation."

"*Ja.*" Michael didn't add more.

But if his friend wasn't right, it meant one thing: Carolyn Wiebe might not be what she appeared to be.

Chapter Four

Michael quietly shut the door to the trailer he was sharing with his friends from Harmony Creek Hollow and stepped out into the cold morning. He didn't want to wake Benjamin or James or anyone else who might be asleep in the other travel trailer parked behind the used car dealership. The two trailers had been donated for the workers rebuilding the homes. He hadn't expected anything so comfortable when he'd volunteered.

Though describing the cramped trailer as comfortable wasn't accurate. With three full-grown men trying to squeeze past each other as they got ready each morning and went to bed each night for the past three days, it was a tight squeeze. However, the narrow bed where he slept had a *gut* mattress.

He looked at his trousers. They were his next-to-last clean pair. The local laundromat had told volunteers that as soon as the business was open in a couple of weeks, they were welcome to come in anytime to wash their clothes for free. Something in the water had left a dirty line above the tops of his rubber boots. The scum might have been gasoline or fuel oil or some other chemical that had leaked into the brook after the flood swept cars and furnaces and everything else along it. He hadn't seen the telltale rainbow sheen, but it might have dissipated enough so it was no longer visible.

The volunteers working in the flooded houses had been given white plastic coveralls as well as ventilating masks. Mold had begun growing as the water receded, so those workers had to be protected when they tore out drenched drywall and tossed the pieces into wheelbarrows that were then taken to big dumpsters sitting at a central spot in town. The plan, as he understood it, had been for the debris to be removed daily, but so far nobody had come to retrieve it. Stacks of reeking building materials and furniture and carpet were piled along the streets.

The rumble of generators came from the village. He walked past a collection of used cars marked with bright orange paint. When he'd asked why, he'd been told the cars would be destroyed. Water was as destructive to an internal combustion engine as it was to a wooden structure.

Michael counted more than two dozen buildings with visible damage before he stopped, knowing there were more with ruined interior walls and drenched contents. Grimacing, he guessed anything in those buildings wore the same dark sheen as whatever stained his trousers.

What a mess! Before he arrived he hadn't imagined the breadth of the disaster.

There was one thought he hadn't been able to shake out of his head as he stared at the brightly colored trees on the mountain beyond the village. If the storm had blasted its way up the other side of the Green Mountains, the settlement along Harmony Creek could have been washed away.

God, make use of my hands and my arms and whatever else You need to help these people regain their normal lives. Let my heart be as eager to help here as it would be to do the same for those at home.

He prayed something similar every morning when he went on a short walk before breakfast. He depended on the prayer to focus him on the work ahead of him. Talking to God also helped him clear his mind of thoughts that seemed to center around the enigma Carolyn was. She'd never explained why she'd reacted so vehemently when Glen spoke about an interview.

Shoving his hands into his pockets, Michael continued toward the village. How had Carolyn coped with this day after day for the past week? Nobody could have been prepared for what had occurred, but except for the single outburst at the school, she'd been calm. He was a bit envious because he wished he knew how she managed the drama surrounding her. Maybe if he could learn how she did it, he'd be able to do it himself.

Michael didn't meet anyone else as he walked past the library. The large two-story building was solid on its foundation, or at least the stone walls made it appear that way. He couldn't say the same for the seafood restaurant next door. The whole building listed to the right, revealing the foundation had been compromised. Several other structures along the street were also off-kilter, one two-story house so tilted the eaves on one side were low enough he could have touched them without rising to his toes. Yellow police tape surrounded the house, a warning that it might collapse.

The odor of mildew strengthened as he continued

along the street. Raw earth scents rose from where trees had been ripped from the ground, leaving gaping holes and thick fingers of roots torn apart. Broken flowerpots lay shattered by front steps, but he guessed they'd once been much farther upstream.

The nearer he got to the brook the worse the damage was. He slowed to stare at the remnants of one house where the first floor had vanished. The upper story sat on the ground about ten feet from the foundation. Another house was tipped over, every window and door intact, as if a gigantic hand had reached down and lifted it off its foundation before setting it on the ground. Not far away, a clock perched over a shop's door. Its hands marked the time the flood had struck the building.

6:47.

As Carolyn had said, if the waters had arrived a few hours later, people would have been in bed and might not have had time to escape.

Michael sent up a prayer of thanks for the lives saved through God's providence. Many villagers had lost everything, but they had their most precious possessions—their lives and their families' lives.

What stopped him in his tracks, however, was the sight of the covered bridge on the north side of the village. One half hung precariously over the water. The rest of it had vanished except for a pair of boards. The top of each arch was more than twelve feet off the ground, and he tried to imagine water reaching high enough to tear the bridge apart.

Destruction spread to the horizon on both sides of a brook he could have waded across in a half-dozen steps. Trees were lying on their sides, on the ground or propped on top of broken roofs. Water pooled everywhere. He'd been wandering through this disaster for three days and still hadn't seen the full extent of the destruction.

"Can't believe your eyes, can you?" asked James as he came to stand beside him. His stained pants were stuffed into the tops of his boots. He held out a cup of *kaffi* to Michael.

Taking the cup with a nod of gratitude, he answered, "I can't get accustomed to the randomness of it all." He pointed along the brook toward where a garden shed sat on an island, separated from its house by ten feet of water. "Both buildings look fine, but Washboard Brook now runs between them instead of behind the shed as I assume it used to."

"I've heard there are plans to put the brook back into its original banks."

"I've heard that, too, but I'm not sure if the state will go to the expense of reconnecting a house and its shed."

"Then it may be left to the homeowner to reroute the water."

Michael arched his brows, knowing such a task would require excavating equipment and permits. Maybe some rules would be relaxed for the rebuilding, but he guessed most would be kept in place to protect the village and its inhabitants from a repeat of the disaster.

For the first time he wondered how long it would take Evergreen Corners to return to normal.

Or if it ever would.

At breakfast, Michael had had a chance to greet Carolyn and receive one of her pretty smiles, but he didn't have time to say anything more before he had to move on to let others get their food. It was long enough for him to notice the dark circles under her eyes, and he wondered what had kept her awake. The *kinder*? The house? Something else?

Pondering the questions kept him silent through breakfast. He was quiet as he walked with James and Benjamin and the other volunteers toward where they'd be clearing debris from the site of Carolyn's house. At least, he told himself, they could reassure her the project was moving forward.

Jose shared apples from his orchard. The man was one of the hardest workers at the site, and Michael wasn't surprised to learn Jose had volunteered at other disasters throughout New England. Each day, he came with a treat to share. Though Jose said the apples had been harvested a few weeks ago, they had a crispness that put any apple Michael had ever had in Pennsylvania to shame.

"Our weather in Vermont is perfect for apples," Jose said. "Warm summer days with cooler nights. When we get plenty of rain—" He scowled as if he'd found a worm in the core of the apple he was eating. "I mean *regular* rain, not flooding rain like they had along these valleys. When we get lots of nice, steady rain, the apples are juicy. After drier summers like this one, the apples aren't as juicy, but they're sweeter. Either way, they're great for eating, cooking and making cider."

Trisha, who'd worked with him in the past, laughed. "You sound like an ad for the Vermont apple growers' association."

"Hey, a guy's got to be proud of what he does." He turned to the other men. "Right?"

Michael hastened to agree rather than explain pride—

hochmut—was seen as a negative among the Amish. He doubted the *Englischers* would be interested in hearing about plain life, and he didn't want to cause any sort of gulf between the plain volunteers and the *Englisch* ones. He glanced at his friends and gave the slightest shrug. He got grins in return.

Noise met them before they reached the remains of Carolyn's home. Generators rumbled, waiting for electric tools to be connected to them. The sound of circular saws battled the whir of gas-powered chainsaws cutting through the debris blocking the brook, creating pools where there shouldn't be any. Small clouds of blue-gray smoke marked each spot where someone was slicing through wood that might once have been a house or a fence.

As they emerged from the trees separating her property from her neighbor's, large land-moving equipment was being maneuvered toward Carolyn's cellar hole. The tons of gravel deposited by the swollen brook onto her yard crunched under large tires and caterpillar tracks. Two skid steers, which looked like a *kind*'s toys compared to the massive vehicles, were shoving fallen trees into a pile near the brook. He knew they would be burned later but were being shifted out of the way so the massive equipment could do its work.

Glen Landis stood near stone steps that had led to the house. From there, he could supervise workers removing the debris, filling in the old cellar hole and laying out the new foundation. Michael and James were put to work marking the location of the new house with sticks and bright orange string while the others focused on finishing the cleanup.

When the evaluation had come back on Carolyn's

house the day before yesterday, the decision had been clear. The old house, as Michael had suspected, had been built too close to the brook. Though it'd been almost twenty yards away, the building hadn't been spared during what people were calling a thousand-year flood. He didn't have much confidence in their time-table. The flood caused by Hurricane Kevin had been the fifth in the past hundred years.

Michael wondered if Carolyn had been consulted about the new location, which would set the front porch a few yards from the road. She had around six acres on either side of the brook, but most was wooded, so putting the house near its original location seemed the best idea.

Though he was focused on his task of trying to make a perfect rectangle with James's help, Michael knew the instant Carolyn arrived in the clearing. Some sense he couldn't name told him she was nearby. He couldn't keep from smiling. She had a white crocheted shawl over the shoulders of the pink dress that looked to be far too big for her. It had, he guessed, come from the bins of donated clothing. She'd cinched it with a black apron, accenting her slender waist. Her gold locket twinkled around her neck.

She scanned the work site and smiled. That expression softened when her gaze caressed his, pausing for a single heartbeat before moving on. Was it his imagination that her smile had grown a shade warmer when their eyes connected?

"Is this the spot for the next stake?" James asked in an impatient tone that suggested he'd already posed the question once or twice.

Michael concentrated on his task. As much as he

enjoyed looking at Carolyn, he couldn't let his attention wander. He squatted and placed a laser level on the ground so the red line marked where the next few stakes should be driven.

His sleeve was grabbed, and he struggled to hold his balance in the awkward stance. Putting his hands on the dirt, he pushed himself to his feet when he realized Carolyn must have rushed down to them.

"Was iss letz?" he asked. When she opened her mouth, he said in *Englisch*, "What's wrong?"

A flurry of emotions stormed across her face before she looked away to point farther down the hillside. "Where's the wood we pulled out of the brook?"

He squinted through the bright morning sunshine. "Right there." As he was about to add more, a skid steer moved toward the stack. The forks started to slide under the wood. "Did you tell them to move it?"

"No."

Running at a pace that threatened to send him falling face-first, he managed to slide to a stop before he reached the one-man forklift.

The man inside was so riveted on his task, he didn't see Michael waving his arms. Michael leaped forward and grabbed the end of one of the boards rising on the forklift.

A curse battered his ears, but he ignored it as he motioned to the man controlling the skid steer.

"Are you crazy?" demanded the man, poking his head out of the small vehicle.

"The owner wants to hold on to these boards."

"Why?" asked the operator. "She's getting a brand-new house."

"She collected them to rebuild her chicken coop."

He pointed toward where a half-dozen chickens were pecking at the ground near where an old tree trunk had been removed. A feast of bugs and worms must have been uncovered.

"Those chickens aren't going to be long for this world if they keep wandering around here. Nobody's going to be watching for them." The operator gave a twisted grin. "They're gonna be flat chickens in no time."

Michael knew the guy was right. "I'll take care of them."

"They're in the way."

"Okay." He held up one hand. "I'll be back in five minutes."

The man switched off the skid steer. "I'll wait here." His tone suggested Michael was wasting everyone's time defending a pile of water-soaked wood and a few chickens.

Striding up the hill, Michael explained what the skid steer operator had told him.

"I'll talk to Glen." Carolyn walked away before anyone could reply.

Michael turned to his friends. "We've got a new job."

"What's that?" asked James, stretching as Michael had done a few minutes ago.

"How are you at catching chickens?"

Benjamin groaned. "Don't tell us you volunteered *us* to round up Carolyn's chickens."

"All right, I won't tell you, but let's go. We need to get them before—" He grinned when a chicken let out an ear-splitting squawk as it flapped away from a bulldozer, leaving a cloud of feathers and dust in its wake. "I, for one, don't want to explain to Carolyn and her *kinder* why their chickens have gone bald."

With a laugh, the men went to capture the hens. It wasn't the day Michael had planned, but he'd already learned, despite the plans Glen and his team had made, there were going to be plenty of surprises while rebuilding Carolyn's house.

Carolyn scrubbed the last of the muffin tins from breakfast in the community center's kitchen. She'd returned to work there after being reassured by Glen that her small pile of boards would be kept safe so she could build another chicken coop.

During the walk to the community center, she hadn't been able to keep from smiling as she thought of Michael taking off at top speed to stop the skid steer operator from tossing them onto the pile with the rest of the debris. If the ground had been covered by snow, he would have looked like a reckless snowboarder on Mount Snow.

Yet, he'd saved the boards, and she appreciated his interceding on her behalf. He seemed to be a *gut* man.

But so did Leland when you first met him.

She shuddered at the thought of her brother-in-law and her own father, who'd derided her mother every chance he had. Others had acted as if they admired both Leland and her father. Others who hadn't seen the truth hidden by charming smiles. She didn't want to believe Michael was the same, but she'd be a fool to leave herself and Kevin and Rose Anne vulnerable to another man.

He wouldn't be in Evergreen Corners for long—another reason not to get too close to him. She'd keep her distance.

Just in case.

"Hey! Guess what? There are more Amish folks here."

Carolyn's ears perked up at the words spoken by someone on the far side of the community kitchen.

More Amish? A shiver of dismay sliced through her. What if Leland had secreted himself among these plain people and come to Evergreen Corners with them? What if she was recognized as Cora Hilty from Indiana?

She put the last muffin tray in the drainer and squeezed out the dishrag. Draping it over the faucet, she said, "I'll be right back."

The other women looked at her in obvious confusion.

She gave them a wide smile and whirled to leave before someone could ask a question she'd have to evade as she had so many others. When she had embarked on this new life, she hadn't given any thought to how hard it would be to protect the truth from those she called friends. So many times when she'd stopped to chat with Jenna in the library, she'd been tempted to spill everything.

But the burden was hers and hers alone until Kevin and Rose Anne were old enough to be told the truth. She tried not to let herself think about what their reactions would be.

When Carolyn emerged from the community center and hurried to the center of the village, she saw four plain people standing in the middle of the green and looking around as if they didn't know what to do first. The three men, all wearing black hats, were bachelors because none had beards. The lone woman had a black bonnet over her *kapp* and wore a black wool coat, so Carolyn couldn't guess which community they came from. A single suitcase and three paper grocery bags sat on the ground by their feet.

"Can I help you?" Carolyn asked as she reached the quartet.

"We're here to help," said the tallest man. "Do you know where we go to meet with the project director?"

"The high school." She smiled. "I'll show you the way. I'm Carolyn Wiebe, by the way."

"Isaac Kauffman," the tall man answered. "This is my sister Abby, and our cousins, Danny and Vernon Umble."

Danny appeared younger than the others, not much more than a teenager, while Vernon looked the oldest of the foursome, probably in his early forties. He wore thick glasses that perched on the end of his nose. As Carolyn greeted them, he pushed up his glasses, but they slid down again when he reached for one of the paper bags.

The cousins fell in step behind Carolyn and the Kauffmans as she led them across the green. She kept her sigh of relief silent when they told her they were the only ones from their community able to spare time to help with the rebuilding.

"Ours is a newer settlement," Abby said with a friendly smile. "In the Northeast Kingdom."

Carolyn knew the term as everyone who lived in Vermont did. The Northeast Kingdom consisted of the counties abutting Canada and New Hampshire.

"I hadn't heard about any Amish in Vermont."

Abby smiled. "We don't broadcast we're here."

Flustered, Carolyn hurried to reassure the woman she knew enough about Old Order Amish to understand they wouldn't make a big deal out of the monumental task of building a new settlement. She sighed. Walking the fine line between pretending she was curious about the Amish and yet disguising how much she knew was becoming more difficult. Mennonites and *Englischers* never seemed to notice when she revealed a fact only someone who'd lived a plain life would know. Nobody had questioned—not once—what sort of community she'd lived in before she came to Evergreen Corners.

As more Amish arrived to assist, she needed to be more cautious, or the fragile house of cards she'd built would tumble down and make her and the children more vulnerable to being found by Leland. She must curb her tongue before she destroyed what she'd created over the past four years.

"How do you like Vermont?" Carolyn asked, knowing she mustn't get lost in her thoughts and make the newcomers curious about *her.*

"The winters are much colder than we had in Pennsylvania." Abby gave an exaggerated shiver.

Carolyn's smile became more sincere. "Is everyone in your settlement from Pennsylvania?"

"So far."

"That's nice. You've got a sense of community from where you lived before." She pushed aside her ever-present fear that the newcomers were from Indiana and might recognize her.

She hoped those blessings would continue, and she wouldn't find herself face-to-face with Leland Reber when she least expected it. She wasn't sure what he'd do, but she was certain of what she would. She'd take the children and flee again, leaving everything and everyone else behind.

Chapter Five

Michael hoped nobody else could hear his stomach grumbling. The midday meal was more than an hour away, but his gut wasn't ready to be rational. He was hungry and another of Jose's apples had only taken the edge off those pangs.

But right now, he needed to find someone named Isaac Kauffman. Glen had said the man with the skills of a master mason should have arrived today in Evergreen Corners. No more work could be done on any of the houses until Isaac reviewed the dimensions of the foundations and approved them. Isaac had worked on other projects with Glen, who'd come to depend on his expertise.

Michael looked across the village green, a small open park with a veterans' memorial stone at one end and a damaged gazebo big enough to hold a band at the other. Over by the high school, he saw Carolyn with people he hadn't seen before. Their clothing announced they were Lancaster County Amish.

When she laughed, he admired how she seemed to take each challenge as it came and maintained her positive attitude. He'd seen dismay shadowing her eyes and knew she was haunted by the flood, yet she made an effort to put everyone around her at ease.

What would she say if he told her what *he* had been thinking while working today? Would she be shocked he wanted to talk to her about living and worshipping as a Mennonite? God might have brought him to Evergreen Corners to give him a chance to consider his future without input from well-meaning friends and family. Even if he chose not to be baptized as a member of the *Leit*, he wanted to live a plain life. He knew nothing about the day-to-day lives of other plain sects or how they praised God in their churches. He'd always attended services in a neighbor's house.

But now wasn't the time to ask his questions. Not when she stood with an Amish woman and three plain men.

Michael smiled when Carolyn motioned for him to join her and the others. She introduced him to the Kauffmans and the Umble brothers. He learned they'd come from northeastern Vermont, where a Pennsylvania daughter settlement had been established.

When Isaac switched to *Deitsch*, Michael wanted to chuckle at the choice of topic. Deciding which family or friends they might have in common was the Amish way of meeting new folks. Somewhere along the line, everyone shared ancestors.

Glancing at Carolyn, he saw her brow was ruffled in concentration as she listened to them. Was she trying to pick out words she understood? Or did she comprehend more than a few words? She'd seemed to know what he and his friends were talking about when they spoke in *Deitsch* at the school.

"Glen has been waiting for you to arrive, Isaac," Michael said after they'd established they had a common ancestor six generations back.

"How many foundations are you preparing?" asked the man who was taller than James. His light brown hair was streaked with blond from hours of working outside.

"Three."

Isaac laughed. "Glen likes to keep lots of balls in the air at one time. I keep telling him it would be more efficient to start one house, finish the first step of it and then start the next house."

"Like singing a round?"

"*Ja.* Exactly." He switched to *Englisch* with a guilty glance toward Carolyn. "I'd best check in with Glen."

"I hope he'll give us a chance to move in before bedtime," grumbled Vernon. The older man took off his black hat, revealing a balding pate that glistened in the sunlight.

When the newcomers went into the school, Carolyn said she needed to return to the community center. Michael walked with her because he should get back to the building site and let Glen know Isaac had arrived.

But he had another matter on his mind. "Do you speak German?"

Her dark brown eyes widened. "That's an odd question."

"I was watching you while Isaac and the others spoke. You seemed focused on every word." He was bumbling through what should have been simple. "You looked like you were trying to puzzle out what we were saying."

"I could understand names. There were a lot. Do you know all those people you named?"

"Some I know. Some the Kauffmans and the Umbles know. A few we both know or know of."

"That's amazing! You live in New York State, and they live on the Canadian border. Yet you have friends in common."

"All of us have roots in Lancaster County, Pennsylvania."

Her face became less tense as the hint of a smile brushed her lips. "Ah, I get it."

"And you didn't understand anything but the names?"

She bent to pick up a paper cup and tossed it into a nearby trash barrel. Wiping her hands, she said, "Some words sounded like English. If I offended you by listening, I'm sorry."

"Of course you didn't offend."

"I'm glad." She gave him a smile, and his heart lurched in his chest. "I can't ever forget what you and the others are doing for us. I wouldn't want to make you think I was unappreciative."

"Why do you think we'd feel that way?"

She shrugged, her smile losing a bit of its brilliance. "I know...that is, I've heard... People have told me the Amish like to keep separate from the world. I didn't want you to think I was trying to intrude."

"Will it make you feel better if I tell you I'll let you know if you do anything to offend me?"

"Yes!"

He laughed at her sudden enthusiasm. When she looked at him as if he'd lost his mind right in front of her, he hurried to say, "I was teasing you, Carolyn. You've got enough to worry about without worrying you might be crossing some imaginary line."

"If you're sure..."

"I'm sure." He patted her shoulder as he would have his brother when he wanted to assure Gabriel of something.

But the tingles scurrying along his arm were nothing he'd ever felt with his brother.

Or anyone else…not even Adah.

The memory of the woman who'd played him for a *dummkopf* and then left him for another man in front of all their friends was like a bucket of icy reality poured over his head. He'd decided at that moment to expel any kind of drama from his life, and he had.

Until now, when he'd come alive as never before with a chaste touch.

He turned away, mumbling about seeing Carolyn later at the building site. If she replied or if she went on her way without any reaction was something he'd never know because he didn't look back as he walked away.

How could he have forgotten the incident when Adah had paraded her new boyfriend in front of him so she could squeeze as much drama out of the situation as possible? He'd begun to question everything in his life. If he could be so wrong about Adah, how could he be certain of anything else?

It was something he couldn't allow himself to forget again.

Sleep refused to come.

Carolyn tossed and turned and punched her pillow, searching for a comfortable place on it. The pillowcase seemed too wrinkled, or when she tried to pull it tight, it puffed, striking her in the nose. When she finally got comfortable, her right cheek itched. She gave in to the need to scratch it, and the process of finding a good spot on the pillow began all over again.

More than once, she considered getting up and walking around until she was so tired she would collapse into bed and sleep. She couldn't do that without risking waking the children and the others in the stables.

There were now only two other families with them. The rest had been able to return home or had moved in with relatives. She and Kevin and Rose Anne didn't have kinfolk in Evergreen Corners. As far as she knew, she wasn't related to anyone in the whole state of Vermont.

She tried not to think of the *aentis* and *onkels* and cousins in Indiana who might still be wondering where she and the children were. Tears swelled into her eyes when the *Deitsch* words came into her thoughts. *Aenti* and *onkel* were two words that once had been as common as breathing. Though Carolyn missed her life in Indiana, she had turned her back on it, never expecting to encounter an Amish person again.

Then the flood swept everything away and good-hearted volunteers came to help.

Amish volunteers.

Michael's face filled her mind along with a pulse of guilt. She couldn't blame him for leaving abruptly when they'd been talking on the village green. In her efforts to pretend she didn't know about *Deitsch*, she'd sounded ludicrous.

Why didn't you say that you spoke German even though you don't?

The answer was simple. She didn't want to lie, though she was avoiding the truth every day. However, she had a good reason. She was protecting the children from their brutal father. Being dishonest with Michael about understanding German wouldn't have done anything to prevent Leland from finding her and the children, so she couldn't bring herself to lie.

The thoughts chased around and around in her mind until, exhausted, she fell into dreams as unsettling as her waking life.

Then screams punctured the night.

Carolyn sat up and reached for the light on the table beside her bed. Her fingers found nothing. No lamp. No nightstand. Nothing.

Another shriek jerked her to her feet. She wasn't in her comfortable bedroom. She was sleeping in a horse stall, and the gray fingers of dawn were slipping past the feed sacks covering the windows on the other side of the building.

And a child was terrified.

Grabbing the robe she'd found in the piles of donated clothing, she forced her arms through the floppy sleeves. She rushed to the neighboring stall. Drowsy questions from the others in the stable were fired in her direction, but she paid them no mind. Her toe rammed something on the floor. Tears erupted into her eyes. She half hopped, half ran to the cots where Kevin and Rose Anne slept.

Light flashed from behind her, and she glanced over her shoulder. A shadowed form hung a lantern on a brad by the door. Nodding her thanks, though she couldn't see who'd left it there, she dropped to kneel next to Kevin's cot.

He screeched at the top of his lungs. He thrashed his arms from side to side. His eyes were closed, and she realized he was asleep. On the cot beside his, Rose Anne began to cry in sympathy.

Hoping she was doing the right thing, she soothed

her niece as she put her hand on her nephew's shoulder to keep him from throwing himself off the narrow cot. She didn't call his name or wake him. Instead, she protected him from his own panic.

Slowly, he calmed. When he was nestled again into his pillow, she adjusted the blankets twisted around him. She didn't want him to fall out of bed when he tried to loosen them.

She looked at the other cot. Rose Anne had her thumb in her mouth, a sure sign she was distressed, too. She'd stopped sucking her thumb three years ago, but Carolyn had noticed her doing it since the flood. Again she figured the best thing to do was not to mention it and pray the little girl's anxiety would dissipate as their lives returned to normal.

"You need to get back to sleep," Carolyn whispered, smoothing her niece's blanket, too.

"Is something wrong with Kevin?" the little girl whispered.

"Of course not."

"He was yawling, and I was ascared."

Translating Rose Anne's words, she knew the child meant her brother had been yelling and she'd been frightened. Carolyn bent and kissed her on the forehead.

"You don't have to be afraid," Carolyn murmured. "God is always watching over you, and I'm close by if you need me."

"But Kevin is ascared."

"He was having a bad dream."

The little girl shook her head. "It wasn't a bad dream. It was the rain."

"Rain?"

Rose Anne pointed at the roof. "Rain. Lots of it."

It *was* raining, Carolyn realized. Lost in her terror for Kevin and how he might end up hurting himself, she hadn't noticed rain hammering on the roof.

"We're safe here, sweetheart," she whispered. "You need to go to sleep so you can have fun with Taylor tomorrow."

Kevin sat as she stood. He was wide-awake, and he had his blanket in a white-knuckled grip. "Are we having another hurricane?"

"No, it's just rain." She laughed when thunder boomed in the distance. "A thunderstorm."

"Will we be okay?"

"We'll be fine." She hoped he couldn't see the tears filling her eyes as she wished for a way to banish his memories of the flood. It was impossible, she knew, but that didn't keep her from wanting to spare him more pain.

"Do we need to run away like we did last time?"

She shook her head. "We're safe here." Looking from him to his sister, she added, "The flood never reached here."

"But if it keeps raining—"

"It's going to be okay." She held out her other arm and gathered Rose Anne to her as soon as the little girl had clambered onto the cot. "God is watching over us."

"You said he was watching over us before, but our house is gone."

Tilting Kevin's face toward hers, she said, "Yes, the house is gone, but we're not. God kept us safe because He loves us and we love Him."

"But he didn't save Tip—Tip—Tippy." The child's voice cracked on the name of his stuffed dog that had vanished along with everything else in their house.

And Carolyn's heart broke anew. She'd prayed that somehow, someone sometime would return Tippy to Kevin. Knowing how much she was asking when God had already let them escape the floodwaters, she couldn't silence the prayer from the center of her soul.

She persuaded the children to go back to sleep. She turned to reach for the lantern. She wanted to take it down and extinguish the flame so the others could find another hour of sleep, as well.

Her fingers halted in midair as she saw Michael standing on the other side of the stall door. He took them as he held his own finger to his lips. Drawing her out of the stall, he closed the door and lifted the lantern off the nail. He said nothing as he led her toward the tack room. He set the lantern on a shelf by the door. Lifting the glass chimney, he blew out the flame.

"What are you doing here at this hour?" Carolyn glanced at the window, which was streaked with thick rivers of rain. "And in this weather?"

"I couldn't sleep." He gave her a smile that she could barely discern in the twilight. "And it wasn't raining when I came out. The clouds opened up as I was passing by, so I ducked inside. I was going to wait out the storm, but then I heard Kevin."

"Why were you walking past the stables this early?"

"I try to walk in a different direction each morning while I spend time talking to God about what I can do that day to help. It was by chance I came up the hill this morning rather than down."

Lightning flashed, followed by thunder. The rattle of hail struck the window, and she flinched in spite of herself.

She forced a smile. "I'd say you made a good decision."

"Or God is trying to tell me something." When another clap of thunder shook the building, he added, "Though He doesn't need to be so loud. I didn't realize this was where you and the *kinder* were sleeping."

"We're thankful for a warm, dry place to stay."

"Warm?" He glanced around the stables, though she was unsure what he thought he could see in the dim light. "It's going to be cold here when winter comes."

"All the more reason for you to get my house done." She'd meant her words as a joke, but they fell flat when he didn't laugh.

Concern filled his voice. "Are the *kinder* okay?"

"Yes, they'll be fine." Uncomfortable with his small intrusion into her family, she said, "Kevin had a bad dream and woke us up."

"Because of the rain?"

She wanted to say that was silly, but glad she could be honest with him, she said, "It's possible."

"Rebuilding a structure is easy. Rebuilding one's sense of security isn't."

"That sounds like the voice of experience."

He sighed. "My parents died when I was young, and both my twin brother and I had to learn not to expect something horrible was going to happen without warning."

"I'm sorry." She sat on a small stool. "I should have asked more about you and the other volunteers. I've been wrapped up in my own tragedy."

Squatting in front of her so their eyes were even, he said, "At times like this, nobody expects you to be thinking of anything but getting a roof over your *kinder*'s heads."

He didn't reach out to touch her, but she was aware of

every inch of him so close to her. His quiet strength had awed her from the beginning. As she'd come to know him better, his fundamental decency had impressed her more. He was a man she believed she could trust.

She shoved that thought aside. Trusting any man would be the worst thing she could do after seeing what *Mamm* had endured during her marriage and then struggling to help Regina escape her abusive husband.

When Carolyn stood, wanting to put some space between herself and this man who could convince her to be as credulous, Michael took a couple of steps back to allow her room. She bit back her yearning to apologize because, if she did, he might ask her to explain. She couldn't. That would reveal too much of her past.

"I'm glad you understand why I must focus on rebuilding a life for the children." The simple statement left no room for misinterpretation. "The flood will always be a part of us, but I want to help them learn how to live with their memories."

He stood, but didn't move closer. "I can't imagine what it was like."

"I can't forget what it was like." She edged toward the window. The rain hid any view of the brook.

"Tell me about it." His voice was soft and invited her to share her burdens with him. Oh, how she wished she could!

"It was loud," she said, choosing each word with care. "Very loud."

"The rush of the water?"

"You've seen the massive boulders along the banks. Those were tumbling into each other, though we didn't know what the terrible noise was at the time. They sounded like cars crashing into each other at a high speed, but the worst was hearing the house struggling to stay on its foundation. As I rushed the children down the stairs and outside, I could hear nails fighting not to be ripped out of the boards holding the house together."

She shuddered and wrapped her arms around herself, wishing the conversation hadn't taken this direction. Most of the time, she could keep those memories at bay by concentrating on getting through the day. So many things required her attention that time rushed by until she could fall into her cot each night.

"Were there people to assist you when you got outside?"

She shook her head. "I sent the kids running up the hill while I made sure the chicken coop was open. I didn't want our chickens to drown, either. I reached Kevin and Rose Anne before they got to the road. It's a good thing, because water was rushing along the road, too, and already washing over both sides. I helped the children get across and we kept going. All I could think about was getting to higher ground where the flood wouldn't reach us."

"And you succeeded."

"I stopped when their little legs couldn't go any farther. We sat on a log and tried to catch our breaths. Then we heard screams for help." She closed her eyes, but forced them open as the appalling scenes burst onto her eyelids like a horror film. "People were trapped in their houses because the water had risen so fast their yards were flooded before they realized what was going on."

"But nobody died in Evergreen Corners."

"I thank God for that with every breath I take, and I thank Him for the courage of our neighbors. Several people with four-wheel-drive pickups backed down as close as they dared through the rising water and threw ropes to those who were trapped. At least one had water seeping into the bed of their truck by the time they'd pulled the last person to safety."

"No wonder Kevin was frightened by the sound of rain tonight."

"The children didn't see any of that. I'd taken them to a shelter set up at the school and left them with Jenna who'd fled the library, bringing some of the irreplaceable books and the patrons who'd been there when water began pouring into the basement."

He shook his head. "I keep hearing stories of narrow escapes, and I try not to imagine how many more there were along the brook."

"Not just this one, but every stream and river in this watershed flooded that night." She started to add more, but halted when a soft cry came from the stall where the children slept.

As she excused herself to go and check on them, she could see the pity on Michael's face. She rushed to calm Rose Anne, who was curled into a sobbing bundle on her cot.

Normally, she would have been bothered by someone having sympathy for her, but if pitying her kept Michael from looking at her with his brown puppy-dog eyes that urged her to trust him, she'd accept it. She couldn't trust any man, because she wouldn't let the children spend their lives witnessing what she had.

Chapter Six

Carolyn yawned as she got dressed. All of them were exhausted. She helped Rose Anne deal with her frustration by pretending to be as incapable as the child at closing the buttons on the little girl's coat. It didn't take much acting because she felt as if her hands were encased in inflexible gloves and her feet in leaden boots.

In only twice as much time as it should have taken, she had the children ready to leave for the day. Rose Anne paused to kiss her stuffed rabbit, Hopper. Wanting to hug Kevin when she saw his devastated expression, Carolyn refrained when he edged away from her. How she wished he would grieve outwardly over losing his cherished stuffed friend! She didn't like how he continued to hold in his sorrow. She knew how caustic unhappiness could be.

She herded the youngsters out. She should be grateful they had a place to stay—and she was!—but she longed for a home where she didn't have to worry about Kevin's night terrors waking others. She would be able to concentrate on helping him. In addition, she longed for a bathroom she could share only with Rose Anne and

Kevin. She was tired of brushing her teeth with water from a galvanized bucket and taking showers where hot water was a rare luxury. The idea of a bath where she could soak until her fingertips were wizened was almost beyond her imagination at this point.

The morning's chill caught her by surprise. She should have expected the weather to change after the thunderstorm. Temperatures were capricious in autumn, jumping from summer to fall to winter in the space of a single day.

"What's going on?" Kevin asked, his sorrow pushed aside as he pointed at where a dozen people were gathering between the library and the seafood restaurant.

"I don't know." She squinted through the dim morning light that burned in her sleep-deprived eyes. Gray clouds lingered over the mountains to the west, obscuring their tops in off-white fuzz.

"Let's go see!" He didn't wait for her answer as he pelted down the hill with Rose Anne on his heels.

Though she'd never felt less like running, especially on grass slick with rain, Carolyn gave chase. The rumble of voices got louder as she drew even with the children. She took them by the hand, but continued on, drawn to the crowd by the undeniable anxiety wafting off the group.

Had something else gone wrong?

She couldn't see over the taller people. For a second, she considered putting Rose Anne on her shoulders and asking the child to give her a report. She almost laughed at the idea of what the child would tell her and how little it might have to do with reality.

Seeing Michael with his friends and several other Amish men, she walked toward where he stood. Kevin yanked his hand out of hers and ran forward to greet Michael with enthusiasm.

Michael looked over her nephew's head and gave her a smile that threatened to melt her knees. He'd been so kind to her this morning, letting her go on and on about the flood. Every instinct urged her to believe he was a good man, and she wanted to listen to her gut. It'd never steered her wrong.

Always a first time, her most sensible mind warned as another part whispered, *Oh, ye of little faith, trust in the Lord with all your heart.*

To hide her uneasy thoughts, Carolyn asked, "What's going on?"

"The road washed out last night." He pointed north, then when she stood on tiptoe to try to see what he was indicating, he drew her forward.

She gasped when she saw the rubble lying next to the only bridge still spanning the brook. The bridge remained sturdy, but the rain had undermined the road. It had collapsed, leaving a band of asphalt not much wider than a railroad track.

"At least..." she began, then halted as the rest of the asphalt caved in and slid down into the brook. The bridge's deck ended in midair on the side closer to her. There was a gap of about six feet between it where the road was gone.

"That does it," said one of the Amish men whose name she couldn't remember. "We're cut off from the outside world until the road across the bridge can be rebuilt."

She resisted her longing to shout her gratitude to God. The people around her wouldn't understand why she was relieved. She'd happily accept being separated from everyone else if it meant Leland couldn't get to town.

"That section of road was weak," someone said behind her. "I'm surprised it hadn't fallen in already."

There was a chorus of agreement, but silence clamped on them at the distant rumble of a truck's engine. Michael and two other men raced toward the abutment. Carolyn watched as the men laced their fingers together and Michael put his foot on them. They raised Michael high enough to grab the top of the abutment with both hands. He scrambled onto the bridge like Kevin used to climb onto the roof of their chicken coop. Running to the far side, he waved his arms to get the driver's attention before the truck reached the bridge.

Carolyn breathed a grateful prayer as the vehicle slowed. She drew the children back as other men rushed past to collect ladders from the general store. In quick order, they were leaned against the abutment, and more men climbed onto the bridge, carrying pieces of wood and tools.

Michael finished talking to the driver before stepping aside to let others erect a temporary barrier by the bridge. Orange barrels left along the side of the road were dragged onto the center line.

Mayor Whittaker walked by with her cell phone close to her ear. She wore a bathrobe under her winter coat and had curlers in her hair. "Now! We need warning signs so nobody drives onto the bridge when the road on one side has collapsed."

"Not safe?" cried Rose Anne. "What about Michael?" She ran toward the abutment.

The mayor lowered her phone and stepped forward

to block the little girl. Bending toward her, she said something too low for Carolyn to hear.

Rose Anne whirled and called back, "It's okay as long as Michael isn't in an a-tween wheeler."

"She means an eighteen wheeler," Carolyn translated in case the mayor was bewildered by Rose Anne's response.

Nodding, Gladys Whittaker put her phone back to her ear and continued to demand what she believed her village needed.

Motioning for Rose Anne to come back to where she and Kevin stood, Carolyn frowned. Kevin was watching the bridge, mesmerized by the sight of the men walking along it. She wanted to warn him not to scale it, but decided she shouldn't give him any ideas. She'd talk to him later when the lure of ladders and an empty bridge wasn't right in front of him.

Benjamin lifted Rose Anne and carried her to Carolyn. The little girl giggled as he blew a loud, buzzing kiss on her cheek.

"*Gute mariye*, Carolyn," he said with a smile as he set her niece on her feet. "Have you met everyone here? If not, let me introduce you while we wait for our hero to return." He winked. "You know James, and the other three are his older brothers. Mathias, Enos and Orris. They've been working on the Gagnon house next door to yours."

The men nodded in her direction, but turned back to talk to James. No, not talk to him, but harangue him, she realized.

She tried not to listen. It wasn't easy to hear his older brothers tell him what he was doing wrong. Or what *they* thought he was doing wrong. They spoke in English. Why? Were they determined that everyone understood what they were saying about James? The list of their beefs with him ran from big to minuscule. It didn't seem to matter to them that he wasn't in charge of arranging which house would receive their delivery of concrete first or that the slight changes in his clothing had been made to comply with the *Ordnung* in the new settlement on Harmony Creek. They acted as if James's sole intention had been to annoy them.

"Don't," Michael said, startling her because she hadn't heard him return.

She hadn't thought she'd ever be unaware of him, and she realized how nettled she was by James's brothers' litany of complaints. "Don't?"

"Don't interfere. I understand that you think it's unfair for them to treat him as they do. I got involved when they first came to Harmony Creek Hollow and acted as if James didn't have a single thought between his ears. He asked me to let him handle it."

"You call that handling it?" She flung out a hand toward the four men. "When Kevin starts to get all bossy, I step in."

"But Kevin is a *kind.* Those are grown men."

"So they should know better."

"I agree, but I also agree with James. It's his problem to handle."

Carolyn had to accede, though she didn't want to. Taking her niece and nephew by the hand again, she left, though every particle of her wanted to announce to James's brothers that they should treasure the time they had with him instead of ruining it with accusations. If she were granted another few minutes with her sister, she wouldn't waste a second of it.

"That was cool!" crowed Kevin to Michael who walked with them. "You kept the truck from falling off the bridge."

"The driver kept it from happening by being quick on his brakes. I just warned him."

Kevin refused to be persuaded. "But you're a hero!"

"God put me and the other men in the right place at the right time."

Seeing how uncomfortable Michael was with Kevin lauding him, Carolyn guessed his unease came from being raised Amish and considering pride a sin. She understood that, but Michael's reluctance seemed to hint there was something more bothering him.

"Are you okay?" she asked beneath the children's excitement.

"I'm fine." He sighed, then smiled faintly. "Sorry, Carolyn. I don't like being ensnared in drama."

"Then you came to the wrong place. Everyone in Evergreen Corners is dripping with drama since the flood." She started to add more, then groaned as the clouds overhead opened like a kitchen faucet.

When he grasped her arm, she let him pull her toward the store. The ground was already soaked, and soil quickly turned to mud. Others were already huddling beneath the wide roof of the wraparound porch. He helped her onto the warped boards, and she was relieved when her boots weren't left behind in the mire. He hefted the children up before jumping out of the storm himself.

She moved closer to the store's wall, hoping to escape the spray from the deluge. A shiver ran an icy finger down her back while she looked at where the wooden steps had been. They'd vanished down the brook. Where had they ended up?

She almost laughed. How would anyone ever be able to differentiate one shattered board from another? Paint had been stripped off by the gravel swept along in the water. It had raised the brook's bed almost two inches. Dredging had begun farther upstream, but she had no idea when the equipment would get to Evergreen Corners.

Especially now that the last bridge was unusable while the road was out.

Michael leaned his right shoulder against the wall, so he faced her. When she looked at him, she was astounded by how close his face was to hers. She lowered her eyes and turned away.

What was wrong with her? She shouldn't be imagining how his lips would feel against hers. She'd promised herself—and God—that she would learn the lessons He'd placed before her when she witnessed *Mamm* and her sister with abusive husbands. She couldn't risk making the same error, not when the children depended on her.

"You aren't dramatic, Carolyn," Michael murmured. When she raised her eyes to meet his steady gaze, he said, "You can't know how much I admire how you stay calm in the middle of the biggest tempest." He shook his head as the rain seemed to fall harder. "Maybe we should stop saying words like *tempest, drip* or *pour*."

"Now who's being dramatic?"

She meant her question as a joke to defuse the tension hardening his shoulders into a taut line. When he recoiled from her words, she was shocked.

Though she wanted to ask him why he was leery of

what he called drama, Carolyn simply said, "It shouldn't take them long to fix the road and reconnect it to the bridge. It was quick for the roadbed to be rebuilt last time."

"There's more debris and rocks to move because the whole section collapsed." He gave her a wry grin. "Or at least that's what I was told. I know exactly nothing about building roads."

"We're all learning a lot about things we never thought we'd ever need to know."

He didn't answer as Glen stepped onto the porch with one easy motion. Shaking rain off his baseball cap, the project director said, "Not how I planned to start the day."

"Do we have enough supplies for today?" Michael asked.

"I've got a 4x4 truck if someone needs it." Glen tapped his forefinger against his cheek. "We've been keeping it for when someone needs to travel north because that road out of town has been iffy since the flood. Some of the locals cut a route through the woods behind the diner to reach Ludlow."

Carolyn wasn't the only one on the porch who sighed at the mention of the diner that had been a popular meeting place. Whole sections of the building were gone, but the owner had vowed to rebuild. She hoped he would be interested in buying her baked goods again. A large portion of her income before the flood had been from providing pies and cakes and cookies to the diner. Now she was dependent on her neighbors and groups like the Amish Helping Hands to provide food and shelter for her and the children.

When Glen spoke her name, she focused on the project director again as he said, "We'll be ready later today to begin excavating the new cellar for your house, Carolyn, and we've got plenty of diesel. Of course, we need it to stop raining."

As he spoke, the storm stopped. Everybody laughed at the coincidence.

Carolyn gathered the children because they were late for breakfast. She went with them, though she wished she could have stayed on the porch with Michael until he explained what had dimmed his eyes when he spoke about drama. He was doing so much to help her. It seemed only right she should offer him an ear if he wanted to unburden himself.

Or her lips for a kiss.

Michael stepped back from the cellar hole and tested aching muscles that had been challenged that day. Rebuilding the road had taken almost three days, using machinery brought in for excavating the cellars. The state's equipment had been allocated elsewhere. Glen and his volunteers had assisted the town crew in reconnecting the bridge to the single lane road running through the center of Evergreen Corners. It was only a temporary fix, but it kept supplies moving into town and let concrete trucks deliver their loads.

He couldn't remember the last time he'd done masonry work, and he remembered why he'd avoided it. Cement wasn't like wood, beautiful and intriguing to the touch. The concrete forms outlining the new dimensions of the house had to be level in every direction. Unlike the old cellar, which had been plowed in before they'd begun work on the new foundation, the new cellar hole needed to be waterproof. The old cellar walls had been layers of stone with dirt between them.

He eyed the new foundation. He'd seen Isaac measuring each corner to make sure it was as close to ninety degrees as possible. The newcomer had insisted on making changes to the wall facing the brook because he hadn't been satisfied with the line Michael and James set in place. Though the work of pulling up the stakes and resetting them had been tedious, Michael hadn't complained. He respected a man who took such care with his work. Glen had agreed to bring all the volunteers to work on the Wiebe family's foundation. With the first foundation poured, they would move to the Gagnons' house next door and then on to the third house. That one would become Rhiannon Cadwallader's home. The widow, whom everyone called Rhee, had been rescued seconds before her house crumbled. She currently lived in the basement of the church where she'd once preached.

After working a couple of days with Isaac Kauffman, Michael had no doubt Glen had decided to give in because Isaac wouldn't. He might be the most stubborn, exacting man Michael had ever met, but he backed his demands with precise work. Michael looked forward to using his own skills when it came to adding molding and cabinets to the house.

Taking a piece of rough board and smoothing it and shaping it seemed to bring him closer to God. When he mitered corners or added stain to bring out the beauty of the grain, his fingers created a hymn of praise to the greatest Maker who'd put the pieces of the world together in perfect order.

He bent and lifted one of the stakes that had been

tossed aside because the notch had failed. Turning it in his hands, he pulled out his pocketknife. Four quick strokes cut out a place where the string could be hooked into place. Several had broken while preparing this foundation, so they needed all they had for the next ones.

"Hey, Michael!"

At the shout in a young voice, he looked over his shoulder as Kevin came bounding toward him. Did Carolyn know the boy was here? *Ja*, she was talking to Glen as they bent over a stack of long pages on a large rock. He recognized them as the plans for the new house.

"*Gute mariye*, Kevin," he called back.

"Did you say *good morning*?"

"I did. *Gut* guess."

"That one's easy. They sound a lot alike, and I remember hearing it before." Without a pause, he asked, "What are you doing?"

Michael had to smile. The boy's endless curiosity reminded him of himself at Kevin's age. At first, he'd been given answers. However, as he grew older and learned to read, his adoptive father had provided him with simple books where he could find the answers on his own. The day he'd first entered the public library and discovered the array of resources waiting there had been one of the happiest of his whole life.

Until he met Carolyn and her *kinder* and was able to spend time with them.

He hadn't guessed he'd find youngsters of their ages fascinating. He liked how he never could guess what they'd do or say next.

He showed Kevin the stick and his pocketknife. "I'm making a new stake for the Gagnons' house."

"How?"

Running the knife along the wood, he demonstrated. "It's called whittling."

"Why are you a wit-ling?" asked Rose Anne who'd followed her brother. She peered down into the cellar.

Folding his knife and sticking it in his pocket, Michael swept an arm around her waist. He picked her up so she wouldn't tumble over the edge. Her laugh tickled his heart and made him want to join in. He smiled at Carolyn as she walked toward them.

"She means whittling," Carolyn said.

"I was hoping so, but I guess wit-ling is better than witless." He put Rose Anne down and watched as the two children ran to get a closer look at the bulldozer parked a few feet away. "She knows how to make new words when she doesn't understand something, ain't so?"

"She's trying to keep up with her big brother."

"That sounds like the voice of experience. Did you have a big brother you needed to keep up with, too?"

"No, a big sister." She looked away as if she'd said something she hadn't planned to.

He couldn't guess what it was, but there were many things about Carolyn Wiebe that baffled him.

Deciding the best thing to do was not press her, he said, "What would you think of me teaching Kevin to whittle? He seems interested, and he's about the same age I was when I started."

"Maybe so, but I know how enthusiastic he can get and how he can toss common sense out the window."

"Then we'll work outside."

She frowned at him. He wasn't sure if it was because

of his weak jest or because she was upset he joked about something she took seriously.

Holding up his hands, he said, "Just trying to lighten the mood."

"By showing you can be as absurd as Kevin is when he gets overexcited?"

"Ouch." He put his hand to the center of his chest and rocked back several steps.

"Michael!" Exasperation filled her voice.

He relented. "I'm sorry, Carolyn. I know I shouldn't pick on you when it's something you care about as much as you do your *kinder*."

"I don't like the idea of him cutting off a finger or two." A faint smile tilted her lips. "Or you, either."

He wiggled his fingers. "So far, so good, and I've been whittling since I was five or six. Learning what a stick of wood could become led me to wanting to do more."

"So you became a carpenter. Will you be framing our house?"

"*Ja*, I'll be one of the framers. The work doesn't require much imagination. I like being able to see a piece of wood and figuring out what it could become. A two-by-four is already pretty much all it's going to be." He chuckled. "That's why I'm looking forward more to working on the finish carpentry in your house."

"Me, too, because that will mean the work is almost done, and we can move into a real house again instead of living in two stalls in a stable. I shouldn't complain. After all, a stable was good enough for a very special baby's birth."

"That is very true." He gestured toward the cellar hole. "Do you want to see what we've done? We can start with what Benjamin and I finished." He crooked a finger. "This way."

He walked toward the trees and heard her gasp when she caught sight of the rectangle of chicken wire that made a pen for her vagabond chickens. She ran to it, lacing her fingers through the wire and examining how he and his friends had hooked more wire to the top.

"We didn't want to let your pesky poultry fly out," he said with a chuckle.

"As long as they've got plenty to eat, they're content not to wander." She counted the chickens. "All nine hens are here! You found them all."

"They found us. I think they're happy to be home and safe from predators." He watched her face as she cooed at her beloved hens who came waddling over to her, hoping for more food though corn was scattered on the ground. "And your rooster—an ornery fellow, I've got to say—was captured by a deputy sheriff who took him to a nearby farm. I can find out which one. He's—"

"Doodle."

"I hope that's the name of the rooster and not the deputy."

She laughed, the sound lighter than he'd ever heard from her. "Yes, Doodle is our rooster. I told you the kids chose the chickens' names, though they had help from our friends." She pointed at each of the hens in turn. "There's Henrietta. Henley. Henster is the one at the back. Hendrix and Henmeister. Henna. Little Red Hen and Big Red Hen. And, of course, Henny Penny."

Glad to laugh along with her, he felt a flush of satisfaction—something he hadn't experienced in a while—rush through him as she thanked him for collecting the chickens and building the wire pen. She was more delighted when he told her that he planned to rebuild her coop for her.

"But first," he said, "we've got to get you and the *kinder* into your house. *Komm mol*, and you can have a look down at your new cellar. There's not much to see at this point because it's empty, but I know you'd like to see what progress we've made."

"I don't want to get in the way."

"There's nothing more we can do here until the concrete finishes curing. If we put up walls too soon, we risk damaging the foundation."

"How long will that take?"

"About a week?"

"A week?" The word came out in a squawk.

"Pray for warmer and drier weather because it'll shorten the time, but we want to pour the other two foundations before we start framing your house." He led her to where she could look down into the cellar. "It'll be worth the wait because you won't have water leaking in as you did with your old house."

Her eyes cut toward the sleepy brook, and he wondered if she was reliving how she'd feared for her life and the *kinder*'s. He resisted his yearning to give her a hug as he would have Kevin or Rose Anne. She wasn't a *kind*. She was a beautiful woman shadowed by tragedy.

Ja, she was a lovely woman, and he'd spent too many hours thinking about her and how it would be to hold her close.

But he couldn't. Not until he made his final decision if he'd be baptized or not. The choice must not be influenced by his burgeoning feelings for her, feelings that made his fingers quiver at the thought of touching her.

Chapter Seven

Michael couldn't wait for Carolyn to appear at the neighboring work site four days later while they watched the first concrete truck start pouring its load into the forms for the cellar of the house next door to hers. The news he had for her today should bring one of her gentle smiles. He hoped he wouldn't burst with what he had to share with her.

At last, she arrived. She carried a tray. The cups of *kaffi* on it sent out an inviting aroma that drew the workers toward her like bees to a patch of flowers. Someone grabbed a cup for the guy operating the truck.

As Michael stood to one side to let the others take their cups, there was only one thing more enticing than the *kaffi*'s scent. Carolyn herself. Her blond hair was drawn back at her nape beneath a small round lace *kapp*. Beneath a black apron, her lilac dress was decorated with small flowers in a scattered pattern and accented by her gold locket. The image of a sweet, plain woman was ruined by the heavy work boots someone had given her so she didn't ruin her sneakers in the mud.

"How's it going?" she asked as he took one of the last cups.

"It feels *gut* to be moving forward again."

Michael drained his cup while Carolyn collected empty ones. "Do you have a few minutes?" he asked when she held out the tray to him in a silent invitation to add his cup. "I'd like to talk to you about something important."

"I need to return the tray, and—"

He didn't give her a chance to continue. Putting two fingers in his mouth, he let loose a whistle in the direction of a pair of teens. One *Englisch* boy whose name he thought was Jack turned to look at him. Since work on the Gagnon house had resumed a few days ago, about a half-dozen *Englisch* teens, both boys and girls, had been hanging around after school. They wanted to help, but Glen had been firm that volunteers had to be approved by Amish Helping Hands and the Mennonite project director before they could work.

Michael didn't agree because the teens were as eager as he would have been at their ages to help rebuild their village. Maybe he should mention that to Glen and suggest the teens be found chores at the work sites. He valued Glen's vast experience, but there must be tasks they could ask the kids to do.

Later, he'd make a point of seeking out Glen.

For now, he motioned to the lad he thought was named Jack to come closer. Taking the tray from Carolyn, he handed it to Jack.

"Can you take this to the community center's kitchen?" he asked.

When the boy hesitated, not wanting to miss watching the concrete being poured, Carolyn said, "There are extra cinnamon rolls left over from breakfast. Tell them I said you should get two for bringing back the tray."

"Can we both go?" He pointed toward his friend who'd been listening while trying not to appear to.

Michael glanced at Carolyn and saw her nod. "I'm sure the offer is *gut* for two."

"Thanks!" The kid grabbed the tray and with his friend hurried in the direction of the community center.

"What do you need to talk to me about?" Carolyn asked as another truck reached the site.

So many things, he wanted to reply. He wondered about her life as a conservative Mennonite, and he wondered what had happened to her husband. She never mentioned him. The kids didn't, either, he realized with a bolt of shock. He'd been so involved in the disaster relief work, he hadn't given any thought to Carolyn's husband.

"Michael?" she asked, and he knew he'd been mired in his thoughts too long.

He chided himself for being distracted when at last she was standing beside him and he could share the news he'd been waiting to tell her. Making sure he didn't smile and give away his surprise, he said, "I wanted to let you know you and the *kinder* won't be sleeping in the stables tonight. You're being moved elsewhere."

Puzzlement threaded her brow. "What? Where are we moving to?"

"It's simple." He couldn't halt his grin. "You'll be living in the trailer, and Benjamin, James and I will use the cots in the stable. After all, we're not as susceptible to colds as the *kinder* are."

"You're working hard every day. You need to have somewhere comfortable to sleep."

"We aren't working any harder than you are, and you're taking care of two active *kinder*, as well." He put his hands on her shoulders and bent so he could look into her eyes. "Most important, Carolyn, there's plenty of insulation in the trailer's roof, and that will deaden the sound of rain."

Her eyes widened, and he found himself wondering if a man could get lost exploring their deep brown depths. He looked away before he ended up gawping at her with the same expression her son had worn when Kevin watched the bulldozer push in the foundation of their old house.

"I didn't think of that," she said.

"Those little ones have endured enough, don't you think?"

"But to put you out of your comfortable beds—"

"Comfortable? Three men in such a tiny space isn't what I'd describe as comfortable." When she opened her mouth to protest further, he held up a single finger. "One thing you should know about plain men, Carolyn. When we set our minds on a course of action to help someone else, nothing deters us."

"You're making that up."

"Maybe. Maybe not." He was relieved to see her resistance to the idea crumbling. "But it doesn't matter. We can move our stuff out and your stuff in while the concrete is being poured. We're in the way here anyhow." He waved to his friends who'd waited near the road.

"I don't know what to say."

"Say thank you."

Her shoulders dropped, and her smile softened. "Thank you. I should—"

"No," Benjamin interjected as he and James joined them. "You shouldn't do anything. Let us take care of it." He grinned at Michael. "So glad you got a chance to tell her what we decided. I hope she didn't object too much to what is common sense."

"Not too much." She smiled.

Did it brighten when she aimed it at him? Michael wanted to think so.

Carolyn had to wonder what others must think when she followed Michael, his two friends and the children she'd collected from the day care center in a bizarre parade.

She wasn't surprised to see Kevin trailing Michael as if he were the man's shadow. Rose Anne was dancing around, almost getting in the way on each step. Nobody seemed to mind as they talked and laughed with her nephew and niece.

This was what she wanted for her sister's children. To have in their lives strong, gentle men who would treat them as special gifts from God. She prayed God had concealed any memories Kevin had of his father and thanked Him that Rose Anne was too young to recall the horrific scenes the children had witnessed.

Kevin stopped to peer into some used cars, and Rose Anne had to be lifted to do the same. He decided Carolyn should replace the sedate black sedan that had washed away in the flood with a bright silver SUV. The children were accustomed to her driving a car, a skill she'd mastered when she decided to live as a Mennonite and another example of how far she'd removed herself from the life she'd assumed she would live as an Amish woman. Telling him she'd keep his suggestion in mind, she convinced the children to keep going.

There were a pair of trailers parked behind the dealership. One was small, shaped like a horizontal teardrop and made to tow behind a car. The other was a much grander vehicle with a steering wheel set behind its large windshield. Double sets of tires front and back were needed for such a big RV. She caught sight of a rectangular bay that stuck out the far side to give more room to the interior.

They went to the smaller trailer. Though Benjamin had made it clear all three men had agreed to switching places, she had no doubts Michael was the catalyst behind the idea. Not that he would admit it. No Amish man would lay claim to such a good idea, because to do so would hint of pride.

James opened the door and stepped back. "Be careful. There are three steps in there."

Carolyn thanked him and lifted Kevin and then Rose Anne onto the steps. Inside, the trailer wasn't much bigger than the two stalls at Mr. Aiken's stables. Looking past the miniature kitchen with its dull green appliances and sink, she saw a bedroom at the back and realized the trailer was the size of three stalls. The extra room would give her privacy she hadn't had since the flood.

She gasped when she saw a stacked washer and dryer in the bedroom. "Do they work?"

"*Ja*, they do now," Michael said, coming up the steps. "We fixed them last week and got them hooked up."

What luxury! Their old house hadn't had a washer or dryer, though she'd seen space for them on the plan in the new house.

In front of her was a narrow sofa with cushions covered in striped fabric the same green as the stove. To her right beneath a low ceiling was a table with a curved bench along the outer wall of the trailer. More cushions matched the ones on the sofa.

She edged out of the way as the other two men entered. With all of them inside, she understood why they'd been eager to swap. There wasn't room for them even if she and the children hadn't been there.

"Sorry about the dirty dishes in the sink," Benjamin said, embarrassed.

"I hardly noticed them," she said as she unbuttoned her coat. The trailer had been toasty warm when she stepped in, and now, with all of them crowded in it, the air was beginning to feel as if she'd crawled into the oven. "This is wonderful."

"I don't know if I'd call it *wunderbaar*." Michael laughed. "But it should be much more comfortable for you and the *kinder*."

His words made her think again of how chilly it would be in the stables as the mercury dropped night after night as winter approached. "I can't ask you to give up—"

Her protest was interrupted when Kevin climbed on the sofa and grabbed the edge of the low ceiling over the table. He hauled himself up, rolled onto his belly and peered over the edge. "Can I sleep here?"

"It's a bunk bed with a single bunk," Michael said when her confusion must have been visible.

"I'll sleep in the corner and won't fall out." Kevin clasped his hands together. "Please! I promise to be careful."

Before she could answer, Michael said in a whisper, "We'll rig up something so he won't fall out. A couple of narrow slats will let him climb in and out, but keep him from rolling over the edge while he's asleep."

"All right, Kevin. You can sleep there after Michael fixes it into a bed."

"It's not a bed?" He looked at them in astonishment. "There's a mattress. All I need is a pillow and some blankets."

"We used the area for storage," Michael answered.

Undaunted, her nephew asked, "When can you fix it, Michael?"

"Probably this evening. I need to get some supplies, and then once I'm done, you can sleep there every night until your house is finished."

Kevin's eyes filled with abrupt tears. "Tippy would love being here. It's the kind of place he likes."

Michael looked at her, puzzled. "Tippy?"

She blinked back tears of her own. "Tippy is—he was the stuffed dog he'd had since he was a baby."

"Gone?"

She nodded, glad she didn't have to explain more. As she moved to ask Kevin at which end he'd want to put his pillow, in hopes of distracting him from his sorrow, she heard Michael draw in a deep breath and release it through pursed lips. She wanted to remind him that some things were out of their hands and they needed to trust God had a reason for what had happened along Washboard Brook.

But that wasn't easy when one small boy had lost his only connection to Indiana. She knew Kevin didn't think of Tippy like that. Carolyn wasn't sure how much her nephew remembered of his life before they'd come to Evergreen Corners. It was a topic she wouldn't bring up, and he hadn't asked.

Someday she was going to have to be honest with him and with Rose Anne.

Not today.

When Kevin was calmer, she discovered Benjamin and James had slipped out of the trailer. She didn't see them outside, so she wondered if they'd returned to the Gagnons' work site.

Rose Anne tugged on Michael's pants leg. "What about me?"

"We've got a special place for you. Watch." Michael bent over the sofa built against the wall. When he pulled on the seat cushion, the base rolled out enough to let the cushion on the back fall into place to make a twin bed.

The little girl clapped her hands with glee before climbing onto the cushions and lying down. "My own real live growed-up bed."

Again Carolyn had to blink back tears. They filled her eyes each time one of the children mentioned how they'd been roughing it. How she wished they'd never had to experience losing everything and living in the stable!

Now…

She put her hand on Michael's strong arm and whispered, "Thank you."

"It's nothing."

"No, it's the answer to a prayer." She glanced at where Rose Anne was standing on her bed and peeking into the space where Kevin would sleep. "You've made the children so happy."

"And you?"

"You've made me happy, too." Heat rose up her cheeks, and she guessed she was blushing. "Thank you, Michael."

"I'm glad to be able to help. I know Benjamin and James are, too."

Was that his way of severing the sudden connection between them? If so, she should be grateful because her fingers tingled with a longing to lace them through his as she stepped closer to him. She couldn't do that. Until she knew the children were safe from Leland, she must avoid getting their lives involved with anyone else's.

"Please thank them for us." She edged away. "No, don't do that. Instead, ask them to come here tomorrow night after supper. I'd like to try out this oven and bake a cake."

"Cake?" cried the children as one. "Yummy!"

"How can I resist such an invitation?" asked Michael, his eyes twinkling. "After all I've heard about your baking, we'll be excited to sample it."

"Good. Come tomorrow night after supper."

"We'll have time before tomorrow evening's planning meeting." He winked at the children. "And if we're a little late, it'll be worth it, ain't that so?"

"Mommy makes the bestest cakes in the whole big, wide world," Rose Anne said, crossing her arms over her narrow chest as if daring someone to challenge her assertion. "The *gut-est*, right, Michael?"

Carolyn fought her smile. "Rose Anne, we shouldn't brag about the gifts God has given to us."

"Even when it's the truth?"

Putting her arm around the little girl, Carolyn sat beside her on the extended sofa. "Whether it's the truth or not, it's not something we brag about to the world. We should—"

"Let everyone find out for themselves," said Kevin, looking over the edge.

Rose Anne nodded. "And then everyone will find out Mommy's cakes are the bestest things in the whole wide world."

Giving her niece a hug, she said, "No, you are the bestest thing in the whole wide world." She smiled at Kevin. "Both of you are the bestest things in the whole wide world."

"You can't have two bestest things," he argued.

"Maybe not, but you two are the bestest things in my world."

Her answer set both children to laughing. When a deeper chuckle rumbled underneath their voices, she couldn't help her gaze from rising to meet Michael's.

His warm eyes twinkled as the skin around them crinkled to reveal lines left by frequent good humor. "And if you're wondering, we haven't forgotten about you." He gestured toward the other end of the trailer. "There's a real bed in the bedroom. Not as interesting as the two out here, but it'll give you more privacy than you've had."

"How can we thank you for all you've done for us?"

"The cake will be a *gut* place to start." His easy grin sent a sweet warmth uncurling through her middle.

For the first time, she didn't try to dampen it. Instead, she wanted to savor the luscious sensation while he explained to her that once they had the men's clothing and supplies out of the trailer, he'd help her and the children move their things from the stable. She looked forward to spending the rest of the morning with him.

Enjoying their time together wouldn't last forever, so she intended to appreciate every second now.

Chapter Eight

Eager to discuss his ideas with Glen about putting the village teenagers to work, Michael headed toward the project director's office at the high school the next morning. He undid his coat, glad for the warmth billowing along the empty hallway. Carolyn hadn't been kidding when she said the trailer was more comfortable than the stables. Though the building was heated, the system was meant for horses, not humans. A chill had fallen on everything by morning, making his blanket feel as if it'd been left outside.

On the other hand, he hadn't bumped elbows with James and Benjamin while they got ready for the day. Shaving with the small mirror he'd brought from the trailer and using a water bucket had been simpler than standing at the teeny kitchen sink.

When Michael reached the classroom Glen had taken over as his office, he peered through the big glass window in the door. The scholars' desks had been removed, leaving marks on the parquet flooring. In addition to the teacher's desk, a half dozen folding tables had been brought in for the project director's use. A blackboard held a schedule with each volunteer's name listed under the projects for the three houses. A schedule had been sketched in, though the board showed plenty of erasures.

From another wing of the building, he could hear voices. The students must be arriving for the day. Aromas announced the cafeteria staff was already at work and *kaffi* was brewing in the teachers' lounge.

Michael knocked on the door and nodded when Glen motioned for him to enter. Every flat surface was covered with papers and books and file folders in a variety of colors. Two whiteboards with black markers sitting in the trays at the bottom displayed more lists. Supplies on order, Michael guessed after a quick glance, and delivery dates.

What a task to keep the projects on track with both supplies and workers! Glen must have more patience than Michael ever would have, as well as an ability to see both the big picture for the projects and the tiniest details.

"What brings you here today?" Glen asked, picking up a cup. He took a sip, then grimaced. "This coffee wasn't good when it was fresh. It's gone downhill since."

"I'll bring you some *gut kaffi* from the community center on my way to the work site."

Glen smiled. "A debt I may never be able to repay. This stuff is going to rot my taste buds and my stomach."

"How about repaying that debt by listening to an idea I've got?"

"Ideas can't repay a debt, especially if they're good ones." Motioning for Michael to get one of the folding chairs stored in a corner, he asked, "What's on your mind?"

Michael didn't bother to sit as he spoke about finding work in the afternoon for the teens who were interested in becoming a part of the rebuilding. Leaning his hands on the edge of the desk, he said, "I think it'd be worthwhile for you to arrange for the teenagers, who've been hanging around the job sites, to help."

"We can't be responsible for minors, and getting signed permission from their parents will take time away from other work we need to do." Glen glanced out the windows at the low, gray sky that warned of a mid-November snowstorm. "No matter how much we want to ignore the fact, winter will be here before we know it."

"I'm not talking about them doing construction work. What they could do is be available at each site to run errands so we won't have to spend valuable time chasing down tools or something to drink. I would trust Kevin to do something this simple, so it shouldn't be a problem for teenagers."

Glen leaned back in his chair, folded his hands over his chest and considered the idea. "Y'know, Michael, that's an excellent idea. I must admit asking teens to be errand boys—"

"And girls."

He chuckled. "Errand boys and girls. Usually, when we get involved in such projects, the teens are busy with school and their own lives and don't have time to volunteer."

"They seem eager to help, and we could use the extra hands."

"I agree one hundred percent." Glen closed his eyes

and rubbed his forehead before folding his arms on the papers spread across the table. "Let me talk to Mayor Whittaker. If she's okay with it, let's give it a trial run."

Pushing back from the desk, Michael said, "*Gut.* That's all I have. Anything you want me to share with my team?"

"I hear you, James and Benjamin traded your sleeping quarters."

"That's right. Should we have cleared it with you first?"

Glen waved a hand in his direction. "Of course not, but keep me informed. Okay? If someone needs a list of where our volunteers are, I need to be able to provide it right away."

"Who would need such a list?"

"Someone with too much time on their hands. Nothing we'd know anything about."

"True." He turned to leave, but paused when Glen called his name.

"Well done, by the way," the project director said with a smile.

"The forms for the concrete—"

"I'm not talking about that. I'm talking about you guys offering your cushy quarters to Carolyn and her kids. That was decent of you."

"It seemed like the right thing to do."

"It was." Glen's jaw worked before he said, "If it's none of my business, tell me so, but is there something going on between you and Carolyn?"

Michael knew he couldn't hesitate. Nor could he lie. "I'm Amish, and she's not."

"Things aren't that simple."

"It is for me." Again that was the truth, though he

wasn't going to divulge that. Until he knew what he wanted his future to be, he must not let his heart get involved with any woman beyond casual friendship.

Too bad his heart didn't want to agree.

It wasn't her home, but putting a bowl of steaming vegetables on the small table at the front of the trailer made Carolyn feel more at home than she had in almost a month. She opened the oven and checked the chicken and noodles casserole was browning properly.

"When do we eat?" asked Rose Anne from the sofa where she played with a doll someone had given her.

Unlike the faceless rag dolls Carolyn had as a child, this one had molded features. Its bright purple hair clashed with an outfit of every color in the rainbow. Carolyn's dolls had had sedate plain clothes like the ones she'd worn. They'd had bare feet instead of what looked like a cross between sneakers and a truncated skateboard. But Rose Anne loved the silly doll, and having her happy was what was important now.

"Not until Michael gets here," called Kevin from by the door. "Shouldn't he be here by now?"

"Michael and his friends will get here when they're done with work and have had a chance to clean up." She wagged a finger at the children. "Something you need to do. Go and wash your hands and faces. With soap this time."

Ignoring their grumbling, Carolyn kept her smile hidden until Kevin and Rose Anne somehow squeezed into the minuscule bathroom together. She listened for giggling, a sure sign of mischief, as she opened up the fridge and took out apple butter to serve with the biscuits she'd made earlier. She hoped they were edible because the gauge on the front of the oven seemed to have little to do with the actual temperature inside it.

At a knock on the door, she wiped her hands on a towel and reached to open it. Michael stepped into the trailer, the hair along his face still damp.

"It's cold out there," he said with a big shudder, "but it smells *wunderbaar* in here."

"Take off your coat and sit while I finish." She barely got the words out before the children ran from the bathroom, their hands dripping, to greet him.

Reaching over their heads, she took his coat and hung it in the closet by the bedroom door. There was plenty of room with the few pieces of clothing the kids had. She closed the door and watched Michael listen as Rose Anne introduced him to the garish doll she'd named Brie.

"Like the cheese?" he asked.

"No, like Taylor."

Carolyn stepped forward to say, "Taylor is Rose Anne's best friend, and Taylor's middle name is Brie."

"Ah," he replied, standing straighter so his head almost touched the ceiling, "now I understand."

"Where are James and Benjamin?"

"James's older brothers decided he needed to spend time with them tonight, and Benjamin raised his hand when your village librarian—"

"Jenna."

"That's it. Jenna was looking for volunteers to help carry ruined books out of the building. Apparently she's been stashing some of the older, valuable books in freezers throughout the village in the hope of saving them."

She nodded, though she saw the truth in his eyes. He

believed his friends had come up with excuses to allow him to spend time with her and her family. She should be bothered Benjamin and James had made such an assumption, but she couldn't be. The idea of spending the evening with Michael was delightful.

Telling the others to sit so she could get the casserole out of the oven without the risk of burning anyone, she listened as Kevin and Rose Anne chattered. They were eager to share every facet of their day, down to the smallest details of how one of the other children had spilled his juice at lunch. Twice.

When she placed the casserole on a folded towel in the center of the table, she set a ladle next to it. She went to the refrigerator and got out the small carton of milk. There wasn't room for the gallon jug she usually bought. Setting it on the table, she filled two glasses with water for herself and Michael.

"There's not enough milk for—" she began.

He halted her by raising his hand. "You don't have to explain or apologize, Carolyn. Don't forget. I know the challenges of living in this soup can."

That set the children to giggling again.

Carolyn sat across the table from Michael with Kevin next to him and Rose Anne beside her. When her knee brushed his as she stretched to push her nephew's hair back out of his eyes, heat rose through her. She guessed her cheeks were the color of the bright red bow on Rose Anne's doll.

He shifted to give her room and acted as if he hadn't seen her blush. "Shall we thank God for our supper?"

"I'll say grace!" announced Kevin, raising his hand as if in school.

Carolyn glanced at Michael. Before a meal, the

Amish didn't give thanks aloud, but each person prayed in silence to God in their own words. He caught her eyes and nodded he was fine with Kevin saying grace. She tensed, wondering if she'd betrayed the truth. She let her shoulders droop when she remembered how many breakfasts he'd taken with the other volunteers. She could have observed their heads bowed in silence at any one of them.

Kevin rushed through grace so quickly she doubted she would have understood a single word if they didn't say the same prayer each night. A grin tugged at Michael's expressive mouth, but he said at the end along with her and Rose Anne, "Amen."

"You can say grace next time, Michael," Kevin said with a big grin.

"Maybe you'd like to see how the Amish pray." Michael folded his arms on the table. "We've got a church Sunday this weekend. You're welcome to attend if you'd like."

Carolyn gasped, astonished by his invitation to someone he saw as *Englisch*.

"The service is three hours or so long," he went on when she didn't reply. "We have a communal meal afterward, and the *kinder* always spend the afternoon playing games while the rest of us enjoy the news of the past two weeks."

"Can we go?" Rose Anne asked, bouncing in her seat.

"I want to go!" Kevin never was subtle about his feelings.

"It's not for *kinder* to make these decisions." Michael's gentle scold had an instant effect on her niece and nephew as they quieted and looked at her.

She knew so many reasons she should decline, but heard herself agreeing to go. One day, when she could reveal the truth to the children, they would have a memory of how Amish spent a church Sunday. It might make it easier for them to decide what sort of life they wanted.

Not wanting to discuss the topic any longer, because she must avoid any suggestion that she knew more about an Amish worship service than an *Englischer* should, she tucked a napkin in the neck of Rose Anne's dress. "I hope you're hungry. I made enough for us and James and Benjamin."

"As *gut* as it smells, they're going to be sorry they didn't come." Michael leaned forward toward the casserole. "I see you made wedding chicken." He laughed when the kids stared at him, wide-eyed. "Chicken and noodles are one of the main dishes we serve at weddings."

"But nobody's getting merry," Rose Anne lamented. "No chicken for us?"

Carolyn smiled as Michael scooped out a ladle of the casserole and put it on her niece's plate.

"We'll pretend someone got *merry*," he said with a quick grin in Carolyn's direction. "That way, we can eat as if we're at a wedding party."

And it was a party as they sat at the cramped table in the tiny trailer and ate and laughed. For the first time in longer than she could remember, Carolyn felt as if she could set her burdens of worry and fear aside for the evening. The children were as carefree. Michael had given them a wondrous gift that night.

Chapter Nine

On Sunday morning, with the sun a finger's width over the horizon and a blustery wind battering the trailer, Carolyn heard from the upper bunk in the trailer, "Is today the day?"

Kevin spent most of his time when they were inside up there. Sometimes with his sister, other times on his own. The bunk had become a variety of imaginary places in the past week for her niece and nephew. Last night, it'd been a rocket to the moon. The children had imagined it was a train earlier in the afternoon.

Carolyn paused in folding the blankets that had been tucked around Rose Anne overnight. Looking at where the boy was buttoning his shirt, she asked, "Is today the day for what?"

"Is today the day I should pray Tippy will be found?"

"Kevin…"

He turned away, hearing her hesitation as she struggled to find something to say.

"Kevin," she repeated. "Please listen to me."

He looked over his shoulder.

She clutched the blanket, wishing she could swaddle

him in it and keep all his sorrows at bay. "Every day is a good day to pray. God doesn't get tired of hearing what's in our hearts."

"So if I pray, He'll listen?"

"He'll listen, and he'll answer in His time and in His own way. We have to trust He knows what's best for us, even if it's not always the answer we want to hear."

"You mean, He may not find Tippy for me."

"I don't know." She held his gaze. "Only God knows what's to come. All He asks of us is to have faith in Him."

He considered that, then nodded. She waited for him to ask another question, but he began talking with his sister about the Amish church service.

When Carolyn opened the closet to take out their coats and hats, she caught sight of her own reflection in the full-length mirror hanging inside the door. She hoped God understood why she wasn't wearing the *kapp* she used to wear and why her polyester dress was a bright blue. She shut the door, but couldn't silence her misgivings at how her life had been altered by the man who'd abused her sister and threatened his own children.

It wasn't just the cold morning that sent Carolyn hurrying with Kevin and Rose Anne across the village green. Until Michael invited her to attend the Amish service, she hadn't realized how much she'd missed participating in what had once been normal. The children were curious but a little bit overwhelmed at the idea they'd be sitting with the adults during the service instead of attending Sunday school as they did at the Mennonite church.

However, the morning service was being held in the community center attached to the church because none of the Amish had a home to invite the others to. There was no ordained minister, but she'd heard Isaac Kauffman served as his district's *vorsinger*, so he'd lead the singing.

His sister, Abby, greeted Carolyn as she and the children crossed the road in front of the community center. "Come with me," Abby said, motioning toward the women who were waiting on the right side of the building. "We women sit on one side facing the men." She smiled at the children. "You get to sit with me and your *mamm*. I mean, your mother."

Raising her chin, Rose Anne said, "I know that word. *Mamm* means mommy. *Daed* means daddy, but we don't gots one of those."

Abby gave Carolyn a stricken look. "I didn't mean to remind them of your loss."

She reassured the other woman as Rose Anne waved at Michael and his friends who stood to the left of the entrance. His clothes were the same as the ones he wore at work, but clean and pressed.

Only Isaac had on the traditional black *mutze* coat and trousers Amish men wore to church. She wondered how many bags Isaac had brought with him from the Northeast Kingdom.

"Can I sit with Michael?" Kevin pumped out his chest. "Michael is my friend. He's going to teach me to whittle."

"Is that so?" Abby smiled. "If Carolyn and Michael agree, you may sit with him, but you must stay with him throughout the whole service. You can't switch seats later."

"I want to sit with Michael." He gave Carolyn the

sad puppy eyes that always matched his most heartfelt pleas. "Say it's okay. Please!"

"If it's okay with Michael…" She didn't get a chance to add more as Kevin erupted into a run toward where the men had gathered.

She watched as Michael bent toward her nephew, listened to what Kevin had to say and then nodded. He put a gentle hand on the boy's shoulder and drew him closer to make him a part of the men's group. The happiness slipping through her battered aside the cold morning wind. Michael was what her nephew needed. A good man who treated him with kindness and offered to teach him things a boy should know. Things that, no matter how much she tried, Carolyn knew she would never comprehend in the same way.

Holding Rose Anne's hand while the women filed into the community center after the men, Carolyn wondered how a room that served as a day care center, a cafeteria and a gathering spot for volunteers discussing the next day's work could look so different when it became a place to worship. The sunlight coming through the clear glass on the tall windows made giant checkerboards across the two rows of chairs facing each other. The chairs would be more comfortable during the long service than the usual backless benches. There wasn't a bench wagon in Evergreen Corners to go from one home to the next with all the necessities for a church Sunday, including extra dishes and silverware.

She was surprised when she was handed a hymn book. Abby leaned toward her to whisper that Isaac had brought several with him.

"My big brother always worries about the smallest details," she said.

Carolyn smiled and was startled when Abby didn't. There was some undercurrent between brother and sister she couldn't understand, but she didn't ask. Not only was the service about to begin but asking too many questions about Abby's family would give tacit permission for Abby to ask about Carolyn's. That she couldn't allow.

Kevin and Rose Anne, the only children there, looked around in confusion when the congregation rose. Isaac began to sing a familiar hymn, but so slowly that Carolyn wasn't astonished the children didn't recognize the song, though they'd sung it often in Sunday school. As *vorsinger*, Isaac started each line and the rest of them joined in.

She remained silent, though she longed to sing. *Forgive me, Lord, for not raising my voice in Your praise. And forgive me for not being myself here in Your presence.*

As each verse was sung at the same deliberate tempo, Rose Anne began to fidget. Carolyn glanced across at the men and saw Kevin doing the same. Again Michael bent to whisper something to her nephew. Kevin grinned at him and stopped shuffling his feet.

Without a pause as soon as the first hymn was finished, the congregation began "*Das Loblied*," the traditional second hymn sung at each service. The words she knew so well reached into her heart and knit together some of the wounds that had opened when she left her plain life behind in Indiana. She longed more than ever to sing with the others, but resisted. To open her mouth would betray her secret. She held Rose Anne's hand while the song threaded its way through each verse.

"What are they singing about?" the little girl whispered.

"I'm sure it's about how wonderful it is to be able to worship God together," she answered as quietly.

"When will we sing 'Jesus Loves Me'?"

"We'll have to wait and see." She put her finger to the little girl's lips. "Now we need to be quiet and listen."

"To what? I can't unclestan the words."

"Maybe if you listen hard, you'll *understand* some of the words."

Abby glanced at them and smiled, never breaking the languid tempo that was so different from the four part harmony and quicker pace of Mennonite services.

Facing them from the first row of chairs on the men's side of the room, Michael had a hand around Kevin's shoulders. Her nephew gazed at him with adoration.

Uneasiness swept away her contentment and the joy that had filled her as she heard familiar hymns sung in the familiar way. She had no idea how long Michael would remain in Evergreen Corners, and her nephew was going to be devastated when he left.

You will, too.

As if on cue, both Rose Anne and Kevin became restless as soon as everyone sat so they could listen to a reading from the Bible. She drew her niece onto her lap and pulled a book out of her purse so the little girl could have something to entertain herself.

She looked across at Michael and glanced from Rose Anne's book to her brother. Michael held out his hand. She stretched across the space between the women's chairs and the men's, and gave him a book she'd packed for Kevin. Handing it to the boy, he raised his eyes toward her.

When she mouthed a silent *thank you*, she expected him to return his attention to the older Umble brother who was self-consciously reading the eighth chapter of Genesis, the verses about the flood receding and Noah emerging from the ark. Instead, his gaze held hers. Something shifted deep within her, something with the power of the story of God's grace in giving humans a second chance at redeeming themselves.

She couldn't move her gaze away. She didn't want to.

Later, though she had no idea how much time had passed as she fell into the brown warmth of his eyes, she blinked as if waking from the sweetest dream. Rose Anne was tapping on her arm to get her attention.

Carolyn knew she should be grateful to her niece for diverting her, but all she could feel was sorrow that the wonderful moment had ended. She knew, if she had an iota of good sense, she wouldn't ever let it happen again.

No matter how much her heart longed for her to.

Michael was glad the gathering was small enough that the men, women and Carolyn's *kinder* were able to sit together to share cold sandwiches and pickles and potato salad. He wasn't sure if the Wiebe *kinder* would be willing to wait if the men were served first as was customary. And he wasn't ready for them to leave.

Carolyn stood to help the others clear the table, and he edged nearer so he could talk to her without everyone else being a part of the conversation. When their gazes had collided while Vernon stumbled through the reading he'd been asked to do, Michael had been sure he'd seen more than casual interest in her eyes.

He was far less certain when she said in a tone that suggested they were strangers, "Thank you for inviting us to the service today. I hope Kevin didn't give you too much trouble. It's not easy for little ones to sit through a long service."

"He was fine." Why was she acting cool when her gaze had been filled with such warmth? He struggled to keep his own voice even. "Though he kept asking me questions about what everyone was saying and singing about."

"Rose Anne did, too, until she fell asleep."

"I hope you weren't too bored."

"I'm never bored when I'm with others who are praising God."

He was astonished as a feeling he thought he'd put aside rushed through him. The last time he'd felt anything like it was when he'd been envious of the man walking by Adah's side after she'd told him—and everyone else—she wasn't interested in Michael any longer. It'd taken months to submerge his irritation. He'd thought he'd banished it from his mind forever.

Now envy surged back as he heard Carolyn's simple statement of faith. When she turned to put a stack of plates on the pass-through to the kitchen, he saw the small round *kapp* that announced to the world—and, more important, to God—of her commitment to her faith. She knew who and what she was.

And he was no closer to having that self-assurance about what God expected of him than he'd been when he left Lancaster County to follow his twin brother to northern New York.

Knowing he couldn't let the conversation lag or she might go to talk with someone else, he said, "I suppose Abby translated for you."

"She did during the sermon Isaac gave, but the rest

of the service was pretty self-explanatory." She looked past him and groaned. "Oh, Kevin! He could find mischief in an empty room."

When she whirled past him to go to where her nephew was trying to hold back boxes about to tumble out of a closet, Michael didn't follow. Two of James's brothers rushed to help her, and there wasn't room for anyone else in the cramped space.

However, after the boxes were restored in the closet and stable again, and Kevin had been chastised for peeking into places he shouldn't, Michael had the boy sit beside him on the bench at the back of the big room. The women were in the kitchen, cleaning up, and the other men were rearranging the tables so they'd be ready for breakfast tomorrow morning.

Michael pulled out his pocketknife and opened it. Kevin's eyes grew big as Michael held the haft out to him. Gripping it in his left hand, the boy watched in uncharacteristic silence as Michael picked up a broken stake. He'd cut it to about a foot in length so it'd be the right size for a *kind*.

"Are you left-handed?" he asked the boy.

Kevin looked at the knife in his left hand and shrugged.

"Which hand do you use when you're coloring or writing?"

He started to raise his left arm, but halted when Michael cautioned him.

"I wouldn't have cut you, Michael," Kevin said, chagrined.

"I know you wouldn't have intended to, but any time you're responsible for something that could hurt someone else, you must be extra, extra careful. Always think about where the blade is and where everyone and everything around you is. You'll do that, ain't so?"

Kevin nodded, as solemn as a *kind* could be. In spite of his efforts to show he was mature enough to handle the pocketknife, his face glowed with anticipation for his first whittling lesson.

"Okay, let's get started." He handed Kevin the stake and told him how to hold it. "Always cut away from you." He guided the *kind*'s hand holding the pocketknife to a spot about halfway down the stake. "That way, if your knife slides off the wood in the wrong direction, it won't hurt you. It's a lesson you don't want to learn the hard way. Now you cut with the grain."

"Grain?"

"See the darker lines in the pine?" Michael pointed them out. "That's the direction of the grain. You should always go in that direction, because it'll be easier for both you and the wood. A slow, long stroke along the wood is best."

Kevin jammed his knife against the pine, snagging the blade. He tried to pull it back. It was stuck.

Taking the stake, Michael drew the knife out. "Make thin bites into the wood. You don't want big chunks like a piece of bread, but thin strips like a slice of cheese to put on bread. Watch me."

It wasn't easy keeping his eyes on the knife and the boy at the same time. He needed to have Kevin sit close enough that he could see, but not so near he'd get struck if the knife slid off the wood. He was sure Carolyn would put an end to the lessons if either he or Kevin nicked their fingers.

By the time the others were gathering at the far side

of the room, Kevin was becoming more confident in handling the knife.

"*Gut, gut*," Michael crooned as Kevin managed to make two shallow cuts in the wood. "You're going to be *gut* at this if you keep practicing."

Rose Anne skipped up and grinned when she saw what they were doing. "How long before Kevin can make something pretty like the little wooden bird we used to have?"

Both *kinder* looked at Michael for an answer.

"Tell me about it," he said.

"It was a hawk, which is my mommy's favorite bird."

"Is that so?"

Kevin nodded. "She says a hawk takes the gift of the wind God gives us and uses it to soar high in search of food. It will only kill what it or its babies have to have in order to eat." He cut off another piece of wood. "Unless something attacks its nest. Then it'll go after an animal bigger than it is." He shifted the knife, and a piece of wood popped off.

His sister frowned as she examined the small chunk. "You're making it flopsided."

Michael didn't hold back his laugh at the little girl's pronouncement.

Rose Anne put her hands on her hips. "It's not nice to laugh at someone."

"You're right," he replied as he smothered another chuckle at the pose that suggested she was the older one trying to instruct Michael. "But it's okay to laugh when you're with someone who makes you happy."

Her frown became a broad smile. "Do I make you happy?"

"You do."

When she spun on her heel and ran away, he wondered why. Figuring out the Wiebe women clearly was a task he couldn't master.

He looked at Kevin, who was concentrating on whittling. Before he could say a single word to the boy, Rose Anne rushed back to them. She held up a bright red box kite almost as big as she was.

"Will you help me?" she asked.

He took it. "If you want."

Rose Anne gave him another frown, but this one was easy to translate. She wouldn't have asked him if she didn't want his help.

Trying not to laugh at the expression the *kind* must have borrowed from her *mamm*, he took the knife from Kevin. He told both *kinder* to get their coats. He thought Kevin might protest, but the boy giggled with excitement when he noticed what his sister had given Michael.

He wondered where Carolyn was. He didn't see her in the kitchen. Finding Abby, he asked her to let Carolyn know he was taking the *kinder* outside to fly their kite. The youngsters bounced as they hurried outside with him.

Within a minute, they were standing in a clear section of the village green and the kite was soaring over their heads, far from the trees edging the open space. Both kids begged to hold onto the string. He could imagine a big gust sending Rose Anne skyward along with the kite. However, he gave her the first chance. He knelt beside her and kept his own hand on the string because he didn't want the little girl to get distracted and release it. On such a blustery afternoon, the kite could go sailing a distance and, once it hit the ground, be broken.

Michael took his attention from the kite when Kevin ran off. Where was the boy going? He smiled when he saw a well-bundled Carolyn walking toward them.

Why hadn't he ever noticed that the black coat she'd been given was at least two sizes too big for her? Maybe because the wind kept catching its hem and tossing it around her skirt and apron in every possible direction.

He sighed. Having her join them for the service hadn't revealed anything new about why she seemed to be able to understand *Deitsch*. Perhaps he'd been overly optimistic in his hopes that inviting her to church would answer his questions about her once and for all because the everyday Amish language was different from the High German used during church services.

But it had revealed one vital thing: he wanted to spend more time with her.

A lot more time, more time than he'd planned to stay in Evergreen Corners. He'd told Gabriel he would be home at the first of the year, which was about six weeks away.

Carolyn smiled when she stopped next to him and Rose Anne. "When I came back in from taking out the trash, Abby told me none of you had enough good sense to stay inside where it's nice and warm."

"I was recruited to fly this kite," he said.

"I asked you to be patient, Rose Anne," Carolyn said. "You shouldn't have bothered Michael."

"She's no bother." He winked at the little girl. "And she didn't have to do any persuading. I haven't had a chance to play with a kite since I was a *kind*, so I'm glad I remembered how it works."

"It's souring, Mommy," Rose Anne announced. "See? Up there. Michael says it's souring."

When Carolyn looked baffled, Michael stood. "I think she means soaring."

"You're getting good at translating her unique form of English," she said, laughing.

A half hour later, when the sun was perched atop the western mountains, they reeled in the kite, and he watched Carolyn show Kevin how to wind the string so it could be released with ease the next time they wanted to fly it. She was such a *gut mamm*. He doubted the *kinder* had any idea how blessed they were.

He didn't ask Carolyn if he could walk home with her and the *kinder*. He strolled alongside her as Kevin and Rose Anne frolicked in front of them, their energy far from depleted. There was no traffic on the road on the late Sunday afternoon. For the first time in days, he wondered how the world beyond Evergreen Corners was faring.

Had the roads been repaired enough for traffic to get back to normal? There had been rumors on Friday about the state department of transportation coming next week to the village so every road in and out of town would once again be smooth, two-lane highways. The villagers were eager to be able to get out of town to the big box stores where the selection of food and other goods was far broader than in the small general store.

"Thank you," Carolyn said, "for making sure Kevin kept his ten fingers."

"He's a *gut* student," Michael replied as they moved from one elongated shadow to the next. "Eager to learn and cautious."

"For now. Once he's no longer in awe of the knife, he may be careless."

"Then it's my job to make sure he never loses his

awe of what a blade can do." He gave a short laugh. "If I'd known he was left-handed, I might not have offered to teach him. You're right-handed. Was his *daed* left-handed?"

"No." She paused so long he wondered if he'd made a huge mistake to mention the *kind*'s *daed* before she said, "But we do have other lefties in the family. It's been a challenge teaching him some things, but we've learned to muddle through when I can't see things the way he does."

"When I watch you with your *kinder*, I find myself wondering about what it would have been like to know my own *mamm*. I don't recall much about her."

"That's sad."

He shrugged. "You can't miss what you don't remember having. I do have a few memories of my *daed*, but most of what I knew in my childhood came from living with Aden Girod. When we were eight-year-old orphans, he took Gabriel and me into his home and raised us as his own. He was a *gut* man." Michael sighed. "It was after he died that we moved from Pennsylvania to Harmony Creek Hollow."

"You miss him."

"I do." He stopped by the wooden steps leading to the old mill that now was the town hall. Someone had marked the height of the flood on the wall. It was three inches above the top of his own six feet, making it almost twenty feet above the brook's bed.

She halted and faced him. "But he's always within you."

He drew in a sharp breath when her fingertips brushed his coat over his heart. Her touch was light and so brief that, if it had been anyone else, he wouldn't have noticed. He couldn't ever be unaware of her. He didn't want to be.

"He's the one who taught me to appreciate wood," he said, needing to share this memory with her. "Once he saw I enjoyed making things by whittling, he introduced me to carpentry and woodworking. I never was interested in making furniture, but cabinets fascinated me. I liked—and still like—how a series of wooden boxes can be arranged in such a useful pattern."

"What a gift he gave you!" She began walking toward the trailer, and he matched her steps so the *kinder* didn't get too far ahead.

"I'm grateful every day he didn't hesitate to become our *daed*. He always said a family is a family, no matter how it comes into being."

"I like that." She smiled at him, and he had to clamp his arm along his side before it moved of its own accord to encircle her shoulders.

Then they were standing in front of the trailer, and he knew he needed to bid them *gut nacht* and leave before he couldn't fight his longing to pull her into his arms. He turned to the *kinder* when Carolyn prompted them to thank him. Was she as aware of the electricity arcing between them like lightning knitting together storm clouds?

Rose Anne mumbled something, but Kevin said, "Thanks for teaching me to whittle, Michael. Can we do it again tomorrow?"

"I'm not sure about tomorrow because we may be working late on your house if the weather holds, but we'll whittle again soon. *Danki* for joining us today, Kevin."

The boy stood a bit taller when Michael offered his

hand. He shook it with a rare solemnity. "I hope God heard my prayers today."

"He always hears our prayers," Carolyn said in a strained voice.

Glancing from her to her son, Michael asked, "What were you praying for, Kevin?"

"That God would find Tippy and make sure he's okay. If He can't bring Tippy back to me, then I hope He finds some other boy for Tippy to spend time with. Someone who needs a best friend." Tears bubbled into his eyes as he flung the door open and ran into the trailer with Rose Anne on his heels.

Carolyn bit her lower lip, trying—and failing—to keep it from trembling.

"I'm sorry," Michael said, hating the trite words. But they were the truth. He was sorry she and the *kinder* had lost so much.

When she spoke, her voice cracked. "It's my fault that Tippy is gone. I thought I'd grabbed Kevin's stuffed dog, but in our hurry to escape, I took a blanket instead."

"By the time you realized that, it was too late to go back."

She nodded as the lights came on in the trailer, revealing her haunted eyes. "The water was already halfway to my knees in the house when I got the children out. I didn't dare go back with them, and I couldn't leave them outside alone."

"Of course you couldn't."

"Kevin's been talking more about Tippy." She closed her eyes, trying to hold in her own tears. "I know he's praying for Tippy to be returned."

"I can put the word out among the volunteers to be on the lookout for a stuffed dog."

"Thank you, but I don't want to get his hopes up only to have them dashed again."

Or your own, he thought. How much sorrow had Carolyn carried on her slender shoulders before the flood tore her life apart? How much more since?

Chapter Ten

The knock interrupted breakfast. Before Carolyn could remind Kevin she should answer the door in the trailer as she had when they'd had a house, he'd thrown it open. Not that she expected Leland at the trailer's door while it was so difficult to get into Evergreen Corners, but she couldn't let down her guard.

"Michael!" her nephew crowed as if having the man on the other side was the greatest surprise ever.

Or the best gift, because the boy began firing questions about what the construction teams would be doing and wasn't it great that Kevin didn't have school today because it was a teacher in-service day and he could join the workers and so what did Michael think he could do to help? It was all said without her nephew taking a single breath. He might have kept on going until he ran out of oxygen and keeled over right in the middle of the kitchen if she hadn't put her hands on his shoulders and turned him toward the table.

"You need to finish your breakfast," she chided, "before you think about what you're going to do today."

"I'm going to help Michael." He grinned at the man who stood on the steps into the trailer. "I am, right?"

Without looking over her shoulder, she asked before anyone else could speak, "Do you want to join us, Michael?"

"We're having flipjacks," Rose Anne announced through a full mouth of pancakes.

"Flipjacks?" asked Michael as he entered. "Another Rose Anne-ism?"

"She seems to have one for every occasion." Carolyn moved to the small stove, glad for the excuse to put some distance between herself and Michael's shoulders, which seemed wider in the cramped space. Their heartfelt discussion yesterday on the way back from the church service had created a bridge she'd been trying to keep from forming. With it now in place, she couldn't think of a way to dismantle it without hurting Michael. "Would you like pancakes, or did you eat over at the community center?"

"The line was long there, so I just grabbed a cup of *kaffi* and a couple of biscuits. If you've got enough batter, I'd appreciate some flipjacks." He gave Rose Anne a wink, and she giggled, wiggling on the bench like an adorable puppy before she moved over to give him room.

"I've made plenty, and if I run out, it's easy to mix more." She didn't look toward the table as she heard the creak of the banquette when he slid in beside the children.

Pouring batter onto the griddle, she took another plate out and listened to Michael tease her niece as Kevin kept interjecting questions about the day's work that waited at the building site.

"We'll be putting up the roof rafters today so we can begin the sheathing next week," he answered. "The house will be closed up before the weather gets much worse."

"So soon?" she asked, half turning in her excitement. The house had been a skeleton for the past few days with only her imagination filling in the spaces between the rows of two-by-fours.

"Just in time," Michael said before adding his thanks when she put the plate with two skillet-sized pancakes on the table in front of him. Reaching for the bottle of syrup, he added, "It's getting colder every day. Any rain we get now will leave everything covered with ice."

"Our autumns are beautiful in Vermont, but we sometimes have snow before the leaves are off the trees. When that happens, lots of branches come down making a mess of the roads and yards and roofs. Who would have guessed this year, instead of an early snowstorm, we'd get a late hurricane?"

"We can predict the weather a few days out, but that's about it. Even the almanacs get it wrong sometimes." He poured syrup over his pancakes, catching a drop on his finger before it could fall onto the table. Sticking his finger in his mouth, he raised his brows. "This is delicious!"

"It's maple syrup. *Real* maple syrup." She laughed. "You're in Vermont, and we don't serve anything but the real thing. It may be against the law."

Kevin sat straighter. "Really?"

"She's joking," Michael said before she could. He nudged her nephew with his elbow, and both laughed.

She was amazed how easy Kevin and Michael's relationship was. Her nephew hadn't grown close to any other man in Evergreen Corners. Should she have asked Michael right from the beginning not to let the children get too close to him? It was too late to protect them now, because they already adored him. She couldn't deny her niece and nephew the chance to enjoy his company. When the time came for her to tell them the truth about the man who was their father, she would remind them of how nice Michael had been to them, so they'd be reassured not all men were violent to those they loved.

But that was years from now, and she wished she knew a way to keep them from being heartbroken when Michael's stint of volunteering came to an end and he left.

Kevin pouted after Michael went to work without him. Climbing onto his bunk, he refused to speak to either Carolyn or his sister. Not even fresh cookies could lure him down, so she gave up trying to explain Michael couldn't be distracted while he was working.

As if Kevin's mood was infectious, Rose Anne became irritable, too. Again, Carolyn's warm cookies didn't seem to help, though her niece did try one. She acted reluctant but out of the corner of her eye Carolyn saw the little girl take two more, handing one to her brother before clambering up to join him.

Carolyn felt their eyes on her as she took the last batch of cookies out of the oven and set the cookie sheet on top of the stove. As always, she checked to make sure she hadn't accidentally turned on one of the burners. She didn't want to scorch the cookies or ruin the tray belonging to the family that was loaning them the trailer.

A yawn surprised her, but then she remembered she hadn't had a second cup of coffee that morning. She'd given the last in the pot to Michael before he went out into the cold. She decided to finish her housework. It wouldn't take long to clean the small trailer, and then she would take cookies to the volunteer builders.

Going into the bedroom, she folded their clean clothes, grateful for the washer and dryer in the trailer. Before the flood, she'd used the laundromat, toting baskets of clothes there and back each week. She'd heard it was open again. It hadn't been flooded, but the water supply had been cut off for a couple of weeks. She put the clothing in the appropriate drawers. As always, the children's looked as if they'd pawed to the bottom every day. She glanced into the single drawer she used, and it wasn't much neater. They didn't have a lot of clothing, but they could have used more storage.

Carolyn walked back into the main room of the trailer. "Let's go…"

The children were nowhere to be seen.

"Kevin? Rose Anne?" she called.

She didn't get any answer. Opening the closet, she saw their coats, mittens and hats were gone.

Carolyn knew where the children would be. Kevin was fascinated with the building process and wouldn't stay away from Michael. Rose Anne was interested because her big brother was. The little girl had been trailing after her brother from the time she could walk. Both of them knew the rules for crossing the street, and before the flood Kevin had begun to walk the short distance to the elementary school on his own.

Grabbing her own coat, she pulled it on and hurried down the hill. She shivered in the icy wind as she watched a large delivery truck drive past where she stood on the sidewalk near the library. She tried to keep her skirt from flying up as the truck rushed by her. Dust rose from the road covered with dried mud. It seemed every rain storm brought more loose soil onto the narrow line of asphalt. Until the ground froze, it would repeat with each storm. She grimaced as she thought of how it would begin again with the first spring thaw.

But by then, she and Kevin and Rose Anne would have moved into their new home. She'd heard during breakfast that the diner was under repair and the owners hoped to have it open by the New Year. If so, she hoped they would again buy baked goods from her, so she could save for the furniture and clothes her family would need in the coming months.

By then, too, Michael and the other volunteers would be long gone.

Every joyous thought she had of living in a real house again was tinged with sadness at knowing he would have returned to his own home. Her memories of the meals he'd shared with her and the children in the trailer gathered around her with each breath. Brushing them away was impossible, because she wanted to hold them close. They banished the pain of seeing *Mamm* belittled and Regina abused and her own life shadowed by threats of the same violence.

She waved aside the dust, coughing and scowling as she saw the fine layer clinging to her black coat. Shaking it off, she crossed the road once the truck had disappeared around a corner. She followed the brownish cloud past where Rhee's cellar was now topped off by sheets of plywood ready for the framing to begin.

Nobody was on that site, so she kept going. The Gagnons' site was also abandoned, but she heard noise from hers. Rushing forward, she glanced around, searching for her nephew and niece. When she saw them standing with Benjamin by the pen where the hens now lived, she breathed a grateful prayer. She didn't look forward to scolding the children, but they must learn they couldn't run off.

As she walked toward them, she couldn't resist a look at the house. On the far side, men were hauling large sections of rafters up to form the roof. It was exciting to see the house take shape.

She bowed her head to send up more heartfelt gratitude to God Who had sent these helping hands to Evergreen Corners. She wasn't sure what she would have done otherwise.

Raising her eyes, she saw Michael standing on the far side of the house. His gaze connected with hers, and she forgot about rafters and concrete and breathing. Her pulse resonated in her ears. She wasn't sure if he moved first or if she did, but somehow by taking a few steps, she found they were standing face-to-face.

"Hi," she said.

"Hi," he answered.

She gazed at the slow smile that eased the tense lines of his wind-scoured face. A delightful warmth flickered within her, and she leaned toward him, halting when the mittens she hadn't realized she was holding instead of wearing struck his hard chest.

Somehow, she collected the tattered remnants of her composure and said, "I'm here to find two naughty children."

He smiled. "I thought that might be why you're here with your coat unbuttoned and without your bonnet." He laughed when she touched the round *kapp* on her hair. "When I saw them arrive, I assumed you wouldn't be far behind."

"They slipped out when I wasn't looking."

"I was worried they might do something like that. I've been sprinting back and forth from here to the road between helping lift each rafter. I was about to believe they had better sense than to take off without you when I saw them. Benjamin and I have been taking turns watching over them."

"Thank you."

"It was my pleasure."

Michael realized the trite words were true. He'd been happy to keep an eye out for Kevin and Rose Anne... and Carolyn.

"James and his brothers left this morning to return home," he said to keep the conversation going. "He needed to go back to Harmony Creek Hollow and his work as a blacksmith because our *Leit* depends on him to shoe their horses."

"Maybe his brothers didn't want to stay when he wasn't here for them to boss around."

"Why, Carolyn Wiebe, what a thing for a *gut* Mennonite to say!"

"We're taught to speak the truth." When he grinned, she hurried to add, "And the truth is I'm grateful for everyone's help."

"James said to tell you he'll be back after the New Year. By then, Glen will have us starting on a new trio of houses. James's skill with metal will be valuable for the steel-reinforced concrete in the cellar walls."

She looked at the work site that was humming with activity. "So you're short-handed now?"

"No, a group of plain folks arrived this morning from Pennsylvania and were waiting here for us when we got to work. We have about a half dozen extra sets of hands here, and the two women have gone to help at the community center."

"Good. I'll meet them when—"

Shouts came from every direction. The voices were swallowed by a great crash and the clatter of wood against stone and concrete.

Carolyn's eyes were riveted on a stack of boards falling in what seemed like slow motion. Her niece stood too close to it. She saw Benjamin leap forward to grab the little girl. Both of them vanished in a cloud of dirt and dust.

For a moment, it was so silent the brook's gurgling was the loudest sound. Then the air exploded with shouts and pounding feet as everyone ran toward the spot where Benjamin and Rose Anne had been visible seconds ago.

With her feet moving before she had a chance to think, Carolyn pushed through the others to reach her niece. She gave a sharp cry of dismay when she saw the little girl lying on the ground while Benjamin was pushing himself up to sit. Their faces were gray with pain.

"Rose Anne!" She knelt by her niece who was staring at the collapsed stack of wood as if she couldn't believe it had moved. "Are you all right?"

Instead of answering, Rose Anne shifted her gaze from the wood to her left arm. It hung at a grotesque angle, as if she had a second elbow between her wrist and her real elbow.

"Don't move," Carolyn cautioned.

"Mommy!"

"Hush, sweetheart. Just be still." Looking up, she saw Michael behind her. Kevin stood next to him, his face as pale as his sister's. She met her nephew's eyes steadily. "Her arm is broken."

Michael's head swiveled as he glanced at his friend.

Benjamin said in a strained voice, "You need to get her to a *doktor* and get it set before she does more damage to it."

"There isn't a doctor in Evergreen Corners," she said.

"Where...?" asked Michael.

"The closest one is at the urgent care clinic. It's on Route 100 heading north toward Ludlow."

"So let's go."

She stared at him. "We can't. The bridge is still out between here and there."

He'd started to turn, but halted. "There's got to be something we can do."

More shouts and a loud sob from Rose Anne kept her from answering. Looking through the open walls of their home, she saw a dark-haired woman hurrying toward them. She wore the pleated *kapp* of a horse-and-buggy Mennonite. Her steps were uneven, because she wore a plastic brace on her right leg over her black stockings.

"Over here!" Carolyn called when she realized the woman was carrying a medical bag.

The crowd edged back to let the dark-haired woman past. She looked from Rose Anne to Benjamin, then knelt beside Carolyn and her niece.

"I'm Beth Ann Overholt," the woman said as she ran her hands along Rose Anne's sides and tilted her head with gentle hands. "Look at me, little one." She pulled a light from her bag and flashed it in the child's eyes. "Good. It doesn't look as if she was hit on the head."

"Are you a doctor?" Carolyn asked.

The woman shook her head as she stood and went to give Benjamin the same examination. "No. I'm a midwife."

"Midwife?" Benjamin's face twisted, and he clamped his mouth shut when her fingers brushed against his right side. Any color his face had vanished.

Beth Ann sat on her heels. "I've had enough medical training to know the two of you need to see a doctor immediately. Your ribs are, at best, bruised. At worst, you've broken one or more."

"I thought I'd jumped back far enough," he said, breathing shallowly as if he'd run the full length of the Green Mountains. "I miscalculated."

Surprised anyone could make a joke while injured, Carolyn fought to keep frustration and fear from her voice. "How do we get them to a doctor? An ambulance will take too long to get here."

Michael asked, "Didn't Glen tell us he's got a vehicle that can navigate the rough path through the woods between here and Route 100?"

"How rough?" She glanced down at the little girl whose face was growing taut with pain.

"Rough," he replied, "but it's the only way to get her to a *doktor* now."

"Where's Glen? Have you seen him today?"

He hooked a thumb toward the village. "Probably in his office."

"I'll get him!" shouted a man from the back of the crowd. She didn't see who it was before he ran to get the project director.

With every bit of care she could muster, Carolyn lifted Rose Anne into her arms. She cradled her as she had when her niece was a newborn, but made sure she didn't bump her broken arm. Kevin looked on, horrified, as Michael and Isaac assisted Benjamin to his feet.

Again the volunteers stepped aside as Carolyn carried her niece toward the road. Quiet words of good wishes and offers of prayers flanked her, and she nodded her thanks while she kept her eyes on where she placed her feet. She didn't want to slip and jar the little girl, adding to her pain. She wished she had another arm to put around Kevin as she heard him crying.

She spared a look over her shoulder and was relieved to see Michael had one arm supporting his friend and the other on Kevin's shoulder as they followed her to the road. She knew her nephew had no idea how precious Michael's consoling touch was, and that lifted her heart, which had plummeted into her stomach when she saw Rose Anne disappear as the stack of wood gave way. Kevin trusted Michael and she wanted to, as well.

More than she'd imagined she'd ever be willing to trust a man. She waited for the warning that should have flashed through her at that thought. When it didn't come, she told herself it was because she had more important things to worry about.

Like making sure Rose Anne's arm was set before it could be more badly injured. It was easier to concentrate on that than her feelings, which she'd been sure would never alter...even so slightly.

Michael made sure Benjamin was steady when they reached the road. Only then did he bend and draw out a handkerchief and give it to Kevin, who was sniffling as thick tears ran down his cheeks.

"Everything's going to be okay," Michael said as he squatted in front of the boy.

"She's broken."

"*Ja*, but God was wise when He made us. We can be fixed as *gut* as new."

"What if Tippy is broken, too? Who's taking care of him?" Kevin's eyes grew round. "God is, isn't He?"

"*Ja.*" He gave the boy a quick hug. To keep Kevin from asking more questions—especially ones he couldn't answer—Michael added, "For now, though, let's get your sister and Benjamin fixed. Okay?"

"Okay."

As he stood, he saw Carolyn watching him.

She whispered, "Thank you."

He nodded, not wanting to say more in front of the *kinder*. He thought about offering to take Rose Anne, but knew Carolyn would be worried about bumping the little girl's arm during the transfer. Then he knew what he wanted to do was put his arms around Carolyn and comfort her.

When Glen rushed along the road toward them, Michael released a quick breath of relief. Fighting his own desire to hold Carolyn was becoming more difficult with each passing minute.

Glen frowned at the sight of Rose Anne in Carolyn's arms. "How bad is it?"

"A broken arm," Michael answered. "And Benjamin has done some damage to his ribs. We need to get them to a *doktor*. Carolyn tells me the closest one is out on Route 100."

"Take my 4x4 truck. It's the only vehicle that can make it through the woods. Can you drive, Michael?"

"I did a bit in the fields when I was a teenager."

"That's not the same as driving a utility vehicle on

a busy road." The project director turned to Carolyn. "You know how to drive, don't you?"

"Yes."

Fishing in his pocket, he pulled out a single key on a simple chain and handed it to her. "Then you drive. We can't chance wrecking our sole emergency vehicle. Sorry, Michael."

"I'm glad to have Carolyn drive as long as she'll trust me with Rose Anne."

He wasn't surprised to see a myriad of emotions swirl through her eyes. As protective as she was of the *kind*, she was battling with herself over letting him hold her daughter during the trip to the *doktor*'s office.

Sorrow hammered him. She must have been hurt by someone she'd thought she could rely on! Her husband? The thought unsettled him further. He hadn't asked any questions about Carolyn's husband, and he wondered, as he hadn't before, if she never spoke of the *kinder*'s *daed* because he had been a disappointment to her during their lives together. Was the secret she hid that her husband had done something to betray her faith in his love for her and the *kinder*?

Michael was glad the next few minutes became a whirlwind of activity that kept him from being able to ponder those tough questions further. The 4x4, a garish green truck with two sets of bright yellow seats and a flat board over the back wheels to allow for cargo to be strapped on it, was brought to the building site. Kevin was sent with Beth Ann, who agreed to take him to the day care center. Jenna would watch him until they returned to Evergreen Corners. Workers began gathering the wood, sorting the ruined pieces and restacking the unbroken ones.

With utmost care, Carolyn slid Rose Anne into Michael's arms. The little girl began to screech with pain and thrash, but her *mamm* remained calm, stroking her daughter's hair back from her face and murmuring to her until Rose Anne stopped tossing herself against him.

What an amazing woman Carolyn Wiebe was! In the midst of any catastrophe, she was serene.

He walked behind her toward the truck, then looked back. "Aren't you coming with us, Benjamin?"

"There's nothing a *doktor* can do for bruised ribs." He winced on every word.

"They may be broken."

"Nothing a *doktor* can do for that, either. When my older brother cracked a rib, he was told to take it easy and…" He groaned.

Carolyn scowled as she slipped behind the wheel of the truck. "Enough! Get in, Benjamin!" She inserted the key into the ignition, and pulled the seat belt around her and snapped it into place.

"You heard the lady," Michael said, motioning with his head toward the vehicle. "Do you need help getting in, Benjamin?"

"I'll manage."

Michael suspected his friend regretted his hasty words as Benjamin's face grew more ashen while he pulled himself into the back seat. Pretending not to notice because he didn't want to embarrass the other man, Michael slid onto the other front seat without jostling Rose Anne.

"Put your feet on the seat, Benjamin," Carolyn urged impatiently.

"My boots—"

"Don't worry about something that can be cleaned later." Her voice softened as she added, "Putting up your feet will relieve the tension on your ribs and maybe ease your ride a little bit."

"Danki," Benjamin murmured as he shifted with care.

"All set?" she asked.

Michael knew he wasn't the only one not being honest when he replied, *"Ja."*

He looked down at the *kind* curled against him. The trip was going to be rough on each one of them, but this little one most of all.

Chapter Eleven

Michael guessed someone had called ahead to let the medical clinic know they were on their way. There had been plenty of time, because it'd been slow going through the woods on a path strewn with rocks and branches. On each bump—and there had been so many he'd lost count—he'd seen Carolyn wince.

The ride was smoother when they turned onto the highway, but the adults were kept busy watching for cars behind them. When possible, she drew the truck over onto the shoulder to let cars pass them. Several cars beeped at her when there wasn't a place to edge to the right, and he realized they weren't *gut*-natured honks.

He wanted to shout to the occupants of what Carolyn called a glorified golf cart on steroids that they were in a hurry, too. He didn't, not wanting to upset her or their injured passengers.

As soon as she steered the vehicle into the parking lot of a pristine single-story building, the front door was thrown open. Two people wearing long white coats emerged, a man and a woman. He wasn't sure which one was the *doktor*. Maybe both were because they went to work examining Rose Anne and Benjamin.

Questions were fired at him and Carolyn. He had to let her answer everything about her daughter, and Benjamin, though in more pain with each passing second, was able to share information about medical allergies and what had happened as well as Michael could. As soon as the man and woman realized that, they ignored him.

The woman lifted Rose Anne off his lap and carried her into the clinic with Carolyn following close behind.

"Can you help?" asked the white-coated man.

Michael realized he'd been staring after Carolyn and not paying attention to the conversation in the rear of the vehicle. "Me?"

"It'll be easier if one of us is on each side of Benjamin while he goes inside." The *doktor* looked at him as if he wondered if Michael had been injured, too. A head injury would make him incapable of being able to discern the most obvious thing.

"Certainly." He swung out of the vehicle and followed the *doktor*'s instructions to stand beside them as Benjamin slid out.

Michael heard his friend grunt in pain on each step as they walked to the clinic. He continued to pray. He'd reassured Kevin their injuries were easily repairable, and he didn't want to disappoint the boy.

Inside, the clinic looked like any he'd visited. On the sterile white walls hung pictures of scenery that could have been Vermont or anywhere else with mountains. A glass enclosure cut the space in half. He counted four desks on the far side, but only two were occupied.

The chairs in the waiting room were empty, and he sat in the closest one to the door through which the *doktor* led Benjamin. As he'd guessed, the chairs had been selected for their clean lines. Straight backs and seats too low to the floor made him sit at an uncomfortable angle. Unadorned side tables held magazines and a few games for *kinder*. A pair of televisions hung high on the wall and broadcast health information without sound. He ignored them and stared at the door Benjamin had used.

Time moved at a snail's pace as he sat by himself. He'd hoped someone would come out and give him an update, but the doors remained closed. Maybe he shouldn't have insisted on Kevin remaining in Evergreen Corners. He would have enjoyed the boy asking him the hundred and one questions Kevin seemed to have each day. At least that would have made the time move. He looked at the clock and was ready to assert it was running backward.

The door to the parking lot opened, and two men came in. One was supporting the bloody hand of the other. They went to the desk. The woman there took one look at the man's hand and told them to follow her. A soft buzz unlocked the door, and they vanished through it.

He waited for the door to open again with news about Rose Anne and Benjamin. It didn't happen. A man he hadn't seen before walked out, stopped at the desk and did some paperwork before he left holding several pages. He wondered how many people were being treated.

Bring each of them Your healing, God, he prayed, halting when the outer door opened again.

Three more patients entered, each one with a companion. Two, one man and one elderly woman, were suffering from bad colds, and he couldn't guess what had brought the third one, a man with a bushy brown beard, to the clinic. In turn, each of them was called to the back.

And still nobody came out.

"Are you the father of the little girl?" called the woman behind the window.

He faced her. "No, a friend." He gave her a wry grin. "To both of your patients from Evergreen Corners."

"All right. I'll take the paperwork to her mother." She rose and left before he could ask if there was any update.

Not that she would have told him anyhow. Such information was overseen by so many privacy laws that he'd need signed permission from Carolyn in order to hear the answers. That he'd held the little girl all the way to the clinic didn't matter.

But what if he were to become Rose Anne's *daed*?

He shook that out of his head. Nothing had changed. He couldn't make a commitment to anyone until he decided what his commitment to God would be.

Have you put off making up your mind on one issue so you can avoid making up your mind on the other?

He sat straighter as the unexpected thought resonated through him. He needed to be baptized before he wed. Had he been using God as an excuse to keep his heart barricaded away from another woman who would toss it aside and stomp on it publicly as Adah had? In an effort to avoid more drama, was he shutting himself away from the parts of life he should be relishing now?

The door opened, saving him from having to answer his own silent questions. Benjamin inched into the waiting room. He moved more tentatively than before.

Michael jumped to his feet and assisted his friend to

an armless chair. He didn't want to chance Benjamin bumping himself as he sat.

"How bad is it?" asked Michael.

"Two broken ribs and another that's cracked." Benjamin gave a wry grin as he lowered himself into the chair. "I don't do anything halfway, I guess."

"Sorry."

His friend started to wave away the sympathy, but his breath caught as he moved his right arm. "I guess I'm going to be left-handed for a while."

"Did you see Carolyn and Rose Anne back there?"

"No. All the doors were closed. I didn't see anyone other than the *doktors* who examined me and their nurses."

Though he was anxious to hear about Rose Anne, Michael asked, "What did the *doktor* say?"

"He gave me some pain pills and told me to take them. When I said I don't like taking medicine, he said it's important because I need to be able to breathe normally. Shallow breathing can bring on pneumonia."

"You need to listen to the *doktor*."

"Easy for you to say. You're not the one who's going to be sitting around while everyone else is working." He closed his eyes. "The *doktor* said I can get back to light duty in about two weeks. He's got instructions for me to take home."

As if on cue, the receptionist called, "Mr. Kuhns?"

"I'll get it," Michael said, jumping up again.

The woman handed him a clipboard with several pages on it and a pen. She told him he could have Benjamin tell him the answers and sign it for his friend.

Fifteen minutes later, Michael knew more about Benjamin than he'd ever thought he would. He'd written down information about when his friend had snagged his finger on a fish hook and had to have stitches, as well as a broken finger when he was a teenager. Taking off the advisory pages the doctor had sent out for Benjamin to use during his recovery, Michael signed the papers and gave them back to the nurse.

"Do you know how much longer Mrs. Wiebe and her daughter will be?" he asked.

"I'm sorry, sir. I don't have that information." She took the clipboard and turned to her computer.

Michael forced himself to sit, though he longed to work off his nervous energy by pacing. He didn't want to disturb the others waiting in the silent room. Beside him, Benjamin sat, panting as if he'd run a marathon.

The door opened again, and the man with the bloody hand came out. He and his companion left. They were followed by the woman who'd been coughing hard when she arrived and a man who was probably her husband.

At last, the door swung open and a wheelchair came out. Rose Anne sat in it, her smile shaky. She was excited to be able to ride in the chair, but was hurting too much to enjoy it. The cover over the cast running from her left wrist to her elbow was the brightest pink he'd ever seen.

Carolyn stepped aside as the door opened again, and the bearded man emerged. He glanced at the wheelchair, scowled and edged around it as if it had been put intentionally in his way. He stared at Michael and Benjamin, and Michael guessed the *Englischer* had never seen a plain man before.

Michael ignored the stranger, who hurried to the receptionist's desk. Kneeling beside the wheelchair, he asked, "How's the bravest girl in Evergreen Corners?"

"Bravest?" Rose Anne's eyes glistened as her smile grew a bit stronger. "Me?"

"*Ja*, you've been as brave as your *mamm*, who is the bravest woman I know."

He watched that adorable color rise in Carolyn's too-pale face before she said, "I need to get Rose Anne's paperwork. I'll be right back."

"We'll be right here." He continued to talk to the little girl who seemed to be fading off to sleep. Putting his hand under her head, he kept it from drooping forward and leaving her with a pain in her neck as well as her arm.

After what seemed a ridiculously long time, the bearded man finished his business at the window and left, looking back to stare once more. Michael again paid him no mind.

A few minutes later, Carolyn returned and gazed down at her daughter.

"The doctor gave her something for the pain while he set the bone and cast it," she said.

"And let her pick out the cast cover?"

"Once she saw the pink, she didn't want to look at anything else. I was tempted to suggest the bright green because that would have made her visible when she's near the work site."

"I don't think anyone's going to miss seeing that pink."

"The doctor assured me it'll darken as the cast gets dirty." She sighed. "I'm going to have to figure out how to keep *her* clean for the next six weeks. You know she won't miss coming to the new house any chance she can. She's as excited as Kevin about the construction, and she misses helping me collect the chickens' eggs."

"Another reason to pray rain stays away for the next few weeks."

She smiled, and his heart began to beat at a crazy

speed, as it had when he saw the wood falling. But this sensation was pleasurable.

He reached across the chair and took her hand between his. Her fingers stiffened, then uncurled like a waking butterfly. He cupped them as if they were as fragile.

"Let's get the little one," he said, not wanting to rouse Rose Anne by saying her name, "and Benjamin home."

"Yes, let's go home," she whispered, and he found himself imagining other questions he could pose that she would say yes to.

The day's light was fading into twilight when Carolyn trudged up the hill to the trailer along with Benjamin and Michael, who was carrying Rose Anne. Jenna was waiting with Kevin and her daughter, Taylor. The librarian insisted on taking Benjamin to her neighbor's house.

"I checked with them," Jenna said. "It was the least I could do after all the help you've given to me at the library in the past week. My neighbors, the Zielinskis, have an extra bed in their den for you. You remember them, right? They emptied their big chest freezer so we could put books in there to keep them from getting moldy. The Zielinskis agree you shouldn't sleep in a barn while dealing with your injury."

"I'll be fine there." His voice remained wispy, and Carolyn noticed how hard he seemed to be struggling for each breath.

Michael must have heard that, too, because he said in his most no-nonsense voice, "Don't try to be a hero, Benjamin. These people want to help you. Let them."

"Listen to Michael," Carolyn said, not wanting the debate to keep her from her children. "Basia and Walter are wonderful people, and they've been disappointed they haven't been able to help. They're elderly, so can't do much as far as the rebuilding or cleanup. However, they'll keep you on your toes, Benjamin. Don't let them talk you into playing trivia. You're guaranteed to lose."

Benjamin nodded reluctantly. "All right. It's not easy to accept charity from someone I've never met."

"Isn't that what I did when you and Michael and the others came to Evergreen Corners to rebuild my house? We'd never met."

"Seems hard to believe, ain't so?" Michael said as he carried a drowsy Rose Anne into the trailer and set her on the sofa bed that Jenna had open and ready for her. "Benjamin, you're skilled with making things from the wood pieces left over at your sawmill. You can make them something nice to repay them." His brows lowered again. "Once you're feeling better again."

Carolyn took the plate of cookies she'd intended to deliver to the building site that morning. Such a short time ago. It seemed as if it'd been a week since she'd gone flying out of the trailer after the children. Now Kevin sat too quietly in the bunk, and Rose Anne was lying on her bed, her little face wrinkled with pain. And Carolyn's own nerves were taut, making every word and every action vibrate along them.

"Here. Take these with you." She held out the plate to Jenna. "Basia always asks when I'm going to make oatmeal date cookies again."

"Oatmeal date?" asked Michael, and she noticed his voice sounded as casual as she'd tried to make hers. Was he hiding behind a facade as she was? Whether he was or not, she appreciated his sanding the edges off the tension in the trailer. "I've never heard of them."

"I got the recipe from Abby."

"Isaac's sister?" Jenna asked.

Carolyn nodded, glad her friend didn't ask any more questions before she took the plate and motioned for Benjamin to follow her and Taylor, who'd been silent as she stared at the cast on Rose Anne's arm.

Carolyn closed the door in their wake. Though she wished she could lose herself in sleep as her niece had, she must offer Kevin solace. Her nephew had been as quiet as Taylor, and that wasn't like him. She climbed into his bunk and, despite the cramped space, huddled with him. Putting her arms around him, she listened as he wept out his terror that she and Rose Anne wouldn't come back. She consoled him in the gentle whispers that always reached through his fear, knowing the day's events had dredged up the one when she'd had to tell him his *mamm* couldn't be with him again until he joined her in heaven. Though she'd done all she could to take Regina's place, her nephew's scars hadn't healed.

When he admitted he was hungry, a sure sign he was feeling better, Carolyn climbed out of the bunk. Michael lifted Kevin down to sit at the table so he didn't disturb his little sister, and told him about the drive through the woods until the worst of the fright had vanished from her nephew's face. At the same time, Carolyn heated the leftover soup she'd planned for their midday meal. She realized Kevin was the only one who'd had anything to eat since breakfast. She let Rose Anne sleep while she served the soup and grilled cheese sandwiches, but she left the teakettle simmering.

Through the meal, Michael kept the conversation light until Kevin yawned. Sending the boy to get ready for bed and reminding him to brush his teeth and wash his face—"With soap this time, Kevin!"—she cleared the table. She was shocked she'd finished every bite in her bowl and on her plate.

When Kevin closed the bathroom door, Michael stood and took a cup from the cupboard. He poured hot water over a tea bag from the box on the shelf over the sink. "Do you need help getting Rose Anne ready for bed?"

"I think I'll let her sleep. It'd be a shame to wake her up to put on her pajamas. I saved some soup in case she wakes later and is hungry."

"Do you think she'll sleep through the night?"

"I hope so." Her gaze met his. "I need to tell you again how grateful I am, Michael, that you and Benjamin and James let us use this trailer. I don't know how we would have managed in the stables."

"You would have found a way." He handed her the steaming cup of tea. "I suspect you always do."

She lowered her eyes. What would he say if she revealed the truth of the past four years?

If he noticed her action, he didn't speak of it as Kevin came out of the bathroom. Michael waited for her to listen to her nephew's nightly prayers, which now included a request every night for Tippy to come back, and then lifted the boy into his bunk.

Once she knew Kevin was asleep, Carolyn went to hang up their coats, which had been tossed on her bed. When she heard the crackle of papers in her pocket, she took out the sheets the receptionist had given her. She sorted them, putting the ones for Rose Anne's care to one side so she could refer to them during the next six weeks until her cast could be removed.

She flipped over one of the pages and gasped.

"Was iss letz?" asked Michael.

So shaken she didn't care he'd spoken in *Deitsch*, she replied, "I didn't realize until I looked at the forms they gave me at the clinic. Today is exactly one month from the night of the flood."

He stepped forward and drew her into his arms. She leaned her cheek over his heart. Its pace jumped as her own had when he touched her. Being held to him was like coming home after wandering, lost, for all her life. She closed her eyes and drank in the scent of him.

"I'm sorry," he murmured against her hair. "If I'd realized, I would have... I don't know what I would have done, but I wish I could make this easier for you."

"You are." Her arms curved up his back as she nestled closer. She might be acting like the greatest fool in history, but she didn't care. The comfort he offered was what she hadn't realized she'd been looking for. "You're making it easier by being here."

"I'm glad." His voice was low and husky, inviting her to stay where she was as long as she wanted.

But she drew back, knowing if she remained enfolded to him she wouldn't ever want to leave. All too soon he would be returning to his own home, and their lives might never intersect again. Before he'd come to Evergreen Corners, she would have told herself it was for the best...and she would have believed it.

Now she wasn't sure what to believe.

Chapter Twelve

Michael pulled his scarf around his collar and listened to the muffled clank of his tool belt beneath his heavy coat. He'd heard the winters in Vermont were rougher than what he was used to in Pennsylvania, but hearing it and living it were two different things. In the week since the accident on the work site, it seemed every morning was much, much colder than the previous day.

Benjamin was spending time at the library helping Jenna and other volunteers determine what was salvageable and what had been ruined beyond repair. He'd returned to the stables after two nights at the Zielinskis' house, grateful for their hospitality but overwhelmed by Basia's determination to coddle him as if he were her own *kins-kind*

Each day, Michael got updates on Rose Anne from Kevin, who seemed to appear wherever he was working. The little girl was already complaining about wearing a heavy cast, because it kept her from chasing after her brother.

The previous evening, when he'd given Kevin another lesson in whittling after supper at the trailer, the boy hadn't been able to talk about anything but when it would start snowing. He couldn't wait to go sledding. The fact he no longer had a sled didn't bother him because he was planning to go with his best friend.

"My best *kid* friend," he'd told Michael. "You're my best *grown-up* friend."

Michael had heard Carolyn laugh at the comment, and he'd acknowledged what he'd been trying to ignore. He liked being in Evergreen Corners and spending time with the Wiebe family.

He liked it a lot.

A real lot.

"What if I don't want to go back to Harmony Creek Hollow?" he mused aloud, the wind snatching the words away as soon as he spoke them.

He kicked a stone along the asphalt and listened as it tumbled over the broken side of the road. Why should he leave when he'd discovered someone who—other than not being Amish—fit the criteria he would have looked for in a wife? Carolyn was kind and funny and, most important, calm.

When he'd first stepped off the bus, he'd assumed her serenity was because she was numb from the shock of the flood. His opinion had changed in the wake of her daughter's broken arm. Carolyn had been as imperturbable as one of the trees growing along the road through the whole disaster and in the days afterward. A bit subdued, perhaps, but cheerful and optimistic...and calm.

Had God brought him here in answer to his questions about his future? He was beginning to think so.

"Hey, Michael!"

At Kevin's familiar shout, Michael looked back to see Carolyn and the *kinder* walking toward him. Rose

Anne seemed to be moving more naturally each day as she adjusted to her cast, which was hidden beneath a bulky coat so big the hem dropped below her knees.

"Aren't you supposed to be in school now?" he asked the boy, though his gaze settled on Carolyn, who looked lovelier than usual with her cheeks rosy from the cold.

"Tomorrow's Thanksgiving!" Kevin crowed. "We had only a half day."

"So you decided to take a walk?"

"We decided to remind ourselves," Carolyn answered before her son could, "what we're grateful for."

"The freezing weather?"

"Not that." She gestured along the road. "We're grateful for everyone who has come to work so hard on our new house."

"Have you seen it since the shingles were put on?"

Her eyes twinkled with excitement. "No! Can we go now?"

The work site was empty because the crews were doing framing and setting the rafters in place on the Gagnons' house next door. Michael smiled as the family delighted in the sight of what looked like a house now. Spaces for windows and doors had been cut into the sheathing, and he pointed out where each room would be. His face ached with his grin, because he wasn't sure who was more excited: the *kinder* or Carolyn… or himself.

Rose Anne flung her uninjured arm around his leg and hugged it. "I love my new house." She looked at him. "Can we make it a pretty color?"

"Whatever color your *mamm* wants it to be."

"How about sky-blue pink?" the little girl asked.

"We'll see what we can find at the paint store." He winked at Carolyn over Rose Anne's head.

Carolyn took her daughter's hand. "We've got to go one step at a time. Remember? We've talked about this. Wood first and then paint."

"I know. I know." The *kind*'s voice took on a world-weary tone. "We gots to follow plopper pole-scissors."

"Yes, *proper procedures* are important."

Michael put a hand over his mouth before he could burst out laughing. He was glad Carolyn had "translated" that Rose Anne-ism.

When he strode down the hill to the stack of wood he'd helped Carolyn pull out of the water when he first came to Evergreen Corners, Kevin bounced after him.

"What are you doing? Can I help?" the boy asked.

"Ja." He looked across the grassless yard to where Carolyn was guiding Rose Anne closer to the chicken pen. "We'll let them keep the chickens distracted while you and I build your chickens a new home."

"Now?" Kevin let off a cheer that set the chickens to racing around, frightened, in their pen.

"Remember what I've told you about being quiet and careful around tools?"

The *kind* froze, then nodded. "I'll be quiet."

"And careful."

"Yep."

Picking up two long planks, Michael lifted them to his shoulder as he walked toward the house. "Where would you like your henhouse, Carolyn?"

"Near the fallen log would be good. The ground is flat, and it's far enough from the house so the smell won't invade when we open the windows. Yet it'll be close enough for collecting eggs. But you don't have to do this today."

"Why not?" he asked as he put the boards on the ground. "If Kevin can have a half day off from school, I should be able to take a half day off from work."

"So you can do different work?"

He liked how her eyes shone when she teased him. "You know what Proverbs says about idle hands, ain't so?"

"All right, but I can't stay to help. I was supposed to be at the kitchen to work on preparations for tomorrow's big feast about fifteen minutes ago."

Though he wished she wouldn't go, he nodded. "Don't let me make you later."

"We're having a gathering tonight at the community center to count our blessings as well as peel and cook all the potatoes we need. Why don't you come and join us?"

"So I can help peel potatoes?"

"I'm sure you'll be exempt after your work out here today."

He nodded. "I'll see you then."

"Can I stay and help?" Kevin asked as Carolyn motioned for her son to come with her.

"It's fine with me, Carolyn. Anytime." Michael was surprised how much he hoped those words would prove to be true. If he remained in Evergreen Corners...

He silenced that thought as he watched Carolyn walk toward the road with her daughter. He'd promised to build the chicken coop, so he'd better get to it before the sun set, making the air colder.

Until Kevin asked him what the song was, Michael didn't realize he was whistling as he collected a few discarded two-by-fours and began to measure them.

He couldn't remember the last time he'd whistled. Back when he was a carefree kid? Then he realized it'd been before Adah had dumped him. He'd let her melodrama steal his happiness and leave him in a grim place.

Now he wanted to whistle like a robin welcoming back spring.

He worked with the boy to complete the structure for the small building. Located where it was, it wouldn't be in the way of finishing Carolyn's house, and the chickens would be protected from the cold tonight. He built a roof, but just set it on top without attaching it to the coop. After Thanksgiving, he'd find some time to remove the roof and put in a shelf where nest boxes could be set.

"Hey, Michael," Kevin said as he sat on the log. "You know what?"

"What?" He squatted to cut out a doorway. A small piece of plank on simple hinges would allow access to the interior but allow Carolyn to shut in the chickens if she needed to.

"I hate my name."

"Why?" He looked back at the boy. "It's a *gut* name. When I lived in Pennsylvania and was about your age, I had a friend named Kevin."

"That's the problem," the boy grumbled.

"That I had a friend named Kevin?" Sometimes the course of the *kind*'s thoughts eluded him as much as the meaning of Rose Anne's odd words.

"No! The problem is I don't want to share my name." Kevin jumped to his feet, his small fists pressed closed by his sides. "Not with that stupid, stupid hurricane."

He kept measuring the doorway. "Why? The storm

has come and gone, and there won't ever be another one named Kevin."

"But everyone talks about Hurricane Kevin. Sometimes they just say Kevin, and I think they're talking to me. Then I realize they're not. I'm tired of it."

"I understand."

"You do?"

Michael let his measuring tape roll back into its case with a snap. "Do you have any idea how many Michaels and Mikes there are around here? Amish ones and Mennonite ones and *Englisch* ones and lots of other ones. Every day I hear someone use my name, but they aren't talking to me. They're talking to someone else."

"Don't you hate it, too?"

Michael shook his head and gave the boy a gentle smile. "Not any longer. It used to annoy me, but I realized it was such a *wunderbaar* name it needed to be given to many different people. My twin brother's name is Gabriel, and I know only one other person with his name. He used to say, when we were kids, he wished he could have a friend with the same name like I did."

"Not me. I wish I could change my name. It's not unusual for people to do that, y'know?"

"Who do you know who's changed his name?"

"My mom. Her name wasn't always Carolyn Wiebe. It was something different. If she can do it, why can't I?"

He tried not to laugh at the boy's sense of unfairness in his situation. Of course, Carolyn would have changed her name after she married. All plain women did.

But why did she never talk about the man she'd wed? Could something have happened, something that caused the shadows in her eyes? She held on to secrets of her past as tightly as she did the *kinder*. He wasn't sure where she'd moved from. She'd mentioned an older sister, but then changed the subject so fast he'd nearly gotten whiplash.

She's wiser than you, taunted a small voice in his mind. *She's put her past to rest while you let yours dog your every step through life.*

He halted the saw in midcut. He'd never looked at the situation from that angle.

"Are you okay, Michael?" asked the *kind*.

"I'm fine. Just fine."

He distracted the boy and himself by building a door to set into the doorway he'd cut. When it became too dark to work any longer, he took Kevin to the community center.

He opened the door and saw Carolyn on the other side of the long room with Jenna and Abby. Her sweet laughter drifted across the room to him, enthralling him in its lyrical song. He thought they were sharing a joke, and then Jenna stepped aside. On the floor, two pies were smashed to pieces.

"It's all right," Carolyn was reassuring her friend. "We can make more pies. Jose has made sure we've got plenty of apples."

"But," Jenna moaned, "look at the time we've lost. How can we make more pies and have time to do everything else?"

Abby glanced at the clock. "It's getting late, and we need to finish preparing the evening meal before everyone gets here."

Unperturbed by either the pie filling oozing across the floor or her friends' despondent tones, Carolyn said, "We've got enough time if we get started now. Once we get this cleaned up, Abby, you can start making more crusts while Jenna and I peel and cut the apples."

None of the women looked at Michael as they hurried into the kitchen. It was for the best, because his face must have displayed his admiration for how Carolyn handled any crisis, no matter how big or small. He couldn't imagine her making a mockery of someone else to turn all eyes to her.

Michael closed the door, backed away and walked down the hill. He paused by the brook and switched on his flashlight. It shocked him how such an innocuous trickle had caused the damage he'd seen in the village. The soft whisper of the water flowing over the stones was almost lost in the sound of voices coming from his right. He saw the lights were on in the diner by the road over the bridge. The owners must be working so they could open after the first of the year as they'd announced.

Though they were busy with their own work and hadn't seen him by the brook, he continued downstream. He had a lot to think about tonight, but most especially he needed to decide if he should make the change in his future that would allow him to pose an offer of marriage to Carolyn.

Though she wondered why Michael hadn't come in when he'd brought Kevin, Carolyn didn't have time to find out. After she helped with the pies to replace the ones that had slid off Jenna's tray, she made batch after batch of brownies for the workers who were coming in to get their suppers. The cold seemed to make everyone ravenous.

"Why the long face?" Jenna asked as she came into

the community kitchen. With the pies baking in the large ovens, she'd regained her good spirits.

"Brownies used to be one of my favorite treats." Carolyn glowered at the bowl in front of her. "But after stirring my tenth batch today, I'm not sure I ever want to smell one again."

Jenna dipped her finger into the bowl and licked it. "Ah, chocolate! One of God's best creations." She reached for an apron from the stack on the counter. She pulled out one in shades of bright red and green and tied it around her. "I know you like chocolate as much as I do, so stop grousing. You'll be at the front of the line anytime someone is passing out warm brownies."

"How's Benjamin doing at the library?"

"Helpful, but impatient to get back to working on the houses. Kind of like Rose Anne, but larger." She laughed as she reached for a bag of dried bread and began to cut it into cubes for the stuffing they needed to make before they left tonight. "He wants to do everything he usually does, but then gets a reminder he shouldn't."

"Rose Anne hasn't slowed down much. When I checked on her last night, I found she'd climbed into Kevin's bed so she could sleep with him."

"With a cast on?" Jenna smiled. "Ah, to be young and unaware of what you should and shouldn't be able to do with a broken arm."

The sound of the back door opening was accompanied by a whoosh of air so cold it conquered the hot kitchen. At the call of her name, Carolyn whirled to see Michael slipping in. He closed the door and pulled off his scarf, then motioned for her to come over to where he stood.

"Why are you coming in the back way?" she asked. "Hurry!"

She glanced at Jenna, who shrugged. Walking toward him, she said nothing as he looked around as if to determine who else was in the kitchen.

"What's going on?" she asked.

He put a paper bag on the floor, and she heard something rustle inside as it settled to the bottom. As he began to unbutton his coat, he said, "I didn't want Kevin to see me until I had a chance to talk to you first."

"Why?"

"Because I wanted you to see what I've got before he does."

Every word he spoke confused her more. "Michael, if this is your idea of a joke, it's not—"

"Look." He grabbed the bag and thrust his hand into it.

She gasped when she stared at what she'd never expected to see again. The tattered toy had been stained by mud and debris, but she recognized the floppy ears and the once-bushy tail, though it was almost two inches shorter than it had been. Her fingers quivered as she reached to take it from his icy fingers. The toy was damp, but not soaked. Turning it over, she saw the spot where she'd stitched a rip closed last summer.

He whispered, "Is it Tippy?"

Unable to speak as tears rushed into her eyes, she nodded. She cleared her throat once, then a second time before she could ask, "Where did you find him? *How* did you find him?"

"The how part was simple. I stumbled over it while I was walking along the brook tonight."

Her head snapped up. "You were walking along the brook in the cold and dark? Have you lost your mind?"

"I needed to sort out some important things, and walking always helps me do that."

"And you found Tippy?" She ran the back of her hand under her eyes to dash away the tears that refused to stay put. "Where?"

"Down along the curve of the brook. There's a car stuck on the bank." He sighed. "I think it's yours. It's black. Both the front lights and the rear ones are shattered, and there are small rocks behind the portions of the intact glass. I waded out into the brook to see if the license plate was on it. When I was bending down to aim my flashlight at the front, I saw something stuck among the torn plants and small trees embedded in the space between the bumper and the radiator. I was curious because it was above the water."

"Tippy," she whispered, unable to believe what she held in her hands.

"I wasn't sure if it was Kevin's, but I figured I'd bring it back here. If it wasn't his, some other kid would be looking for it."

"It's his. God put you in the right place at the right time."

"Me and Tippy."

"Yes, both of you were in the right place at the right time to find each other." She brushed the ruffled fur back into place, then reached out and grabbed Michael's hand.

He chuckled as she pulled him into the other room. Did he think she cared if everyone in Evergreen Corners saw her holding his hand now? She didn't slow until she reached the corner where Kevin was helping his sister choose a crayon out of a big plastic box. She pushed the stuffed dog back into Michael's hands. He'd recovered it, so he should be the one to give it to her nephew.

"Kevin," she said in a shaky voice.

Both *kinder* looked up at the same time.

"Michael has something for you," she went on, stepping aside.

Holding out the battered toy, Michael said, "Here's someone who's been missing you."

Kevin jumped to his feet and cried out his toy's name. He snatched the stuffed dog from Michael's hands and stared at it, then he looked at her. When she nodded, he pressed the dog to his chest. With his cheek against the dog's head, he began to sob as he folded to sit on the floor.

She knelt and put her arm around him. Seeing his sister ease closer, she drew the little girl within the arc of her arm, too. She took Michael's hand. There were no words to thank him, so she didn't try.

He gazed at her with tears in his own eyes. No one else moved as her nephew welcomed home a dear friend he'd thought was lost forever.

Suddenly, a timer went off in the kitchen, and the world flowed into motion again as the bakers rushed out and conversations began everywhere.

Everywhere but where she held her children and the hand of the man she wanted to love. Could she put aside her trepidation and dare to trust him with her heart?

She had from now until year's end to find out. Not only if she could trust him with her heart, but if she could trust her heart itself.

Chapter Thirteen

The last thing Carolyn expected was for Michael to stop at the trailer at dawn on Thanksgiving morning. The children were in her bedroom watching Tippy roll over and over in the dryer. Though she'd been anxious the toy would fall apart when she washed it, the stuffed dog had come through its bath looking almost as it had before. Kevin had discovered one of its eyes was missing, and Carolyn had promised to sew on a new one as soon as they could buy a button.

"Do Mennonites have Christmas trees?" Michael asked as he poked his head past the door.

She didn't glance up from the German chocolate cake she was frosting. It felt wonderful to be baking again. She'd finally mastered the quirks of the trailer's oven and now was able to make sponge cakes and bundt cakes and coffeecakes. She'd forgotten how much she missed putting gooey dough into an oven and a short time later pulling out aromatic, spongy cake layers. Too much else had been on her mind, but mixing the ingredients and enjoying the results had kept her focused instead of anxious as it had ever since…

Since she'd left Indiana with the children.

Propelling that thought into the back of her mind, she was able to smile as she motioned for Michael to come in. His kindness during the past month was one of the reasons she felt a contentment she'd thought she'd never experience again. She had spent half the night awake as she sought the right words to thank him for bringing Tippy back to Kevin. Everything she thought of seemed too vapid to convey the depths of her appreciation.

"Christmas trees?" she asked. "It's almost a month before we celebrate Christmas. Why are you asking?"

"But do you Mennonites have Christmas trees?" He came in and closed the door.

The small trailer seemed to shrink more as his broad shoulders and vital personality filled the space. She gave herself a moment to savor the sight of his strong features. A quiver ran from her heart right to the tips of her toes as she recalled his hand holding hers the previous night. Yes, she'd grabbed his first when she dragged him into the main room, but he hadn't released her fingers until she had to return to work on the feast for this afternoon.

Despite her heart urging her to believe he was the man he appeared to be, she had to select her words with care. It was the same walk across a tightrope she'd been doing for four years. She wouldn't lie, but she had to avoid spilling the truth that could lead to a disaster greater than the flood.

"Some Mennonite families have trees," she replied, applying more coconut-pecan icing to the cake. "Some don't. It depends on how conservative a family's beliefs are or what their traditions are. Sometimes the differences range from family to family rather than from district to district as with you Amish."

He pulled off his black felt hat and brushed his too-long hair back from his eyes. The man needed a haircut. Should she offer? That was the job of an Amish woman. Maybe she should suggest to Abby that it was time for the plain men to have their hair trimmed.

"I guess I should have asked if *your* family has a Christmas tree," he said.

"We do."

She had relented and gotten Kevin and Rose Anne a tree their first year in Evergreen Corners. In part, it'd been so their house didn't stand out as the one without a tree. But the main reason she had given in was that her sister had put up a small tree every year because she'd lived an *Englisch* life, and Kevin had faint memories of those. Decorating the tree with popcorn strings and handmade ornaments and not putting on lights had eased Carolyn's regret about another sign of how far she'd moved from the life she'd known.

The life she'd always expected to live.

The life you could have again if you told Michael the truth and he became part of the family.

She silenced the thought. Going to live in an Amish community could give Leland the lead he needed to find them.

"Why are you asking?" she asked.

He grinned, and she looked at the cake before she couldn't resist his smile and grabbed his hand again. This time to pull it around her waist as she stepped into his arms.

"*Englischers* seem to have a tradition," he explained,

"of putting a Christmas tree on top of any building project in progress at this time of year."

"On the roof?"

"Ja."

"So you're going to put a Christmas tree on top of the brand-new shingles on my roof?"

He smiled and leaned a shoulder against the upper cabinets. As before, she was astonished by how little space there was between his shoulders and the cupboards on either side of the tiny kitchen. "I had the same thought, Carolyn. I was told, in this case, the trees would be put in front of the houses, so they could be seen from the road." His smile faded. "The other two houses belong to *Englischers*, and they're thrilled with the idea. I wanted to check to make sure you're okay with it, too."

"The children will be excited about it." She hedged, hoping it was enough of an answer.

It wasn't, because he asked, "How do *you* feel about it?"

"I'm grateful for what you are doing for us. I wouldn't care if you wanted to put a dancing elephant in front of the house." She wagged a finger. "But no elephant on the roof."

He caught her finger in his broad hand, then ran his finger along hers, catching the frosting on his rougher skin. Popping the frosting into his mouth, he gave her a slow, enticing smile. "Delicious."

The familiar frisson rippled through her center, but she laughed to break the invisible connection between them. "You sound like the kids when they plead to lick the spoon."

"Some things a guy shouldn't grow too old to try.

Baseball, horseshoes and beguiling frosting or raw cookie dough from a skilled baker."

She scooped out a generous spoonful of the icing that was as rich as fudge and offered it to him. "Here you go."

"Me, too?" asked Rose Anne from behind her as she and Kevin rushed from the bedroom. "Can I have some?"

"Can I have *lots*?" chimed in her brother.

As she handed each child a small taste of the frosting, Rose Anne asked, "Sit with us at supper, Michael, okay?"

"That's the best invitation I've had all day," he replied. "As long as it's okay with your *mamm*."

"Of course it is." Carolyn was glad her voice didn't convey the excitement going off in her like a fireworks show finale. Michael would have Thanksgiving with them.

Like a real family.

Oh, how she wished that was possible, but no matter how much her heart begged her to give it to Michael, she must keep the children safe.

She was relieved she didn't have to say more before Michael headed out and the children returned to the bedroom to watch Tippy's wild journey around the dryer. When she was alone again in the kitchen, she took a deep breath, wondering when she'd last drawn a steady one. Not since she'd heard Michael's voice as he came into the trailer.

Her fingers tightened around the spoon until the wood creaked. Loosening her grip, she drew in another slow breath. All she had to do was keep her heart under control until Michael returned to his brother's farm.

* * *

Opening the door to the community center, Michael smiled. The place was bustling as church members and other villagers, including the mayor and most of her council, joined the volunteers for a Thanksgiving meal. It was made up of dishes from the many different groups in the room. Amish noodles and chow-chow were set on the table beside Mennonite dishes that ranged from brimming casseroles topped with crispy browned cheese to a pear and walnut salad drizzled with maple syrup. Homemade breads from white to pumpernickel were displayed with sweet rolls in baskets along the long tables set in a giant U in the center of the room. Potatoes and yams and green beans had been placed in the centers of the tables while butternut soup had been ladled into bowls on top of each plate.

He looked forward to sampling, but most of all he wanted a piece of the German chocolate cake Carolyn had been frosting a few hours ago. Its aroma had been astounding, and the frosting the best he'd ever tasted. He wanted to try both together. However, first there was the meal to consider.

"Nobody's going to go away hungry," Benjamin said as he struggled to get his coat off so he could toss it atop the others piled on chairs by the front door.

Michael almost offered his help, but knew his friend would turn him down. Benjamin was determined to be able to return to doing everything he could before the accident…even if his mulishness injured his healing ribs more.

Shouts came for everyone to take a seat. Michael hurried to where Kevin and Rose Anne sat with Jenna's daughter, Taylor. Streaks of red on the festive tablecloth announced little fingers had already been in the cranberry sauce.

Cheers broke out just as Michael sat, leaving one empty chair between himself and Kevin. Benjamin gave him a grin, then chose the seat on Michael's other side. The cheers became applause as the stars of the day arrived in the common room. Not the six women who'd been working in the kitchen, but the turkeys they carried on large platters. Abby led the way, holding up a perfectly cooked bird.

"That one's as big as me," Rose Anne said loudly.

Her words brought more cheers as well as convivial laughter.

"Then it should go right by you." Jenna put the turkey she'd brought beside where Rose Anne and Taylor sat.

After placing the turkey she'd brought out in front of Pastor Hershey, Carolyn hurried to the empty chair between Kevin and Michael. She smiled at him, but looked down the table as the Mennonite minister rose.

The room hushed while Pastor Hershey asked each person to thank God for His blessings in his or her own way. Soft prayers flowed through the room like a breeze on a perfect summer day, though the Amish were silent. When the minister said, "Amen," every head rose and silverware clicked as they began to enjoy the soup.

Jenna smiled along the table. "When I was growing up, we'd say what we were thankful for. Michael, why don't you start?"

He was surprised she didn't ask Benjamin first, but said, "I've got many reasons to be thankful this Thanksgiving. My brother is happily married and has the farm he's wanted since we were kids. I'm getting ready to do the work I love in what will be three *wunderbaar* homes. And I'm blessed with many new friends."

He watched Carolyn's face while he spoke. Did she have any idea *she* was what he was most thankful for this year?

Kevin was next. "I'm thankful Michael brought Tippy home," the boy announced, and smiles along the table broadened.

Carolyn spoke of her gratitude for the volunteers who'd come to Evergreen Corners. "And, as Michael said, you've become our friends."

Everyone's smiles widened more when Rose Anne announced she was grateful for the pies waiting to be served for dessert.

"Which is your favorite?" Benjamin asked.

"Pun-kin." Rose Anne giggled as she added, "I'm going to have a big piece with whip-it cream on it."

"Whippet?" asked Michael as he leaned toward Carolyn. "I hope you aren't putting small greyhounds on top of the pies."

"I wasn't planning on it." She spooned some mashed potatoes onto Rose Anne's plate before stretching to do the same for Kevin. She gave him another half spoonful when he offered her a mournful glance. "I figured I'd use regular whipped cream."

"Sounds delicious."

"But no dessert for anyone who doesn't finish their supper," she said as she aimed the same unrelenting frown at her daughter and her son and then on to him.

That she included him brought peals of laughter from her children and Jenna's daughter. As others spoke of why they were blessed, Michael let himself relish the merriment and the gratitude. Now was the time for feasting and laughing and sharing each other's company.

There was time enough later to speak to her about what he'd decided as he walked by the brook.

Carolyn rearranged the trailer's small refrigerator for the third time and managed to squeeze in the two servings of green bean casserole Jenna had insisted she bring home with her. Straightening, she sighed. It had been a good day, but a long one. She was glad they could live on leftovers for the next few meals. She picked up her cup of tea and carried it to the table where Michael sat nursing the decaf coffee he'd made while she got the children into bed.

Checking both children, she saw they were asleep. She sighed again, this time with happiness, at the sight of Kevin lying with his cheek on Tippy.

"Can I get your opinion about something important?" Michael asked when she put her cup on the table.

"Of course."

She slid into the banquette across from him. Her joy tempered when she noticed his fingers tapping the table. What was he nervous about? "Do I need to make some decision about the house?"

"No, nothing about the house or the *kinder* or you." He paused, and his gaze slid away from hers as if he were ashamed of what he was about to say.

She couldn't imagine what it might be. He was a good man, the best she'd ever met. Putting a gentle hand on his arm, she said, "Tell me."

"I'm not sure I want to be baptized Amish."

She was struck speechless by his words. Not be baptized Amish? Did he have any idea of what he would lose if he decided not to become a part of the *Leit* in Harmony Creek Hollow? Images of her past, spending time with neighbors and friends who offered her an escape from the cruel words in her house, zoomed out of her memories. The love and acceptance of her plain community had been the bulwark God had offered her against the secrets hidden behind the Hilty family's walls. She should tell Michael how much she missed those connections and that community.

But she couldn't.

She bit her lower lip and stared at her clenched fingers laced together on the table. When she'd embarked on the path she was sure God had set out for her, she'd never imagined she'd come to such an impossible crossroads. She ached to trust Michael, but feared sharing her secret with anyone risked the truth leaking out to the whole world.

Including Leland.

She ached to speak from the heart, but pushed aside her own pain as she thought of what she might call down upon the children.

"It must be a big decision." She loathed herself as soon as the platitude came out of her mouth. Michael was hurting as he sought the path God had created for him. Instead of comforting him, she was offering him a useless cliché.

"A huge one." He sighed.

"Are you unhappy with your Amish community?" If she kept him talking, she might find a roundabout way to help him, a way that didn't endanger the children.

"No." He folded his hands in front of him. "My twin brother and his family are part of it. So are James and

Benjamin. Our neighbors made us feel welcome from the day we arrived in Harmony Creek Hollow."

"It sounds like a lovely place."

"It is." He gave her a lopsided grin. "In fact, Evergreen Corners reminds me a lot of it. You may not be Amish, but the people here are a community that cares for one another. In the month since the flood, nobody has backed away from offering to help."

"But if you're happy there, is it because you question your faith?"

"Who hasn't questioned their faith at one time or another? That's part of the weakness of being human. I'm thankful God is patient enough to keep loving me as a *kind* who has much to learn and accept and rejoice in."

"Then why…?" She wasn't sure what else to ask.

"Once I'm baptized, I'll be expected to find an Amish girl to marry, so we can raise a family in our faith traditions. Marrying someone outside our faith would mean being put under the *bann*."

She stared at him, her mouth agape. He couldn't be thinking of putting off being baptized because of any feelings he had for *her*, could he? Her heart sank. If he was making his choice because of her, he was making it without knowing the truth. How could she let him make such a life-altering decision while she withheld information from him?

But she couldn't tell him the truth.

Nothing had changed, she realized. It wouldn't until Rose Anne and Kevin were old enough to understand why she'd taken them from their home in Indiana and brought them to Vermont.

Wanting to hear him say he loved her as she loved him, she knew she must set aside that dream as she had others. She couldn't let him give up the life he knew and the family he loved based on what he believed she was.

But she couldn't tell him the truth.

"If you want my advice, Michael, don't make your decision now," she said, hoping to calm her roiling stomach. "At least, not while you're in Evergreen Corners."

His breath sifted past his clenched teeth, and she got the feeling she'd missed something. Something he hadn't said, but had wanted her to know.

"Take the time," she urged him, "to pray on it and see what guidance God offers you. He knows what you should do, but He may not let you know until His time is right."

"Rather than my own timetable, you mean?"

She nodded, biting back her own answer. If she said *ja* now, he might think she was making fun of his way of talking. She didn't want him to think that, and she couldn't explain how tough it was to avoid slipping into *Deitsch* when they spoke of their faith.

"That's *gut* advice." He gave her a rigid smile, then set himself on his feet. "*Danki* for listening, Carolyn. I appreciate the perspective of someone who's not Amish. You're right. This is between me and God and will be resolved at the time He deems right."

Her heart didn't know whether to jump in celebration that he was going to make his decision through prayer and patience or whether it should tumble in despair that he considered her an outsider not involved in his life.

And why shouldn't he? demanded the logical part of her brain. *He doesn't know you were raised Amish.*

"I know you'll make the best decision," she said, again falling back on the trite.

"If I heed God's guidance, I will." He cupped her cheek.

She yearned to lean her head into his strong, work-hardened palm and tell him how she longed for his arms around her again, how she wanted to share the secrets stalking her, how she wished she could tell him about her heart dancing with joy whenever she saw him or heard his voice. She didn't say anything.

"Gut nacht," he said as he pulled on his coat and reached for his hat, which he'd left by the sink.

"Good night," she whispered, but he was already gone.

She went to the door and looked out the small window. She watched him fade into the darkness. She stood there for uncounted minutes, turning only when she heard Rose Anne give a half sob. Going to check her niece, she ignored the tears running down her own face as she wondered if, somewhere, Leland Reber was laughing at how he'd ruined her life, too.

Chapter Fourteen

As he walked across the village green, Michael scratched his nape beneath his wool coat. It was always itchy in the wake of getting his hair cut. He should have been grateful Abby had come to the community center with her scissors and a battery-powered razor to give the plain men the opportunity to have their hair trimmed. He wasn't the only one who'd gotten tired of hair falling into his eyes when he bent to drive a nail or measure a length of wood. There had been seven men standing in line when he got there. Piles of hair in every possible shade had littered the floor.

Looking at the boy beside him, Michael smiled. Kevin had insisted on getting his hair cut, too, because he'd declared himself a full member of the volunteers. Carolyn had given her permission, so Michael had put Kevin in front of him in the line.

Carolyn was an excellent *mamm*, stern when she needed to be but willing to let her *kinder* make choices when she could. He'd seen her glance at little *bopplin*, and he guessed she wanted more *kinder*, though she'd shown no particular interest in any of the bachelors in the Mennonite community.

Or any interest in him, according to her response on Thanksgiving night when he'd opened up to her about his uncertainty regarding baptism. She'd given him every argument to become a member of the Harmony Creek Hollow *Leit*. Or, as she'd said more than once, he should let God guide him and not hurry the decision.

Those were the exact words he'd debated with himself about for months. If he'd sought his twin's advice, he would have expected Gabriel to make almost identical suggestions. Eli, the district's minister, wouldn't have told him anything else, and if his *daed* were still living, he'd have advised Michael the same way.

But he'd hoped for something more from a woman he'd been ready to propose to. A woman who seemed to be what he wanted as a wife. Had he been wrong about the light sparkling in her eyes when she looked at him? He didn't want to think so, but he'd been wrong about Adah.

Somehow, he'd let more than three weeks pass without talking to Carolyn about anything else important. He kept telling himself he'd speak to her about his feelings…tomorrow. Not that he had much time because she'd been busy with the *kinder* and village events for Christmas. He'd been as absorbed working on the houses, even being drafted to go with Glen and Jose twice to get supplies in Massachusetts.

Excuses, he told himself as he had before.

Now, as he walked through the biting cold with Kevin, he knew he couldn't put off being honest with her. He was scheduled to finish his volunteer stint in ten days.

"It's Christmas Eve eve," the boy said, as if Michael had been sharing his uneasy thoughts.

"That's right." He made himself chuckle. "So that makes yesterday Christmas Eve eve eve, ain't so?"

"Don't be silly!" Kevin rolled his eyes with a skill he'd likely hone further as a teenager. "There's no such thing!"

"I'm glad I've got you around, buddy, to keep me straight on things."

"So why don't you stay around?"

"I'm not sure what you mean."

"I mean why don't you stay here instead of going back to Harmony Creek Hollow?"

"My family is there."

"Your family could be here," Kevin said with the certainty of a *kind*.

He shook his head. "My brother won't want to move away because he can't wait to get working his fields this spring. You should come to Harmony Creek Hollow. You could visit Gabriel's cows and his wife Leanna's goats."

"Goats?" Kevin grimaced. "Don't they eat your clothes?"

"Only if you're *dumm* enough to leave them in a pile in their pen."

"I don't think I'd like goats."

"Maybe you'd like the soap Leanna makes out of their milk."

"Ugh!"

Michael swallowed his chuckle. He wasn't sure if Kevin was disgusted at the idea of goat milk soap or soap in general. "You might change your mind if you came to visit."

"I know what you should do," Kevin said as if Michael hadn't spoken.

"Do you?" He nodded to a bundled-up man walking across the green.

He wasn't sure who it was, now that many of the *Englischers* were growing beards for the winter. The man hurried past them without speaking. Michael didn't blame him. The wind seemed to be getting more frigid by the second.

"Yep, I do!" Kevin didn't seem bothered by the cold as he turned and faced him. "I know what you should do."

"What's that?"

"You should marry Mommy, and then you could be my uncle."

A buzzing had erupted in Michael's head when Kevin said "marry" and "Mommy" in the same breath. That had to be why he'd misunderstood the rest of the boy's words.

"You mean your *daed*, ain't so?"

Kevin's grin grew so wide it almost escaped his face. "Yes, you can be my daddy-uncle. Like Mommy is my mommy-aunt."

He didn't want to insult the boy by saying Kevin was confused. Or was he? Kevin was an intelligent *kind* with an agile mind and a vocabulary far beyond other boys his age.

"What's a mommy-aunt?" he asked.

"Guess it should be aunt-mommy. See, first she was my aunt and then she became my mommy after my other mommy died."

Every word the boy spoke made more questions blossom in Michael's head. Asking Kevin wouldn't get him anywhere. He needed Carolyn to explain. It was long past time to learn about the past she'd been hiding from him.

Putting the last cookie sheet away in the drawer under the stove, Carolyn closed it quietly. She didn't want to wake Rose Anne, who was napping on the narrow sofa. The thought of taking a nap gave birth to a big yawn. She surrendered to it, hoping letting it escape would leave her with enough energy to mop the floor before she began supper.

Twelve dozen cookies.

A gross of chocolate chip cookies and snickerdoodles and oatmeal raisin nut cookies were packaged and waiting to go to the community center tomorrow. They'd be served at the Christmas Eve caroling on the green. She'd been so pleased to be asked to contribute, though it had been a challenge to mix, bake and store so many cookies in the cramped kitchen.

She glanced out the window. Michael should be bringing Kevin back soon. They'd been gone almost two hours, and the line for haircuts couldn't have been too long. There were fewer than a dozen Amish men in town.

Her smile returned when she remembered how Kevin had taken his pocketknife with him so Michael could show him more tricks to whittling. Her nephew was eager to learn, and there wasn't room in the trailer. With the arrival of winter two days ago, it was too cold for them to sit on the steps.

Maybe in the spring...

Her breath caught when she remembered that by spring, Michael would be living in Harmony Creek

Hollow over fifty miles away. She didn't want to think about a time when he wouldn't be close by.

A knock on the trailer door made her square her shoulders and paste on a smile. She opened the door and started to speak. She paused when she saw Benjamin standing beside Michael and Kevin.

"What a nice surprise, Benjamin!" she said. "Come in."

"Carolyn, will you get your coat and take a walk with me?" Michael asked, his voice so serious she gripped the edge of the door frame. "Benjamin will watch the *kinder* for you."

Looking from one man to the other, she nodded. What was going on? She rushed to get her coat, hat and gloves. Pulling them on, she slipped past where Benjamin was edging to sit at the table. She invited him to try any of the cookies still on the counter.

"The ones on the trays are for tomorrow night," she said. "There's coffee and—"

"We'll be fine." Benjamin smiled. "Enjoy your walk."

She realized the circumstances couldn't be so serious if Michael's friend was grinning. Pausing only to tell Kevin his haircut looked good, she went out to where Michael stood with his gloved hands beneath his folded arms.

She wasn't surprised when they walked toward her new home, but she was shocked Michael said nothing. The silence pressed on them, and the sound of children playing football on the other side of the green barely intruded. She wasn't accustomed to feeling uncomfortable with Michael, but she sensed he had something important on his mind.

Will he tell me he loves me? She had to keep herself

from twirling around like Rose Anne at the thrilling thought. If that was what he wanted to talk to her about when they were walking out together—she tried not to laugh at the thought of the Amish words for courting—she must not rush him. Hearing him speak from the heart would be worth every second she had to wait.

When he paused outside the library that was a dark hulk as the sun sank behind the mountains, he asked, "Why does Kevin call you his mommy-aunt?"

She put her fingers to her lips, but her gasp escaped. She'd thought Kevin had forgotten the phrase he'd used right after she brought the children to Vermont.

"Because it's the truth." Saying the words was a relief as she put down a huge burden she'd been carrying too long.

"You can't be both his *mamm* and his *aenti*."

"But I am."

"He said he had another *mamm*. Is that true?"

She motioned toward the steps. "You should sit because this is a long story." She gave a terse laugh. "Actually, it isn't that long, though it felt like forever when we were living it."

He didn't move, so she launched into how Leland Reber's cruelty to Regina had led to Carolyn leaving Indiana with the children and moving to Evergreen Corners after her sister's death. She didn't downplay her fear or how she doubted the court granting her custody of her niece and nephew would have done anything to protect them from their father.

"So you lived in a Mennonite community in Indiana?" he asked.

Closing her eyes, she prayed God would give her strength to say what she must and that He'd open Michael's ears and his heart to listening to her. She looked at him and said, "No, I lived in the Amish district where I was born."

"You're Amish?"

She nodded, dropping her gaze because she couldn't bear to see what was in his.

"So everything I know about you is a lie?"

She recoiled from his harsh tone. "The only things I changed were our names and the children's ages."

"Kinder." The single word was clipped as if he'd cut it in half with a circular saw.

"What?"

"You might as well use the *Deitsch* words," he said in the language of her childhood. "I know you understand them."

"I do." She wished he hadn't switched to *Deitsch.* For her, the language of the Amish should draw people together rather than tear them apart. "I tried to be careful, but I know I made mistakes."

"You did." He shifted to look at the library. "So did I."

She ached to tear down the walls he was building between them, moving farther from her than he'd ever been. "What would you have done if you were in my situation?"

"I would have sought help from the *Leit.*"

"And what *gut* would that have done if Leland had come to demand I turn Kevin and Rose Anne over to him in spite of me having legal custody?"

"Then you could have contacted the police."

She clamped her arms together in front of her. "Nobody in our district would have gone to the *Englisch* authorities without talking first to our bishop."

"Then you should have gone to your bishop."

"I couldn't. He's Leland's great-uncle and was fixated on Leland coming back and being baptized." She shook her head. "Maybe the bishop could have forgiven him for putting my sister in the hospital more than once with his abuse, but I couldn't." She blinked back tears. "You don't know how many times I tried, Michael, but I can't. And maybe that's why it's best I left my *Leit.* How can I be Amish when I can't forgive Leland or myself?"

She didn't give him a chance to answer. Instead, she raced away across the green toward the sanctuary of her trailer, dragging her ragged hopes with her.

Christmas Eve dawned with lazy snowflakes falling beyond the stable windows. Like the cards Michael had seen in the project office, the scene of great pine trees frosted with fresh snow seemed the perfect setting for celebrations of the Christ Child's birth. The snow on the mountains glistened in the subdued sunlight sifting through the clouds, but a sparse inch of snow perched atop the grass and leaves. It should have imbued the view with happy anticipation of the holidays.

Instead, all he felt was disbelief. Carolyn had been false with him. Just as Adah had been. Though she hadn't tossed him aside spectacularly, she'd listened to the troubles of his heart and never once admitted she'd had to make a decision herself to stay among the Amish or leave. *Ja,* the circumstances were different, but he'd given her the opportunity to be honest with him on Thanksgiving night.

He swung his feet over the side of his cot, but didn't stand. Cold crawled up his legs. He should shove his feet into the slippers he'd been given after he moved into the stables.

He didn't.

He sat and stared at the floor. It should have been covered by hay and bits of oats dropped when the horse that lived in the stall was eating. And he should be somewhere else.

Where?

He didn't know where he should be, but coming to Evergreen Corners had been a mistake. No, that had been fine. He shouldn't have gotten involved with Carolyn and her family. Why was he tempted to laugh when there wasn't anything funny about the blunder he'd made when he thought she was as averse to drama as he was?

She was a walking, talking bundle of drama.

Everything he told himself he didn't want in his life. Wasn't that so?

He put his head in his hands and tried to pray, but he wasn't sure what he wanted to ask God for. To harden his heart so it didn't ache? No, he didn't want that.

"Gute mariye," came Benjamin's voice from the other side of the stall. The wall between them creaked, and Michael knew his friend had folded his arms on top of it. "Late night last night?" When Michael didn't answer, he went on, "You look like you've been run over by one of the big excavators. Twice."

Michael raised his head, but didn't bother to try to smile at Benjamin's teasing. Nor did he explain to his friend how he'd spent the night tossing and turning, unable to sleep. He hadn't kept Benjamin awake, because a steady snoring had come from the other stall throughout the night while Michael waited for the darkness to thin into the first cold light of dawn.

"Trouble sleeping," he admitted, hoping if he did then his friend would let the matter go.

Benjamin didn't. "Did you and Carolyn have an argument?"

"Why would you ask such a thing?"

He shrugged. "I can't think of any other reason why she came back to the trailer alone and looked as if she was trying not to cry. I waited for you to say something last evening, but you stomped around like you wanted to drive your boots a foot deep into the ground."

Standing and reaching for his work clothes, Michael said, "I'm confused. That's all."

"About how you feel about Carolyn? Because let me tell you, if you're confused, you're the only one. Everyone else can see how much you care about her and the *kinder*. Then why—?"

Michael aimed a quick prayer of gratitude up to God when Benjamin was called away by one of the other volunteers now sharing the stable. He regretted such an insensitive prayer. Benjamin was trying to cheer him, but repairing a broken heart was a much tougher task than building a house.

And he knew it would take much, much longer.

Chapter Fifteen

"Mommy, what's wrong?" Rose Anne leaned against Carolyn's leg as they found a place among the villagers on the green. The Christmas Eve concert was being performed by the unified choirs from several churches in the village in front of the still unrepaired gazebo. Light from the waning moon, not much more than a slender crescent, shone down on the gathering.

"Nothing you need to worry about, sweetheart." She ruffled the little girl's soft curls that refused to stay beneath her cap and made sure the knit band covered her niece's ears. The temperature was going down fast, though the air remained dank with the odor of snow.

"But you look sad, and that makes me sad."

"Me, too." Kevin pushed his hands into his pockets, standing stiff, a sure sign he was upset.

Her heart filled more at their concern for her. Forcing a smile onto her lips, she bent toward them. "I've got a lot on my mind. So many decisions to make about the house."

Both statements were true, but neither spoke of the

pain clamped around her heart because she'd refused to admit another truth.

Not to others this time, but to herself.

She loved her niece and nephew with her whole heart, but she wanted her heart to belong to Michael Miller. So many fantasies she'd created, dreaming he might love her, too. She'd imagined him coming in his mud-stained work clothes and boots to propose. She'd thought of him asking her to be his wife while he wore his *mutze* coat and vest. The same clothes he'd be wearing when they stood side by side in front of the ministers and bishop marrying them.

What a mess she'd made of everything! But she couldn't imagine anything she could have done differently. She'd have had to tell him the truth sometime. She'd planned to when…

She flinched at the realization she'd never given thought to choosing the best time to tell him about why she and the children were in Evergreen Corners. But she'd intended to tell him.

Hadn't she?

Listening to the choir begin "Joy to the World," she wrapped her arms around herself. She couldn't hold the cold out when it gnawed deep within her heart. She had fallen in love with Michael, but hadn't been ready to trust him. The legacy of secrets and abuse she'd witnessed prevented that.

"Mommy!" Rose Anne tugged on her coat.

"Yes?" she asked beneath the sweet, soaring notes.

"Can we go and see Taylor?"

Carolyn looked at where Jenna and her daughter were coming out of the community center. "All right. Don't cross the street."

"I know. I know. Stay on the green," Kevin said in a singsong voice.

Her aching heart lifted, or tried to, at her nephew using the tone of an adolescent who'd been reminded of a potential transgression too many times. She shooed them on their way and turned to watch the choir so she could avoid scanning the green to discover if Michael had joined the crowd.

"Mommy!" came a muffled cry that was abruptly cut off.

Carolyn stiffened. Rose Anne! She looked toward where her children had gone to meet Jenna. She saw her friend and Taylor, but not her nephew and niece.

Where were Kevin and Rose Anne?

She whirled to scan every direction across the snow-covered green. She couldn't see them anywhere.

Someone waved from the far side. The children! They weren't alone.

Who was with them?

She gasped when she saw a man had Rose Anne by the arm and was dragging her across the street. He stepped into the glow from a streetlight and glanced back at Kevin who was in pursuit. His face was illuminated as clearly as if he stood in sunshine.

Carolyn pressed her hands to her mouth to silence her scream, then began to run to stop him from taking her niece.

She'd never mistake that face and square jaw that had been visible in the bright light through his bushy beard.

Leland Reber!

People around Michael applauded as the choir finished the rollicking Christmas carol that was so different from the slow tempo of Amish hymns. The multipart harmony added both a lilt and a depth to the song unlike any he'd ever heard.

He'd come tonight at Benjamin's insistence. He hadn't wanted to stand in the cold with Carolyn a short distance away and try to act as if he weren't aware of everything she said and did. All day, she'd been on his mind. So much he'd pounded his thumb with a hammer, something he hadn't done since he first learned to drive nails. His hand throbbed, and his thumb was swollen to twice its normal size. He'd put some ice on it after supper at the community center, but its pain dimmed in comparison with the anguish searing him each time he thought about the grief and betrayal on Carolyn's face when she'd left him standing in front of the library last night.

Motion on the far side of the green, close to the main road and almost hidden by the tall pine tree beside the general store, caught his eye. He squinted, trying to bring the forms into focus. So many people had gathered on the green for the carol singing.

A faint cry teased his ears as the choir began their next song, but he recognized it. Kevin! The boy was calling out for help.

Help?

What was wrong?

His eyes widened when he saw Carolyn racing across the green. He yelled her name.

When she didn't stop, he started to shout after her again. He clamped his mouth closed when he heard her cry of horror.

"Leland, no! Don't take them!"

Her few words told him everything he needed to know.

Leland Reber!

The *kinder*'s *daed*.

He was in Evergreen Corners?

No time for answers. He needed to get to Carolyn and the *kinder* before the man hurt them.

"Was iss letz?" asked Benjamin, reaching to grasp his arm.

With a quick sidestep, Michael eluded his friend's grip. He paid no attention to the shock on Benjamin's face. "I've got to go. They're in danger."

"Who?"

"Carolyn and the kids."

"What? Why?"

Another question Michael didn't respond to, though this time he knew the answer. Leland Reber! The man who'd been married to Carolyn's sister, the man who was the *kinder*'s *daed*. How had he found her and the *kinder*? More important, what was Leland going to do?

The answer came stark and appalling into his mind. To Benjamin he ordered, "Call 911! Now! Before he can hurt them more!"

As he gave chase, Michael heard his friend shouting for someone's cell phone.

The pounding of his boots on the ground echoed the name *Leland Reber*. He ran through a maze of people, all staring at him as if he'd lost his mind.

Slowing at the edge of the green, he looked in both directions. Where had they gone?

A childish shout came from the far side of the old mill in the center of the village. Was that one of Carolyn's *kinder* or someone else's?

He knew he couldn't wait to be sure. He had to take a chance. As he ran beside the three-story building, empty windows gave him no clue to what might be happening on the other side. He came around the end and stared down the steep bank toward where the brook was held back by the remnants of an old dam. Water rushed over it. If he shouted to Carolyn, she wouldn't hear him.

Ahead of him, a man with a bushy brown beard and mustache had Rose Anne under one arm. He was running toward the half-demolished covered bridge. Kevin was struggling to reach the man with Carolyn close behind.

He had no idea what Leland would do once he got to the bridge. Did the man know that route was cut off by damage from the flood? Would he turn like a trapped rat and attack? Leland had been raised plain, but Michael knew not everyone clung to the principles their elders tried to instill in them as *kinder*.

Then he saw a dark car waiting on the far side of the bridge. That must be where Leland was heading. The boards across the bridge were narrow, and he carried a struggling *kind*. Was the man crazy? If so, Carolyn was, as well, because she was closing the distance between them.

Spurring his own feet forward, Michael knew he wouldn't get to the bridge before Leland was on it. No matter. He had to stop the man from abducting Rose Anne.

Suddenly the bank dropped away. His feet slid out from under him, and he found himself sliding down the slope. Jamming his feet into the half-frozen ground, he kept himself from catapulting into the brook or over the dam. He pushed himself to his feet and groaned.

Not in pain, though he'd crushed his thumb against the hillside, but in horror as he watched Leland run across the pair of boards between the two open sections of the arches supporting the bridge. He held Rose Anne as if she were a bag of potatoes. Carolyn and Kevin were about to climb onto the bridge to follow him. Would the boards in the arch hold beneath them?

Save them, God. He didn't bother calling. Nothing would stop Carolyn or Kevin from trying to get Rose Anne back.

Carolyn screamed as Kevin wobbled beyond her outstretched arms.

Michael raced forward, though he was farther away. They couldn't let the boy fall twelve feet straight down into the stone-lined brook.

When Leland reached back and grabbed the boy, he yanked him toward the car. He held Kevin with one hand and shoved Rose Anne inside with the other. The little girl scrambled across the back seat and tried to open the other door. It wouldn't budge. She pounded on it with her tiny fists and shrieked in frustration.

"Stop!" Carolyn screamed.

Michael reached her in the shadows beneath the bridge's wrecked roof. "He's not going to listen. Stay here." He moved toward the man and the frightened *kinder*.

He doubted Carolyn would heed him. Nothing, not even her own safety, would prevent her from protecting Kevin and Rose Anne. When she pushed past him, he caught her by the shoulders at the far side of the bridge.

"Stay back!" shouted Leland.

"How did you find us?" Carolyn asked, her voice as placid as if her brother-in-law were a welcome visitor.

"I saw you at the urgent care clinic. Your boyfriend mentioned you lived in Evergreen Corners, so I decided to pay a call." His nose wrinkled. "Lousy place. Half the town is gone, and the rest of it stinks."

Michael couldn't hold back another groan. *He* had been the one to give Leland the way to burst back into her family's lives.

"Don't," she whispered. "Don't listen to him. He twists everything in the hope it'll hurt everyone more."

He nodded, knowing her composure might become their sole weapon against the man who was trying to push Kevin into the car, too. The boy fought, but couldn't escape his *daed*'s greater strength.

"Then I saw that locket," Leland taunted. "Did your sister ever tell you what I did when I discovered she'd wasted my hard-earned money on it?"

"Yes."

The simple dignity of her answer amazed Michael, who'd thought he couldn't be more astonished by Carolyn's quiet courage. She faced this horrible man in terror, for her hands quivered, but she refused to let him daunt her.

"I wasn't sure if these were my kids because they weren't the right ages." Leland snickered a derisive laugh. "Then I realized you'd changed their ages as well as their names. My seven-year-old son, Devon, became your five-year-old son, Kevin, while Rosina lost a year on her age and became Rose Anne. I didn't think you were that devious, Cora."

Cora?

Michael flinched. Had Cora been her name before she came to Evergreen Corners? He remembered Kevin saying she used to have a different name.

Something in his face must have betrayed his thoughts, because Leland laughed. "Guess you didn't tell your boyfriend everything. Maybe you're not so different from me when it comes to toeing the line on the rules."

"Let them go," she pleaded as she stepped from beneath the overhang at the edge of the bridge. "Please, Leland. I'm sure we can work out something so you can have time with them."

He sneered at her, then snarled at Kevin to behave. The boy ignored him as Leland laughed with contempt. "Supervised visits with some social worker looking down her nose at me if I speak to them? No way! They're my kids, and they're coming with me."

"We're not your kids!" Kevin swung his foot and hit Leland hard in the shin.

The attack shocked Leland enough that his grip on the boy loosened. Giving his *daed* a shove out of the way, Kevin broke free. He reached into the car for his sister. Leland threw the boy to the ground.

Michael didn't hesitate. All his plans to avoid someone else's drama and live a peaceful life had been *dumm*. More than *dumm*. They'd been selfish. God hadn't put him on Earth to go through the motions of living while he kept his existence on an even keel. His Heavenly Father had given him something important to learn, and Michael had spent his life trying to avoid any situation where he might have to face that lesson.

No longer.

Stepping forward, he scooped Rose Anne out of the car. She tried to cling to him, but he put her next to her brother and ordered, "Kevin, go back to Carolyn."

The boy was scrambling to his feet. "But, Michael—"

"Go!" He kept his gaze locked with Leland's.

The other man seemed shocked by his overt defiance. So shocked he was frozen in indecision. Like other bullies, Leland didn't know how to react to someone standing up to him.

Rage twisted the man's face as he spat, "What do you think you're doing?"

Michael wished he could have prevented the *kinder* from hearing the curses spewing from their *daed*'s mouth. He didn't reply. Nothing he said would lessen the man's fury. At the same time, he intended to do all he could to keep Leland from taking the *kinder*.

A slim hand settled on his coat sleeve. "Let's go, Michael. We've got the children. There's nothing else for us here."

Leland pushed past Michael, raised his hand and drove it into Carolyn's face. She fell with a soft cry. The *kinder* screamed in horror as they knelt by where she sprawled on the dirt road.

Michael curled his own fingers into fists. How could he have been so stupid? He should have known Leland wouldn't attack a man his own size. Instead, he'd turned on Carolyn. As he took a step toward Leland, he heard her soft voice.

"Don't, Michael. It's not our way."

Our way? She'd walked away from her Amish life four years ago, taking the *kinder* with her and cutting them off from their faith and their heritage.

That was true, but she'd made what must have been a terrible choice in order to protect her nephew and niece from the man he faced, a man who'd struck her in a fit of fury that he hadn't been willing to expend on someone who might fight back.

Our way...

Her simple words proved she'd never set aside the life she'd loved, the life she would have given the *kinder* if she hadn't been trying to protect them from the one person who never should have been a threat to them.

Looking from her cheek that was already an angry red to his fists, he heard her voice echo in his mind. *Our way.*

A life of nonviolence was their way. Both his and Carolyn's. He couldn't set that aside. He'd prayed for more than a year for God to lead him in the direction he should go. It was with Carolyn and her *kinder.* It was among the Amish. It was a life of seeking peace.

He watched Leland make a fist again. Had his face revealed his thoughts? If so, there was nothing he would do to change what was going to happen. He steeled himself for the blow.

Carolyn cried out in horror as Michael wobbled and almost dropped to his knees when Leland hammered his fist into Michael's face. Blood exploded from his upper lip and his nose. Had Leland broken it?

God, forgive me for bringing him into this mess. Help us find a way out before the children are hurt, too.

Kevin stepped forward, but she pulled him back as she saw the triumphant smile Leland wore.

What could have been better for a bully who took delight in others' pain than to fight a man who wouldn't strike back?

Turn the other cheek to the evil-doer.

Michael was doing that, but she couldn't let him bear the brunt of Leland's cruelty.

"Kevin, Rose Anne, stay here," she ordered as her brother-in-law began to curl his hands into fists again.

If the *kinder* protested, she didn't hear them. Her heart was beating louder than thunder as she rushed forward. Thunder? In the winter on a cloudless night? The sound must be inside her battered skull.

She stepped between the men. "You aren't taking the *kinder*, Leland," she said as she confronted the brute with every bit of dignity she had in her.

"No? Who's going to stop me? You and your buddy, who doesn't seem good for much but being a punching bag?"

"You aren't taking the *kinder*."

Michael's hands clasped her shoulders, but she yanked them off, moving forward another step. He couldn't, with the best intentions aimed at keeping her safe, prevent her from protecting Kevin and Rose Anne.

"I'm done with running away," she said. "I'm done with hiding. I'm done with not being able to live a truthful life with God, but I'm not done with making sure these *kinder* are safe."

"Big words. You want to hear what I have to say? I'm done wasting time on you. Those kids are mine!" He drew back his arm.

She closed her eyes, trying to brace herself for another concussive blow.

It didn't come.

Feeling small arms encircling her legs, Carolyn opened her eyes to an astounding sight. Leland's arms were being held by Benjamin and Isaac and a couple of other men she couldn't identify in the clump of bodies.

Suddenly Leland popped out from among them. He dove into the car, started it and sent it skidding away from the bridge.

She heard sirens and realized the police had arrived.

They were sent in pursuit of Leland's car, their tires squealing like a wounded animal.

Their rescuers came rushing to ask if they were okay. She didn't answer them as she threw her arms around the *kinder*, then reached out to Michael to draw him into their small circle. As he held them to his broad chest, she began to cry for all that had been lost and found in the past four years.

Chapter Sixteen

As soon as the trailer door was opened, Kevin and Rose Anne led Michael and Carolyn inside. Michael longed to close his eyes and lean back against the cushions and shut out the world until it stopped spinning like a maddened top. His head ached, and he couldn't see past the swelling around his left eye. Breathing made him sound like a beached trout, because he had to gasp for air through his mouth. His nose might not be broken, but it sure felt that way.

He was grateful they hadn't had to maneuver back across the weakened boards of the covered bridge. Her neighbors had assisted the *kinder*, Carolyn and him to where someone had built a wooden footbridge across the brook. He wondered how he'd missed that way across the brook earlier.

Everyone else stayed outside the cramped trailer. He heard someone offer to go for a *doktor* and someone else suggested opening the kitchen at the community center because it might be a long night while they waited to hear if Leland had been apprehended.

He sat on the narrow sofa while Rose Anne ran to the

bathroom. Her brother followed her, standing outside the closed door in a clear message that he didn't intend to let anyone threaten his sister again.

"Are you okay, Michael?" Carolyn whispered.

"I will be once Leland is caught."

"They'll catch him." She looked toward where Kevin now sat on her bed where he could keep an eye on the bathroom door.

He wished he shared her optimism. The authorities were on Leland's trail, and if he was nabbed, he'd be arrested. But only if they caught him.

"I'm sorry you got drawn into this." Her slow, careful motions warned she was hurting worse than she'd admit to.

Glen walked into the trailer without knocking. He gave them a grim nod, but motioned for them to stay where they were.

Michael realized the project director had taken on the same job Kevin had, guarding a door. People kept coming to the trailer, asking questions and trying to sort truth from the rumors raging through the village. Some of the tales were *dumm*, like the one that suggested the *kinder* had encountered a bear and were either dead or maimed.

Ja, they'd confronted a beast, but a human one.

He was relieved Glen was handling the door. Every time Michael spoke, his lip started bleeding again. He watched when Carolyn went to comfort Kevin, who was shaking so hard he feared the boy's slight body would come apart.

A rush of anger swelled as fast as his lip. What they'd witnessed tonight no *kind* should have to see and hear. If Leland had been thinking of anyone but himself, he would have realized he risked scarring his *kinder* for the rest of their lives. The thought of Kevin and Rose Anne being in their *daed*'s control sent a shudder of disgust through him.

"Michael?" asked Carolyn as she walked back to him.

Knowing she'd sensed his increased tension, he reached for her hand. He winced when he moved his thumb.

"I'm okay," he said past his split lip. "Confused my hand with a nail earlier today."

"Remind me not to let you teach Kevin how to use a hammer."

His smile became more sincere. She was doing what she always did. She was trying to make those around her feel better, though her own heart must have been hurting.

As soon as the bathroom door opened, Kevin jumped from the bed and threw his arms around his sister, startling her. Rose Anne began to cry. The poor *kind* had feared a man who was a stranger to her would take her away from the only *mamm* she knew.

Carolyn reached into the raised bed where Kevin slept. She pulled down the well-loved stuffed toys the *kinder* kept close each night.

"Here are some friends who want to see you," she murmured, her voice distorted by her bruised cheek, as she handed the dog and rabbit to the *kinder*.

Both Kevin and Rose Anne tossed the toys aside and threw their arms around her, clinging to her. Michael heard a sob slip through her lips, a sound she hadn't made even when she was knocked off her feet.

But he realized as he watched her put her arms around the *kinder*, her reaction was one of joy.

"I'm sorry," Kevin moaned.

"For what, dearest?" she asked.

"I was wrong," he said. "I like my name. I don't want the name that bad man gave me."

She knelt by the *kinder*. Though he knew how painful it must have been, she smiled. "He didn't give you those names. Your *mamm* did." She brushed the tearstains from their cheeks. "Devon, the name she gave you, Kevin, means divine because you are a gift from God. She chose Rosina as your name, Rose Anne, because it was the name of her favorite flower—a rose— and Ina, our mother's name, two things she cherished almost as much as she did you."

"Really?" asked Rose Anne.

"Really. You can choose if you want to be Kevin or Devon, Rose Anne or Rosina."

The two *kinder* looked at each other, overwhelmed. Carolyn must have seen that, too, because she stood, kissed them both on the head and said that no decision had to be made until they were ready.

The trailer door opened, and Glen stepped aside as Beth Ann walked up the steps. The midwife's eyes grew big as she stared at him and Carolyn, but she quickly recovered.

She had the *kinder* sit at the table and served them some orange juice she found in the refrigerator. From the tiny freezer, she pulled a tray of ice cubes. She put them in a bowl and frowned.

"Glen, have someone go over to the store and get some ice out of the box there." She didn't wait to see if he followed her order while she wrapped a handful of cubes in a dish towel. Handing it to Michael, Beth Ann said, "You will be using this for twenty minutes. I'll set the timer on the stove. When it beeps, take the ice off and let your skin rest for twenty minutes. Then keep repeating at least until the bleeding stops. Better yet, until the swelling starts to go down."

"All right." He was more than happy to spend the next twenty minutes sitting beside Carolyn, who was given a similar bundle of ice.

"Don't let the ice press directly against your skin," the midwife cautioned. "You don't want to cause more damage. Look at me, Michael."

He did, and she aimed a flashlight at each of his eyes before doing the same to Carolyn.

"Any double vision?" Beth Ann asked.

"No," they answered as one.

He smiled at Carolyn, who smiled back…and they both winced at the same time. But for the first time in a long time, he felt something he'd almost forgotten.

Happy.

When the children didn't protest going to sleep in her bed, Carolyn was astonished. Beth Ann had given Michael and her a cursory examination after they'd used the ice for twenty minutes and had said there were no signs of physical trauma, other than the skinned knee Kevin got when Leland shoved him away. Last Christmas Eve, the two had been too excited to sleep as they waited to unwrap the presents she'd bought for them as well as the ones she'd made.

This year, their gifts had been washed away in the October flood. The void in her heart that opened each time she'd thought of what they'd lost usually sent an ache deep within her. Tonight, she was celebrating she hadn't lost what was most precious to her.

"You need to use this again," Michael said, handing her an ice pack.

"It's been twenty minutes already?" She hadn't realized how long she'd been standing by the door, watching the children drift into their dreams and praying the nightmare they'd endured wouldn't follow them into their sleep.

"Ja." He took her hand and drew her back to sit beside him on the sofa.

She longed to lean her head on his broad shoulder, but brushing her aching cheek against his shirt sent a bolt of pain through her. She contented herself with sitting close enough to him that she could feel each shallow breath he took. Wondering how long it would be before he was able to breathe normally again, she hoped the doctor would arrive soon.

A soft knock came at the door. Was that the doctor at last? No, because Benjamin came in with Pastor Hershey on his heels. Without speaking, they motioned for Carolyn and Michael to remain where they were.

Only after the two men had joined Glen at the tiny table did Pastor Hershey ask, "Where are the children?"

"Asleep in the bedroom." She pointed toward the door that was slightly ajar.

"Can you make sure they're asleep?" Glen asked.

She started to nod, but halted as pain streaked through her head like a bolt of lightning. She pushed herself to her feet. When Michael stood, cupping her elbow, she whispered her thanks. Assuring herself the children were sound asleep, she walked back to the sofa.

Pastor Hershey spoke into the silence. "I've been informed Leland Reber is in custody."

"They caught him!" She breathed a sigh of relief.

"Not exactly."

"I don't understand."

Benjamin said quietly, "Leland either drove his car off the road or lost control of it. Whatever happened—and the police will determine that—he was discovered in the car, injured. He's on his way to the hospital now."

She started to put her hand to her lips. She caught herself before she could touch her aching face.

"He's going to be charged with assault and battery as well as abduction of a child. The last is the big felony. If convicted, he'll go to jail for a long time." The minister wore a grim smile. "Long enough for the children to grow up."

"Will they have to testify at the trial?" she asked.

"Let's deal with each problem as it comes," Pastor Hershey said, "and trust God to watch over His children, both big and small." He invited them to join him in prayer, and new tears fell down her cheeks when he included Leland in his supplications.

"Thank you," she said when he was finished.

"Of course." He stood.

Glen did, as well. "Let's get a good night's sleep tonight and tomorrow night before we head back to work the day after tomorrow. Installing drywall is nobody's favorite job. We'll start bright and early on Thursday on your walls, Carolyn."

"You're going to finish my house?"

Glen exchanged a bewildered frown with Benjamin before he looked at Michael as if hoping he'd explain what she meant. "Why wouldn't we finish your house, Carolyn?"

"I wasn't honest about who I am. I'm not a single mother, and I'm not Carolyn Wiebe. I'm Cora Hilty."

Glen put a calming hand on her shoulder. "You never told me or anyone here a lie. You *are* responsible for these two children, and you *are* in need of a home for them. What you call yourself isn't important. Nothing else matters to me or the organization I represent." He turned to Michael. "I assume the same could be said for Amish Helping Hands."

"I don't speak for the organization," he replied, "but I can't imagine any of us walking away before the house is finished. Especially me because I haven't had a chance to do that finishing work I've been looking forward to tackling."

Shortly after, with wishes for a Merry Christmas, the three men left, and for the first time that evening, it was quiet in the trailer.

Michael took her hand. When she looked at him, suddenly shy when she thought of everything they'd left in limbo, he said, "It's over, Carolyn."

"Cora," she replied. What would her real name sound like on his lips?

She almost laughed at how his split lip distorted every word he spoke, but the laughter would have been laced with tears. After four years of fearing Leland Reber was ready to ambush her and the *kinder*, tonight she didn't have to pray another day would come and go without his finding them.

"You're going to need to decide what you want to do now, Carolyn." He grinned. "I mean, Cora. It's going to take me some time to get used to your new-old name."

"Me, too."

"What do you plan to do?"

"First I have to forgive Leland."

"Can you?"

"I must." She closed her eyes, but opened them again when anguish swelled through her head. "Something is wrong in his heart. I saw it just after he struck me. He was terrified you would hurt him. I don't know when or how or who, but someone, sometime, somewhere hurt him, and it did something to his heart. I will pray he finds healing in God's love."

Michael regarded her without speaking, then leaned forward and pressed his lips to her forehead. "Will you be able to forgive yourself, too, when you did the only thing you could to safeguard the *kinder*?"

"I'm going to try. I'm going to write my friends in Indiana and let them know where we are."

"I'm sure they'll want you to come there."

"Most likely."

"I see."

She hesitated when she heard all the emotion vanish from his voice like water down a drain. Tossing aside all caution, she asked, "What do you see?"

"What do you mean?"

"Are you going to sit there and tell me you don't care if Kevin, Rose Anne and I go back to Indiana while you return to your life in New York?"

His eyes snapped as they had on the bridge. "Of course I care. But I won't let my yearnings get in the way of what you think is best for the *kinder*."

"What's best for them is to be with someone who loves them as much as I do." She put her hand on his uninjured cheek. "And that's you. Kevin has adored you since you met, and Rose Anne, like always, wasn't far behind him. However, this time, I wasn't, either. I want you in our lives, Michael."

"Are you asking me to marry you, Cora Hilty? Proposing to a man isn't something a plain woman would do."

"You need to know that I intend to live an Amish life…starting tomorrow."

"So you can propose to me tonight?" His eyes twinkled with merriment. "Well, you're too late."

"What?" She sat straighter, then wished she hadn't when pain arced across her head. "What do you mean I'm too late? Have you made up your mind about baptism?"

"*Ja*, I've decided. But Kevin already asked me to marry you and become his *daed-onkel*."

"He did?"

"When he mentioned you were his *mamm-aenti*." Leaning his forehead against hers, he said, "I never gave him an answer, and then I was a complete fool when you told me about Leland." He told her what he'd decided on the bridge when he faced Leland and made his choice of the life he wanted. "God opened my heart to Him and showed me that my life should be lived as an Amish man."

"I'm so happy for you, Michael."

"And be happy for yourself, because my answer to Kevin's proposal and yours is *ja*. I want to marry you, even if I can't remember what to call you right now. Why don't I call you my future wife?"

"*Ich liebe dich*, Michael Miller." She kissed him on his cheek.

He traced a feathery line along her lips. "As soon as I can, I want a real kiss."

"As many as you want, especially if it takes the rest of my life to give them all to you."

Epilogue

"And here are the keys to your new home," Pastor Hershey said after blessing the completed house.

Applause exploded through the cold, crisp day. Cameras clicked as many of the witnesses, who'd also participated in rebuilding the charming house that overlooked Washboard Brook, raised their phones to record the family taking possession of their new home. Two dozen red, white and blue balloons rose into the sky.

Mr. and Mrs. Gagnon, both leaning on walkers, smiled before taking the keys and opening the door to the second house finished by the volunteers in Evergreen Corners. Cheers rose through the cold afternoon, and the nattily dressed anchors from the local TV stations followed the elderly couple into the house.

Standing in the shadows of the trees separating her new home from the Gagnons', Cora clapped. The joy on the Gagnons' faces was a testament to the hard work and the faith of the community in coming together to rebuild. Glen's grin had barely fit onto his face as he accepted congratulations from several state government officials and spoke to a reporter from the high school newspaper.

Michael crossed the snow-covered yard that would be planted with sod in the spring. Unlike her, he bore a scar from the encounter with Leland. It was a small half circle near where he'd been struck in the mouth. She thought it made him look rather rakish.

Beside him, Kevin and Rosina were sharing a box of popcorn. She smiled as she watched them acting like normal *kinder* as they giggled at something Michael had said before running off to see their friends.

Kevin had insisted on keeping the name she'd given him, but his little sister changed her name back to the one given to her by her *mamm* in honor of the *gross-mammi* she'd never known. Remembering Rosina's name was becoming easier, and everyone in town seemed comfortable changing from Carolyn to Cora. There were slipups, but they all laughed them off.

"It could have been your celebration," Michael said when he reached her. They walked back through the woods toward the charming little house where she and the *kinder* lived. "Now that Leland is in jail, you don't have to worry about him seeing you and the *kinder* on TV or in the newspapers."

"I didn't need a celebration." She smiled as she laced her fingers through his when they climbed up the steps to the inviting front porch where she planned to put rocking chairs once the weather warmed. "How can I expect Kevin and Rosina to embrace their plain heritage if I step in front of a camera?"

"They seem happy with learning to be Amish."

"Except for complaining about having to sit still during church services."

He laughed. "As Gabriel and I did when we were kids."

"Regina and I did, too." She smiled at the memory that was no longer tainted by one man's cruelty.

"Do you want to join the party next door? I don't want you to miss this one when you missed having one of your own."

"You volunteers came to the house when it was blessed and Glen gave me the keys. Besides, it doesn't seem right to have a celebration when we won't be living here for long."

"For at least six months. It'll take that long before we can have our wedding."

She smiled. "I'm glad you could come here today for the celebration."

As planned, Michael had returned to Harmony Creek Hollow on New Year's Day and had been helping his brother prepare for planting. He'd also been taking classes so he could be baptized in the spring. When he could, he caught a ride in one of the *Englisch* vans to Evergreen Corners bringing volunteers for a short stint.

He grinned. "I didn't come for the celebration. I've got lots of kisses to collect, as you recall."

She didn't have a chance to say she was ready when he was because Gladys Whittaker walked into the yard. "May I speak with you, Michael?"

He arched his brows at Cora, then went down the steps.

Wondering why the mayor wanted to speak to Michael, Cora went into the house that already felt like home. She took off her boots and hung up her coat and bonnet on the pegs by the door. Touching the Amish *kapp* she wore once again, she looked around her. The stone counters glistened like the wood floors beneath the rag rugs she'd made. The living room was partially furnished, but thanks to her work for the diner and other orders for baked goods, she'd been able to buy a sofa where she cuddled with the *kinder* at day's end. She was home schooling them, focusing on the topics they'd study in a plain school. After three months, Kevin and Rosina were doing lessons at their true grade levels.

As it did every time she came into the house, her gaze went to a small shelf on the living room wall between the two windows that offered a view of the brook. The house's sole decoration, other than a calendar hanging in the kitchen, was set on the shelf. The small sculpture of a hawk with its wings spread wide to capture a thermal sat there. It wasn't the same pose as the statue that had been swallowed by the flood.

When Michael had brought it to her and explained how Kevin had spoken of the wooden hawk, she'd been awed by Michael's artistic skill. She'd seen only the rough birds and boats he'd taught her nephew to whittle. The hawk, which was less than six inches high, looked so real she half expected it to rise up off her palm and soar into the sky.

Pounding his feet, Michael came into the house and took off his boots. He set them beside hers. Knowing this man would put his boots next to hers for the rest of their lives sent happiness pulsing through her.

Before she could ask what the mayor had told him, he asked, "Are you sure you want to leave Evergreen Corners?"

"No, but there's no Amish community here."

"What if someone started one?"

She looked at him in astonishment. "Are you saying you're willing to stay?"

"Why not? You've got six acres here. Not enough for a farm, but enough for a family garden and a chicken coop and a shop for me to work in while I'm building new library shelves for the ones ruined in the flood as well as supervising the repairs on the first floor of the town hall."

"What?"

His eyes were bright with happiness. "Gladys offered me enough work to keep me busy for a year or more. By the time I'm done with work for the village, I should be able to find other jobs to keep me busy."

"But what about your baptism classes?"

"We can travel to Harmony Creek Hollow every other weekend. It's about time you and the *kinder* met my brother and his wife and their *kinder*. I can take baptism classes on Saturdays, and then we can attend the services on Sunday. It will give Kevin and Rosina a chance to see what it's like to live in a plain settlement. What do you think?"

She grasped his hands as she stood face-to-face with him. "I think you're *wunderbaar*, Michael Miller."

He chuckled as he did whenever she spoke in *Deitsch*. "You're pretty special yourself, Cora Hilty, and I think I need to start collecting my kisses starting now."

His lips brushed her cheek, and she closed her eyes as delight danced through her. His broad fingers curved on her shoulders as his mouth found hers. His kiss was as gentle as a spring breeze luring a leaf to unfurl, and she softened against him. After so many dark years, he'd brought joy into her life and she could not wait to spend every day and night together for the rest of their lives.

He raised his head when noise came from the front porch.

"Sounds like the *kinder* got tired of playing in the snow," she whispered, running her fingertips along his strong jaw.

"So I hear." He kissed the tip of her nose. "Well, in that case, I'd better get to work."

"You're starting on the library shelves *now*?"

"I need to work on your house. On *our* house." He leaned toward her and whispered, "I don't know how the other volunteers are going to feel about me pulling out their wiring to make it a real Amish house."

"We'll break it to them when they're in a *gut* mood."

"And when will that be?"

"When they come to our wedding celebration."

"You have the best ideas, *liebling*." He laughed again. "Or as Rosina would say, the *gut-est*."

* * * * *

AMISH
CHRISTMAS HIDEAWAY

Lenora Worth

To all of the friends I've made while writing
Amish fiction. Thank you to our loyal readers!

Why do the heathen rage,
and the people imagine a vain thing?
—*Psalm* 2:1

Chapter One

She'd stopped here on a whim. Tired from a lengthy deposition in Philadelphia, Alisha Braxton planned to find a strong cup of coffee. She needed to stay awake to drive the two hours from the city to the small community of Campton Creek in Lancaster County to celebrate Christmas with her grandmother Bettye Willis.

This quaint Christmas market on the outskirts of Philadelphia beckoned her with the promise of something warm to drink and maybe something wonderful to nibble on while she traveled. Too busy to shop for gifts before now, she decided she'd do a quick browse and buy her grandmother something special. And maybe Mrs. Campton, too.

The two elderly women lived together in the carriage house at the Campton estate, now called the Campton Center. Alisha did several hours a week of pro bono work at the center. It was a good chance to visit with her grandmother and help out the community.

But this week she wouldn't be working as much. A whole week with Granny—a gift from her firm. Five days before Christmas. Her boss had insisted and, as much as she loved her career as an associate with the law firm of Henderson and Perry, Alisha needed a break.

She looked forward to spending the upcoming holidays there with her grandmother, who'd been Judy Campton's assistant for years and now her companion since they were both widowed. A week off and then she'd get back to her paying hours at the small law firm near Reading where she'd worked since law school. The firm was a satellite branch connected to the main firm in Philadelphia. Alisha hoped to work at the big firm one day, but for now she was paying her dues and working her way up the firm's ladder.

Taking in the bright lights lining the marketplace that had once been a town square on the outskirts of Philadelphia, Alisha pulled her small blue sedan into what looked like the last available parking place. A couple strolled by together, holding hands and laughing, packages hanging from their arms. The man smiled down at the woman then tugged at her long dark hair.

A surge of longing hit Alisha, causing her to sit there in the dark while the couple kissed by a stark white sports car parked directly across from Alisha. After putting their packages in the tiny trunk, the man helped the woman into her seat and hurried around to get inside.

They looked so happy, so in love.

Would she ever have that? Probably not. She'd sealed away her heart and focused on work. No time for romance or anything that followed. Once, she'd fallen in love. Once. Putting her memories away, Alisha took in her surroundings.

Dusk moved over the sparkling Christmas trees decorating the tiny square, causing the whole scene to shimmer and glisten. People bundled in scarves and jackets strolled along the busy open market, sipping hot drinks as they laughed and took in the lovely holiday displays. Beautiful but so deceptive. She'd seen the underbelly of life too often lately to appreciate the forced facade of a commercial Christmas. And she sure didn't need to sit here longing for something she'd never have.

"When did I become so jaded?" she said out loud before opening her car door. She needed caffeine and maybe something with pumpkin spice.

She lifted one booted foot out onto the asphalt parking lot, the chilly air hitting her in a burst of December wind. Hoping the snowstorm headed this way would hold off, Alisha watched a vehicle approaching at high speed. The black SUV came to a skidding halt behind the white sports car now trying to back out of the parking space across from where Alisha had just pulled in.

Before she could exit her car, a window came down on the SUV. Then the air shattered with the sound of several rapid-fire gunshots, aimed at the sportscar.

Alisha screamed and sank down in her seat. When the shots kept coming, she crouched low and watched in horror as the couple in the sports car scrambled to find protection.

The gunman kept shooting. And they had no way out.

Alisha looked up and saw the gunman's face in the bright lights from the twinkling decorations and the glow of streetlights. His cold, dead gaze stopped and froze on her.

She got a good look at him.

And…he got a good look at her.

Ducking back down, she held her breath. He'd try to kill her, too. She'd seen him. Bracing for a bullet, she heard people screaming, heard footsteps rapidly hitting the pavement as pedestrians tried to scramble away.

Dear Lord, please help these people and protect me. Help me. Alisha's prayers seemed to freeze in her throat as she waited for more gunshots.

Instead, the vehicle's motor revved and then the dark SUV spun away, tires squealing, the smell of rubber burning through the air. Only a few seconds had passed but the scene played over in Alisha's mind in slow motion as she relived the sight of that face and then the screams from inside the tiny car. And then…a stunning split second of silence.

She heard people running and screaming. Quickly pulling out her phone, her hands shaking, she called 911 as she wobbled onto her feet and hurried to the car that now looked like it had been in a war zone, bullet holes scattered across it, the heavy vinyl convertible top split and torn.

"A shooting," she said to the dispatcher. "At the Christmas market near West Fairmount Park." She named the street and told the dispatcher what had happened. "I… I witnessed the shooting."

People had gathered around and a security guard stood staring into the car, his expression full of shock. "What in the world?"

The dispatcher confirmed the location and told Alisha to stay on the phone.

"Officers on the way," Alisha said to the scared guard after the dispatcher had told her as much. "Secure the scene and get these people back."

She stepped away, her stomach roiling at the carnage in the two-seater car. Blood everywhere and both passengers slumped over, holding each other, their bodies riddled with bullet holes. They'd been smiling and happy seconds before and now they were obviously dead.

The other vehicle was long gone but while she waited she managed to give a description to the dispatcher.

"Large black SUV." She named the model. "A driver and one shooter but I couldn't make out the license plate. I didn't see anyone else inside."

But she remembered the shooter's face. A light scruffy beard and stringy long dark hair covered by a thick wool cap. His eyes—black as night and dead. So dead inside.

Alisha stayed on the phone but heard the sound of sirens echoing through the chilly night. Her boots crunched against something as she tried to scan the surrounding area. She looked down and saw the delicate, gold-embossed Christmas ornament that had decorated the now-shattered streetlight hovering over the sports car. A star shape, shimmering white.

The ornament laid broken and crushed underneath her feet.

Hours later, Nathan Craig heard a ringing in his ears that would not go away. "Stop it," he groaned, coming awake to find a weak slant of moonlight filtering through the darkness of his bedroom. He wiped at his sleepy eyes and glared at the dial of his watch.

Eleven o'clock.

Exhausted after an all-night surveillance and a day full of reports to his client, he'd gone to bed early and at his own place for once. Now he'd never get back to sleep.

Then he realized his phone was ringing. Not so unusual. Being a private investigator meant he had a lot of late-night calls from either clients or informants. And sometimes, from the angry subjects of his investigations.

Sitting up, he grabbed the annoying device and growled, "This had better be good."

"Nathan?"

The voice was winded and scared, his name a whisper from a raw throat. But that voice held a familiar tone that hit deep in his gut.

"Alisha?"

"Yes."

Now he was wide awake.

Knowing she'd never call him unless she was in trouble or really mad at him again, he said, "Alisha, what's wrong?"

"I... I think someone's trying to kill me," she said, the tremor in her words destroying him.

He stood and grabbed his jeans, hit his toe on a chair and gritted his teeth. "Where are you? Are they after you right now?"

"I'm almost to Campton Creek. Just a few miles from the turnoff. I know they're following me but I don't see the SUV behind me. He'll be back. I saw his face, Nathan. I witnessed a man shoot and kill two people. And you know what that means."

"Hold on," he said, his mind racing ahead while fear held his heart in a vise. "I can be there in fifteen minutes. You stay on the line with me, okay?"

"Okay."

Then he thought better. "Have you called the police?"

She heaved a deep breath. "I had a police escort following me, watching my back. Two officers."

"Where are they now?"

"Dead, I think. Someone shot out their tires and they

crashed on the side of the road. The patrol car exploded. I should have stopped to help."

Nathan closed his eyes and tried to focus. "You didn't stop. Smart move."

"I wanted to stop but… I saw the SUV. I sped up and rounded the big curve near Green Mountain." Heaving a sigh that sounded more like a sob, she said, "I pulled off on a dirt lane but it's a dead-end. I think the SUV went on by but I'm afraid to get back on the road."

Nathan knew that curve. Just enough time to get her out of view of any car following her but also a dangerous place where someone could hide and wait for her.

"Did you call anyone else?"

"I called you," she said through a shuddering sob. "Because this won't end with the local police, Nathan. I witnessed a double homicide that looked like a hit job. Those two officers are probably dead. The FBI will probably be called in and I'll need to testify."

FBI? Now he was tripping over his own feet. "Alisha, I know the road you're on. Find an Amish farm and wake someone up. Stay with them until I get there. Do you hear me?"

She didn't speak.

He held the cell between his ear and shoulder while he grabbed at more clothes and found his weapon and wallet.

"Alisha?"

"I know a shortcut," she said, sounding stronger. "I'll take that route once I hit the turn. I'll try to find a house, I promise. My cell battery is low. I have to go."

"Alisha, tell me what to look for."

"Black Denali SUV. Two men in the vehicle. I have to go."

"Alisha, don't—"

She ended the call.

Nathan stood there in the dark, the images playing in his mind a terrible torment. If anything happened to her…

He'd been through this kind of terror before. He would not go there again.

With that vow in mind, he finished putting on his clothes and hurried out of the cabin toward his big Chevy truck. His heart pumping adrenaline, he headed toward Green Mountain. Once underway, he called his friend Carson Benton at the sheriff's department. While per Pennsylvania law, the deputy couldn't apprehend the suspects, he could serve in tracking them down and alerting the state police and the FBI if needed. He could also help in transporting them if they were apprehended.

Nathan and Carson went way back, had been friends for years. Carson sometimes helped Nathan in an unofficial capacity with missing person cases.

"This had better be good," Carson said, echoing the same words Nathan had uttered about ten minutes ago.

"I need you to check on a woman driving alone and headed toward the turnoff just past Green Mountain, toward Campton Creek. She thinks someone is following her. Someone dangerous. She witnessed a shooting near Philadelphia and she had a police cruiser following her but the perpetrators ran the patrol car off the road."

"Hello to you, too," his longtime friend said with a grunt. "Got it. Who's the woman?"

"Alisha Braxton," Nathan said, one hand on the wheel as he broke the speed limit. Then he described her vehicle. "I'm on my way."

"I know how you drive, Nathan. You'll beat me

there," Carson replied in a tart tone. "I'm on it." Then he asked, "Hey, isn't she the one who—"

"Yeah," Nathan said. Then he ended the call.

Alisha Braxton.

The one who got away.

This had to be bad if she'd called him.

Because Nathan knew he was the one man on earth she'd never want to call for help.

Why had she called him?

Logic told Alisha her first call should have been to 911. But she'd panicked after she'd seen the patrol car behind her bursting into flames and when she'd grabbed for her phone, Nathan had come to mind. He lived close by when he wasn't traveling. Thankful that she'd caught Nathan at home, Alisha knew he could get to her fast. And he'd act first and ask questions later.

He was the kind of man who took matters into his own hands.

He was also the kind of man who broke all the rules, one of the reasons she'd given up on him long ago.

Now it was the only reason she wanted him by her side.

The one man she didn't want to call was also the one man who could help her escape from a couple of killers.

The irony of her situation made her laugh a tiny hysterical laugh while she slipped her car back onto the main road and kept watch behind her. She'd seen the SUV and now it had disappeared. But she wasn't imagining this. If she turned down Applewood Lane and hooked a left back to the old covered-bridge road, she could throw them off. Then she could take the back roads to Creek Road and then Campton Creek proper.

She'd be safe soon. She knew these roads, had traveled them as a child.

Had met Nathan in a park out by the creek when they were both in their late teens.

Nathan, who'd been Amish then.

Nathan, who now had few scruples when it came to bringing justice to this world.

He no longer lived among the Amish but for close to fifteen years, he had made it his life's work to always help and protect the Amish. Because he had to help others seek their loved ones so they wouldn't have to live with the pain he carried in his heart.

His younger sister had gone missing after Nathan and his father had fought about his relationship with Alisha. Hannah had been found dead a few weeks later.

Nathan blamed himself. Alisha lived with that same guilt.

She shouldn't have called him tonight. She had her life in order, had her routines down, worked hard, rarely dated. She'd learned to be her own hero. Because she never wanted to go through that kind of pain again, either.

Nathan could complicate all of that.

He could also save her life.

Alisha checked her mirror again and tried to stay calm. She knew how to take care of herself. She'd given the police her statement, described in detail the vehicle and the man she'd seen, left the officers and detectives her contact information and finally had been given permission to leave.

"Will you be all right, Miss Braxton?" one of the detectives at the gruesome scene had asked her.

"I will be when I get to my grandmother's place," she'd replied, glancing around the empty parking lot.

The marketplace had been shut down until the crime techs could scour the scene. By then the authorities had questioned all of the witnesses, but most of them had just heard gunshots and seen the SUV speeding out of the parking lot.

Alisha had been the only eyewitness to the murders.

"We can give you an escort," one of the detectives had suggested.

"That might make me feel better," she'd admitted. "It's about two hours from here."

They arranged for a patrol car with two officers to follow her, staying close. She'd watched their car through her rearview mirror, feeling safe, until she'd heard screeching tires and gunshots.

And watched the patrol car careening off the road and into a rocky incline. It had burst into flames.

Now she prayed for those two officers, but she knew in her heart they were probably dead. If the crash hadn't killed them, the shooter would make sure they were dead.

She would be next.

Hurry, Nathan.

When she saw a car approaching, Alisha gasped and watched as it zoomed close. Dark, big, gaining on her.

Alisha couldn't tell who was behind her, but the driver had a lead foot. Coming up on another curve, she took a quick glance in the rearview mirror. The big vehicle was still gaining on her.

Then she saw the headlights of another vehicle off in the distance, coming from the other direction. Her turnoff was up ahead but the on-coming car could be the SUV retracing the same route. Could she make it before either vehicle caught her? She'd have to speed up and make a hard right turn. Checking again, she gauged the distance and monitored the oncoming car, hoping she'd be past it before she spun to the right. Meantime, she prayed the vehicle behind her would keep moving ahead instead of following her.

The night was dark and cloudy, with a possible snowstorm headed across the state. Out here, where few streetlights existed, the hills and valleys looked ominous and misshapen. The ribbon of road twisted and turned and meandered like a giant gray snake.

The vehicle behind her gained speed. When it came close enough to tap her bumper, Alisha let out a gasp and held tight, bracing for a collision. But the vehicle didn't hit her. The driver stayed close but never made contact.

It was now or never.

Taking a breath, Alisha held onto the wheel and watched for the turnoff. Then with a prayer and another gulp of air, she slowed enough to turn the wheels of her car to the right onto the narrow road. Her car wobbled and fishtailed her heart bumping and jumping while she tried to keep control. If she lost the wheel, she'd go careening down into a deep ditch. Or worse, a rocky embankment.

Her nerves tightly knotted, Alisha managed to regain control of the car and stay on the road. Letting out a breath, she gathered her wits and glanced into the rearview mirror. To her dismay, the car that had been approaching from the other direction was now following her.

They'd found her.

Chapter Two

Nathan hit the steering wheel again, wishing Alisha's phone worked. Her battery must have finally fizzled out. He couldn't reach her. But he'd been tailing her for two miles when he looked up and saw another car coming down a hill toward them.

Then he'd watched in horror when Alisha had made a sharp right turn, his heart stopping while he watched her car careening wildly.

She'd made it off the main road and he was headed to follow her when a big dark SUV coming from the other direction turned onto the same route she'd just taken, cutting Nathan off as it whipped in front of his truck.

"No." Nathan slammed on his brakes to avoid a collision and then hit the gas pedal again. "Where are you, Carson?" The deputy sheriff should have been here by now. Carson would have alerted the town police, too, since he didn't have the authority to make any arrests.

But if those men saw the deputy tailing them, they could have shot at Carson, too.

Lord, please protect my friend.

The silent prayer felt foreign and raw inside Nathan's

head. He rarely prayed these days, but he still believed deep down inside. Right now, he needed the Lord to hear him on a lot of accounts.

Alisha needed him. He had to get to her.

He slipped and slid onto the turnoff, noting where Alisha's car had gone, his heart doing that jumpy thing it always did each time he came back to the place he'd once called home.

The place where he'd fallen in love with a beautiful *Englisch* girl who had her own dreams and ambitions. The girl who'd walked away from him because she felt as if she'd only remind him of the worst night of his life.

If he didn't find her, *this* would be the worst night of his life. He might have lost his sweet little sister Hannah, but he would not lose Alisha.

Not this time.

Nathan hurried along the dark, deserted road and noted the two vehicles up ahead. The big SUV hovered near Alisha's sedan. He had his weapon concealed in a shoulder holster and he'd shoot first and ask questions later.

When Alisha's vehicle swerved around a curve, Nathan took off and caught up with the SUV following her. While the sleek vehicle inched closer to her, Nathan did the same with the aggressive SUV.

He knew a certain spot up ahead where if he hit at its back bumper just right, he could force the SUV off the road long enough to allow Alisha to get to safety.

Preparing, Nathan kept his eyes on the two cars up ahead. Then he looked in his rearview mirror and saw another vehicle approaching. A traffic jam on this road late at night? Unbelievable. He hoped Carson had found them.

His cell buzzed. Careful to keep his gaze on the road, he let the call come through his truck's Bluetooth.

"I'm behind you," Carson said. "The locals are out in force since they've heard what happened. There's a BOLO out based on the eyewitness description."

"They're following that witness," Nathan replied, relieved for the backup. "I can't let them get to her."

"I'm trying to catch up with them."

"They have to be the same people who killed someone in front of Alisha earlier."

"Why did she come here?" Carson asked.

"She's afraid and…she must have been coming to see her grandmother. I don't know. She panicked, I think."

She had to have panicked to call him, Nathan reasoned.

"Dangerous situation," Carson replied.

"Be careful," Nathan warned. "They're armed."

"I won't do anything stupid," Carson said. "I'm here to observe and help with transport, if needed."

"Okay. I'll tail them until we meet up."

Carson ended the call and sped around Nathan to alert the town police up on the main road out of town. Nathan watched the road ahead. His friend had the authority to stop them for speeding if nothing else. But these people were dangerous. Carson shouldn't take that risk. Smarter to get the police out here.

Nathan focused on the vehicle behind Alisha. The big vehicle bumped against Alisha's car. The driver tried to force her off the road. Nathan gunned his truck, thinking he'd smash into the other vehicle.

Too late.

He watched in horror as the SUV bumped hard against Alisha's sedan again. Unable to help, Nathan shouted as her tiny car went spiraling across the road and headed into a deep ditch.

"No," Nathan said, slamming on the brakes as he came up on the scene.

The SUV took off, speeding away. The town police should be waiting up ahead. Nathan had to check on Alisha.

Nathan put the still moving truck into Park, left it running, and hopped out and hurried toward Alisha, pulling open the driver's-side door.

Nearly out of breath, he called, "Alisha?"

"I'm okay," she said, her hands tight on the steering wheel, her head slumped over. "I'm all right, Nathan."

She didn't sound all right. More like out of breath and going into shock. "I'm calling for help."

"No." Grabbing his arm, she said, "Just get me out of here, please."

He looked at her and then looked down into a dark abyss. She'd somehow managed to stop the car against a jutting rock, but most of the car sat nestled against an old jagged tree trunk. A rotting and weathered trunk that could give at any minute.

Mere inches away from what looked like a sizable drop-off into a ravine.

"I've got you," he said. "C'mon, take my hand."

She nodded. "My bag."

"Okay, grab it. But careful."

She lifted the big businesslike leather bag and handed it to him. Nathan set the bag on the ground and gently tugged at her. "Turn slowly toward me, okay."

She nodded, the car rocking with each movement. Once she twisted and managed to put her legs on the ground, the car moaned and slipped another inch into the old tree trunk.

Nathan's heart slipped right along with the vehicle, his breath caught. That old stump wouldn't last much longer. "On three," he said. "One, two, three."

His hands on her waist now, he tugged her up and out and then pulled her away from the now shaking car. With a groan and the hissing of tires and metal, the car plummeted against the weak tree trunk, causing the weathered wood to crumble into a hundred powder-dry pieces. Nathan held Alisha down, the sound of the car's front right fender scraping against the rock as it slid over the edge of the ravine and crashed down below with a last moan. A hard crash and then the sound of metal breaking apart echoed out over the hills.

They fell together onto the grass near the curve in the road. Nathan held her close, shut his eyes and took in the sweet scent of her hair.

"Alisha."

She suddenly sat straight up and scooted away from him. "What?"

He lay there, checking her over, the urge to hold her close still strong. "Are you all right?"

"Yes. But my car… It's gone."

Nathan took in her dark golden hair all scattered and wispy around her heart-shaped face. "I'm sorry about that, but I had to get you out. Too late for your car but I need to get you away from here."

Brushing at her hair and clothes, she let out a long, shuddering sigh. "I still owe on that car."

Still practical, he thought, his pulse pounding like a jackhammer in his ear. "You have insurance?"

She gave him a nod, her expression blank now. "Did you call reinforcements?"

"Yes—a friend nearby and the locals waiting down the road. Tell me if you hurt anywhere. Did you hit your head?"

"No. I mean I bumped against something but I'm okay. When they rammed me, I tried to steer the car toward a tree. I found a rock and a tree. Bounced a bit. I could have died if you hadn't come along."

She was shaken but Nathan knew this woman. Tough and stubborn.

"Okay, but you did not die." He stood and offered her his hand. She hesitated and then grabbed on while he tugged her up, the touch of her skin against his fingers jarring him with a current of awareness. "I called my friend Carson Benton. He's a deputy sheriff who helps me out a lot."

"Unofficially, I'm sure. I hope he chased them away."

"Unofficially, yes. I hope they don't shoot him."

Looking her over, he took in the boots and straight black skirt, the tan leather jacket and black turtleneck sweater. Classy. "Alisha, listen, they don't know you're still alive. That gives us time. We need to get you somewhere safe, okay?"

"I'm going to Campton House."

Just as he'd thought, and the closest place to hide for now. "Good. Mrs. Campton has a state-of-the-art security system."

"I know. I told her to get a system installed because of the sensitive nature of some of our cases. It serves as a safe house at times, too."

"Well, that will come in handy since we have to hide you until I can figure this thing out. The longer they think you died in that car, the better our odds of keeping you alive."

"You mean, until *we* can figure this thing out. I'm the one who witnessed a double murder."

He liked her spirit but heard that stubborn tone in her voice. "And I'm the one who'll protect you and help you find justice. You have to stay hidden."

He took her by the arm. "I'll report the crash from the truck. And before you start up, it's too cold out here to argue about this right now."

"I'm not going to argue," she said. "I'm exhausted."

Nathan's heart went out to her. "Alisha…"

"Don't," she said, holding up a hand. "Don't baby me, Nathan. Just get me to my grandmother's house."

Nathan grunted and let her open her own door. Then he grabbed her big leather bag and hopped in on the driver's side. "Here's your purse."

"This is *not* a purse. It's full of work, my laptop and a flash drive, clothes. And my phone. My life is in this bag."

And hidden chocolate, if memory served him.

"That's a lot of life crammed into one fancy lady purse."

"I don't have a life," she said. Then her gaze met his in sheepish surprise. "It's a briefcase."

"You didn't mean to admit that, did you? The part about not having a life."

"I'm tired. Not making much sense."

"Well, if I have it my way, you'll have a lot of life left in you."

His cell buzzed. "It's Carson." Hitting Accept, he said, "Did you find them?"

Carson's voice came over the Bluetooth connection.

"Saw them, followed while the locals gave chase and we had them surrounded."

"But?" Nathan glanced over at Alisha since she could hear the call. Her expression held dread.

"They crashed the SUV near the main highway down the mountain. Got out and ran away on foot. We've got men searching the area and we've called in the K9 unit, but I have a feeling they had another ride coming. It's still not safe." Then he added, "One of the escort officers is alive but critical. The other one died at the scene. I'm sorry, Nathan. The police are up to speed and they've alerted the proper authorities in Philadelphia, including the FBI."

Alisha let out a sob, her hand going to her face.

"Thanks." Nathan said, glancing at Alisha. "I have Miss Braxton with me. I got her out of the car, but it went into the ravine. They'll send someone to circle back around to make sure she's dead. I'd like them to think that for a while. Just until I get her somewhere safe."

"Understood," his friend said. "But you know how this will end, right?"

"Yeah. With me bringing these people to justice." Nathan ended the call and turned to Alisha. "So you heard. Your pursuers managed to escape. You're not safe."

He saw the shudder she tried to hide. "What they did was horrible. I can't get it out of my head." Looking out into the darkness, she whispered, "I should have done something for those officers."

"You did the only thing you could do—you got away. It was probably too late for the one who died at the scene and hopefully, the other one won't die."

He didn't want her to meet that same fate.

"That will be in the news, too. His poor family. To lose him at Christmas. Maybe I should have gone back to Reading."

"No." Nathan couldn't tell her that he was glad to see her, glad to help her. "No. You need to be with family right now."

She nodded, her head down.

"Tell me what you saw tonight," he said in a gentler tone, wishing he could touch her, hold her and make her feel better.

But that would be the worst idea he'd ever had and he'd had a few bad ones at times.

She nodded and started speaking, her voice strained and weary. Once she'd finished, Nathan couldn't stop himself. He reached over and took her hand. This reeked of a professional hit. But he wouldn't tell her that until he did some digging.

"You'll be safe at the Campton Center for now."

She stared down at his hand and then pulled hers away. "Of course I will. It's solid."

"And I'll be there to make sure."

"What exactly does that mean?"

"That means we'll be spending Christmas together," he replied with a soft smile. "Because I'll be staying there with you until we find these killers."

Chapter Three

"Oh, no," Alisha replied, the shock of his statement overtaking the shock pumping through her body. "That is not going to happen."

"It's happening," he retorted as he took all the back roads she'd planned on taking. "I'm not leaving you alone."

"I won't be alone. I have my grandmother and Mrs. Campton."

"Right. Two elderly ladies who have to use an elevator to get downstairs."

He had a point but Alisha wasn't ready to concede. "And a good security system."

"That helps but we both know a good criminal can work around that."

Right again. But Alisha wasn't about to let him hang around. Yes, she'd called him in a moment of panic but reason was taking over now. "Nathan, I'm a big girl. I can hide out there while I do some checking. For all we know, they might give up on me and go into hiding."

"I'm not willing to wait and see if that happens. Are you?"

She shook her head. "No. I have a week before I go back to the office in Reading the day after Christmas."

"Call your boss and make that two weeks. Just until the New Year."

"I can't do that."

"Yes, you can. Explain the situation. Take some vacation time."

"I'll take the time I have allotted and I'll use that time to track these killers."

"You do realize Christmas is not the time to work, right?"

"Yes. But watching a gunman shoot up a Christmas market five days before the holidays kind of puts a damper on things."

"Are you going to tell the ladies the truth?"

"I have to," she said, hating the idea. "They need to be warned so they can be aware."

"And they need protection, too."

"Maybe I should stay somewhere else."

"No, this is the best plan for now. But, Alisha, I'm going to stay there with all of you whether you like it or not. I know the place has a couple of extra bedrooms in the main house. I'll bunk in one of those."

Bad idea. So why did she feel safer, just knowing he'd be nearby?

Because she was frightened, shaken and... She'd need his help. Nathan Craig was good at his job and he could go where others didn't dare go. He found people. Good people. Scared people. Lost people. And sometimes, the worst of people.

"I can see those wheels turning inside your head," he said when she didn't retort right away. "What are you thinking?"

She twisted to stare at him as they turned onto Creek Road. "I don't have much of a choice. I need you—I mean I need your experience and expertise."

Her head told her to be logical, while her heart shouted that she did need him, too. She'd always needed him.

But she'd been fighting that need since she'd first met him the summer after her senior year. Funny, how he'd been on the fringes of her life for most of her life. Around but always out of her reach. Once, they'd been so close. Teenage sweethearts. But they were both adults now. Professional and on a case. Nothing more. Because neither one of them had anything more to give.

Tonight, he'd saved her. Alisha couldn't forget that.

"Don't worry," he said in a tight tone, as if he knew exactly what she was thinking. "I'll stay out of your way. I'll have plenty to keep me busy."

Justice. The man always wanted justice.

Well, so did she, but she sure hadn't planned on getting it with Nathan's help. She didn't want to spend her holidays chasing after a killer, but her instincts told her the murderers would keep chasing after her.

"I'll be busy, too," she said. "I just want this over."

"Are you referring to this murder investigation or being forced to keep me around?"

"Both," she admitted.

Nathan pulled the truck up to the quiet, looming house and switched off the motor. "We'll have to wake them and I'll need to hide my truck in the garage."

Alisha stared at the stately redbrick mansion trimmed in white columns, the rows of tall windows now looking vulnerable instead of comforting, the big evergreen wreath on the door reminding her of all the holidays she'd spent here.

Too many memories for tonight, coupled with Nathan being here beside her. A great weight of fatigue and shock pushed at her soul. "Yes. Let's get inside and do what we have to do."

Nathan quickly came around the truck and opened her door, his gaze scanning the old oaks and high shrubs and then the driveway and parking areas. "At least the backyard is gated and fenced."

"We have security lights and alarms everywhere."

He helped her down, his hands on her waist. Alisha stared up and into his eyes, really seeing him for the first time in a long time. He had always been good-looking, but that world-weary cragginess that shadowed his face made him handsome and mysterious. His eyes, so cobalt blue and shimmering, held too many secrets and his dark hair, always unruly, curled against his neck. A rogue sweep of heavy bangs shielded his frown while his gaze held hers.

He was off-limits and yet, right now, she wanted to reach up and brush those thick curls off his forehead.

"Thank you, Nathan," she said instead.

"You can thank me when this is all over," he replied, removing his hands as if he'd been burned.

Alisha accepted that, the loss of his touch already moving through her with aching clarity. Grabbing her briefcase, she hurried to the double doors of the carriage house entryway, where an open portico separated the garage and the upstairs apartment from the main house. Glancing up at the enclosed upper breezeway, which allowed people to move from the garage and second-floor apartment to the main house during bad weather, Alisha breathed deeply and shivered in the late-night cold. She had a key but she rang the bell instead so she wouldn't scare her grandmother by slipping into the house.

"Alisha?"

Hearing her grandmother's sweet voice over the intercom brought tears to Alisha's eyes. "Yes, Granny. It's me. Sorry I'm so late."

"Come on up," Bettye said, buzzing the door open.

Relief filled Alisha's soul but with it came the letdown of adrenaline and the horrible realization of what she'd witnessed. Her hands started shaking but she held her briefcase with a death grip to keep from falling apart.

Nathan stepped up and placed his arm across her shoulder, tugging her close. He then took the heavy bag. "I've got you," he whispered as he pushed open the door for her. "Don't fall apart on me now, okay?"

Alisha swallowed her fears and the delayed reaction to everything she'd been through in the last few hours. "I'll be all right." She didn't want to fall apart and she didn't want him to be kind to her.

But she didn't push him away. She *did* need Nathan. And not just to help her stay alive. The strength of his grip reminded her that he'd once made her feel so secure. That feeling had returned tonight, but she'd have to get it out of her system.

Bettye Willis met them at the landing where the stairs from the portico doors met the second floor in a wide entryway. A small table held a sparkling ceramic Christmas tree, the smell of cinnamon-and-spice potpourri lingering in the air.

Bettye took Alisha into her arms in a tight hug. "Alisha, we were beginning to get worried." Stepping back to get a good look, she said, "I sent Judy on to bed."

Then her grandmother saw Nathan there in the shadows. Her surprised gaze moving from Alisha to him, Bettye asked, "Mr. Craig, what are you doing here?"

Nathan smiled at Bettye. "That's a long story, Mrs. Willis."

"He's here to help me, Granny," Alisha said, hoping her grandmother wouldn't press. "We can explain in the morning."

Bettye scoffed that away. "I was up reading," she said. "Come into the kitchen and I'll make you something to eat. And then you can tell me what's really going on."

When they hesitated, her grandmother put her hands on her hips. "You do realize that while I'm old, I'm not completely hapless and senile. Alisha, you would not bring Nathan Craig here in the middle of the night without an extremely good reason."

Alisha shot Nathan a warning glance. "I'll explain then, Granny. No need to keep you up all night wondering."

"That's unbelievable," Bettye said after Alisha retold what had happened to her. Turning to where Nathan sat in front of a half-eaten roast beef sandwich, she patted his hand. "I'm so thankful Alisha thought to call you, Nathan."

Nathan stared at the cookie waiting by his plate and then glanced at Alisha, concern hitting him in the gut. What if he hadn't answered his phone? What if he hadn't been at the cabin?

He wouldn't think about that. He was here now with her and she was safe. "Me, too, Mrs. Willis."

"Call me Bettye," the older woman said. She wore a blue flannel robe to keep warm in the wee-hour chill of the spacious art deco–style kitchen. "More coffee?"

Nathan held up his cup, thinking he wouldn't get much sleep tonight anyway. "Thank you."

Alisha sat holding her mug, absorbing the warmth. Her grandmother had found her a cozy sweater and a pair of jeans. Alisha kept some clothes here since she often worked pro bono into the late hours and spent the night now and then.

"So, you're going to be our protector," Bettye said, nodding her head. "We'll explain all of this to Mrs. C in the morning. She'll certainly agree that this is the safest place for both of you right now."

"I don't want to put you or her in any danger, Granny," Alisha said. "This is just for a couple of days."

"Until after Christmas," Bettye said. "Remember, you have the whole week off."

"Maybe until the New Year," Nathan repeated again.

"I hope it won't take that long," Alisha replied, a stubborn glint in her green eyes.

"No matter," her feisty grandmother replied. "As you know, Alisha, the center will be closed for the next few days and we have lots of baking to do and packages to wrap. We go visiting the Amish during Christmas. You can help with all of that."

"Okay, Granny," Alisha said. But her voice held little enthusiasm. She would work day and night to solve this thing.

"I'll take a room in the main house," Nathan said to Bettye. "But at least I'll be on the premises."

"I feel better already," Bettye replied. "Now, let's get you both settled in. I'm sure you are exhausted. We'll continue this discussion in the morning." Getting up, she added, "You two must not have been hungry."

"I'll save my cookie for later," Nathan said.

"I'm sorry, Granny. Hard to eat." Alisha took her own sandwich to the sink. "I'll do the dishes and then I'm going to my room."

Nathan lifted his eyebrows, questioning.

"Relax," Alisha said. "My room is right across from Granny's. This place has three bedrooms. The big suite where Mrs. Campton stays and two smaller bedrooms across the hallway, with a bath and small sitting room between them."

"It's quite cozy," Bettye said with a shrug.

"Yeah, cozy. I vaguely remember the layout." Nathan thought of all the things that could go wrong. "Do I need a key or a code to get to the main house?"

"I'll show you," Alisha said, her tone anxious.

"I'll wait here then," Bettye said, her grandmotherly gaze taking in all the undercurrents flowing around them. "Then we'll lock up tight."

Nathan nodded and thanked Bettye for the food. "I'll be close if you need anything."

Remembering the house from his time here before, Nathan guided Alisha to the glass door that led to the enclosed breezeway, where two rows of windows provided views of the big front yard and the sprawling tree-lined backyard and lighted pool area.

"Too many windows," he said, holding her elbow while he scanned their surroundings.

"I've never worried about that before," Alisha admitted. "Granny will feel better, having you close by."

They made it to the matching set of doors on the other side of the breezeway, bypassing wicker chairs and tall parlor ferns.

Alisha keyed in the code and the doors clicked open. Then they moved into the upper hallway of the estate house, now a center to help the Amish and anyone else who didn't have the money to pay for doctors, lawyers and counselors.

"The elevator is to the left if you ever need it," Alisha reminded him, her words echoing over the big upstairs floor. Then she pointed to the right. "There are two bedrooms on the front of the house. And two more on the back. The master is up here on the other side down another hallway. It faces the backyard. We put mothers with children in there."

"I'll take one to the front," he said, "since the back should be fairly secure, but the front yard could be compromised."

Alisha nodded and took him to a bedroom that had a direct view to the street and to the carriage house. The yard was well lit, at least.

"Sheets and towels are in the linen closet in the bathroom," she said, pointing to the adjoining door. Then she turned at the main door. "I guess I'll see you in the morning."

Nathan reached for her arm. "Are you sure you're all right?"

Alisha nodded but he could see the fatigue and worry shadowing her eyes. "I'm good now that I'm here. I doubt I'll sleep but I'll be okay."

"I can walk you back across," he offered.

"You don't need to do that."

"I'll go as far as the doors to the breezeway, to be sure."

She nodded and they walked back up the hallway together.

"This is an amazing house," he said once they'd reached the breezeway.

Alisha nodded. "The Camptons founded this town

over a century ago. It's sad to think the Admiral and Mrs. Campton lost their only son Edward. He was killed in Afghanistan. He was a navy SEAL."

"I've heard about him," Nathan replied. "I still have friends around here who tell me the latest news."

"And family?"

Her question threw Nathan. They never discussed the past.

"A few," he said. "My parents will always be here."

He was about to tell her good-night when he heard a noise outside and then saw a flash of light.

Without thinking, he pushed Alisha down beneath the windows and went with her, shielding her.

"Someone is in the front yard," he whispered, his heart hammering. "Don't move."

Alisha nodded. "Granny—"

Nathan put a finger to her lips, his grip on her so tight he felt her heart beating against his. "I'm going to check it out. You stay right here."

Alisha gave him a wide-eyed frown. "Nathan, don't do that."

When they heard another noise, he gave her a quick nod.

"If I'm not back in five minutes, call 911, okay?"

Then he turned and headed back across the breezeway so he could sneak out the garage door downstairs, the beat of Alisha's heart still racing through his pulse.

If these goons had found her here this quickly, how did he have any chance of protecting her and keeping her alive?

Chapter Four

Alisha huddled underneath the windows, the cold floor making her shiver while fear for Nathan made her shudder. Should she go after him? Alert her grandmother? Find a weapon?

Granny. What if someone hurt her grandmother?

Deciding a weapon would be good, just in case, she hurried back into the big, dark house and went to the master bedroom. Moving past the eerie glow of all the sconces, she stood at the bedroom door and spotted the big fireplace inside. Then she hurried to find the fire poker.

The wieldy iron poker in her hands, she slipped to the windows lining the room and checked the sloping backyard. Shadows cascaded out over the grass and shrubs to reveal a quiet stillness. The yellow glow of the security lamps gave her courage. But she needed to get back to the front of the house and check on her grandmother and Nathan. Had it been five minutes?

Alisha moved quickly back up the wide hallway, going past the stairs. When she heard a noise coming from the front yard, she stopped. Should she go down or call 911?

Before she could decide, a strong arm pulled her close. She tried to scream but the sound caught in her throat. Then a hand clamped down over her mouth and a man breathed close.

Frantic, she tried to raise the poker.

"Be still and don't make a sound."

Nathan.

He released her and touched his finger to her lips. Then he whispered close. "I've got this."

Relieved but wanting to kick him for scaring her, Alisha whispered, "Who was out there?"

"Carson," he said. "He was done with the search and decided to drive by to see if we'd made it here safely. But he did spot a prowler. We met up in the front yard. He's still out there rattling around."

"Why didn't you just say that instead of scaring me?"

"I didn't want to startle you and cause you to scream."

"What makes you think I'd scream?"

"Why didn't you stay put?"

Tired and still shaking, she glowered at him. "I went to get this," she said, holding up the poker. Her hand shook so she held it down again.

Nathan's frown darkened. "I told you to stay where you were."

"I was worried about you and my grandmother. I had to do something." Then she checked him over. "What happened?"

"I'm fine. The prowler ran away and got in a vehicle about a block from here. Carson's off-duty, working on his own time to see if he can find any prints."

He took the poker from her. "Are you all right?"

Nodding, she turned toward the breezeway. "I need to check on Granny."

"I went over there when I couldn't find you," he said. "Her door is closed. The lower door is still locked. Everything's okay over there."

Nathan's phone buzzed. "Carson, all clear inside. I'll meet you at the front door."

Alisha followed Nathan down the stairs and put in the code to unlock the door.

The deputy came in, shivering and nodding. "So we had a visitor."

"Yep." Nathan turned to Alisha. "Alisha, this is my friend Deputy Carson Benton."

Alisha shook the man's hand, noticing he was about the same age as Nathan but his hair was clipped and close-cut and he was built like a linebacker. "Thank you for all of your help, Deputy Benton."

"Call me Carson," the deputy said with a smile. "Nasty business, but we'll get things going. The town police will want to get your statement, Miss Braxton. We can do that in the morning." Then he glanced toward Nathan. "And we can talk more in the morning. I want to help but I'll need information."

"Why not now?" Alisha said. "I can't sleep and it's quiet here. We can go in the office."

Carson's stern expression never changed but his gaze moved to Nathan. Did he have to get the PI's approval? "I'll need to call the officers who worked the scene where your car went over. They'll be the ones working this side of the case."

"I would expect all of you to follow proper protocol," Alisha replied, daring Nathan to argue with her.

"You heard the woman," Nathan said. Then he turned

to Alisha. "I know you're antsy but you're gonna crash and burn if you don't get some rest."

"I want to find these killers," she replied, moving ahead of them. But she couldn't deny that she was sinking fast. Turning at the stairs leading down, she waited. "The sooner I get this report done, the sooner I *can* rest."

Carson shook his head and shrugged at Nathan. "We all agree on that." He walked aside to call in one of the officer who'd been on the scene earlier.

Alisha motioned them along the downstairs central hall. Soon they were settled in the big office that used to belong to Admiral Campton. She kept the blinds closed and turned on a desk lamp while she wondered if someone could still be lurking around out there.

Once the other officer arrived, they all sat down across from the desk, quiet and observant until they got down to business.

Officer Cantor looked sleepy, his salt-and-pepper hair thick and unruly. "Once I take your statement, I can work with the state police to get on with this investigation. They'll put out an APB on the vehicle Nathan described, the same one you saw. The Philly police issued a BOLO on the two suspects who are now wanted for the double homicide that you witnessed and for murdering a police officer and injuring another one, and for your attempted murder. We've got men searching the woods but I have to believe whoever showed up here tonight had to have been one of those men. Or both."

"They might not even realize we came here since my truck is hidden in the garage," Nathan said. "Maybe they were looking to steal a ride."

"Or finish the job," Carson pointed out.

"So let's start at the beginning," Officer Cantor said. "I know you told the LEOs back in Philadelphia what happened but whatever information you can give the town police will help them to coordinate with Philly to make sure we're after the same driver and shooter, got it?"

Alisha nodded. "I'm a lawyer. I've got it."

Carson's appreciative glance eased her worries a little. She had to wonder what Nathan had told his friend about her. She wondered about a lot of things regarding Nathan Craig. He was back in her world in a big way so she needed to handle this with a logical approach. Not a good time to get all tangled up in the past and what might have been.

For the next few minutes, she talked about what had happened hours ago in Philadelphia. When she was finished, she had no energy left. Retelling the horror of watching two people die had outdone her.

Nathan held up his hand. "That's enough for now. Alisha needs to get some rest. I'll stand guard."

"You need to sleep, too," she said, glad he was here but still holding out reservations on how this was going to work.

"I don't sleep much," he said, his tone quiet, his eyes shuttered.

"Okay." His friend stood and crossed his arms over his chest while Officer Cantor gathered his things. "You two work out the details on who's more tired and I'll get back with you tomorrow to see how you're doing."

Alisha didn't argue. "Thank you, Deputy Benton and Officer Cantor." Then she added, "You'll probably hear from the Philadelphia FBI field office. I'm more than willing to talk to them, too."

"We can arrange that," Officer Cantor said. "Bring you into the station."

Nathan walked them to the side door and then came back to where she stood in the hallway. "Okay, upstairs. You need sleep."

Alisha wanted to fuss at him but fatigue made her dismiss that idea. She had a feeling they'd have lots of discussions before this was over.

When would it be over?

Nathan walked her back to the upstairs door to the carriage house. "Alisha."

"I'm all right, Nathan. I just want a shower and sleep."

"Okay." He turned to go across the breezeway, but pivoted to stare outside, checking. "It's snowing," he said.

Alisha looked through the windows on both sides of the wide room. "So it is. I used to stand here on nights like this, waiting for the snow to fall. This has always been a beautiful place, the one place where I felt loved and happy."

"Alisha," he said again, something raw in the way he said her name. "I know you don't want me here but... I can't leave now. This is dangerous, too dangerous. You have to know that we might not be able to stay here."

"*I* might not be able to stay here," she retorted, her heart battling a mighty war. "You can go on about your business."

"No, I can't," he said, his tone sharp. "I'm in it now. They know my vehicle and they must know I brought you here."

What if they hurt Nathan? She hadn't considered that

he was in trouble, too. "I shouldn't have involved you. I wasn't thinking straight."

"I don't mind being involved and I want to find these people, same as you. We have to work together and that means we might have to leave together."

So he could protect her and seek justice, not because he wanted to be near her. She wished she'd never called him. "But we don't know who was out there in the yard."

"Yes, we do. They sent someone here because they know everything about you now. The minute you looked into that hit man's eyes, they started digging and now you're on their list."

"So you believe this was a professional hit?" She'd suspected that herself.

He lifted his chin. "The way you described it, the way they came after you, yes. It had to be."

Alisha leaned against the door jamb. "This is bad. I should have left and gone far away from here."

"But you didn't. I'm glad you didn't. Now I can help you and protect you... That is, if you let me."

With that he turned and went to the other side of the rambling old house.

Alisha shivered and closed the door between them, thinking there was a lot more between them than just a hallway in a house.

More like a lifetime of regret and longing across a broken bridge that couldn't be mended.

God, if you had to send me a hero, thank you for sending this one. Even if I didn't want him here. Thank You, Lord.

With that prayer centered in her head, she went into the tiny room with the window alcove she'd always loved, showered, threw on some old pajamas then sprawled across the purple chenille spread her grandmother had turned down.

And promptly fell into a troubled, nightmarish sleep.

Nathan sat in a chair by the window in the room across the house from Alisha, his eyes burning from fatigue while he noticed every little thing in the muted darkness below. The snow silenced most of the noises, but years of stakeouts and doing surveillance that kept him up in the wee hours made him tense and alert. He'd told Alisha the truth. He never slept well.

While he sat in the shadows, he remembered the girl he'd fallen in love with. He'd been willing to give up his way of life for this girl but as it turned out, he'd had to give up the Amish community for another reason. That reason had opened a chasm between Alisha and him, all of their dreams shattered and broken in one long horrible night.

A night so different from this one but full of the same kind of fear and angst.

Summer. With a full moon and the world at his feet.

Sitting there, he drifted into sleep, his memories an aching reminder of the family he'd left behind. Just a few miles from here but so far away.

He thought of Alisha with her long golden-brown hair and bright green eyes, laughing in the wind, her sundress long and flowing. He'd been out in the garden right here helping his father work the soil and plant a butterfly garden for Mrs. Campton. Alisha had been visiting her grandmother and she'd been sitting by the pool, reading a book but also watching them at work.

He'd met her briefly once before when her grandmother had come calling at his family's house. And he'd never forgotten looking into her pretty eyes.

Now she was staring at him, smiling at him.

After he'd clumsily dropped a whole crate of plants and sent dirt flying everywhere, she'd hopped up to help him salvage what he could before his father saw what had happened. They'd become fast friends and Nathan had gone home with a big crush on a girl he was forbidden to like.

"You're different, Nathan. You're like no one I've ever met."

He'd felt the same about her. Always.

We were so young and carefree that summer.

And so naive.

Nathan came awake with a start. Had he heard something outside? Or had he been dreaming?

Standing, he grunted in pain, every muscle in his body protesting. Wiping at his eyes, he noticed the time on his watch. Four in the morning. He'd slept in this cushioned chair for over an hour.

Wide awake now, he studied the front yard and saw that it was now covered in snow. No alarms had sounded and the motion-detection lights hadn't triggered.

He was imagining things.

But his gut told him to be cautious so he washed his face and decided he'd do a walk through the old house and wait for the sun to come up.

For good measure, he grabbed his weapon. He'd been licensed to carry a concealed weapon for years now but he rarely had to use the thing. Still, he'd learned that being out alone in the wee hours could be dangerous.

He padded in his socks up the wide upstairs hallway,

the wooden floors creaking here and there underneath his weight.

He made it to the master bedroom and took his time checking on the backyard. It stretched like a white blanket down to the deep creek that ran through this town. He remembered swimming and fishing in that creek with his younger siblings.

"Tag, you're it."

"I'll find you," Nathan would call to his two younger brothers. He'd always been the one who looked after the *kinder*.

Then he thought of Hannah.

"Nathan, do not leave us. We love you. You must not leave. What about me, Nathan? I won't have my big brother. Don't go. Please don't go."

Tears formed in his eyes. He'd left his little sister crying. "I'll find you, Nathan. I'm come and bring you home."

Only she'd become the one who'd never returned.

Too many thoughts crowding his mind. He'd never planned to be back here under these circumstances.

Nathan turned back and went downstairs, amazed at the size of this mansion. He checked two other bedrooms and then moved toward the large den where a massive fireplace took center stage. Beyond the den with all of the family portraits and fancy trinkets and treasures, he saw the sunroom that formed a rectangle at the back of the house.

More windows here, rows and rows of them, with two sets of French doors leading out to the terrace and a huge pool that was covered for winter.

The yard looked the same from the lower floor, white

and stark against the security lights. But he knew a criminal could be hiding out there, alarms or no alarms.

He headed to the front of the house and went to the dining room window to peek through the heavy curtains.

Then he saw something that had him on high alert again.

A fresh set of heavy footprints had marred the beauty of the new-fallen snow. Someone has passed through the front yard while he'd been moving through the house.

Chapter Five

Nathan hurried upstairs and across the breezeway, checking both sides of the yard as he went. Nothing in the back and nothing, no one, in the front. Maybe someone walking to work had cut through the yard, but this place was so stately and secluded he doubted that. The Amish would respect the property and stay on the roads or sidewalks. Anyone else would drive to work. Why would anyone walk through the snow on private property this early in the morning?

Knocking softly on the door, he waited, hoping Alisha would hear and check through the peephole since her room was the closest. When he heard movement behind the door, he did another sweep of the front yard. Other than those glaring, man-size footprints in the powdery white, the world looked serene and safe. Like a Christmas card.

Alisha opened the door, a cup of coffee steaming in her hand, her expression wary. "What are you doing?"

"I couldn't sleep." He swept past her. "What are *you* doing up?"

"I couldn't sleep much, either. I've been up a while."

Not into small talk, he said, "I saw footprints down in the snow."

She puttered in thick red socks to the windows of the tiny sitting room across from the big kitchen.

Nathan tugged her back. "Hey, don't get too close to the windows."

"I want to see."

"Trust me—the footprints go right through the yard."

Giving him a sleepy stare, she said, "What should we do?"

"Nothing for now since they're gone and we don't know if they were just passing through or not." He eyed the coffee.

"Go get a cup," she said, reading his mind.

Soon, they were nestled in the dainty sitting room. The deep burgundy brocade covering the furniture looked old and comfortable, worn in all the right places but adorned with feminine things like doilies and crocheted blankets. He watched as Alisha curled up with one of the blankets, papers and folders scattered all around her.

Nathan inhaled a sip of the good coffee and then watched her while the brew burned all the way to his stomach. "What have you been working on?"

She gathered the papers and shoved them to the side. "A case regarding a divorce. Nothing for you to worry about."

"And this?" He pointed to a bullet-point list and skimmed the information. "You're building a case for what happened last night, right?"

"I'm jotting down things as I remember so I can sort through them, yes."

"That's very lawyerly of you."

She took a long sip of her coffee. "Did you sleep at all, Nathan?"

"No, but the one time I did fall asleep someone decided to take an early morning stroll through the yard. Some bodyguard I am."

"You don't have to do this. I don't expect you to watch me 24/7."

For a brief instant, he wondered what it would be like to have her around day and night. But he pushed that dream away, like he always did at three in the morning when he ached with loneliness and hopelessness. "I told you already, I want to do this."

Picking up her list, she studied it for a moment and then dropped it back on the couch. "I stopped there to get coffee last night. I wanted to shop since I'd been so busy. Everything looked so pretty. Like Christmas. I thought it would put me in the spirit."

Nathan's heart, so hardened and withered, crumbled a bit. She wasn't ready or willing to collapse and she sure wouldn't do it with him in the room. She'd always been strong, sure, secure. Now her world had been shattered.

Now he was back in her world and she would fight him every step of the way. "You can talk to me, you know."

She bobbed her head in acceptance. "I don't even know the names of the victims. I mean, I heard the crime scene people talking, but I don't remember. I remember so many details, so why can't I recall that? I need to find out who those people were."

"We can do that," Nathan said, thinking the shock was still messing with her head. "We'll get a full report and compare what you told the police to what the police in Philadelphia have. You can stay in contact with all of them, but you don't have to leave here to do that."

"We won't get anything done if we don't go into action."

"I say we lie low here today," he told her. "You need some time with your grandmother. I'll start digging into things."

"I want to dig with you."

"Well, we can do that but first, try to relax and enjoy being here, okay?"

"Is that possible after last night?"

"I said *try*."

"I won't put them in danger."

"I'm going to map out a way for us to slip out of here if we need to do so. I'll also coordinate with the police about beefing up security for them if we do run."

"I don't plan to spend the rest of my life on the run," she said. Standing, she held her cup and watched the dawn breaking, careful to stay back from the opening in the drapery. "It looks so peaceful out there, doesn't it?"

"Yes."

"But that's the thing about life. The surface covers so much more. So many undercurrents and hidden things. That couple last night obviously had it all but they knew something—or were hiding something—that caused someone else to want to murder them."

"Or they could have done things that made someone extremely angry."

Nathan also wondered if the couple had witnessed events they didn't need to see or if they'd managed to make dangerous people put a hit on them. Probably both.

Thinking about Alisha's jaded view of life, he waded through the undercurrents in this room. His chest hurt with trying to breathe while being this close to Alisha again. As grim as it was, working on this murder would help him to clear his head. He'd barely had time to process being in her life again or having her back in his in such a shocking way. The last time he'd seen her here, they'd both wound up working on a missing person case involving an abandoned baby in the Amish community up the road. He'd found the young mother and reunited her with her older brother, who was now married and raising the girl's baby with his new wife.

He and Alisha had worked together, grudgingly. But they both wanted the same things—justice and helping those in need.

"Are you hungry?" Alisha asked, her gaze touching on his face and moving on.

"Starving."

"I can cook some eggs and toast. Maybe some bacon."

"I'd like that."

They moved to the kitchen and worked in a comfortable silence since Alisha didn't want to wake her grandmother or Miss Judy. But the smell of coffee and bacon acted like an alarm clock.

"Well, what do we have here?"

Nathan turned to find Alisha's grandmother smiling at them, hope in her crystal blue eyes. She wore the same robe that covered her from neck to feet and fuzzy reindeer slippers complete with red noses.

"Granny," Alisha said, smiling for the first time since Nathan had entered the apartment. "Did we wake you?"

"Child, I have been getting up at five-thirty in the morning for most of my life," Bettye said as she shuffled into the kitchen and found a mug. It read: Be Still and Know. The mug had a butterfly motif on it. "But I have to admit, that bacon smells good."

Nathan smiled and flipped the bacon onto a plate

lined with paper towels. Used to eating solitary meals, he enjoyed the coziness of this kitchen. Too much.

Bettye filled her cup and glanced down the long hallway. "I usually wake Judy around six-thirty. She has a nurse who comes and helps her with her bath and makes sure she's had her medication. She still insists on dressing for the day—usually in a pastel pantsuit. I fix her a tray for breakfast and make a light lunch, sit with her while I knit or crochet and then I cook supper. We watch television—she loves romantic movies—and I read to her in her room. We lead a pretty boring life."

"Sounds good to me," Nathan said while he delivered the bacon with a flourish to the small four-top breakfast table. "Your food is ready, madame."

Bettye giggled like a schoolgirl and came to sit by him. "It's so good to see you again, Nathan. I know we run into each other from time to time, but having you here is a blessing despite the reason for you being here."

Nathan knew Bettye Willis to be a good, faithful woman even though she'd done the same as him—jumped the fence and left the Amish. He appreciated her sweet declaration. She'd found love and happiness in the outside world but she'd sacrificed seeing her Amish family since she'd moved here from another community. Her husband Herbert had been alive when Nathan first met Alisha. A great man with a larger-than-life personality. He had worked for the Camptons, too, as their maintenance man and groundskeeper.

"I'm glad to be here," Nathan said, glancing at Alisha. "I hope we can find these people before they commit any more crimes."

Bettye buttered her toast. "I'll explain to Judy when I

go in to wake her. She's fuzzy in the mornings but once she gets going, she is still wise and spry."

Alisha sat down beside her grandmother. "Nathan and I plan to work in the main office today, Granny. We want to crack this thing but we have to be watchful."

"Of course you do," Bettye said. "I have plenty of supplies for the holidays, so I'll cook us a hearty supper. Judy loves company and she's looking forward to seeing you, Sugar-bear."

Alisha's eyes widened in embarrassment as she looked over at Nathan, a becoming blush moving over her face.

Nathan couldn't stop his grin. "You hear that, Sugar-bear? Supper cooked by the best of the best. We're in for a treat."

"If you call me that again, you won't be invited to supper," she retorted, but her eyes held a twinkle.

Bettye smiled her sweet smile and sipped her coffee.

Nathan remembered calling Alisha that long ago after he'd heard her grandfather calling her Sugar-bear.

And Bettye Willis must have remembered, too, since she looked pretty smug and proud of herself. Matchmaking during a murder investigation.

That was a new one.

Alisha silently cringed while she washed up the breakfast dishes. *Sugar-bear?* Why had Granny brought up that old nickname?

Maybe because the handsome man sitting at the breakfast table had made her grandmother's pragmatic mind go completely giddy?

Nathan had that effect on people. Which made him a great investigator since he could get people to talk, but it also made him too dangerous for most women.

She should know. She'd been smitten with him ten years ago and even now, when they were forced to come face to face on cases, she had to fight not to revert back to being a wide-eyed schoolgirl.

Deciding that couldn't happen, she hurriedly got dressed and gathered her files, shoving them into her briefcase. Her grandmother wanted her to find love and be happy but pushing Nathan back at her wouldn't take Alisha back down that road. The man had a quest that took all of his time. And she had her own sense of justice which meant long hours and sleepless nights. She was still an associate at the law firm since she'd only been practicing a couple of years. But one day she hoped to make partner. Which reminded her, she needed to call her boss and explain what was going on here before anyone saw it on the news.

"I'm so glad we got to visit," her grandmother said from the kitchen when Alisha came out of her bedroom. Granny was making cinnamon bread, one of Alisha's favorites. The place smelled divine.

"So am I," Miss Judy said from her dainty chair by the small fireplace. "What a good day to stay in and bake."

Judy sent Alisha a soft smile. Even in old age, Judy Campton as still a regal, beautiful woman. Her hair was white now but clipped in a precise short bob. She wore a blue cashmere sweater and her famous pearls, classic and commanding. "Can you come and sit by me before you head to work, darling?"

"Of course." Alisha crossed the room to settle on the ottoman by the chair. "I hope we didn't upset you with our news, Miss Judy. I won't let anything happen to either of you."

Judy scoffed at that. "Alisha, your grandmother and I are tough old birds. We've seen a lot in our lives. We have faith that God is always in control."

"His will, not ours," Bettye echoed, her hands moving with grace over the bread dough. Granny still had the Amish doctrine ingrained in her.

Judy patted Alisha's hand. "You are safe here. Your grandmother and I will pray all day while you and your handsome protector do what needs to be done. God gave us brains to help in His work, you know. You might be terrified, but He put you in that spot at that time for a reason, Alisha. You fight for the underdogs and you fight for those who can't help themselves. You will bring these evil people to justice."

"I hope so," Alisha said. "It's something I can't get out of my mind. I've worked a lot of cases since law school but seeing a murder will stay with me a long time."

"Seeing justice done will help you come to terms with that image," Judy said. "Now we have security and Mr. Craig has assured me the authorities are aware of the situation. I can rest easy and enjoy all those cute Christmas movies on television. You know, they are so romantic."

Alisha laughed at that. "I rarely have time to watch but my friends sometimes force me to sit for popcorn and love stories."

"We all have love stories," Judy said, nodding. "You have one yourself."

"I think I'm a little late for the love department," Alisha said, thinking of the man waiting for her on the other side of the house. "I love my work so I'd better get going."

"All work and no romance can make a girl tuckered out," Granny said. "Be kind to Nathan, Sugar-bear. He still cares about you."

Alisha wasn't sure how to answer that, so she said, "I'm thankful that he's here, that's for sure."

"Yes, we are too," Miss Judy said with a serene smile. "Bettye, finish up and we'll watch this movie while the bread rises."

Alisha left them talking back and forth about which holiday movies they loved the most.

She really did need to get a life outside of her brief-case. And she really needed to get a handle on the way Nathan made her heart bump and skip all at the same time.

I'm fighting a battle, Lord. Please give me the strength to stay away from temptation.

But when she got to the office across the way, that temptation was sitting on the old leather loveseat with his eyes closed and his booted feet across an ottoman straight in front of him.

Alisha had to swallow. He looked so at peace, asleep there in the sunlight that had slipped through the blinds. So beautiful, so young, so amazing.

Was he as soul-weary as she felt?

Had God brought them together for a reason besides finding a killer?

Get to work, she told herself. *Focus on what needs to be done. Or you won't live to figure out that question.*

Standing here, watching Nathan sleep, Alisha sure wanted to live for a long time to come.

Chapter Six

Nathan woke with a start and tried to remember where he was. Campton House. He sat up, removed the blue chenille throw someone had placed over him then rubbed his hand down his face.

The office, with midmorning sunshine streaming through the blinds, its brilliance casting off the last of the snow. Everything came back to him and he became fully awake, a panic setting in.

Where was Alisha?

The office door stood open and the house breathed quietly, the few creaks and sighs from old age as comfortable as the air around him. But that sinister shadow of death and fear surrounded him too and he jumped up, hit his boot against the coffee table and mumbled to himself as pain shot through his already sore toe.

Hurrying to the hallway, he called out. "Alisha?"

No answer.

Nathan sprinted up the long hallway toward the kitchen, his breath catching against his chest. Why had he fallen asleep?

"Alisha," he called again.

"In here," she said, emerging from the powder room midway between the kitchen and the office. "I'm sorry. I was taking a break."

Seeing the concern and surprise in her wide eyes, Nathan nodded, took in a breath, and then raked a hand over his mussed hair. "Sorry. I woke up and you weren't in the office."

"I *was* in the office for two hours," she said. "I didn't want to wake you so I came out here to talk to Mr. Henderson and assure him that I'm safe and then I took a break."

"Don't do that again."

"What, go to the bathroom? That might be hard considering all the coffee I've been consuming."

"You know what I mean. Don't let me sleep."

Putting a hand on his arm, she said, "Nathan, you needed to sleep. It's daylight with bright sunshine everywhere. I think we're safe for now."

"These people don't care about daylight," he said, pulling away.

"I should take my boss up on his offer to come to his estate near Philadelphia. Talk about security." Alisha's boots clicked against the wooden floor, right on his heel. "Because I shouldn't have called you. You'll take this on and work yourself into a frenzy while you shadow me like a guard dog."

"You've got that right," he said, whirling so fast he had to catch her with his hands on her arms to keep from knocking her down. Holding her there, he stared into her eyes while memories filled his head. Sweet memories of summer nights and the wind lifting her hair. Nathan didn't want to let go—of her or the memories. But he shifted back, accepting that they'd been young and full of idealistic dreams back then. Things had changed so much since that sweet summer.

"I'm okay," she said, lifting away to move past him in a quick rush. "I'll be all right, Nathan. Please don't make a fuss. Let's just do our jobs."

"Is that a hint to back off?"

"Not a hint. A request. We have to remain professional and focus on this case. You have to trust me."

"I do trust you, but I also need to make sure nothing happens to you."

She went behind the big desk and sank down into the chair. "Nothing is going to happen," she said. "I hope that with all my heart and I'm thankful that you're willing to drop everything to help me. But you can't panic every time I leave a room."

"Okay, all right," he said through a breath. "I was tired and I woke up in a different place. Don't make any rash decisions about going back to the city. That's the last place you need to be and I don't care what your boss thinks."

"Well, that's understandable because you're tired, same as me. I don't want to seem ungrateful for what you've done for me but I have another option at least. I was in a panic last night."

"You had to be to call me," he said, wishing he could be the first person she called instead of the last.

"I'm better now and regretting that I dragged you into this. But you're allowed to get some rest even if it's on the office couch."

"Sorry," he said. "Waking up like that is part of my job since I move around so much."

He wouldn't tell her that he woke in hotel rooms a lot but this was different. Hotel rooms were impersonal and sterile to the point of being boring. This house, which was now a community center, still held the charm and homey feeling that he remembered so well. Being here again brought it all back, the many hours he'd spent with Alisha, walking the grounds, falling in love and trying to figure out his future. A future he'd hoped to have with her. He'd never imagined that summer so long ago, that being with her would change his life forever in both good and bad ways.

"I understand." Her green eyes softened. Was she remembering, too? "Do you ever stop thinking about her?"

"Who?"

Alisha's eyes held his for a few ticking seconds. "Hannah."

Nathan's heart lurched each time he heard his sister's name. But hearing Alisha say it with a quiet reverence almost did him in. So he turned sarcastic. "No. Never."

"That's what I thought," Alisha said. "I think about her a lot, too, especially around the holidays."

"Can we change the subject?" he snapped, wishing he could wipe some of his memories away. Then because she looked so crushed and her cheeks blushed a bright pink, he added, "It's still hard, Alisha. I'm sorry."

Alisha nodded and studied the notes in front of her. "All the more reason to remember why we need to keep at this and get it over with."

"Agreed," he said, wanting to fight with her some more. But he couldn't bring himself to do that. She blamed herself for Hannah's disappearance and death, same as he did. But it wasn't her fault.

He was solely to blame for his little sister leaving

the house that stormy summer day. Hannah had gone looking for him. She'd gotten lost and...

Closing his eyes, he tried to get the image of his sister calling after him out of his head and instead focused on Alisha and her open laptop. "What have you got?"

"I found the names of the victims," she said. "Joshua and Tiffany West."

"Hmm. Common names. Could be aliases."

"You don't trust anyone, do you?"

"I've had too many Tiffanys in my life."

"Oh, really?"

"Here and there."

"I'd say more here than there. Do you date a lot, Nathan?"

"Here and there. Jealous?"

"Nope. Just curious."

"What about you? Got anyone special in your life?"

"*That* is *neither* here *nor* there," she retorted, her tone telling him she could be a tad bitter about any love connections.

He thought of her briefcase and how she carried it like a shield. Same as him, she was married to her work. They both wore the armor of indifference to hide the brutality of being hurt.

Back to business. "What else did you find?"

"Well, they live in an upscale part of the city in a new development. A modern condo in a building that went up about eight months ago. Comps sell for a million and over."

"How did you find out all of this while I slept?"

"I have my sources, PI Craig, same as you. My firm has been more than willing to help. As I said, Mr. Henderson had offered me protection, too."

Her firm would have investigators. "Probably not as good as me, though."

"They found the information I needed and during a holiday week at that."

"Touché," he said, admiring her determination. "Anything else I need to know?"

"Mitchell Henderson recognized the West couple, told me he'd been at a fund-raiser or two where they'd been top donors. He claims they like to flash their money."

She studied the screen and then let out a gasp. "Dr. and Mrs. Joshua West. He has a family practice and—this is interesting—she's a pharmaceutical sales rep, which my boss failed to mention. That explains the fancy sports car and all the shopping bags."

"Those things didn't save them," he replied.

"No, but their lifestyle might have something to do with the way they died. I mean, a doctor and a big pharma rep. Are you thinking what I'm thinking?"

"Illegal drugs? Now who's not trusting?"

"Look, we know it had to be a professional hit," she reminded him. "I'm trying to get a report from the crime scene but my connections only go so far."

"So *now* you need me around," he teased, a sense of relief washing over him. He needed to be needed to keep from going to that dark place that kept him up at night.

"Yes, now you can make yourself useful." Her smile softened the edge. "Do what you do best—get to the truth."

"Is that what I do?" He felt the glow of her praise even if she might be sarcastic.

"You do." She nodded and placed her elbows on the desk then cupped her hands together to rest her chin on them while she stared over at him. "And for once, I don't care what nefarious methods you use."

"I have friends in high places," he said. "And some in low places. Let me make some calls and call in some favors. Maybe we can put our own case file together soon." Then he added, "If you think the FBI will get involved, you must believe this wasn't random."

She closed her eyes for a moment. "No. It felt deliberate. Like a professional hit."

Nathan couldn't argue with that. "If that's the case, this could go way beyond just protecting you. You'll be questioned by everyone from Campton Creek police to the state police and the Philly police. And probably the DEA."

"Yes," she said. "I'll tell them everything I witnessed. I just need to get there from here."

"Yes, because we can only hide you for so long."

Giving him that lifted-chin attitude, she said, "I'll do whatever needs to be done to find these killers."

"That's what I thought," he said with a grim smile.

She gave him a grim smile back. "Meantime, I'll go and find us some lunch."

"So far, so good," he replied watching her walk out into the hallway. "Be aware."

She turned at the door. "Always."

Nathan marveled at her calm nature. But then Alisha had always had a good head on her shoulders and a sense for doing the right thing. That's why she'd walked away from him.

A flash came through the window, causing Nathan to reach for his gun and rush to the hallway door. Grabbing her, he said, "Get down."

Alisha crouched with him as he guided her into the

hallway. Nathan held a hand on her back and whispered, "Get in the powder room and lock the door."

"My phone—"

"No time. Now."

She did as he told her while he slipped to the front window and peeked out. No one. Nathan circled to the portico door and keyed the code to open it. After slipping out, he reset the code to lock the door behind him.

Broad daylight and someone was already messing with them.

This situation would not go away until they did something about it.

Easing through the shaded portico, he felt the chill of the day in spite of the sun. When he heard a noise near the west side of the garage, Nathan skirted some old-root camellias and slid up against the house. Then he did a quick glance around the corner and spotted a man with a huge camera.

A reporter or someone who needed to prove she was alive and hiding here?

The news of the murders had been all over the papers, television news and online sources. Someone must have gotten Alisha's name. He'd take care of this intruder.

"Hey," he called as he climbed out of the camellias with his gun in plain sight. "What are you doing?"

The man jeered at him. "I'm just doing my job. Heard a woman staying here might have some information on those murders in Philadelphia the other night."

"You heard wrong. No one here to talk to you."

The scruffy man came close, his beard and hat covering most of his face. Nathan studied him. He looked disheveled and his posture held an edge that reeked of someone posing as a photographer.

Nathan didn't waste any time. The man gave him a quick glance and made his move, lifting the camera in the air to strike at the same time Nathan grabbed him with one hand and pushed him up against the side of the brick home, causing the camera to fall into the bushes. Placing his handgun against the man's ribs, he said, "I suggest you tell me who you really are and who sent you here."

Alisha came out of the powder room and ran to the office to find her phone. She pulled on her heavy sweater and dropped the phone in the pocket. After searching the room, she grabbed a small porcelain statuette that was probably worth more than a week's salary. But it would make a good weapon.

After searching all the rooms downstairs, she came back to the stairs and crossed over to the carriage house, keying in the code for the door to open.

"Granny?"

"We're right here, Alisha."

She sighed and rushed inside the sitting room to find her grandmother and Mrs. Campton working on a Christmas-inspired jigsaw puzzle. "Are you two all right?"

"Why wouldn't we be?" Miss Judy asked, her elegant eyebrows lifting. "We've both had some soup and it's about time for our afternoon naps. You should rest, too. You look exhausted."

"Did you hear any noises? See a camera flashing?"

"We don't hear very well," her grandmother pointed out. "And we have the drapes shut to stay warm."

"Good," Alisha said, hurrying to the window. Then she saw an official-looking SUV, lights flashing, as it turned into the drive up to the house.

"Now I see something flashing," Miss Judy said, pointing to where Alisha stood. "Do we have company?"

"The state police," Alisha replied. "And Nathan's dragging a man toward the vehicle. I'd better go down."

"No, young lady, you stay right here with us," her grandmother admonished. "Whoever's intruding on our property shouldn't see you here. He might think you're here, but he doesn't need to verify that fact."

Impressed with her spry grandmother's way of thinking, she said, "I think he already knows I'm here." She watched as Nathan shoved the man toward Deputy Benton. "His camera flash alerted us. I guess Nathan found him and obviously called the police."

"You should let Nathan know you're with us," Granny said, nodding. "He'll worry if he can't find you."

Remembering how concerned he'd been this morning, Alisha nodded. "Good idea."

Alisha texted Nathan: *I'm with Granny and Mrs. C. We are all safe in the carriage house.*

She watched and waited. He tugged at his phone, read her text then turned to the window. Without showing her face, she quickly put her hand out, waved then stepped back. He'd be mad at her. Again.

That seemed to be the only relationship they had right now. One annoyed with the other, it usually involved him breaking the rules while she tried to abide by the law.

But she also knew that Nathan was an honest, good man who'd do anything to help someone in need. Even her.

"Everything okay?" Mrs. Campton asked in her serene way.

"Apparently, the intruder has been neutralized and is now taking a ride in an official SUV," Alisha replied. "Mind if I wait here for Nathan? I was supposed to stay locked in the powder room."

Her grandmother stood and tugged her close. "I'd feel better if you stayed right here, but the powder room was a good plan."

"He won't like me leaving the powder room. He tells me to stay put but I can't do that when people are prowling around."

"Men consider it their duty to protect the women they care about," Miss Judy said with that same serenity she'd always held.

Alisha stood back and stared at both of them, her heart bursting with love and a bit of bittersweet regret. "How did you both do it?"

"Do what?" Granny asked, her expression puzzled but pleased.

"Love the same man all of your life."

Her grandmother glanced at Miss Judy, their eyes holding some sort of secret message.

"Oh, that's easy," Miss Judy said with a smile. "It was our duty to protect them, too, in our own way, which is with prayer and understanding and by trying to meet them halfway in compromise. But mostly, we stayed with our husbands out of love. That's what commitment is all about—we love through the hard times and love through the pain and anger. Love conquers all."

Alisha didn't know how to respond to that. She wanted to believe those words, however. "Wow. That's amazing."

"That's life, darling," Miss Judy said. Then she slipped in a piece of the puzzle. "Aha! That piece has been nagging me all day!"

Alisha smiled and shrugged. "I think that's my problem. I feel like pieces of my puzzle are missing."

"You just have to find the right fit." Judy shrugged back with a giggle.

"I'll make you some tea," Granny said. "And I'm guessing you haven't had lunch."

Alisha relaxed in spite of her worries. "That sounds nice, Granny."

She couldn't confess, but each time Nathan ran out that door to protect her she worried fiercely for his safety and she remembered how much she'd loved him once.

Did that mean she was doing her duty to him?

Chapter Seven

"So our roaming photographer isn't talking much," Carson told Alisha and Nathan later that day while they sat huddled in the office. "Word is getting out, no matter that the authorities are keeping this on the down-low. People will figure out that Alisha is alive and well and hiding out in Campton Creek."

"Here's what we know about the man the police took away this morning," Nathan said, thinking they'd have to do this one step at a time. The newshounds smelled a good story and they'd want to interview the only eyewitness to these murders, even if it put that witness in danger.

Alisha lifted her chin, ready to do battle. "Tell me everything."

"Corey Cooper. He actually is a reporter-photographer, but his shady tactics have given him a pretty impressive rap sheet—petty stuff such as trespassing on private property, breaking and entering and one assault charge since he's become aggressive in doing his job."

"Well, now he's got an even more impressive rap

sheet," Carson noted. "Trespassing and another near assault—on you."

Alisha shook her head. "I guess he'd make money getting a scoop on the unidentified witness everyone wants to talk to—and that would be me."

"He's been fired several times over," Nathan continued. "Now he's freelance and struggling, desperate. Says the person who hired him left a big wad of money in a safety deposit box at a bank in Philadelphia. The Philadelphia police are checking into the bank since a manager had to give him access per the client."

"So he won't talk because he doesn't know who hired him?" Alisha asked.

"Or he won't talk because he *does* know who hired him and he's afraid he'll be next on the hit list," Nathan replied, still sore that she'd left the powder room. He decided there was no point in telling this woman what to do. She'd always been independent and stubborn.

"Probably the latter," Carson said, nodding. "They'd need proof that you're here. Hiring a somewhat experienced reporter known for snooping on his own allows them to keep their identity a secret." He stood and gave them both a stern glance. "You two stay out of trouble. I'll check on you later today."

"Thank you," Alisha said, her gaze touching on Nathan. "I'm worried about Mrs. C and my grandmother but they seem to be taking all of this excitement in stride."

"A formidable pair," Carson said. "Those two are solid in their faith."

Nathan didn't voice what he was thinking. His parents were solid in their faith, too, but that had not brought his sister back. Nathan couldn't accept that

Hannah's unsolved death was the will of God. Now he was being overprotective with Alisha. But the thought of something happening to her gave him chills.

Alisha watched him as if she knew his every thought. "I don't want to continue this—putting them in danger. These people are vicious."

"You're still in the best place possible," Nathan said, meaning it. "Strangers tend to stand out around here and news travels fast. Even though no one has identified you publicly and most people don't know you're here, I'm sure the whole town is on the watch whether we realize it or not. The shooting has been reported all across the state and we have an officer dead and one in the hospital because of this. Not to mention a car that went over a ravine not far from here."

"Anyone can trace the license plate back to me." Alisha shook her head. "This is such a mess. I should go into hiding somewhere far away from here."

"You know they'll find you," Nathan said. "Look, this place is a stronghold. Carson's gone out of his way to help and the state police have agreed to place officers around the property. And… I'm here. I won't let you go out there alone."

Her twisted frown and straight-out stare indicated frustration but her eyes held apprehension. Both echoes of how Nathan felt but he wouldn't tell her that. Of course, he'd shown her *his* apprehension over and over. No wonder she was ready to bolt.

"I have to go," Carson said. "I do have regular duties to carry out."

Nathan walked with him to the door. "We'll compare notes later."

After Carson left, he turned to find Alisha staring

at him with that stern expression on her heart-shaped face. "What?"

She lifted away from the door jamb. "Are you and Carson telling me everything?"

"Of course. You've been right here the whole time we've talked."

"But you two have a thing."

"A thing?"

"Yes. He goes out of his way to help you, even so far as sharing the details of an open, active case."

"A lot of law enforcement personnel share with private detectives and investigators. It's how we get things done."

"I understand but how did you two become friends?"

Chafing under her scrutiny, Nathan moved past her and back into the office. "I knew him growing up and then when I left Campton Creek, he was one of the few people I stayed in touch with. He suggested I become a private investigator."

"Because you were born to do that or because you feel the need to help others find their loved ones? So they won't have to go through what your family did?"

So she wanted to get to the core of what drove him and made him tick? He didn't want to bring up Hannah's death. "A little of both, I think. And I don't want to talk about that."

"*That* is like the elephant in the room, Nathan."

"It doesn't concern you."

"Right. Hannah will always concern me."

"No," he said, anger washing over him. "She is not *your* concern."

"But I was part of the problem that night."

"I tried to tell you then and now—I don't blame you for what happened to Hannah."

"But Nathan, you blamed me when you came to me in the park after…after they'd found her. You said we should have never been together that night."

Shaking his head, he stood silent before responding. "I was angry at the world. I didn't handle any of it very well." His expression softening, he added, "I wish I could take back what I said to you but…maybe things worked out for the best with us."

"Then why won't you talk to me? Be honest with me."

He couldn't do this. Not now when he was already antsy and wired. "Alisha, let it go, okay? She's gone. I can't change that."

"So you do still blame me."

He didn't want her to keep thinking anything was her fault. Hannah's death was on him and they both knew it. "I'm the one to blame. Me, alone. She would have never run out into a storm that night if I hadn't left. And we need to get back to trying to figure out who's trying to kill you. That's my priority right now."

"I wish I'd never called you."

"Well, you did and now you're stuck with me, so that line is getting old."

They had a stare-down right there, just inches between them but so much distance, Nathan knew they'd never reach a peaceful compromise.

He'd keep her alive and then he'd be out of her life again. This time for good.

Two hours later, Alisha pulled the last of the sugar cookies out of the oven. "Okay, Granny, this batch makes six dozen cookies. I hope that's enough for the baskets we're putting together."

Frazzled from searching for answers on the two men who were now wanted by the law, she'd offered to help her grandmother make cookies. The reprieve had cleared her head, at least.

"Plenty, darling," her grandmother replied. "Why don't you make us some Christmas tea while these finish cooling? Then we'll ice them and hopefully we can deliver them tomorrow."

The kitchen smelled of sugar and spice, the familiar scents making Alisha wish this was an ordinary day during the Christmas season. A day where she could go for a walk near the creek or stroll through one of the garden trails.

Alisha wanted to help deliver the cookies, but Nathan had warned her she needed to stay hidden here on the estate. Growing up, she'd always enjoyed baking and decorating Christmas cookies and then going on the deliveries afterward. Her grandmother knew a lot of people within the Amish community so they'd bundle up and head out in Granny's sturdy station wagon and go door-to-door visiting with several of the Amish families, Miss Judy all warm and cozy in the back seat. They'd come home with baked goods and handmade trinkets from their Amish friends.

The first time she'd ever seen Nathan had been during one of those deliveries. A senior in high school, she'd been fascinated with the Amish for a long time. Her parents didn't like coming here much, called it country and boring, but Alisha loved the quietness of this quaint village and the history behind it even if her mother, who'd been raised here, resented it. Charlotte

Willis Braxton, married to a successful Boston lawyer and herself a tenured professor, loved the big city and her society friends but Alisha loved Campton Creek.

One smile from Nathan and she'd become even more intrigued with the Amish. He might have jumped the fence but when he smiled now, she saw that rugged, handsome boy who'd taken her heart over a basket of freshly baked cookies.

Pushing away that memory and those of the summer afterward, when she and Nathan met again and became so close that they fell in love, she thought about the faith and strength in this community.

Admiral Edward Campton Senior's grandfather had owned most of the land on both sides of the winding creek that deepened near the big covered bridge in the middle of the community. When an Amish couple with six hungry children had knocked on the door of Campton House one cold winter, Mr. Campton had invited them in and his wife had fed them and then they'd let the family stay in their home until they could make arrangements for them.

That led to the couple moving into another home the Camptons owned—their original farmhouse. The couple worked the land and helped them around the estate to pay them back. Mr. Campton gifted them with the land and the rental house so the Amish family could stay. Then word got out.

Soon, he was selling off land to the Amish until all he had left was the estate grounds. The story went that Grandfather Campton could never turn down anyone in need and that the Amish around here had stayed by his side until the day he died. Then they'd helped his widow and now Miss Judy after the Admiral died. When the

Campton's only son Edward Junior, a navy SEAL, had died in combat, the Amish had been the first to show up and organize everything while they grieved.

Alisha had looked forward to this week, but now she was back under the worst of circumstances.

The teakettle whistled rudely, bringing her out of her memories. Alisha made two cups of tea and found her grandmother in the little sitting room with two iced tree-shaped cookies.

"There you are," Granny said. "Let's enjoy the fruits of our labor. And while we're at it, let's talk about what's going on."

Alisha sat down in the cushioned chair beside the sofa. "A murder case. Not what I wanted to bring for Christmas."

"I know all about that horrible incident," Granny replied, her eyes warm and knowing. "I'm sure the authorities will find these evil people. I'm more concerned about you."

"I'll be okay," Alisha said, wanting to reassure her grandmother. "I'm being careful and alert and we have people watching out for all of us."

"I mean you and Nathan."

"Oh." Alisha glanced over at her grandmother. "Do you think I was wrong to turn to him?"

"No, I'm thankful that you called on Nathan for help."

"Then what are you fretting about?"

"I know how intense things got with you two long ago. Your mother might not ever forgive either of us for that."

"Mom knows how to hold a grudge but I can't change that," Alisha said. "It ended and... I have a good life now."

"But you're alone and so is he."

"And that's the way it has to be for now, Granny. You aren't suggesting that Nathan and I—"

"Get back together?" Her prim grandmother looked a tad too guilty. "The thought did cross my mind. He's no longer Amish and you're still single."

Alisha shook her head. "I'm sorry but that can't happen. We're two very different people now. I have my work and…he lives for his work."

"Work isn't life, darling."

"But it's all I have."

Alisha put a hand to her mouth. "You managed to force that confession right out of me and with a cookie to bribe me."

Bettye laughed. "I suppose I did at that." Putting down her china teacup, she took Alisha's hand in hers. "I'm so proud of you but I want you to be happy. Not just content. But truly happy the way your grandfather and I were."

Alisha had long ago given up on that kind of happiness. "So you never regretted leaving your family?"

Granny stared across the room to the one card she'd received early on from her mother, telling her that she would always love her. She'd framed that card, a beautiful sketching of Amish country in Ohio. "I regret nothing. I've missed them, no doubt, and we did finally reach out to each other and I've kept in touch enough to attend funerals and send Christmas cards, but I knew I belonged with your grandfather and so, no, I've never regretted that. I loved him enough to leave everything else behind."

Alisha could see that love in her grandmother's eyes. "I think that might be the problem with Nathan and me, Granny. He loved his sister and now she's dead. He thinks he'd not worth anyone's love. And he sure doesn't want to be with me, especially when I'm partially to blame."

Granny shook her head. "No, ma'am, you are not to blame and neither is Nathan. *Gott*'s will."

Alisha couldn't accept that. "So God wanted Nathan's family to suffer and automatically accept Hannah's death and then just move on?"

"No, God knows their anguish and he knows their strength. But we can't question the ways of the Lord. There is a reason for everything. I know your analytical brain can't quite accept faith the way I do, but I also know that you depend on the Lord same as me."

"I do depend on God because you taught me that and I pray every day that Nathan can get over Hannah's death and finally find some peace in his life. He's always out there searching, trying to help others. But why can't he heal and move on with his own life?"

The door to the apartment slammed, causing Alisha to come out of her chair and whirl around.

Nathan stood there staring at her with such anger she actually took a step back. "What business is it of yours whether I find any peace of not?" he asked. "You don't know me anymore and you certainly don't need to waste your prayers on me. What *you* should do is let go of that heavy blame *you* want to keep. You have no part in this."

Chapter Eight

"Nathan."

He turned and whirled back to the door. Alisha glanced at her grandmother. "What should I do?"

"Go talk to him," Granny said, nodding, her tone solemn.

Alisha grabbed a wool wrap, hurried across the breezeway and spotted him out in the back garden, staring off toward the water beyond the trees. Without thinking, she ran into the big house and hurried down the stairs toward the sunroom. When she opened the French doors out onto the terrace, a burst of cold, late-day air greeted her, pricking at her eyes and causing them to water.

Or maybe she was crying real tears for the man who stood hunched over, his hands in the pocket of his jeans. How long would he carry this burden?

As she drew closer, she called out. "Nathan?"

He pivoted, the anger she'd heard in his voice still smoldering in his eyes. Stalking toward her, he stopped a few feet away. "You shouldn't be out here."

"I'm worried about you," she said, a cold mist of

breath heaving into the air. "Come back inside by the fire."

He didn't move. He scanned the trees and woods. "I needed some air. And you need to get back inside."

"No, I'm not going in without you. You're exhausted and you need food and rest—not just coffee."

"Don't tell me what I need, Alisha."

"Then don't pretend you don't care. I know what you heard in there hurt you and I'm sorry."

"You've been sorry for a long time now, but I've tried to tell you this is not your burden to bear."

"This burden," she said, advancing toward him, "is all about your need to be a martyr because of Hannah. For Hannah. That's why you left, right? You decided on your own that you were no longer worthy of being Amish. And you decided you no longer wanted to be with me."

Lifting her hand out to make her point, she added, "Have you ever considered how arrogant that is? That you get to suffer but no one else is allowed, that you won't try to turn this grief over to God and let Him help you to heal. We get through these things because our faith gives us strength. And yet, you push everyone away when you could let all of us help you."

"That's right. I decided. End of discussion. You don't get to suffer along with me."

Alisha stopped short and drew back. "What did you say?"

"I said—"

A shot rang out, echoing through the woods and causing the forest animals down by the creek to scurry into action. Nathan dived for Alisha, knocking her to the ground near an arbor with a leafless vine covering it.

"Are you hit?" he asked, his anxious gaze sliding over her face.

"No, I'm all right," she said, too numb to even feel a bullet. "What do we do now?"

He glanced up and then back toward the woods. "A sniper near the water. I told you to go inside."

"I wanted to talk to you."

Another shot hit one of the arbor posts, nicking the wood into splinters that rained down on their heads.

He didn't fuss at her anymore. "We need to find shelter. I don't have my weapon."

Alisha glanced around, checking to make sure her grandmother wasn't peeking out the back window. Then she spotted the sunroom door. "I left the door cracked."

Nathan looked into her eyes. "I'm going to move over and I want you to crawl into the arbor and get behind one of the chairs."

"What about you?"

"Don't worry about me."

Like asking her not to breathe. She'd been worrying about him since the night he'd told her he was leaving Campton Creek. Without her.

"I told you I'm not going back inside without you," she reminded him.

"Stop being so stubborn and do as I'm asking," he replied, a soft plea in his words.

Alisha didn't want to add to their troubles by being stubborn, so she caved. If she did get in the house, she could call for help, at least. "Okay, but...don't get shot."

She knew he wouldn't care if he took a bullet, but she sure would. Admitting that gave her courage. "Okay, let me up and I'll hide over by the table and chairs."

Nathan nodded and lifted up to squint into the sunny

woods. "I see a glint. Could be our man. To the east near that big oak tree."

"I'll take your word for it," Alisha said, afraid to move.

"Are you ready?"

"Yes."

Nathan gave her one last look, his hand briefly touching her cheek as he did a drop-and-roll. Alisha did the same, flipping over to crawl toward the shelter of the old arbor, her wrap caught against her skin and the rocky dirt, tearing, holding her back. Thankfully the chairs underneath were tightly woven black metal, a slight source of protection.

Another shot rang out and Nathan crouched down and ran toward her. "We're pinned in and I don't have my phone."

"I didn't bring mine," Alisha said. "Only open air between us and that door." She shivered, grabbed at her tattered wrap. It was ruined but still warm.

Nathan scooted closer and tugged her into his arms. "I've got you, Alisha. No matter what, you need to remember that."

Huddled in the safety of his arms, Alisha prayed for this brave, tortured man. He'd been in her peripheral vision since she'd been eighteen. But now she was beginning to see him straight on and clearly.

Touching her fingers to his jaw, she said, "I've got you, too. You need to remember that."

The darkness in his eyes shifted and lightened, a brief shard of clarity shining through as he gazed into her eyes.

And her heart was remembering why she'd fallen for him in the first place.

"Nathan, I—"

Another shot hit the still, cold air. The bullet ricocheted off one of the old chairs and pinged into the shrubbery behind them.

"Not a trained sniper or we'd both be dead. But close enough to hit one of us if he doesn't let up," Nathan said.

Then something happened that had both of them sitting up to take notice.

The sunroom door flew back, and her grandmother stood with a high-powered rifle, her eyes, bifocals in place, set against the scope. Bettye stood perfectly still, aimed and fired at least three rounds into the woods.

Alisha heard her grandmother calling, "Run. Hurry. I'll cover you."

They ran quickly, staying against the shrubbery until they were close to the open door. Bettye backed away but kept the rifle in sight of the woods. She kept firing until they were through the door. While they collapsed against the floral porch couch, Granny sent out one more volley and then closed the door with such a proper ladylike slam, they both started laughing.

"Granny, where did you learn to shoot like that?"

"From me," came the voice from behind them. They looked back into the parlor and saw Judy Campton in her wheelchair, a slick pistol centered on her lap.

"I will never forget what I witnessed here today," Nathan said to Alisha.

They sat at the kitchen table, safe and warm, while two officers combed the woods for shell casings and worked on a grid of the yard, hoping they could find bullets to turn over to ballistics. The shooter was long gone, leaving only some muddy footprints by the creek.

After talking to the officers on the scene, Carson told

them to stay in for the rest of the day. Alisha had chosen to remain close to her grandmother, so Nathan followed her and here they sat, eating supper and waiting.

At least they had something interesting to talk about.

"So Mrs. Campton and you learned how to shoot to protect yourselves?" Alisha asked, her tone telling Nathan that she was still shocked. Shocked about the whole episode and about his remarks to her, too, probably.

"I actually learned how growing up Amish," Bettye explained. "But Judy and I have perfected the art."

"So you practiced through the years?" Alisha asked.

"Obviously," Judy said with a serene smile. "I taught her a few tricks I learned from the Admiral."

Bettye laughed and shook her head. "Girls aren't supposed to be interested in guns but I watched and listened whenever my *daed* and brothers would sit cleaning their hunting weapons. They used them to hunt or to scare off predators."

Nathan shot Alisha a quick smile. He was still angry at her but he'd cooled his jets so he could keep his head in the game. He hadn't meant to hurt her earlier but some things needed to be left unsaid. Her accusations against him still stung. How was he supposed to get over his sister's death when he was reminded about Hannah each time his phone rang, each time he had to tell another family that their loved one wasn't returning?

He'd found a lot of people safe and sound but he'd also discovered a few who were dead and gone. It never got easier and he never found any relief. Was he being too self-righteous by refusing to let go of his grief? Should he depend more on God and less on his own tormented assumptions?

He couldn't think about that right now.

"But you never used a gun?" he asked Bettye while they tried to enjoy the meal she and Mrs. Campton had insisting on preparing.

"I had to learn the hard way one day when all the menfolk were in town loading up supplies for the spring plantings. A big snake showed up out near the barn. I think it was a timber rattlesnake. Scared my poor *mamm* almost to death."

"You shot the snake?" Alisha asked, a buttered roll in her hand.

"I tried. Missed the first couple of times but then I remembered how calm my *daed* would be when he held a gun to shoot an animal or a varmint." She gave a dainty shrug. "So I calmed down, aimed and boom, that snake lived no more."

"Your grandmother is a remarkable woman," Mrs. Campton added with a smile. "After they heard that story when we were all still so young, my sailor and your granddaddy got it in their heads they'd take us to target practice in case we ever needed to use a weapon."

"I haven't fired a rifle in years," Granny said, shaking her head.

"Well, today, you did just that," Mrs. Campton said. "Good thing we kept up the practice as long as we did."

"Yes, good thing." Nathan finished the baked chicken and mashed potatoes and stood. "Ladies, thank you for the food. But I need to go and see what the law found out there today."

Alisha glanced up at him. "I'm going to stay here and help clean the table. I'll talk to you later."

He nodded, the moment of silence between them shouting too loudly while the two Annie Oakleys gave each other speaking looks.

Excusing himself, he turned and left before they forced him to eat a piece of coconut cake. The food was great and being pampered reminded him of home, but Nathan knew in his heart he had to control all of these sentimental feelings coursing through his system. He'd find these killers and then he'd be on his way, on to the next case. Finding people was his thing.

What if he couldn't find the murderers, though? Would Alisha have to spend the rest of her life with this threat hanging over her head? She already blamed herself for what had happened to Hannah.

That's partly your fault.

His memories of the past suddenly shouted loud and clear.

"I shouldn't be here with you, Alisha. I should have stayed with my family. Hannah is gone and now I've lost everything."

Nathan could never forget the shattered look in her misty eyes nor the pain and shame he'd seen on her face as they stood in the park one last time.

"You still have me, Nathan."

"No, I can't be with you now. Not like this."

She'd started crying but she didn't beg him to stay. No, Alisha took matters into her own hands. "Then you won't have me in your life anymore. I won't be a reminder of what has happened. I can't live with your resentment."

With that, she'd turned and ran back toward Campton House. He had not seen her again until a couple years ago when the Admiral had died and Mrs. Campton had invited Nathan to the dedication of Campton House as a community center.

If he could take it all back…

He'd said some awful things that night after they'd heard Hannah was found dead. Lashing out at Alisha had made sense at the time but he'd regretted it a thousand times over.

And today, he'd said another horrible thing to her. He didn't want to share this burden, this torment. He'd held it around his heart like an armor of shame. He *had* become a martyr of sorts, pushing away the world he'd so longed to be a part of and shutting out those who loved him the most.

When would he stop punishing himself?

And her?

Nathan texted Carson and told him he'd be in the office.

A knock at the front door brought Nathan out of his dark thoughts.

Carson came in, the cold blasting behind him. "More snow tonight so I hope the bullets and casings they found will provide something to work with."

"But no sign of the shooter?"

"Nah. He must have taken a rowboat up the creek to get here. Then once he was fired on, he had to have jumped in the boat and paddled away to hide out somewhere across the shore. They went around to search and ask if anyone had seen him. Got nothing. But several people did hear the shooting."

"Yes, pretty hard not to hear in such a quiet place."

"Look, Nathan, I have a suggestion."

"I'm listening."

"Word will spread and more people will come looking. The press is hot for a grisly story and this one fills the bill."

"So?"

"So, I think you and Alisha should go deeper into hiding."

"And where do you think we should go?"

Carson scratched his head and stared into Nathan's eyes. "The last place a killer would look for you. Amish country."

"We are in Amish country," Nathan pointed out.

"I mean all the way in. Dress the part, play the part, find someone you can trust to hide you."

"The Amish don't condone violence and dishonesty. I won't bring that on this community."

"It's already here."

"And what about Bettye and Mrs. Campton?"

"Those two won't leave but the town police can assign two officers to patrol the grounds day and night." Then he shrugged. "And from what I've heard about today, I'd say the women can hold their own if push comes to shove."

Nathan turned toward the fire and stared at the flames. "Alisha won't like this."

"What won't I like?"

They both looked up to find Alisha standing in the hallway, her eyes full of questions and her expression full of stubbornness.

Chapter Nine

"Nathan, what's going on now?"

Alisha saw the look that passed between the two men. "One of you had better start talking."

Nathan scratched his head and turned to her. "We need to go into hiding away from Campton House."

"I couldn't agree more but you both told me this is the safest place for us right now."

"We thought that," Nathan replied, his eyes stormy blue. "But they breached the estate from the water today and they'll find another way in."

"Then what's the plan?" she asked as she stepped close to the fire, her shivers coming from the fear holding her like a clawing hand. "Where are we going?"

Nathan looked uncertain and Carson stared at the floor.

"Carson thinks we should hide in plain sight—within the Amish community."

Alisha's shock returned with a jolt. "What? And put more innocent people in harm's way. I won't do it. I'll go back to Reading and rent a hotel room. Or I'll head straight back to Philadelphia."

"You can't do that, Alisha. They'll track your every move."

"And they won't do that here?"

"Out there, they have a better chance of finding you," Nathan said, his gaze beseeching. "The Amish won't condone violence or danger but they will protect someone in need."

"There has to be a better way," she said. "A safe house somewhere."

"The Amish community is safe," Carson finally said. "If we find the right family and you two can blend in and follow the rules, you should be fine."

"But how will we find the right family?" Alisha paced by the fire, her boots hitting the hardwood floor. "I'm not doing this. It's not right to put a family in jeopardy."

"There is one other option," Nathan said, his eyes on her.

She stared him down while Carson looked confused. "I'm listening."

"I can take you to my cabin."

That halted Alisha in her tracks. "What?"

Carson ran a hand down his five-o'clock shadow. "I don't know—"

Nathan held up his hand to stop both of them. "It's on the fringes of the Amish community, deep in the woods. Few people even know it's there. We can dress to look Amish and sneak out after dark." He nodded to Alisha. "I know you keep Amish clothes here, as needed."

"You know too much," she retorted, the thought of going deep into the woods with this lone wolf scaring her in a different way. "But yes, we have the proper clothing."

Carson put his hands on his hips. "You can't take your vehicle. They might have seen it here before you hid it in the garage."

"We'll walk," Nathan said. "We'll bundle up and keep to the paths, not the main roads. My cabin sits about three miles from the main road."

"I can find someone to watch near the woods," Carson said. "I know where a deer stand is hidden near your cabin. We can put an off-duty officer there. So no official vehicles will give you away and he can keep watch and alert you by phone if he notices anyone headed that way."

"This is ridiculous," Alisha said. "They can follow us on foot and then we'll have nowhere to hide."

"Do you want to risk another attack here?" Nathan asked.

"No." She didn't want that but she didn't like *this.* They stood staring at each other until she finally let out a sigh. "I'll have to explain to my grandmother."

"You can tell her you're leaving, but don't tell her where you're going," Nathan suggested. "The less she knows, the better."

"I agree." Alisha gave Nathan one last look, her heart in a panic. Would she be able to do this? To run away with the man she'd tried to forget? Once, leaving with Nathan had been her dream. Now she was living a nightmare.

Nathan reached out a hand to her. "You know I wouldn't do this if we had any other choice. I promise I'll protect you and I'll make sure your grandmother and Mrs. Campton are safe."

Carson nodded. "The Amish are getting word that something is brewing but they tend to stay out of matters of the law. They'll keep an eye on Campton House, too. They will warn of anything strange happening."

Alisha pulled away from Nathan and sat down on a chair. "I don't know. I should have never come here in the first place." She let out a breath but held in her tears. "I just needed to see my grandmother."

Nathan bent down on one knee and took her hand again. "I understand. You wanted to feel safe, right?"

"Yes." She stared into his eyes. They were calm now, a deep blue calm that scared her all over again. "I was so frightened and in shock and I wasn't thinking straight."

He kissed her forehead, a brief touch of his lips to her skin. "It's going to be all right."

She savored that sweet gesture. "But you can't be sure, can you?"

His eyes flashed a pain so deep it cut straight to her heart. He was thinking of little Hannah. "No, I can't be sure. But I'm going to do my best to take care of you."

Carson cleared his throat. "What time do you want to leave?"

Nathan stood, his gaze still on Alisha. "Later tonight. At least, the moon isn't full."

Alisha stood. "I'll go and talk to Granny then I'll find some clothes for us."

Nathan lifted his chin in acknowledgement.

Once she was out of the office, Alisha stopped and stared out into the well-lit backyard. The trees and old shrubs she'd always loved now held a sinister, hulking presence. Leaving had to be the only way.

But the people who were after her wouldn't know she'd left. What if they came after her grandmother again?

Whirling back around, she crashed into Nathan and

grabbed his arms. "We need to put out the word that I've been placed in a safe house. In the city."

At first, Nathan balked and then realization hit him. "So they'll know you're no longer here?"

"Yes. Exactly. So they'll search for me somewhere else. Do you think Carson can make that happen?"

"He probably can. The locals in Philly might not like it. In all this confusion, I didn't get an opportunity to speak to you alone about something else that came up."

"What?"

"The FBI *is* on the case in Philly but they're being tight-lipped about the whole thing. They'll want to question you just as we thought. But they might also want to put you into protective custody."

"Did the town police tell them where I am?"

"Right now, you're classified as unavailable for questioning but you're willing to cooperate. Carson and Officer Cantor both gave the same statement."

"Right, but Carson's helping *unofficially*," she said, doubt in her eyes. "I don't want to get your friend in trouble. I need to meet with the FBI, but I also need to stay alive to do that."

Nathan nodded and scanned the windows. "They know that, so we'll wait to hear from them."

"But they might show up at the cabin."

"We don't have to tell them where you are. They'll get mad and then they'll get on with the job. We can stall."

"I see you're still good at going to ground."

"Been doing it most of my life."

"I'm too tired to argue," she admitted. "Let me go and explain to Granny, please."

"Do you need backup?"

"No."

She whirled to leave but turned. "Thank you, Nathan."

He nodded, watched her cross the breezeway and then turned as she entered the apartment door.

They were in this thing together now, no matter what. Alisha prayed they'd both come out alive.

Hours later, covered from head to toe, Alisha wearing a dark bonnet and black cloak, Nathan wearing a hat and heavy overcoat, they slipped away into the night.

Nathan kept her between him and the open fields as they followed the forest paths the Amish used to come and go around the country side. He had a small flashlight but only turned it on when the path grew heavy with overgrowth.

Alisha was quiet, allowing him to hold her arm as they hurried through the bitter cold. "Are you all right?" he whispered.

She nodded. "Granny is worried for me but she's brave. She'll pray for us. They are aware of the officers patrolling back and front now and the alarm is set."

"Carson and I checked everything one last time before we left," he said to reassure her.

Alisha stumbled and Nathan caught her against his chest. She felt so small and fragile but he knew the strength encased inside this woman's heart.

Staring up at him, she said, "They kept telling me they'd be fine. Their faith is solid—like a wall. But we both know faith can only carry you so far."

He held her there for a moment, accepting that she hadn't pushed him away, taking in her eyes and how innocent she looked. "Faith carries us all the way through," he replied. "Those two know that no matter what, God's will and their faith will see them to the end."

She did pull back then. "I don't want to prove that faith. I don't want one of them to die even if they are ready for Heaven."

"Don't think that way," Nathan told her as he guided her along. "We have to believe we'll all make it through this."

"I wish you and I could have that assurance. I'm trying."

He held her there. "I'm trying, too. And I'm sorry I got so angry today. Your words made me think about how prideful I am, refusing to turn back to God—I mean all the way back, not just when it's convenient."

Her eyes brightened, the sparse light sparkling through like joy. "Nathan, I'm glad to hear that."

"I guess being back here with your grandmother and you has brought out a lot of pent-up memories. I never gave up on God but I did give up on attending church. I hope He listens to a burned-out man with a chip on his shoulder, sitting on a park bench."

"I'm pretty sure He does," she replied, sending him a hopeful glance. "I hope He listens to a tired law associate who has to burn the midnight oil, even on Sunday mornings."

Nathan smiled at that. "I'm guessing He's listening right now as we head out into the woods on faith alone."

They started walking again, wary but less weary. "Up this way," Nathan said. "We have about a mile to go."

"Does that make my faith weak?" she asked, her

voice timid now. "I made that comment about not test-ing faith."

"What? Because you want your grandmother to live?"

"Yes. Does that make me selfish?"

"No, Alisha. That makes you human."

"I keep thinking if I hadn't stopped there, we'd all be oblivious and safe and enjoying the holidays. I would have heard about the shooting on the news but I could have gone on with my life."

"Stop second-guessing this thing," he gently chas-tised. "You can't go back and change what happened—you shouldn't have stopped there, you shouldn't have come here, you shouldn't have called me. None of that matters now. We're here and we have to stay one step ahead of these people. Of everything that you think you should or shouldn't have done, coming here was prob-ably the best decision considering the circumstances."

Easy for him to tell her that when he'd been think-ing along the same lines for years now.

They heard a noise off to the side.

Nathan guided her to a stand of saplings and held her there against a tree, his heartbeat bumping against hers. Putting a finger to his lips, he gave her a quick glance. Alisha nodded and held to him.

When he saw a huge shadow on the path, Nathan tugged her tightly into his arms. "If something goes wrong, run as fast as you can to the east and look for the Schrock farm."

She bobbed her head, her eyes wide with questions he wasn't ready to answer.

Nathan held her with one hand and placed his other

hand on his Beretta. Then he carefully looked around the tree and let out a grunt of relief.

"The big stag. Look. He hangs out in these woods. I've often left him food out my back door."

Alisha peeked over his shoulder and squinted in the scant light from the crescent moon caught between clouds. "Oh, my. He's a beauty."

The stag moved over the forest floor, lifting his head when he caught their scent. He stood majestic and still, the snow falling softly around him.

"A twelve-pointer if I'm seeing right," Nathan replied. "Hard to tell in the dark, but I think he's the one I feed every now and then when I'm home. We've become buddies."

"He's big enough to see us and I'm sure he knows we're intruders."

"Maybe he'll recognize my scent and let us be. He'll run when we make a move."

He took her hand and led her back onto the path, his small flashlight guiding them. "*As the deer pants for water…*"

"*So my soul longs for you, O God,*" she finished. "Psalm 42."

"Maybe God is giving us a sign."

"Or maybe a deer just crossed our path."

The big animal leaped into the air and crashed off through the forest.

"A sign," Nathan said, thinking he had not looked for signs from the Lord in a long time. But here he was with the one woman he could never get out of his system, trying to protect her, trying to find some sort of redemption. A bad idea or a second chance?

His heart filled with a strange sensation. A sense of

peace and home and security. Or maybe he was just cold and tired and seeing things that weren't really there.

But the night sky gave him comfort so he hurried Alisha along toward his tiny cabin. "We'll be there soon."

She gave him a little smile and held out her hand. Nathan accepted it like a lifeline, a thankfulness settling in his heart. Without a word they moved over the quiet snow and came up on the cabin.

"Home," Nathan whispered. Because for the first time in a long time, this place felt like home.

Chapter Ten

Alisha stood near the door while Nathan found the light switch. "I do have electricity," he said. "I didn't go totally off the grid."

"That's good to know."

He turned on a small lamp away from the two front windows, probably so no one would notice they were here. "It's not much and I'm not here very often but it'll keep us warm and, hopefully, safe."

"Do you have a security system?" she asked.

"Yes." He held up his Beretta. "This."

"Well, that's reassuring."

"Don't worry. I have good locks on the doors and the windows haven't been opened in years. We'd hear them groaning."

She took in the impressive fireplace and the worn black leather couch and tan-and-black plaid side chair. The room opened into the tiny efficiency kitchen where two more windows held heavy blinds over the sink.

"Has this cabin always been here?"

"Nope. I built it about five years ago."

The man never ceased to amaze her or surprise her. "By hand, I'm guessing."

"Yes. By hand with salvaged logs and lumber. It's solid."

As solid as the man who lived here alone. If he ever actually stayed here. "Do you come here a lot?"

"Only when I'm not on a case, which is pretty much never."

"You should take time, Nathan. Time for yourself."

Giving her a tightly controlled stare, he said, "I'll consider that once I know you're safe."

Alisha didn't push him. The man didn't ever want to talk about his own life. "I feel safe here," she admitted. The little cabin was cozy and homey but a bit spartan.

"The bedroom and bath are over there," he said, pointing to an open door. "I'll take the couch."

"You don't have to do that."

"Yes, I do. I can guard both the front and back doors."

"In that case, yes, I'll be glad to take the bedroom."

He moved around, checking the shadows, adjusting the curtains and blinds. "If you want to change, go ahead. I'll make us some coffee and we can map out a plan."

"A plan?"

"Just in case we have to run again," he said before turning to the stove.

Alisha took off her bonnet and heavy wool cap but left on her apron and dress. "I'm fine in these clothes for now."

Nathan quickly shed his overcoat and turned to stare at her. "Wow. With your hair pulled back and that dark blue dress on, you do look Amish."

"A lot more comfortable than the suits I usually

wear," she said, holding out the full skirt. "I have too many clothes so I can appreciate the simplicity of this outfit."

"The Amish are innovative and practical. Nothing is ever wasted."

Alisha stared him down. "You look rather Amish yourself."

"It never actually left my system. Old habits die hard."

He wore a deep blue long-sleeved shirt over brown broad-fall pants and dark laced-up boots. Seeing him dressed this way again brought back a lot of memories for Alisha.

"Those clothes are a little small for you," she noted while he washed the percolator and found a tin of coffee.

How could she ignore the way the shirt fit him too tightly? Nathan had always been handsome but now he held a world-weary attractiveness. She needed to remember they were no longer kids with a crush on each other.

But she also remembered what she'd felt for Nathan so long ago had been more than a crush. After they'd broken up, she'd decided to never let her guard down again. She shouldn't do that now.

He turned, checking on her quietness. "Yep. Not quite my size but at least all Amish clothes are made loose. That helps."

"Yes, my skirt is plenty big." She came out of her stupor and twirled around. "And warm."

Nathan was the quiet one now. His gaze moved over her with a deep warmth. Moving closer, he said, "You look beautiful."

"Thank you." They stalled out on the fashion talk. "Nathan, do you think they'll find us here?"

"I hope not. Carson and one of his men who looks similar to me took my truck to a motel out on the main highway and the police put two plainclothes officers nearby to see who shows. So we'll see if they go looking there first."

Alisha wondered if someone had seen them leaving the estate, but they'd circled back by the creek and crossed over the main covered bridge so it would look like they were walking from a nearby farm. The late hour would be questioned, but if stopped they'd had the excuse of visiting into the night with a sick relative.

"Why did you tell me to run to your father's house if something happened?" she asked, remembering his words from before.

"It's the closest one to this cabin," he explained when he brought over two cups of dark, rich coffee. "Just through the woods, about a half mile beyond the cabin. A narrow path but there. Look for the birdhouses."

He'd always loved building birdhouses. She still had one he'd made for her, a small white house with blue shutters and flowers painted on the sides. He told her a bluebird would live there when they built their house in the woods.

Alisha sat down on the cold leather couch, wanting to know everything about him. "Why did you change your name?"

He placed his coffee mug on the table by the side chair and turned to get a fire going. "Craig is my professional name," he said while he gathered kindling and found matches on the mantel. "I took a professional name to protect my family. I didn't want any of my findings to fall back on them."

"Ah, because sometimes you take on cases such as this one. Dangerous."

"Yes." He studied the growing fire and, satisfied, dusted off his hands and then sat down across from her. "I've brought them enough grief without having someone trying to get to me through them."

"And yet, you built a home nearby and told me to run to them."

"This is an unusual circumstance. I hope it won't come to that."

"Because it involves murder or because it involves me?"

"Both."

Alisha wasn't sure how to respond to his admission. The fire crackled in the quiet, its warmth reaching out to her shivering bones. "I won't say what I'm thinking."

Nathan put down his coffee cup and leaned forward. "I know what you're thinking. You tend to blame yourself for a lot that happens in life."

She couldn't deny that. "Yes, I guess I do. Being an only child can sure put a tremendous pressure on a person. Perfection is hard to achieve and so…guilt takes over."

"So you and your parents still don't see eye-to-eye?"

"No. My dad is mad that I didn't join his law firm right away and my mom is so involved in her teaching and research, she tends to forget I exist. I think I'm one big letdown."

"Your parents are stupid."

She burst out laughing at that. "Well, that or too intelligent for their own good."

"Sometimes intelligent people are the stupidest."

"Duly noted." She finished her coffee. "Let's talk about what we know so far on this case."

"So you're not ready to discuss all of our flaws and dysfunctions?"

She wanted to question him about so many things but Nathan would get the wrong idea and peg her as nosy. "No, are you?"

"Not in the least. Not right now, anyway." He grabbed the small leather overnight bag he'd brought with him. "I have written notes and I've saved some things on my laptop."

"Do we have Wi-Fi?"

He pulled out a heavy oval gadget. "Wireless hotspot. It's charged to last thirty-six hours and there's a tower about ten miles away."

"Always this prepared?"

"It's how I roll," he quipped. "I wind up in some sketchy places at times. But I've managed to get some solid information regarding this case. I have the police report."

"I'm not going to ask how you obtained that so quickly."

"Good, because I won't tell you who helped me."

"I've had my people digging, too." She reached for the briefcase she'd insisted on carrying underneath her cloak. "I printed mine out before we left."

"Smart. We can compare notes." Then he asked, "Have you explained all of this to your firm?"

"Yes. I didn't want my boss to hear about my involvement on the evening news or worry that I'd gone missing. I called the main office and talked to him and then asked for an investigator there to help with some online searches."

Remembering Mitchell Henderson's concern, Alisha knew the senior partner would stand by her. "You keep us posted," he'd said during their conversation. "These people need to be stopped."

He'd questioned her in his lawyerly way, asking for details on the shooter. She gave him what she knew which, beyond a description, wasn't too much.

"Do you trust the people you work with to keep this quiet? They can't reveal where you are."

"Of course." Telling Nathan about her conversation with Mitchell, she nodded. "Why wouldn't I trust them? They know this is a bad situation."

"Because whoever is behind this is ruthless and will stop at nothing to get to you, including infiltrating your workplace."

"Do you think they'll go after my boss and coworkers?"

"To get to you, possibly. But since you've warned your firm, I hope they're all on the alert."

"Knowing Mr. Henderson, I can almost guarantee that. We have a top-notch security protocol online and on the premises."

"Okay, just needed to check that off my list."

"Thanks. Now I can add worrying about adding the dozens of people who work with me to *my* list."

"Don't. They'd only take that route as a last resort."

He pulled up his phone files while she went through her papers. "So our reporter isn't going to tell us much," Nathan said. "We can only hold him on trespassing but I'm sure he's lawyered up. We need to find out who his lawyer is, to give us a clue."

"Like that will happen."

Alisha studied the paperwork one of the paralegals had sent her earlier. "Hey, I have a list of some of the good doctor's patients. According to what we've found, these are some nefarious people who don't always want to go through proper procedures to get their medications."

"What kind of medications?"

"Opioids," she said, dropping the page she'd been reading. "So a successful doctor who has high-powered and high-paying clients and is willing to write them prescriptions for whatever they need."

Nathan scoffed. "I'd call that a quack."

"But a rich one, according to his bank account. Owns property in Philadelphia, which we've verified, and owns a fancy beach house in the Caymans."

"Of course, the Caymans. Offshore money and all of that. Not to mention a wife who sells pharmaceuticals." Rubbing a hand down his face, he said, "Let's take the top five on that list and see what we can find."

Alisha got up to find more of the diesel-fuel coffee. She'd be up all night but she couldn't sleep anyway. Searching her briefcase, she found the tin of cookies her grandmother had insisted they bring along and carried it back to the tiny sitting area. "This new information might explain why the FBI is now involved in this case. Philadelphia has a huge opioid problem."

They quickly zoomed on a woman named Andrea Sumter. Nathan read what he'd found. "A widowed socialite with money to burn, travels to the Caymans a lot herself, plenty of photos of her hanging with the Wests at high-society events. Let's keep her high up on the list."

One man on the list was dead. They eliminated two more names. But the last one caught Nathan's attention. "Deke Garrison. Filthy rich. Dirty money. I've heard his name in certain circles."

"Certain bad circles?" she asked, passing the cookie tin.

Nathan took the tin when she offered it and found an oatmeal cookie. "I'd say. You're the only eyewitness, and if he's our man the FBI might already be on this case or they're just snooping, hoping to capture him at last."

"They'll want me to testify if we find these people and bring them to trial. I'll never forget what happened the other night. Those hit men need to go to jail."

"And that's why you're in hiding. We're dealing with dangerous people who've already found you and tried to take both of us out."

She didn't want to think about what would have happened earlier if her feisty grandmother hadn't taken matters into her own hands. "Let's see if we can find out who else the doctor socialized with. He might have kept his drug-trafficking—if that's what he was doing—hidden from his legit friends." The couple I saw shouted rich, entitled and indulgent. Their car, their clothes, their shopping bags said it all."

"And now they can't brag to anyone."

Alisha shivered and then caught herself.

Nathan stood. "Are you cold?"

"No. Just… This is so creepy. I've always dealt in helping people and working with a lot of business contracts, some divorces and some petty criminals. But nothing like this. It's a horror story."

Nathan came and sat down beside her. "Rest," he said, pulling her into his arms. "Just rest."

Alisha knew she should protest but being in his arms again took away all of her horrible memories of the last few days. She felt secure here in this little cabin with Nathan, the fire's warmth lulling her to relax. But this couldn't happen.

She lifted up. "I should go and get some sleep."

"Not yet," he said, his warm breath on her ear, his arms still holding her. "Just let me hold you, okay?" He took an old afghan off the back of the couch and dropped it over her clothes.

Alisha closed her eyes. She needed to get up and move away from him. Too tempting. But sleep took hold of her. Nathan tugged her close so she could lie her head on his shoulder.

She shouldn't feel this safe with him but her limbs felt so heavy and a wave of fatigue moved over her, dragging her down.

"Just for a minute," she said as she drifted off.

Only for a little while.

Nathan woke with a start and glanced around. The fire was out and the room was cold. Alisha lay on the couch, covered in the afghan and another blanket he'd found. She'd fallen asleep almost immediately so he'd lifted her up out of his arms and let her sleep there. He had taken the chair and made do with a pillow and a blanket while he studied the facts they'd gathered.

He'd fallen asleep, his head twisted against the pillow.

Now he was fully awake and hearing things.

A rustling outside brought him out of his chair. Listening, he hurried to the door. It was locked and bolted but that wouldn't stop a killer.

Standing there, he checked his watch. Four o'clock. Nathan found his gun and went to a window to peek out. Maybe the big deer had followed their scent here. Listening, he heard only the wind and the occasional sound of snow falling off of tree limbs.

"What is it?"

He turned to find Alisha sitting up on the couch, her blanket pulled tightly against her.

"False alarm," he said. "Something woke me. Probably an animal passing by."

She didn't look convinced.

"Let me go and check," he said, grabbing his boots and his coat. "You don't go anywhere."

"I won't."

He gave her a questioning stare.

"I do not want to go out there," she said. "I'll make coffee. And you—be careful."

He went out the back and quietly worked his way around the perimeter of the square little cabin. No human prints but lots of animal paw prints. Maybe the raccoon he fed sometimes had returned for a winter treat.

Satisfied, he glanced around the quiet forest and wondered if someone was watching him. The chill took over and he hurried back inside, dusting snow off of his clothes after he closed and locked the door. "All clear. I'll start a fire."

She handed him fresh coffee and headed to the bedroom and stayed there a few minutes. He heard water running so he worked on a quick breakfast. When she returned, she'd changed into sweats and a huge sweater, thick socks covering her feet. Moving toward the fire he'd started, she held her hands out.

"Cold?"

"I might not ever be truly warm again."

He thought about holding her last night and how right it had felt. So right that he'd forced himself away. Then, watching and waiting, he'd fallen asleep in the chair by the fire. And he had the sore neck to prove it.

"We survived the night."

He looked around from where he'd thrown together toast with the freshly baked bread Bettye had packed for them. He had a jar of fresh jam in the pantry. "Yes, we did. So we'll stay hunkered down here and hit hard on piecing this thing together."

"And hope no one interrupts us," she replied, worry sounding in her words, her eyes darting toward the windows.

"Yes."

Nathan kept one ear to the ground while they ate. Because even though he hadn't found any footprints around the cabin, that didn't mean they were safe.

He was pretty sure he'd felt eyes on him when he went out earlier to check. While he watched and waited in here, someone could be doing the very same thing in the woods.

Chapter Eleven

They spent most of the day going back over what they knew, which wasn't much but every little tidbit painted a picture of what looked like a doctor filtering opioids through his clinic with the help of his so-called pharmaceutical rep wife—the perfect cover. Except one of his dealers must have wanted more money or had found out the good doctor was skimming off the top.

"Everything points to Deke Garrison," he told Alisha after they put together pages of handwritten notes. "He's a patient of Dr. West's, they hung in the same circles and their wives are all over social media together. Parties, vacations, holidays. Tight group. A lot of trips to South America and the Caymans."

Lots of possible scenarios but nothing concrete to go on yet. They didn't have the names of the shooter and driver so Alisha couldn't identify them unless she went back to Philadelphia. The law would expect her to come in and look at mugshots but as far as Nathan was concerned she wouldn't be able to do that with killers after her.

"How do we get to him?" she'd asked when they finally took a break earlier.

"We let the *authorities* take what we have and follow every lead."

"Well, that sure is a change of tune for you, PI Craig."

"I have to work this one by the book," he replied, thinking he had to walk the line to protect her from both the bad guys and a system that would demand everything of her in order to catch these criminals.

Now as night settled over the snow-covered woods and hills, Nathan figured they couldn't stay here indefinitely. Maybe he should get her back to Philadelphia fast and let the authorities there take over. He'd be in a world of trouble for taking her on the run, but what else could he have done?

"You look deep in thought," Alisha said from the kitchen. "Are you okay?"

Nathan got up from his chair and walked over to the small dining table he'd made from scrap wood. "Just pondering our next move."

Alisha motioned to the sandwiches she'd made and the can of soup she'd found in the cabinet. "Peanut butter and jelly with chicken soup. Eat and then we'll talk about what's next."

Nathan rubbed the back of his neck and sat down in one of the old rickety high-backed chairs. Watching her move around this usually solitary kitchen made his heart ache with a pain that seared his soul. He'd long ago given up on love and marriage, or a home other than this one.

He was a self-imposed nomad. He couldn't go through the devastation of losing someone he loved again. The night they'd found Hannah's tiny body by a stream still haunted his dreams. He'd lost her and Alisha both that night. And he'd lost them both because of his own selfish actions. Falling for a girl way out of his league had changed his life and made him realize some men weren't meant to have a family. So he helped other families find their missing loved ones.

That system had worked until now. Now, he'd held Alisha in his arms and realized his heart would never heal. In some ways, the pain was even worse the second time around.

"Nathan?"

He looked up to find her staring at him, concern clear in her gaze.

"What?"

"Is there something you're not telling me?"

"No." He couldn't blurt out what he was thinking. "We need to keep moving. I think tonight." Looking at her clothes, he added, "You need to put your dress back on in case we need to move quickly. Keep your bonnet and cape nearby."

"You think someone is out there, don't you?"

"I haven't seen anyone but my gut says yes."

Surprised, she held her spoon in the air. "And where will we go next?"

He studied her and wished he could keep her here, warm and safe with him for a long time. "Back to Philly."

Dropping the spoon into her soup, she said, "What?"

"We need to get you into the police station so we can look at mugshots. They'll want to talk to you again since we've had several obvious incidents that back up your fears and can prove our case. The best way to get to these people is to start at the beginning. Again."

She sat still and silent, her eyes downcast. "I understand. I can't run forever. I should have gone straight to them in the beginning."

He could tell she was growing weary. "You needed a couple of days to debrief and retreat, to get your head together for what might come."

"Except we've been looking over our shoulders for those two days and endangering everyone around us. You're right. This has to be our next move."

She looked up and into his eyes, her heart shining through. "Granny says things happen for a reason. I want you to know, Nathan, that no matter what, I think we needed this time together. And I hope you'll consider visiting your family during the holidays. We need to put an end to the blame and the guilt and live life to the fullest. For Hannah's sake. That's how we can honor her."

Nathan swallowed the lump in his throat and reached for her hand. So many things he wanted to say but he didn't have the right to need her so much. He wasn't worth her efforts but oh, how he wished he could be worthy of her love again.

They ate their meal in silence and afterward, she went into the bedroom and became Amish again. "I'm ready," she said. Then she went to her briefcase and took out some of her notes and her phone. "Just in case."

Tired, they sat on the couch staring into the fire for what seemed like hours, both too wired to sleep.

"I hate putting you through this," he told her as the night grew late. Taking her into his arms, he said, "Try to rest."

She leaned in, her hand covering his, her eyes telling him what words couldn't say. He wanted to kiss her and hold her and protect her.

"Alisha…"

A snap of a twig outside caused them both to freeze.

And then a hard knock at the door brought him out of his seat and diving for his weapon. He motioned to Alisha and she hurried across the room while he held to what he'd almost said to her before they'd been interrupted.

He wanted Alisha back with him.

Who would come knocking unannounced here? Alisha wondered, her heart pounding. The only ones who were aware that they were here knew to call or text first. They'd barely gotten settled and now someone was out there. Nathan had suspected this all along. The thought of a standoff here in the woods frightened her but she wasn't going down without a fight.

A light shined outside. She could see it through the slats of the old blinds when Nathan tucked them apart. He looked ready to do battle.

Another knock hit the door.

So now the killer was going to use manners by knocking first?

That gave her time to think.

Alisha rushed to Nathan's side. "Maybe it's a ploy."

"Has to be," he whispered. "Our guard in the woods would have seen them. They must have spotted him first."

Alisha didn't want another law enforcement officer to die because of her. "How do these people find us?"

"They always find a way," he whispered. "I thought we'd bought some time."

"Our time is up," she said. "Do we go out the back?"

Before he could answer, a booming voice shouted.

"Nathan Craig? FBI. We know you're in there. Open the door or we'll break it down."

Nathan turned to Alisha. "They might not be FBI," he pointed out. "My gut is telling me to be careful."

"Then let's go with your gut."

He eyed the back door. "We could make a run for it, but…if it is the FBI, they need answers and we've done a lot of research. They won't take kindly to us ignoring them while we try to break this case. If we run, they'll track us, too."

"I agree," she said. "But if it's those goons, they might have us surrounded and we'll both get killed."

Another knock. "Craig, let us in. We need to talk to Alisha Braxton."

"Give me a minute," Nathan shouted through the door. He turned to Alisha. "Get your cell and put your cape and bonnet on and be ready to run. Look for the birdhouses."

"I'm not going without you."

"Alisha, don't argue with me. I'll have to hold them off."

She shook her head but went to the bench by the back door to grab the dark cloak her grandmother had loaned her. It wasn't regulation Amish since it had pockets but Granny had shoved it at her because it was warm.

Just to be sure, she gathered whatever she could into her briefcase and placed it behind the couch but kept their latest handwritten notes tucked along with her cell phone in the bib of her apron. When she reached down inside the case, her hand hit her pepper spray. She took it out and dropped it into the deep pocket of her cloak, thanking the Lord for that one secret compartment.

Another knock. And then the door rattled. Alisha's

pulsed pounded against her temple while she tried to take her next breath.

Nathan put a finger to his lips and motioned for her to get behind him. "Remember, if you have to run, look for the birdhouses. They line the trail from the cabin to my folk's place."

Bobbing her head, she prayed she wouldn't have to go anywhere without him.

"I need to see some ID," Nathan called. "I'll open the door and you slip your badge through."

Alisha heard mumbling and shuffling. "I have my badge out."

Nathan kept the chain lock on the door and opened it just enough to see the badge. Alisha peeked at it from behind him.

It looked official enough but how could they be sure?

Before Nathan could confirm, the door flew open with a bang, ripping the chain lock away and knocking both of them to the floor. The breath went out of Alisha but she scooted up, ready to make a move if Nathan would go with her.

Then a shot and the back door swung open, a man with a rifle trained on them filling the cold space. She couldn't see his face in the muted lamplight, but she could tell he stood tall and bulky. The air hit Alisha's warm skin like a cold breath. No way out.

Nathan managed to hold onto his gun, his body a solid wall in front of where Alisha huddled on the floor. "Stay behind me, Alisha," he whispered. "But get ready to run."

"What about you?"

"Don't worry about me. I'll distract them."

Two men entered the house from the front and stood

over them. Nathan held his gun toward the men at the door and then spoke to the one who'd just shot out the back lock. "That was rude."

"It's a little late for you to be whining," the first agent said as he flashed his badge again. "We've been looking for Miss Braxton for two days."

Nathan shook his head then sat up. "Breaking and entering is not a good idea. And holding that rifle on us only makes things worse."

One of the men closed the door behind him. The first one who'd flashed his badge said, "I'm Special Agent Mack Smith." Motioning behind him, he added, "This is Agent Scott Kemp and that fellow over there is Adam Baker. Why don't you relax and put down that gun, son."

Nathan checked the IDs they briefly held up but he didn't drop his weapon. "I guess you want to question my client. So I'll put down my weapon when you do the same."

The one named Mack nodded to the man holding the rifle. He lowered his gun. Nathan carefully placed his weapon on the floor.

"You could say that," Mack Smith replied, his gaze sliding over Alisha. "If it's not too much trouble we do need to question *your client*. I mean, this is a federal case and you're the only eyewitness, Miss Braxton. You don't need to run from the FBI."

"Who told you I was here?" Alisha asked, her tone firm and calm, while her eyes moved over the men. She had to find a way to get them out of this, but they were blocked in.

"We asked around," Mack Smith said with a slight smile.

Alisha had already figured out these people were not FBI, but her radar went up. Something was definitely off. They were all three dressed for the weather in heavy canvas jackets and jeans. But they didn't have the clean-cut look most FBI agents adhered to. The two backups were scruffy. One had a beard and from what she could see, the one standing at the back had long hair.

Alisha studied the two standing nearest and when her gaze moved to the other man—Adam Baker—she glanced at his haggard features and confirmed he had stringy long dark hair. Then she looked him in the eye.

The man stared back, a smug expression moving across his face, his eyes black and cold. Dead inside.

She gasped, causing Nathan to turn his head. That gave the intruders just enough time to make a move. The one holding the rifle rushed across the room and hit Nathan over the head with the butt of the weapon.

Alisha screamed as Nathan moaned and crumbled to the floor. Alisha scrambled to reach Nathan's gun, grabbed it up and shot at the one they'd called Scott Kemp. Her bullet hit his leg. He shouted in pain, his thigh gushing blood, and fell just inside the door.

"Help me," he called to his buddies.

"Leave both of them," Mack said to his partner, slanting his head toward Nathan and the bleeding man. He held the rifle over Alisha. "Drop the gun." Nodding to his buddy Adam, he said, "They can kill each other, for all I care. We came for the woman."

Nathan moaned again and tried to roll over toward Alisha so he could get the gun. The one she'd recognized came at her, dragging her away from Nathan. Alisha held up the gun, determined to shoot it but the man knocked it out of her hand, an ugly grin on his craggy face. Alisha screamed and kicked the gun away with her foot, praying Nathan would see it.

Her heart hammering, Alisha screamed again, kicking and fighting. The man with the long hair—the man she'd seen the night of the killings—had her by her cape collar, his stubby fingers digging into her skin. Leaning close, he whispered in her ear, his hot breath hitting her skin. "It's over now, lawyer-lady. No one will ever find you in these woods."

Alisha tried to scramble away, tried to grab her briefcase so she could use it as a weapon. But they lifted her like a rag doll and tossed her out the back door. The frigid air poured over her, freezing her to the spot for a split second. She turned, screaming for Nathan. A grungy hand slapped at her face and then covered her mouth.

"Scream again and we'll kill him in front of your eyes and then we'll kill you and your sweet gun-toting grandma, too."

Alisha turned back, panic in her throat, her lip bleeding, the cold wind chilling her to the bone. She had to do something. Nathan was injured and there was no way out. She'd wounded the other man but he could still get in a shot and kill Nathan.

Then she heard someone calling her name.

"Alisha!"

Nathan. He'd crawled to the door, his gun in his hand. He shot into the air but missed her captors.

One of them turned and shot back and she watched as Nathan slipped down the outside wall. And didn't move.

Nathan grimaced, the pain shooting through his shoulder excruciating. The bullet had gone through but he'd passed out for a few seconds and bled into the snow. He had to get to Alisha but he couldn't help her if he fell unconscious in the woods.

Dragging himself back inside, he pushed away the dizziness in his brain, a throbbing pain coursing through his temple like a roaring train. He managed to shut the door then he turned to where he'd seen Alisha shoot one of the intruders. The man was gone but he'd left a trail of blood out the other door.

Searching for a towel, Nathan dragged himself up and worked to stop the blood oozing out of his upper right shoulder. With a bit of effort and waves of dizziness, he hurriedly cleaned and bandaged it with supplies from the first aid kit he kept in the cabin. His head wound had stopped bleeding and the dizziness subsided once he settled down. But he couldn't stay settled.

Then he bundled up, checked the magazine on his gun and took some pain medicine for his headache. He'd tried to call for help but his phone's battery had gone dead. Too late for that. He had to track Alisha. Not sure how far ahead they were, he checked his supplies one last time and hurried to the back door. Stumbling, he hit his foot on Alisha's briefcase.

She'd said her life was inside that case. Right now, she didn't have it as her shield. He'd have to be her shield and pray that God was watching over them. His heart hammering an urgent beat, Nathan stashed her case under some clothes in the closet, put on a wool hat and his coat, then rushed out to begin the desperate race to find Alisha before it was too late.

Chapter Twelve

She'd watched for the birdhouses.

Now Alisha saw them up ahead in the gray dusk. If she planned to make a run for it, now would be the time. Checking her pocket again, she held her fingers on the container of pepper spray. It had a stretch gripper band that she'd already slipped over her fingers. She used it mostly for jogging but now she was glad she'd kept an extra container in her briefcase. Being jostled here and there, she'd managed to unlock the safety. She was ready.

"Keep moving," Long Hair, or Ace as his friend called him, growled, hurling her forward. They all had nicknames. Mack the Knife, Ace, and Scooter. "Your man isn't coming to help you."

"He's not my man," she retorted. "But he'll find me. He's good at finding people."

"He's probably dead by now," the other one said. "Scooter wasn't hurt too bad."

She prayed Scooter had either left in a hurry or passed out cold.

Ace held her arm in a tight grip that was sure to leave

bruises in the shape of his meaty fingers, while the other one kept watch behind them. They didn't speak much except to let her know that if she ran, she'd die and then they'd kill her grandmother.

Alisha had to go on faith. She would escape and she would find someone to help her and save her grandmother, too. This wasn't going to end in the cold woods. She'd do as Nathan had told her and run along the birdhouse path and find someone, anyone, to get back to him.

But as the two men pushed her toward the path she planned to take, they veered to the left instead of the right. Left was nothing but deep, snow-covered woods for miles. Right had a path and held hope. She had to act now or they'd have her back on the road and in a vehicle.

And then, she'd never have a chance to save anyone.

Ace yanked at her. "Keep up. We're almost there."

Alisha took a breath and said a little prayer for courage. Then she went limp.

"What's wrong?" Ace snarled, anger flashing in his eyes. "You'd better not be faking."

"I don't feel so good," she said, falling to her knees. I'm so tired and I need some water."

"We don't have water and you're walking," he said, trying to drag her up. "Someone wants to meet you."

Alisha was ready. Pulling her right hand out of her pocket, she sprayed him in the eyes and then turned toward the other man and did the same to him.

While they both screamed in agony, Alisha took off running with all her might. She had to get to the Schrock farm.

Nathan followed the path of the footsteps, thanking the snow for stopping long enough to give him a perfect trail. He was about twenty minutes behind and growing weaker by the minute, but he had to keep going. Three sets of prints until they got to the fork in the path. His pulse pressing against his temple, he blinked away pain and studied the trail. Three sets about five feet into the path to the left and then—

He stopped and knelt down, his mind whirling with the worst-case scenario. The snow was all smudged and gutted here, as if there had been a struggle.

Had Alisha gotten away?

Or had those two dragged her farther into the woods to the left?

He didn't know which path to take.

Lord, I need you. Guide me.

Nathan stumbled toward the other path, his breath fanning out in a cold fog in front of him. His body protested every step, his ears ringing with pain while his head throbbed. The bullet hole in his shoulder wasn't too happy, either.

But he kept trudging.

And found one set of footsteps digging through the deepening snow.

"Did you get away, Alisha?"

He looked around and realized he was on the birdhouse path. Squinting, he put one foot in front of the other and trudged ahead, not knowing if the prints belonged to her or not. But who else would be out here?

When he heard a rustling up ahead, Nathan dragged himself off the trail and hid in the snow-covered undergrowth behind a large pine. Something moved to the east. He could hear footfalls.

He watched, holding his breath, the Beretta Alisha

had left behind tight against his fingers. He hoped she'd kept going.

The air shook with an echo of footfalls. A massive shadow fell across the white snow, casting long in the waning moonlight.

Nathan braced for what might come.

The big stag strolled along the path, heading in the direction Nathan had just come. Breathing a sigh of relief, Nathan watched as the animal stopped and lifted his head, his nostrils flaring, his eyes watchful.

Then he looked in the direction of where Nathan was hiding. The deer didn't move and Nathan was afraid to move.

The big animal seemed to be standing guard, watching, waiting, listening. Then he turned around and took off, leaping back to the right.

Nathan decided he'd follow the stag.

Maybe the Lord had sent him another sign.

The stag left him behind, but Nathan saw a clear path now. The same smaller set of prints moved up the path, past the birdhouses he'd built and placed here, one at a time, from the time he'd moved into the cabin until now. He'd made a birdhouse to represent every celebration he'd missed with his family—birthdays and Easter, Christmas, summer, fall, winter and spring. A dozen or so, each unique and meaningful to him. He'd often walked this path, his creations bringing him joy and a sense of home. He enjoyed watching the birds make their nests there in the tiny houses and he'd watched their babies learning to fly away. He often wondered if anyone from his family had noticed the houses set along this remote path.

He'd never known that one day those little treasures,

along with the stag that he'd befriended and obviously called this forest his domain, would take him back on the path toward home. Or back toward Alisha.

Please let her be safe. Let her be okay. Let her be alive.

He prayed silently and sometimes in soft whispered pleas. He would keep praying until he had Alisha in his arms again.

Alisha blinked and tried to focus. But the darkness seemed to close in around her with the same cloying strength as the men who'd tried to take her.

She'd gotten away and then she'd gotten lost. They'd both left earlier but then she'd heard them again, arguing about what to do, their voices getting closer. She kept running east but she'd gone off the open trail to stay hidden.

The two men had left abruptly due to a scare earlier, but now the darkness made it hard for her to see in the sloping hills surrounding Campton Creek. The cold chill that held her in ice, coupled with the shock coursing through her body, made her disoriented and tired. So tired.

Maybe she'd dreamed the whole thing. The two men screaming after she'd pepper-sprayed them, making sure she'd hit them in the eyes and face.

Ace had grabbed her, knocked her down and dragged her back.

"I'm going to end this here and now. I'm tired of chasing you around these aggravating hills and streams. They can't pay me enough for this kind of stuff."

She'd seen the rage in his dark, red-rimmed eyes.

Evil permeated the air around him. He'd kill her without any qualms.

Then a swooping sound and something big and wild had leaped toward them and practically plowed into the man holding her. He'd been so taken by surprise and so terrified that he'd screamed and run away. After cursing at him, his friend had joined him.

The big deer with the massive antlers had scared off her captors. Alisha had managed to get up and run as fast as she could in the deep snow.

Except she'd veered off the path and now it was dark and the snow had started falling steadily again. Exhausted, she sat down near the trunk of a billowing oak tree.

"I'll just rest for a minute," she said into the night. "Just to catch my breath and find my way out of here."

Her last thoughts before a sweet sleep took over were of Nathan. *Please keep him safe, Lord.*

Nathan prayed all the prayers of his childhood, in both English and the Pennsylvania Dutch he'd grown up speaking, all the while searching with his tiny flashlight for any sign of Alisha. He should have found her an hour ago but the footprints he'd followed had taken a turn into the woods to the northeast and a new snow had covered them. He'd lost her trail.

He was lost and now he feared that Alisha was also.

He was also in pain. His arm and shoulder throbbed but he kept applying snowballs, placing a handful of the white slush over the sleeve of his jacket to cool down the wound and hopefully stop it from bleeding. His forehead had a knot on it that complained with each heartbeat.

But he kept trudging in the way the big deer had charged because with his mind so fuzzy, Nathan was running out of options. He'd follow his only ally in this forest.

A scant moonlight guided him deeper into the woods. When he heard a stream gurgling down the hillside, he watched and listened. He hadn't spotted Mack and the one named Adam, but Nathan knew how criminals operated. If Alisha had gone off into the woods, they'd either hidden to wait for an opportunity or, more likely, given up the chase.

Cowards, but he was glad for that. Their boss wouldn't be happy but Nathan didn't care about that right now. If he could find her before they did, Nathan would be able to hide her somewhere secluded and safe.

He made it to where the stream ran through the foothills and shined his flashlight around the woods, touching it on shifts and shadows. When he spotted fresh footprints in an opening leading down toward the water, he knew he was on the right track.

And that's when he saw her.

Alisha, lying curled up and asleep by a tree, snow covering her body without consideration or discrimination.

A freezing snow.

"Alisha?" he called, a catch in his voice, a rip in his heart. "Alisha?"

She didn't respond. Nathan slid down the rocky hillside, tumbling and tripping until he fell a few feet away from where she lay. Crawling and clawing his way to her, he lifted Alisha into his arms.

"Alisha?" She was cold, almost blue with cold. He

rubbed his hands over her coat and then her face. She didn't have on a hat or gloves.

Feeling for her pulse, he let out a relieved breath when he felt a weak beat. Another hour or so and he might have lost her for good. Now they might have a chance.

Lifting her up, he held her in his arms and leaned back against the tree, the urge to sleep here with her so strong that he had to blink it away. His shoulder throbbed in protest, but he couldn't let her go. "We're going to be okay. We'll find shelter and you'll wake up warm and safe."

She didn't move or respond.

Nathan didn't know how he'd get her up the hillside, but he'd find a way. Reluctantly, he laid her back against the tree and took off his jacket to put over her. His long-sleeved shirt was torn and covered with blood. He didn't care.

Looking up, he pointed his light to the hillside and searched for a way up. Seeing some grooves and ledges up past the tree, he decided that would be the best way to go.

He shined the light up higher and saw something else.

The big stag standing there, his antlers spread out in perfect symmetry, his dark eyes on Nathan.

"Thank you," Nathan called on a hoarse whisper. "We're going to go home now and leave you to stand watch."

The stag lowered his head to the ground, snorted and then shook out his mantle in what could have been a parting gesture. Then he leaped away and pranced off into the woods.

Nathan found the strength he needed. Taking back his jacket, he tugged Alisha's still body up and into his arms and started the slow process of getting her up the hill and back to the path that would take them to a warm, safe place.

His parents' home.

His first attempt didn't work. His boot hit on a wet patch of rock and he slipped down, falling onto his backside, Alisha still in his arms.

"That didn't go so well," he said. With a grunt, he stood and rearranged her, one hand around her back and one holding her underneath her knees. "To be such a tiny woman, you sure are weighty."

But she was strong and buff. High-powered lawyers had to stay in shape.

"My *mamm* will make you the best soup and she'll have Christmas cookies in every cabinet. She'll get you in a warm bed and shoo me away while she fusses over you."

He hoped. He prayed.

Lord, please let them accept us. Please. I pray they won't turn us away.

Gritting his teeth, Nathan kept finding footholds, his mind on one step at a time. One step and then another step. Finally, he reached the top of the hill and worked his way across the woods and back toward the open trail. His flashlight, gripped loosely in his weak hand while he held onto Alisha, showed him the way. He saw hoof prints along the same path.

"Now you're just showing off, Old Stag."

But those hoof prints lead him to the path and then he turned east.

Toward home.

Chapter Thirteen

Nathan didn't think he could take one more step. He'd been walking for over an hour, Alisha in his arms. She was still asleep and that worried him. But he held her so tightly to his shoulder he could feel her heartbeat against his own.

At least she was warmer now, her warmth helping him to stay focused as he trudged through the hills and made it onto the old country lane that led up to the front door of his childhood home.

Heaving another grunt as he shifted Alisha in his arms, Nathan whispered in her ear. "We're here. That house right there is my parent's place. You'll be okay. I promise."

Stopping as the house came into view, Nathan's body surged with a homesick longing. How he'd missed his family. Why had he stayed away so long?

Memories reminded him of why he'd run like a coward and never looked back. He couldn't bear the burden of his family's grief, a grief that he felt so responsible for.

Alisha moaned in his arms, reminding him of the

here and now. He didn't need to be standing here in uncertain fear.

So he started walking, wondering how he'd explain this but hoping he wouldn't need to. He made it halfway up the drive and stopped again, fatigue dragging him down.

"I hope they're home." Realizing Alisha and he had been in the woods for most of the night, he said, "It's almost dawn, so they should be up anyway. Farm work, you know."

"Maybe this is a bad idea," Alisha said in a weak whisper. "They don't approve of me."

Looking down at her, Nathan couldn't help but smile. "You got any better ideas?"

"No." Her eyes closed again but at least she had woken up. That had to be a good sign.

Nathan said another prayer, thinking he'd caught up on his quota in one long, horrible night.

He was within yards of the houses when the front door swung open. Martha Schrock came running down the steps, her dark dress and black apron billowing out around her. "Nathan?"

Nathan nodded and stumbled closer. "Hi, Mamm. It's me."

Martha's face filled with concern. "What has happened?"

"I'll explain, but I need to get her inside and warm first."

Martha stopped as she got closer to them and saw the woman wearing a dark bonnet in his arms. "And who is this?"

Nathan glanced back at the road. "Mamm, I'll explain everything. May we come inside? She's been exposed to the cold all night."

His father stepped out onto the porch, a frown marring his face. His mother whirled to her husband. "Nathan has returned, Amos. He and this woman are in need."

For two heartbeats the morning went silent. Alisha moaned again and snuggled closer to Nathan. He kept glancing back as he inched her and his mother forward, afraid those men would be lurking about.

Finally, he said, "Daed, I need your help. May we please come inside?"

The plea in that question must have torn through his mother. Her eyes grew misty. She turned to her husband. "Amos?"

"*Alleweil*, Daed?" Right now.

Amos Schrock stared at them but didn't move.

"Amos?" His wife's plea sounded as heartbreaking as Nathan's had. "Our son needs our help."

Amos nodded. "*Ja*."

Then he turned and went back inside the house.

Feeling dejected, Nathan moved forward. But to his surprise, his father came back out with two blankets and handed them to Martha. She nodded, unable to speak, and then hurried to cover both of them.

"*Kumm*, and let's get you both warmed up."

Martha shot her husband a sweet smile. "*Denki*, Amos."

Amos nodded and guided them up the steps. When they were inside, Nathan's parents turned to see the woman in his arms.

Martha gasped and Amos frowned.

Martha glanced over at Alisha, unable to speak as recognition spilled over her features. "Alisha?"

Alisha opened her eyes and focused. "Yes, Mrs. Schrock. It's me. And I'm so sorry to bother you."

Then she passed out again.

Nathan interjected, weariness and dizziness overtaking him. "We're in trouble, Mamm."

Martha gave Alisha another concerned stare, as if to say she'd already figured that out. Then she motioned to the downstairs bedroom on the back of the house. "*Druwwel*? What kind of trouble?"

Nathan felt as if he was shifting, his legs going weak. Following his folks, he said, "I... I need to lay her down."

His mother pulled back the quilt and fluffed the pillows. "Put her here."

He gently placed Alisha on the bed and tugged her out of her cloak while his mother held the blanket they placed over her. Alisha came awake, her eyes going wide.

"Where am I?"

"You're safe now," Nathan said, his voice hoarse as he covered her from her neck down, making sure she'd be warm. "Just as I promised."

He blinked, stumbled against the high-backed chair by the bed, his arms throbbing from carrying her for so long, his shoulder on fire. Pushing off the blanket, he tried to stay on his feet. And failed.

"Nathan, you're hurt!"

His mother's frantic shouts echoed all around him before he slumped over in the chair, unable to keep his eyes open any longer.

She woke to voices.

A soft voice. "The poor girl is exhausted. No wonder. She almost froze to death. And you with a hole in your shoulder."

A harsh voice. "You bring her here, to our home? You and your *Englisch* world? I had no choice but to help you this morning, but I won't have it. You can't stay here, Nathan."

A tired voice. "I told you, I have nowhere else to go right now. She needs to stay out of sight for a while."

Sitting up, Alisha glanced around the clean, plain bedroom, the sun shimmering through the windows. A beautiful bed with a colorful diamond-patterned quilt that would be worth hundreds of dollars hanging in a city store, along with a side table and a chair and a small wardrobe. Simple, stark and beautiful. A house full of love.

The sun shined high up in the sky, telling her it had to be mid-afternoon. She'd slept all day?

Her mind foggy, she remembered bits and pieces of conversations. Nathan talking softly in her ear out in the forest. His parents wrapping both of them with blankets, their voices filled with worry and surprise.

They'd taken her in. The parents that had not approved of her long ago had taken her into their home. Because they still loved their wayward son.

But she'd brought conflict and confusion back into this house when Nathan clearly needed to find redemption and peace. She saw clearly now. As clear as the glass vase holding a few pine boughs. A simple gesture to celebrate Christmas in a plain and quiet way.

"What do you plan? To shoot people dead in our yard?"

"Enough," Alisha said to herself in a mumbling whisper. "Enough." She had to get out of here, for Nathan's sake, if nothing else.

Pushing back the warm quilt, she got up to get dressed, a slight dizziness causing her to sit back on the bed. She ran her hands through her hair and padded her way across the old linoleum floor to use the indoor facilities she spotted in a small room across the hallway by the kitchen. After finding her now-clean clothes drying in what looked like a combination mud and laundry room, Alisha dressed and went into the living room to catch Nathan and his father in a stare-off, the large dining table between them. Nathan's arm was now tied with a white linen sling and a cloth bandage covered the wound on his shoulder. He also wore clean clothes. But he looked tired, dark circles underneath his eyes. Had he slept at all?

Taking a deep breath, Alisha said, "I'll leave."

They whirled to see her there. Amos turned an embarrassed red while Nathan fumed in frustration.

Martha rushed toward her. "Did you sleep well?"

"Yes, thank you." Alisha wasn't sure what to do or say. "I didn't realize how exhausted I was."

Nathan came around the table. "You need to eat."

"No," she said. "I need to leave. It's obvious I shouldn't be here."

Nathan shook his head. "No. It's not safe. I saw a truck roaming the roads this morning already. We need to stay hidden for a day or so." When she frowned, he added, "You're tired and recovering and my arm is still not in full working mode. We need to rest."

"She has a *gut* point," his father said, holding his own stare. "You shouldn't be here."

Martha touched Alisha's arm but gave her silent husband a firm stare. "Amos, I think they can stay a while. It is snowing and so cold and those people could still be around here somewhere. I made chicken and dumplings for supper. I'd like to share that with my son and Alisha. They are both wounded and need nourishment."

Amos grunted, the jagged wrinkle between his eyes deepening. "This is not our way, Martha."

"It is not my nature to turn away someone in need," his wife replied. "Especially when it is our son who has come to us injured and asking for our help."

Alisha watched the silent war between Nathan's parents. Amos Schrock caved to no one, except Martha Schrock. Nathan used to laugh about that, proud that his demure mother knew how to get her way when she wanted. Seemed this was one of those times.

"It's all right," Alisha said. "I can call a cab."

Nathan didn't argue with her but his eyes went dark. He looked weary but she was relieved that his shoulder was bandaged. She prayed his wound wouldn't get infected but his mother seemed adept at such things.

"You're not leaving," he finally said. "At least not without me."

Alisha realized his sacrifice. He'd come for her in the woods, wounded and hurting, and carried her all the way to this house. Instead of threatening to leave, she should be thanking him. She'd do that later when things weren't so tense.

Martha shook her head. "I am going to feed you both and let you rest. We will decide about what happens after that."

Amos nodded, silently and without any more arguments.

They'd been given a reprieve. One Alisha did not

want or deserve. But Nathan needed this time with his parents, so she remained quiet.

Nathan watched as his father walked out of the room and then shifted his gaze toward Alisha. "How are you?"

"A little wobbly," she said, holding onto the wall.

"Come and sit at the table," he said, taking her arm.

She didn't argue. The smell of strong coffee captured her attention. Spotting the coffeepot, she refused to be rude and beg for a cup.

Nathan read her mind. "Mamm, may I pour Alisha some coffee?"

"*Ja*," his mother said. "Where are my manners?"

Her tone was kind but hesitant. It had to be difficult, seeing her son again under such extreme circumstances.

"I'd so appreciate that," Alisha said. "I can't believe how long I slept."

"You were in a bad way," Martha said after she handed Nathan two cups of coffee. "You slept through Nathan's complaining about me cleaning his wound."

"It burned," he admitted with a smile. "But Mamm knows her way around an injured son since she has three."

"*Ja*, ain't so?" His mother chuckled and then offered Alisha a warm biscuit with a smear of apple preserves. "To tide you over until supper."

Waiting until she'd sat down at the long wooden table, Nathan took the coffee his mother offered and sat across from Alisha. "I got word to Carson about our intruders. He found out the officer in the deer stand in the woods was injured but managed to call it in. Two officers arrived at the cabin not long after I left but the snow became so heavy, they called it a night on doing a search."

Alisha remembered that thick, cold snow. Thankful for the warmth flowing around her now, she asked, "Are you okay?"

Nathan nodded. "I've been through worse." Then he went on with his report. "I gave Carson the names they used so based on their descriptions and the names, they'll run a check. Searched the woods as they backtracked toward the road and found one man. He's in a hospital nearby, under custody, but refusing to offer up any information."

Lowering her voice while his mother went about her chores, she whispered, "Obviously, they didn't find the other two."

"No. But they found a blood trail from the one in custody. That might give them DNA for evidence against him at least. And they think they spotted the dark pickup the men were driving."

Alisha let go of a shiver. "I don't feel comfortable here."

"And you'd be better off out there?"

Martha called to them. "Let her eat in peace, Nathan."

Alisha dropped things for now and nibbled on the biscuit. It was good but she couldn't seem to get much of it down.

Martha looked at her son. "Nathan, would you go and find your father? Supper will be ready soon."

Nathan hesitated and then did as his mother asked.

After he'd gone out the back door, a blast of cold air sneaking through before he shut it, Martha turned to Alisha and pointed to a stool. Then she brought her own cup of tea over.

"I think this is a good time for you and me to have a nice talk, Alisha Braxton."

Alisha didn't know whether to run back to the bedroom or just head out the front door and meet her fate.

Martha waited, a slight dare in her blue eyes.

"Of course, Mrs. Schrock," she said, taking the stool.

Chapter Fourteen

While he wondered how his *mamm* and Alisha were faring alone at the house, Nathan silently helped his father check on the animals and freshen their hay. The horses, milk cows and goats had mostly been fed their big meal early this morning, depending on their feeding schedules. His father had an internal alarm clock that had him up before the sun, checking on animals and going about the work of the farm. Unable to sleep earlier, Nathan had watched his *daed* out the window from his old room upstairs. He hadn't gone down then, afraid his father wouldn't want him to help.

But now, he'd gotten beyond his earlier hesitance. His *daed* might resent him being here and disapprove of all that Nathan had become, but he was home and Christmas was coming in a couple of days. Time to find the courage to face his father.

So here he was doing the chores that came back to him as easily as eating his mother's pancakes. And all the while, scanning the horizons and the edge of the woods for any lurkers or intruders. He'd not seen any trucks roaming the road but he had to wonder who could be lurking just beyond the hills and valleys.

But the land sat settled and quiet, as old and comfortable as the clothes he'd borrowed and wore now. No signs of anyone waiting to attack. He hoped things would stay quiet for a while.

Once Amos seemed satisfied with the animals, he moved on to the chicken coops to make sure the hens were warm and safe. The ornery rooster chased after Amos, but his father ignored the arrogant bird. Nathan followed, waiting for his silent *daed* to speak.

Amos moved on to the woodpile and grabbed an ax.

He offered it to Nathan, who, surprised but pleased, took it and watched as his father found another. Together, they began to chop wood to use to back up the propane tanks they kept to run appliances. His mother still loved her wood stove and used it during the worst of winter.

"Christmas Eve is tomorrow and then we have Christmas and visiting day after that," Amos said, pointing out the obvious. "You can stay through Christmas but I expect you to honor your faith by not bringing the *Englisch* violence into our home."

"I will do my best to keep this situation nonviolent."

"What if these men show up here, Nathan?"

"I'll lure them away from the house and keep everyone safe."

He hoped. He'd have to find his weapon and create a distraction. But Nathan decided he'd fight that battle when it came.

"How does the violent work you do honor the Lord?"

"My work isn't always like this," Nathan tried to explain. "I've helped a lot of people, mostly Amish, locate their kinfolk. I also help solve crimes by finding the truth."

Amos looked out over the fields. "Such as this one?"

"Yes, such as this one."

Following his father's example, he placed a round log on the chopping block and then looked at his father. "I never stopped honoring God. I just do it in a different way now."

The *Englisch* way," Amos said, hitting wood so hard it easily split into kindling.

"Yes, different traditions but the same God."

"So you attend church regularly?"

He had Nathan on that one. "When I can."

"When you are not out there searching for evil people?"

"Or missing people." Nathan couldn't admit he hadn't darkened a church door in a long time. "Yes, when I can," he repeated.

"Your mother has missed you."

Chop, split. Chop, split.

"I've missed all of you, too." Nathan chopped a few more logs and laid them in the wheel barrel. "How are my brothers?"

"Gideon works at the Bawell Hat Shop which has expanded into a big retail business. Raesha Bawell married a man named Josiah Fisher a year ago. Josiah has taken on some of the work at the shop so Raesha can raise their children. They are raising his niece and Raesha is expecting her first baby this spring. Gideon loves his work there. His wife Emma is also with child so she and Raesha have bonded over motherhood."

"That's good news. He always did have a crush on his Emma."

"*Ja*, and finally admitted it and asked for her hand in marriage."

Nathan grinned. His father had spoken more than a few words. He was sharing real news. "Maybe I can see him during Christmas."

"They are coming the day after. Don't bring any harm on him."

The silence after that remark marred the conversation and caused Nathan to glance up again. A movement in the woods caught his eye. When a covey of quail flew out of the brush, he chalked it up to an animal moving past. But the hair on the back of his neck stood up anyway. Glad Alisha was safe inside, he watched for a moment longer but saw nothing.

Nathan tried again with his father, hoping to shake off his jitters. "And Thomas?"

Amos looked out over the fallow, snow-covered hills. "He is *gut*. He likes his life in Ohio. His wife's family *wilkumed* him with open arms. He loves her two children like his own."

"I'm glad they are both okay," Nathan said, meaning it. "I have visited Thomas a time or two. Beautiful community."

Winded and spent, Amos slapped his ax against the chopping block and turned to face Nathan. "How are you, son?"

Nathan's eyes pricked with a wet sheen, whether from the cold air or the kindness in his father's quiet question.

"I've had better times, Daed. I can't let anything happen to Alisha."

Amos rubbed a hand down his beard. "So you still to this day have feelings for this woman?"

"I'll always have feelings for her," Nathan admitted. "We might have been wrong for each other but... I can't forget her. And when she needed me, I had to go to her."

"So she *did* get you involved in this?"

Nathan looked for the condemnation in his father's stormy eyes, but was surprised and relieved to find none. "She witnessed a horrible murder and then they came after her to silence what she saw. Tried to run her off the road."

Amos nodded. "We heard two officers were in a bad accident near Green Mountain. Does that have something to do with her?"

"They were following her to make sure she got here safely."

"And someone caused their accident?"

"Yes." Nathan stared at the house, the cold settling over him as the wind picked up. "She witnessed that, too. She called me out of desperation, Daed. I couldn't say no."

Amos dusted his hands and turned toward the barn. His frown didn't show much but his eyes had softened. "That must have been a terrible burden for her to bear. I can see why she'd call someone she trusts."

Floored, Nathan could only nod. "I suppose so."

Did Alisha trust him? She'd come here under duress and because she was terrified. But he knew she could bolt and try to outrun these people on her own to protect his family and hers.

Once they reached the big double doors, Amos glanced around. "I'm sorry I was harsh earlier but seeing you at our door was both a joy and a shock. Your *mamm* is right, though. I can't turn away a family member in need. What is your plan?"

"I'm making that up as I go," Nathan admitted, accepting his father's apology as a victory. "If I can keep her hidden until we figure out who's coming after us, then we can put them away and she'll be able to testify in a court of law as to what she saw that night. I can't believe she managed to get here safely after they came after her so fast."

"But she brought harm on her *grossmammi* and Mrs. Campton."

"She needed a safe haven. They didn't question that. We have security at the Campton Center day and night and officers on patrol there. We also put out the word that we were headed back to Reading, but unfortunately, that didn't fool them."

"Reading?"

"She works for a law firm there that also has offices in Philadelphia."

"Where do you live?"

Nathan thought about his secluded little cabin. As far as he knew, his family wasn't aware it belonged to him. "I travel a lot and stay in rented apartments or hotels."

"That is no way to live."

"It's the only way I know."

Amos waited for him to enter the barn. "But you are home now, son. And for that, I am thankful."

Nathan let out a breath he'd been holding for over a decade. "Does that mean I'm forgiven for leaving?"

"There is nothing to forgive. God will see us through."

"But you were so angry—"

Amos held up a hand. "I was angry about a lot of things but I've had many days and nights to think about my actions since then. That was a bad time for all of us, but we accept it as God's will. I should not have taken out my anger on you."

Nathan wanted to ask his father about Hannah. Did he ever wonder why this terrible thing had to happen to one so innocent? Did he believe that what happened to her was God's will? But he held off on that. He wouldn't upset his father after such an honest talk. He'd do what his father had suggested. He'd accept things for now because he had to keep Alisha alive so they could get these people put away for a long time.

After that, Nathan would become that nomad again, wandering and always on the move. But he didn't think he'd ever be able to chase his pain away.

Alisha looked into Martha Schrock's eyes and wished she could figure out what Nathan's mother truly thought about her. "What would you like to discuss?" she asked, cutting to the chase.

"You've been through a terrible ordeal," Martha said, shaking her head. "To witness something so horrible. What a shock for you."

Surprised at the compassion in Martha's blue eyes, Alisha bobbed her head. "It happened so quickly and then I had to go into hiding when they came after me. But I was concerned for my grandmother and Miss Judy. So we went on the run again and then they came again. I think the shock caught up with me."

"More than shock," Martha replied as she got up to stir the good-smelling soup. "You almost froze to death. Nathan was right to bring you here."

"But now, we've put you in danger—if those men find us."

"I'm not worried about that," Martha replied, her

hand touching Alisha's arm. "I am more concerned about my son."

"You're worried about Nathan?"

"*Ja.*" Martha moved her hand away but her smile was brief and soft. "He's been through some terrible things, too. I know he left because he blamed himself for our little Hannah's disappearance and…death. He and his father said things in anger that night that they both need to ask forgiveness for."

Thinking about what Nathan had also said to her, Alisha lowered her head. They were way past that now. "He wants to do that, I think. He told me he had unfinished business here with both of you."

"And yet, he brought *you* here."

"Do you resent that?"

"It's not my place to resent anything," Martha replied. "What I'm trying to say, what you need to see, is that he brought you here to help with that unfinished business. He wants to resolve things with us but he also wants to resolve things with you."

"He's trying to save my life. That's all," Alisha said, not wanting Nathan's mother to misunderstand. "Once I'm safe, Nathan will take off again."

Compassion lightened Martha's eyes. "Is that what my son does, takes off?"

Alisha wanted to be honest and Nathan's mom had a way of bringing out the honesty in people. "He's been running for over a decade now. He thinks he'll find all of the lost people in the world."

"He might," Martha said, her whisper so low Alisha barely heard it. "But then, he might not. Sometimes, they are found but…they are in the hands of God."

Wanting to bring Martha some comfort, Alisha said,

"But sometimes Nathan finds them alive and reunites them with the people they love. That's important to him. It's his calling."

"So his calling keeps him from coming home to us?"

"No, his guilt takes care of that. He left all of us behind when he left Campton Creek."

"You still care for my son?"

Alisha wasn't ready to answer that. But she did nod. Then she said, "I'll always care for Nathan."

Now more than ever.

"I had to walk away because he couldn't stay," she admitted. "He couldn't stay with me and he couldn't come home. He's become a wanderer, a nomad without a permanent home. He can't move past what happened that night."

"But God sometimes moves those who can't find their own way," Martha said, tears misting in her eyes. "Nathan left us because of you and because of Hannah. Now, he has come home to us—for you and I think to find some peace with his sister's death. So despite what brought you both here, I pray he can let go of the pain and guilt of her death and just rest. Saving you from harm might actually bring my son his salvation."

Chapter Fifteen

The next afternoon, Nathan and Alisha sat at the dining table wearing more borrowed Amish clothes. Earlier that morning, Alisha had helped his mother with the washing machine, which ran with a paddle powered by hand. Martha had shown her how to clean their clothes with lye soap. They worked together in the small side room off the kitchen, where Alisha and Nathan had taken turns freshening up.

This room was used for laundry, bathing and as a mudroom—clothes hanging on a stringed line to dry over a small propane heater along with coats, boots and work shoes lined up along the wall underneath the clothing pegs. All neat and tidy and simple but with efficient indoor plumbing discreetly hidden behind another small enclosure. For which Alisha was eternally grateful.

While they'd worked, Martha had talked about Nathan growing up here with his younger brothers. She even mentioned Hannah a couple of times.

"*Gut kinder*, but rambunctious," Martha said, shaking her head. "But Nathan always did have a curiosity about life outside of Campton Creek. Wanderlust, I think. I prayed he'd come home after his *rumspringa*, but God had other plans for my son."

Alisha wanted to tell his mother she was so sorry that she'd interfered with those plans. He might have returned home if she hadn't become his forbidden sweetheart.

But before she could voice that, Martha turned to her and gave her a hesitant smile. "It wasn't his fault, you understand. And it wasn't your fault, either. You both left because of a terrible thing. I think God has used this current horrible tragedy to bring you both home."

Logic told Alisha she'd been in the wrong place at the wrong time when she'd pulled into that little Christmas market. That two people possibly involved with criminals had lost their lives and she happened to be the only person around to witness that. But here, in the quiet of this kitchen, another kind of logic took over. Had she been exactly where she should have been the other night?

Martha's eyes met hers. "You don't seem so sure about what I've said."

"I want to be sure," Alisha admitted, "but if God wants to bring us together, why does it have to be in such a violent way? With evil men murdering people, chasing us and threatening everyone we love?"

"Hmm, seems that happened in the Bible a few times, ain't so?" Martha let that observation hang in the air and then went back to her work, her deft hand holding Nathan's shirt against a scrub board.

"Good point." Alisha hung the dress she'd worn yesterday on the line and watched to make sure it wouldn't drip everywhere.

"Time will show us why, Alisha," Martha replied,

her tone firm and calm. She carefully helped to hang the rest of their wet clothes on the taut line stretched across the mudroom. "But I believe that sometimes, we have to walk through the fire to find the calm we seek. Think about it. If you both survive this, you can survive anything, and your feelings will be stronger than ever. If that is *Gott*'s will."

"And what if someone else loses their life?"

"God's will always stands—and we must accept that no matter the pain."

Now, sitting here wearing a clean dress and apron, her hair pulled back in a ponytail and covered with a white *kapp*, Alisha marveled at how Nathan's parents had allowed them to stay. She felt secure inside these sturdy walls, cocooned by the snow outside. Their forgiveness now was in sharp contrast to what she remembered that awful summer way back. This home was roomy and simple, but full of God's grace. Why had it taken so long for Nathan to come back? Did time heal all wounds?

He might not have returned, if not for you.

Martha had been convinced of that. Alisha had to consider being here a blessing at least. No matter the circumstances, Nathan was back in the house he'd loved. She hoped that would bring him a time of healing. She didn't expect he'd return to the Amish, but if he could still visit with his family and be a part of their lives, it could all be worth it.

Alisha looked around, marveling at the simplistic beauty of the place. "It's Christmas Eve," she blurted, her gaze lifting toward Nathan. "I'd almost forgotten."

"Yes, it is." He gave her a smile. "We get to spend it here together."

His gentle words made her blush but she couldn't give in to all these erratic impulses she'd been holding so close. So she glanced around the room instead, searching for signs of the holiday.

The kitchen was sparse and neat, with a huge table that had to have been handmade years ago, along with matching high-backed chairs. A deep farmhouse sink held a pump for drawing water and a refrigerator that ran on propane sat full of prepared dishes for tomorrow. Alisha had offered to sweep the floor after dinner but Martha had shooed her away.

"I do that every morning to start the day fresh. You can do it tomorrow morning if you wish."

The home held bits of Christmas, but no tree or lights. Christmas cards from family and friends, most of them handmade, lined the wooden ridge of a big, practical sideboard across from the table. It held three freshly baked pies—pecan, sweet potato and apple—and two different cakes—a coconut layer cake and a pound cake that had been made from exactly a pound of each ingredient. Tomorrow, they would have a big meal of baked turkey, mashed potatoes, vegetable casseroles and all sorts of other side dishes.

"After devotionals and exchanging simple presents, we'll share the meal," Nathan had told her earlier. "If Christmas had been one day earlier, we'd have gone to church."

Alisha longed to see her grandmother, but today they were trying to map out their next move. "I should be there with Granny and Mrs. Campton," she whispered to Nathan. "I've waited all year to spend the holidays with them. It was the only gift my grandmother wanted." Shrugging, she added, "It's the only gift I want this year, too."

He stared over at her, both of them mindful of his mother puttering in the kitchen and his father sitting in his rocker reading an Amish newspaper. Alisha could tell being here had helped Nathan so much. She didn't want to mess with that.

"I'm sorry," he said, his hand touching hers in a brief brush. "If I could make this all go away, that would be my gift to you."

"Your parents have been more than kind to me," she said, "so I don't mean to sound ungrateful. I just wish—"

"We both have our wishes," he said, his eyes going a dark blue that reminded her of a deep lake. "I'm going to get you back to your grandmother soon."

Since phone service was sketchy, and because they wanted to honor the rules of the house, they didn't use their phones to work. Their laptops were still at the cabin, she hoped. She missed her big briefcase with the shoulder straps. Her shield, her work companion. Nothing to be done about that now, though. Instead, they put together on paper a timeline of events based on the research they'd done already.

"The doctor had some major debts to pay," Nathan whispered. "The cars, the homes and too many charge cards. All a facade."

"That is a great motive to start selling opioids illegally," Alisha replied. "And to get in over your head with some nasty people. But the money had to be enticing."

"Yes, from what we've pieced together, I think he

owed them money or drugs maybe, and when he couldn't pay up, they decided to off him and his wife."

Alisha stared at the timeline. "But that won't get these people their money back."

"No, but they could easily find a way to break into his offshore accounts if there's any money left in them."

Jotting a note to find out about those possible accounts, she asked, "But how do we nail Deke Garrison for this? The man is like a ghost. Nowhere to be found."

"He's hiding," Nathan said. "The hit was completed but you saw the whole thing. He'll kill his own men because they keep messing up. You got away over and over."

"Thanks to you," she said, her words low.

Nathan didn't respond with words, but his expression softened and shifted and for a brief moment, he looked like the boy she remembered.

Confused and too aware of him, she read over the names of the men, thinking about their clothes and faces. "I hope we get a hit on one of these men. They're relentless."

"The one they're guarding in the hospital should be easy to identify, even the name Scott Kemp has to be an alias. They've got his prints so that might get a definite hit. Since we can't get online here, I hope we hear soon."

Nathan leaned close. "After Christmas, I think we should go back to our plan and head into Philly. We can meet with the real FBI there. We'll have to be careful and we'll have to stay in disguise."

She glanced at his mother, wondering if she could hear them. "This is a federal case and we need all three of these men in custody. If I can identify one or more of them, I'll become a federal witness. I can't withhold what's been happening here any longer."

"Okay, so we plan to do this as our next step. But after Christmas. My folks will go visiting the day after tomorrow and they could have lots of visitors, including my brothers, the next day. We'll stay here after they leave and then we'll find a way to get to Philly."

"Okay, but I'd like someone from my firm there to represent me and guide me through the interrogations."

"Good idea."

It sounded like the best solution. Her firm could put law clerks on this and hire people to help protect her. She couldn't stay here indefinitely and keep putting both of their families in danger.

"I'll call my boss first thing day after tomorrow," she said. "Let him know I do need his help." Mitchell Henderson would meet them in Philadelphia if necessary. Having someone she trusted to represent her would be wise.

"Are you two finished plotting over there?" Martha asked, her expression neutral. "I need help with a few things."

"Yes, Mamm," Nathan said. "I hope we didn't disturb you."

"You did not," his mother replied. "But this subject matter is terribly disturbing. I want you both safe."

Nathan got up to help his mother put away some food and baking dishes. "We'll let this go until after Christmas," he said, giving his mother a reassuring smile.

Martha touched a hand to his jaw. "I think that is a *gut* plan, Nathan. Tomorrow we celebrate not only the birth of our Lord Jesus, but we also celebrate the return of our oldest son." Then she added, "If you can't stay for Second Christmas, I understand."

Alisha couldn't help but hear. Second Christmas was always the day after Christmas where more casual visits took place, but still with lots of food and festivities. A visiting day, but the best time for them to leave since the roads would be bustling with Amish buggies.

After they'd helped Martha move the table to add more chairs in case they had visitors tomorrow, Nathan turned to Alisha. "I'm going to try and reach Carson and bring him up to speed. I'll be right outside."

"Okay. Be careful."

"I'll hide in the corner of the porch where the house takes an L-shape."

She smiled. "Watch out for Santa."

Watching him go, she let her heart do that little jumpy thing it seemed to want to do whenever he was near. She'd tempered her feelings for Nathan a long time ago, but even in the midst of fear and danger, he still made her heart beat too fast. He was her protector, her friend, someone she'd fallen in love with years ago and someone she'd tried to put out of her mind since. She'd never dreamed he'd come back into her life in such a big way.

She'd never dreamed anything like this could happen to her. Up until now, she'd been self-involved and focused on her work, lonely at times, but content and fulfilled.

She now appreciated all of that and more.

"*Kumm* and sit with us for a while," Martha said. "I have a few books and devotionals by my chair if you'd like to read a bit."

"Thank you." Alisha sat down across from them. "And thank you for everything."

Amos looked up at her but didn't speak. Martha nodded and glanced toward the door. "I am thankful you are both alive and well and here with us."

Alisha lifted one of the books off the table. A midwife story. That made her think about Nathan and marriage and children and...things she shouldn't be considering. Pretending to read the book, she instead held a vision of Nathan holding a child in his arms. He'd make a good father.

When Nathan came through the door, she exhaled the breath she'd been holding. Would she ever feel truly comfortable around his family? His folks, obviously feeling the same way, said good-night and went upstairs to bed, leaving them alone.

"Want to sit by the stove?" he asked, motioning her over to where the wood stove still held some heat.

Alisha didn't know why all of a sudden she felt shy around him. They'd been together for days. But it was too quiet here, too silent to hide the awareness that seemed to be simmering right below the surface of their fatigue and apprehension.

She sat in the cushioned rocking chair his mother had vacated, the scent of the locally made cinnamon candle sitting on a shelf still lingering in the air. "Did you talk to Carson?"

He hesitated and then nodded. "Yes. First he told me that my truck is being watched 24/7, according to his sources in Reading. Same dark SUV-type vehicle's circling the hotel parking lot."

"They've probably harassed everyone at the hotel to find out if you're there or not."

"Right. But that means they don't know where we are for sure. But they've managed to slip away before anyone can track them, so that's a problem."

"So we keep moving."

"Yes. Carson offered to escort us to the city but in an unmarked car. So we'll continue to dress Amish and take him up on that offer. That won't be so unusual this time of year with people visiting each other."

"If I show up dressed as an Amish woman, my boss will faint dead away," she said with a giggle as she stared down at the burgundy dress and white apron she was wearing. In spite of the seriousness of this situation, she had to laugh at that scene.

"I would think so, although you look pretty pretending to be an Amish woman." His eyes held hers for a brief moment and then he quickly gazed at the old potbellied stove. "We can't go back to your place in Reading. They're probably watching it."

"And they've probably already been inside," she replied, her heart skipping at that thought. She'd have to move. She didn't want to go back there at all now.

"So I'll rent us two rooms in a place I use in the city."

"That's fine."

Lifting an eyebrow, he said, "You don't sound so sure."

"It's just I never thought I'd be having this kind of conversation with you."

Nathan's gaze washed over her again and she saw it there in his eyes—the same longing that poured through her heart each time she looked at him. "No," he said, leaning close, "I always thought one day we'd go on our honeymoon and share a room, as man and wife."

Shocked at those words, Alisha looked down at her lap. "This sure isn't a honeymoon, is it?"

"No," he said. Then he reached across the side table and took her hand in his. "But a double murder and scary hit men aside, I wouldn't want to be anywhere else tonight."

Alisha took his hand and savored the warmth of his fingers curling over hers. "Merry Christmas, Nathan."

"Merry Christmas, Alisha."

He walked her to the door of her room but when he heard a rustling outside, he tugged her close. "Go upstairs."

Alisha watched from the landing as he went to a side window and stared out into the dark night. Hearing another noise, he motioned to her. "Go and get my gun from my room."

She hurried barefoot into his room, hoping she wouldn't disturb his parents. Since their door was shut and the small room he'd taken was down the hallway from theirs, she made it to his room and grabbed the weapon he'd put in the bottom of a small armoire when they'd first arrived.

Then she moved silently back down the stairs to find him roaming from window to window.

"Is someone out there?"

He nodded, waiting, a finger to her lips. "Go to your room but stay by the door."

Alisha didn't argue. She had to stay quiet. If his folks woke up, they could get caught in the crossfire.

Nathan came away from the window and called to her through the partially cracked door. "Listen to me. I'm going to go and check the barn. If I'm not back in five minutes, wake my *daed*, all right?"

She nodded, anxiety making her breath come too shallow. "Where does your father keep his hunting rifles?"

"You don't need to worry about that."

"Nathan, I know how to shoot a gun."

He shook his head. "He keeps them in the barn, locked in a cabinet. We can't get to them, so just stay in your room."

Alisha watched as he carefully opened the back door down the hall past the mudroom. She couldn't stay still so she went to her room and peeked between the modesty curtains, the moonlight shining brilliantly against the whiteout.

Nathan hurried in a hunched run toward the barn.

Then she saw a lone shadow moving around the west corner of the looming structure.

Grabbing a shawl she'd left on the bed, she hurried around to the back door. She had to warn Nathan.

Chapter Sixteen

She'd made it to a mushrooming old oak tree when she heard what sounded like a grunt, followed by an animal's whinny. After that, she heard muttered voices. Then she saw that same shadowy figure running toward the woods. Nathan came around the barn, watching as the man took off in a fast getaway and dived over the corral fence.

Nathan stood watching and then turned back toward the house. When he got close, she called softly. "Nathan?"

Surprised, he whirled and stomped toward where she stood hidden behind the massive tree trunk. "Why do you always insist on leaving your post?"

"Why do you always try to be a hero?" she retorted. "You could have been killed."

He took her in his arms and held her close, the tree blocking them from the house and the woods. "The same with you."

Alisha held him tight, feeling his heartbeat moving with hers. "Did you get a look at him?"

"Not a good one. But I warned him I had a pistol

trained on him and I would shoot to kill. Then while he was pondering that, one of the old male goats gave him a run for his money. I'm surprised the noise didn't wake my parents."

"I heard a few grunts," she said, relief washing over her. "Do you think he's gone?"

"For now. He'd be an idiot to come back tonight."

Alisha looked up and saw Nathan gazing down at her, his eyes a deep blue in the shimmer from the moonlight. "We can't keep doing this," she said. "Because they won't give up."

"I know." He studied her as if he were trying to memorize her face and then reached a hand up, digging his fingers in her hair. "I know." Then he leaned down and touched his lips to hers. "I won't give up, either, Alisha."

His touch caused Alisha to pull him close and kiss him back. This wasn't like the adolescent kisses she remembered from the past. This was a grown man holding her in his arms, his lips conveying what he couldn't say and telling her they'd lived a million lifetimes since he'd last held her this way.

But the moment ended too soon. He pulled back to stare down at her again, a deep burning agony covering his face. "It's cold. We should get inside."

Alisha couldn't speak. He put his hand against her backbone and guided her toward the back door. They moved inside without making any noise, the house warm and quiet and still, as if holding its breath in the same way she was holding hers.

Nathan once again tugged her toward the door to her room. Then he shoved his pistol into her hand. "Keep that close. I'm sleeping in the living room tonight."

With that, he was gone, pulling her door shut before she could respond.

Alisha doubted either of them would get any sleep. They still had a lot between them—bad people wanting her dead, his family having to deal with all of this and the feelings they were both trying so hard to fight.

How would she ever make it through any of this? But how would she have made it this far without his help?

After she'd put on the billowy nightgown Martha had given her, Alisha lay in bed and said her prayers, the memory of that midnight kiss staying with her.

We need mercy, Lord. We need guidance. We need You. I've drifted away from my faith. I got caught up in work and loneliness and life. But I know You are there, always. I need You as my shield now. Nathan needs you. He's been carrying this horrible burden for a long time and he's forgotten how to love. Maybe we can show him that's still possible.

After she'd prayed, she closed her eyes and thought of how she'd felt when he'd held her and kissed her. She'd felt at home and at peace. If only she could feel that way forever.

The next morning, Alisha got up early to help Martha in the kitchen. After she'd dressed and made sure she looked as Amish as she could by wearing her hair pinned up underneath a white *kapp*, she checked her apron and dress and decided her own black boots didn't look too out of place since the heels weren't very high. Nathan had suggested they dress to blend in. Although his parents didn't expect any visitors until tomorrow, they had to take every measure to look the part. Especially after what had happened last night.

She wondered how exactly Nathan had slept, but figured he'd found a quilt and pillow and curled up by the stove. She also wondered if his parents had found him that way and asked for an explanation. She only knew something had changed between them there underneath that sheltering oak tree.

They'd both let down their guard. That could be so good or it could turn out to be the worst thing for both of them. She had to talk to him and make sure he understood this could never work.

But when she walked into the living room, she didn't see Nathan or his father. Or Martha either.

A sense of panic overcame her. Where was everyone? She checked the side room and didn't find any of them. Then she went to the back door and searched the yard before looking out toward the fields and barn.

When she spotted Nathan coming out of the barn with his father, her relief was so great she closed her eyes and fell against the wall to gulp in deep breaths.

"Alisha, are you not well?"

Alisha looked up to find Martha standing in the kitchen, holding a basket of wrapped gifts.

"Oh, I'm sorry," Alisha said. "I couldn't find any of you and I got worried."

Understanding flowed through Martha's eyes. "I went into my chest upstairs to bring out our gifts," Martha explained. "I had to wait until the men were out of the house. Nathan was already up and out tending the livestock when we came down."

So that explained that. He'd probably gone out to the barn to search for any signs of that intruder.

"I can help you put the gifts out," Alisha said, her heart still racing. "Silly me. I'm not usually so jumpy."

"Understandable." Martha gave her a head-to-toe check, however. "You look very pretty this morning."

"Thank you," Alisha said. "Do you want me to take that?"

"We'll leave these things in the basket," Martha said, taking the beautiful woven basket over to the chairs. Placing it by the woodstove, she said, "When they return, we'll get started. But you can help me with breakfast."

"I'll be happy to."

When Martha started fluffing pillows, Alisha relaxed a little. But something about Martha's busy work shouted that the other woman, usually so serene, had something on her mind today.

Holiday stress? Or had Nathan told his parents about the intruder who'd been snooping around?

Alisha took another deep breath even as she sensed something was off. What were they all hiding from her?

Nathan and his dad waited outside the barn, Nathan to watch for any more interlopers, and his father to make sure their big surprise actually took place.

"They should be here by now," Amos said. "Are you sure your friend will be able to get them here?"

"Yes. I told him to come early," he replied, rubbing his hands together. "But those two have a mind of their own and they only move at one speed."

"Slow?" Amos laughed. "They are your elders so be mindful."

"Oh, I'm mindful," Nathan said. "They can hold their own."

Amos stood silent for a moment, one old boot caught

against the fence railing. "Did you and Alisha take a moonlight stroll last night?"

Nathan tried to form an answer and decided to go with the truth. "We did. I heard a noise so I wanted to check the animals. She asked to come with me."

His father gave him a slanted glance. "I thought I heard voices. Your *mudder* said I was dreaming."

"We didn't stay out here long," Nathan replied, memories of their shared kiss warming his skin. "It was chilly."

Amos looked into his eyes. "Are you sure everything is all right?"

"Today, everything is perfect," Nathan replied, praying it so. "Or at least it will be when they get here."

He wondered if his father knew more but decided he'd explain later. After kissing Alisha, Nathan felt in over his head with trying to protect everyone and deal with his growing feelings again. He'd locked away those feelings forever, or so he'd thought. Getting all tangled up in these aching emotions did no good right now. He hoped Alisha would understand that.

Amos watched the road. "There, son. They are here."

Nathan's heart filled with joy. He couldn't wait to see Alisha's face. Would she like his Christmas surprise?

"Let us get to it then," his *daed* said with a soft smile. "Merry Christmas, Nathan."

"Merry Christmas, Daed."

They hurried to the house and had just entered the back door when they heard the buggy coming up the drive.

Martha turned and winked at him. "We have some very early guests arriving."

Nathan looked at Alisha and saw the apprehension in her eyes.

"Should we hide, Nathan?" she asked.

The fear in her voice flooded him. Who was he kidding? He'd walk through fire to protect her and hold her in his arms again. "I think we're safe."

Amos waved his hand in the air. "No hiding. These are *wilkum* guests."

Alisha's frown went from fearful to curious. Moving to the front of the living room, she peered out the window. "That's Josiah Fisher. Is he bringing his family to visit?"

"*Neh*," Martha said, holding a hand to her lips. "He is doing a favor for a friend."

Nathan couldn't hide his grin. "You'll see."

He moved to stand by her, so he could watch her face while she watched the buggy. Alisha shot him one of the questioning glances he remembered before...before they'd become close again.

"Just relax," he whispered. "It's Christmas. Nothing bad can happen to us today." He'd make sure of that.

Then he motioned to the buggy.

Alisha followed Nathan's gaze and waited. What was he up to now? Did he plan to whisk her away and put Josiah in danger, too? She knew they were close since Nathan had helped Josiah find his missing sister Josie. Now the young woman lived with Josiah and Raesha and Raesha's former mother-in-law Naomi. She'd helped them with the same case, which had involved an abandoned baby that they were now raising. A happy ending.

But why involve Josiah in *this*?

Josiah waved to them and then went to the back of

the buggy and untied what looked like a folded wheelchair. Then Nathan went out to carefully help the two Amish women out of the enclosed buggy, a slow process since they both appeared to be elderly. Unable to see who they might be since they were covered from head to toe in bonnets, shawls and cloaks, Alisha waited patiently.

After all, this wasn't her house. She couldn't make demands or run and hide. The others seemed so excited, she figured these two must be matriarchs of some sort.

After Josiah had one of the women in her wheelchair, he turned and nodded, a smile crossing his handsome face. Then the two women smiled.

"Let's go and greet them," Martha said, moving toward the door.

Nathan came hurrying back and took Alisha by the hand.

She watched as the two women looked toward the house and then she saw their familiar faces. Gasping, she glanced at Nathan as he hauled her to the open front door. "Is that…my grandmother and Mrs. Campton?"

He bobbed his head. "It is. My Christmas gift to you."

"Nathan." She couldn't speak. Her eyes pricked with moisture. "Nathan."

His eyes grew misty, "Just for today, we'll pretend that everything is okay."

Amazed and touched, Alisha reached up and kissed him on his jaw. "Thank you."

Then she took off down the steps to hug her grandmother tight.

The next few minutes were a blur of hugs and happiness and both her grandmother and Mrs. C talking at once.

"We planned the whole thing—with Nathan's help, of course. And that sweet Carson. He is a true lawman—a hero. He's kept us up-to-date and coordinated things with our police department and so our place has been surrounded with guards."

"We decided we'd have fun with it and dress up in disguises in case anyone was watching. But we've been fine at our house. Those mean men know you're no longer there and that we have those dedicated guards always checking on us."

"And Josiah was so kind to leave his family to bring us here. He'll get extra cookies for his efforts, of course."

"They are staying for dinner," Martha explained after Josiah had said his goodbyes, a container of snickerdoodles on the buggy seat next to him. "And we will exchange gifts later."

"I don't have any gifts to give," Alisha said, her heart filling with love for their bravery in sneaking out to come here.

"Being here with you today is the best gift," Granny said, her eyes welling up with tears. "We have prayed for both of you and when Carson let us know you were here, we were so relieved. We understand Nathan was injured and you ran away into the woods."

Alisha nodded as they all gathered in chairs by the warm stove. Martha and Nathan stayed in the kitchen preparing coffee and bacon along with homemade cinnamon rolls to tide them over until the big meal. She glanced up at Nathan and thought seeing his smile was the best gift she could ask for. He'd risked a lot, bringing these two women here to share Christmas with her. She'd never forget that.

"I did get away from the cabin," she said, taking a deep breath, the horror of that night still with her. She didn't go into too much detail. "After they shot Nathan, I was afraid they'd kill me, too. I had some pepper spray in my pocket and I used it. Then a big stag we'd seen earlier came charging through the woods and scared them away."

Nathan put down the dessert plates he'd taken down out of the cabinet and held his free hand against the sling his mother had changed out earlier. "Alisha, you saw the deer again?"

"Yes. I didn't think to tell you. He came along the path and almost rammed one of those men holding me."

"I saw the stag later too," he said. "In fact, spotting him helped me to find you." He shrugged. "Almost as if he led me to you."

Mrs. Campton, her bonnet still on, clapped her hands and smiled. "God's creatures can sense fear and danger, even evil, I believe. You are both blessed to have had some of nature's help that night."

"Amazing," Alisha said, remembering how they'd quoted part of Psalm 42 to each other. "He was beautiful," she said, her eyes holding Nathan's. "I hope that big deer stays safe out there. He obviously likes the birdhouse path."

Martha spoke up. "I've seen those beautiful birdhouses. We've often wondered who owns that land. Did you say you were hiding in a cabin?"

Alisha's gaze crashed with Nathan's. "Yes."

Nathan looked back and forth between his parents. "I own the cabin. I bought the land and built the cabin

even though I don't get to stay there as often as I'd like."
He shrugged and lowered his gaze. "And, Mamm, I
made the birdhouses."

Martha gasped and reached out a hand to him. "All
this time, they brought me such joy and to know they
were made by my son. *Denki*, Nathan. That and now
knowing you've been nearby all this time. Another gift
to cherish."

Nathan held his mother's hand tight but he didn't
speak.

Soon, they had the whole story. Amos sat still through
all of the chatter. "If I may speak," he said, a gentle tone
in his voice.

"Or course, Amos," Mrs. Campton said, her smile
beaming.

"I am glad we have our Nathan back. I have prayed
toward that end. And I'm happy to share our home with
all of you today."

Judy Campton straightened in her chair. "But?"

Amos shook his head. "What makes you think I have
more to say?"

"Just a hunch," Mrs. Campton replied, biding her
time.

"But there is danger out there. We don't abide by
this kind of violence but… As my wife has pointed out,
Gott verlosst die Sein nicht. God doesn't abandon one
of his own so I cannot turn away a loved one in need."

"But you still want us gone, right?" Nathan said,
coming to stand by where Alisha sat.

"It's not that I want you gone," Amos replied, his
gnarled hand moving down his beard. "I am thankful for your return but I want that evil out there gone."

"We all do," Granny replied. "We all do. We have

prayed for that and with the help of Nathan and the authorities, we hope that will come to pass."

Nathan's gaze touched on Alisha. "We have a new plan and we don't want to involve any of you in it," he said. "But that's for another day. Alisha and I need this reprieve. It's been a long time coming."

"We can all agree to that," Amos said, standing. "Martha, *kumm.*"

Nathan's mother motioned them to the table. Nathan and Alisha served the coffee and passed the food, unusual tasks for a man in an Amish house but Alisha appreciated him doing it.

Soon they were passing gifts. Alisha received some knitted gloves from Martha and Nathan was handed a basket full of preserves and jellies.

"I'll keep them here for you," his mother had whispered. "For when you return for home-cooked meals with biscuits and bread."

"That is a plan, Mamm," he told her.

Everyone received a small token and no one complained. Alisha took this simple Christmas morning as an example to use when she returned to her life. If that day ever came.

The day passed too soon and while her grandmother and Mrs. Campton were strong and spry, they needed their rest. So after the early dinner feast was over, Amos offered to take them home before dusk settled.

"It's not safe for you," Bettye said, shaking her head.

"If it was a trip you were willing to make, then I can certainly do the same," Amos retorted. "I will not even need a disguise."

"I'll come with you," Nathan offered. "I can wear a hat and coat and no one will know it's me."

"Do you think that's wise?" Martha asked.

Alisha's heart went into overdrive. "Nathan, maybe we should get word to Josiah? You're injured and can barely use your left arm."

"Josiah said he'd come back if we needed him," Bettye added. "I have my cell with me, just in case."

Nathan lowered his head, thinking. "I shouldn't leave you alone but I don't want Daed going into town by himself."

"Then you should go," Alisha replied. "Josiah knows we'll use the phone booth or Granny's cell to call Raesha's work cell if we need him."

Nathan took her to the side. "I'd feel better taking them back. My *daed* will insist on going so I should go with him. Use the gun I gave you last night if anything happens. We should be there and back in less than an hour."

In the end, Alisha couldn't argue with him. She wanted her grandmother and Mrs. Campton to get home safely. So she hugged them tight and thanked them for taking this risk. Then she stood with Martha and waved goodbye to them, her heart pulled in so many different directions, she wasn't sure she'd ever breathe normally again.

Nathan had made this happen. In the midst of running for their lives, he'd brought her a gift she'd never forget.

Now she just had to worry about Nathan and his father making it back without any problems.

Chapter Seventeen

Martha walked up to where Alisha stood by the front window.

Close to an hour had gone by and the snow was falling again in soft, silent flakes. It would be fully dark soon.

"Here," Martha said, holding up a cup of tea. "Meadow tea, mostly mint and sugar but good for calming us down."

"It's getting late," Alisha said, taking the tea, her eyes still on the road. "Thank you, Mrs. Schrock."

"Call me Martha," the other woman said. "We don't stand on formality around here."

Alisha turned away from the window, the last of the sun's feeble rays casting out in a golden sheen over the snowy yard and woods while the snow clouds hovered, waiting for nightfall. "I wanted to thank you for today," she told Martha. "I was so touched by what Nathan did and how you welcomed my grandmother and Mrs. Campton into your home."

"Nathan thought that up and made it happen," Martha explained. "He knew you wanted to be with your *grossmammi* today." She glanced around. "Judy Campton has always been a friend to the Amish and we all adore your *grossmammi*. It was a pleasure to host them today."

"I so wanted to spend Christmas with her," Alisha replied, sipping the herbal tea, the cup warming her hands, the scent of mint lifting to her nose. "I'll never forget what Nathan's done for me. And not just his kindness today. He has always been a protector."

Martha patted the chair next to her rocking chair. "*Kumm*, Alisha. The food is put away and tomorrow, we'll celebrate again with other family members. Sit and finish your tea. If the men are hungry when they return, we'll allow them a snack."

Alisha's skin felt hot, her nerves on fire with worry for Nathan and his father. This nightmare seemed to go on forever. Tomorrow, they would go back to Philadelphia and get moving on finding a way to end this. She should have done that in the first place but fear and a need to be with her grandmother had held her back. But in her heart, she knew she'd called Nathan that night because she needed him—his strength and his ability to make others feel safe. Admitting that she couldn't do it all alone would have made her feel weak before. But now, she could understand that the hole in her heart could only be filled with the kind of courage love brought. She couldn't live in a spirit of fear and she'd always considered herself fearless. But having Nathan back in her life had shown her how she needed her faith to give her strength. She also needed Nathan—to pour her love out on.

Had could she have let this happen? Falling for him yet again? There could be no good end to that so why did it feel so right?

She sank down next to Martha and put her cup of tea on the table, her hands shaking. "I...want this over."

Martha took up her knitting. "I know you do."

"He's been right there, protecting me all this time."

"You mean, from those horrible men?"

"Yes, and even before then when we had to work some cases together. He always overstepped and somehow tried to help. It was annoying at the time but now I can see so clearly that he wanted to do whatever he could to find that justice we both keep seeking." With a resigned sigh, she added, "And he was watching over me like a guardian."

"Because he still loves you."

"What?" Alisha's head came up, her breath catching in her throat. Did his mother see that she still loved Nathan, too?

"My son loves you," Martha said, her serenity intact, her eyes void of any judgment.

Alisha wanted to tell Martha she might be wrong, but she couldn't breathe. She could very well be having a panic attack.

But before she could break down and confess to Martha that she loved Nathan, too, they heard a noise outside.

"They're home," Alisha said, getting up to race to the window, relief allowing her to take in air again.

Then she saw the vehicle parked near the edge of the woods.

Turning to face Martha, she turned a cold, still calm. "It's someone else. We need to prepare."

Martha went into action. "The barn. Amos told me to run to the barn if anyone came."

"I don't know if we can make it," Alisha replied,

searching the front yard. "I don't know how many might be out there."

When they heard a footstep on the broad front porch, Alisha nodded. "The barn has weapons."

Marth bobbed her head. "*Ja*, and it also has animals that will put up a ruckus and give us time to hide."

Rushing to the mudroom, she grabbed two dark cloaks. Shoving one at Alisha, she whispered, "Put this on. It will shield you from the cold and hide you in the dusk."

Alisha put the cloak on and hurried to her room to get Nathan's Beretta. The weapon would also shield her. Because she'd use it to protect Nathan's mother and herself.

Taking Martha's hand, she followed the older woman out the back door then pulled her into the corner Nathan used to hide when he was making calls. After checking the yard and woods, they hurried past the few trees that offered protection and then sprinted toward the front of the big, hulking building. While Alisha watched, Martha unfastened the heavy hinges and motioned Alisha into the big, dark barn. Then she carefully closed the doors and looked into the darkness that engulfed them.

After her eyes adjusted, Alisha spotted a big rake standing against the wall. Grabbing it, she worked to slip it through the inside handles of the doors. "To give us some time," she whispered, taking Martha's hand in hers. "Where should we hide?"

Martha guided her to an empty stall in the far corner where stacked hay stood behind a cluster of feed sacks, milking buckets and hanging harnesses. Crouching, they huddled against the hay behind the feed sacks.

The milk cows danced in a restless anxiety, thinking they might be fed or taken care of.

The big draft horses shook out their manes and neighed softly.

Martha had been correct, just as Mrs. Campton had said about the stag in the forest. The animals sensed something was not right.

"They could hear the animals and come to look," she whispered as she and Martha crouched in a corner near the gun cabinet.

Martha adjusted her cape and did a quick peek around a feed sack. "Maybe the nervous animals will scare them away. I heard that happened last night."

So Nathan had told them about that. Remembering their kiss underneath the oak, Alisha wondered if Martha knew more than she'd voiced. That didn't matter right now.

Outside, the goats voiced their own alerts, their displeasure rising in a confused harmony as they bawled and bayed.

"That old male goat doesn't like anyone messing with his female companions," Martha whispered. "He has a pair of painfully sharp horns."

Then the women heard someone trying to get inside the barn upfront. Through the doors.

They'd secured the main doors but not the doors opening to the goat room and pen. "They'll come around and try." Alisha started searching for things to put in front of the back door. She could move a couple feeds bags to trip them, or tie a rope across the doors to slam them back toward the goats.

"They'll get rammed if they enter that goat pen,"

Martha said with assurance. "The goats will gather around and stall them until we can run."

Alisha thought about that and tried to form a plan that would protect Martha. "We'd have to head to the edge of the woods, near the road. Then I can run to the phone booth."

Wishing she'd grabbed her cell, she listened for footsteps.

They heard the doors jarring again, the pounding and knocking coming quickly this time. With a grunt, someone crashed against the massive, heavy doors. Then Alisha heard the sickening sound of a silenced gun.

"They're trying to shoot the locks off. That won't matter, but the rake won't hold forever," Alisha whispered.

Martha gave her a questioning glance. "We can send out the drafts."

"The horses." Alisha had always admired the sturdy draft horses they used to farm the land. "What if one of your horses gets shot or hurt?"

"Better than one of us getting the same," Martha replied.

They formed a plan. Alisha would pull the rake out of the door handles and allow the man to crash through. Martha would rouse the big drafts and have them waiting and then at the exact same time, she'd send them running.

Hopefully, the animals would knock their intruder right off his feet so they'd be able to get away and also help Alisha and Martha escape. The plan didn't go much further than running to the woods, however.

"On three," Alisha said as they moved slowly toward the doors. The barn had saved them from being assaulted in the house but now, they had one chance to make a run for it.

"If this doesn't work," Alisha said when they approached the heavy doors, "then you run, Martha. Run as fast as you can and I'll deal with whoever this is."

"How can I leave you?" Martha asked, her eyes shining with dread and fear.

Alisha lowered her voice but made sure Martha heard her. "Just do it. I won't have your death on my head, too."

Nathan turned the old buggy into the lane, relieved that they'd gotten Bettye and Judy settled. The two women had insisted they bring home cake and cookies even though they'd barely dented the feast his *mamm* had prepared. He'd gain ten pounds if he stayed here much longer.

"Go and get warm, Daed," he told his father. "I'll put away the buggy and rub down Petunia." The ornery mare lifted her nose and snorted her approval on that.

"*Denki*," Amos replied, nodding as Nathan stopped at the side of the house to let him off.

Nathan clicked the reins and started Petunia toward the barn, but his dad came running to stop him. "Nathan, the front door is open."

Nathan stopped the mare and hopped from the buggy, his heart surging as he sprinted past his father. "Stay by the buggy," he called, using his good arm to wave his father away from the house.

Nathan crashed through the front door, his heart fighting to burst from his chest. What had he been thinking, leaving the women here alone? He'd enjoyed the drive with his father but he'd been concerned about leaving Alisha and his mother here. And for good reason.

Now he hoped he wasn't too late.

After moving through the house to check the dark rooms and finding no one, he sprinted to the back door and out into the yard, careful to stay behind the trees until he could get his bearings. The crescent moon hung low in the sky, causing shadows to cast wide from the woods and the barn. When Nathan felt a hand on his arm, he whirled, ready to fight, and found his father standing there holding a shovel. "Use this if need be."

Nathan let out a breath. "I'm afraid to call out. They'll take them if they know we're here."

His father shot him a grim look, but thankfully, didn't remind him that this was his fault. This couldn't be happening all over again. He wouldn't lose another family member to evil and he would not lose Alisha again—to that same kind of evil.

Then Amos lifted his head. "Listen. Do you hear that?"

Nathan squinted and listened. "The barn? Someone's trying to get in the barn."

Amos rushed past him, but Nathan held him back. "They must have hidden there and now someone is out to find them."

"We must go," Amos said, lifting away.

"You stay. I'll go," Nathan said, a gentle plea in his words.

"Bring your mother back to me," Amos replied, that same plea caught in his words.

Nathan hurried toward the barn but when he was about to make the last sprint toward where a man stood trying to pry the door open, he heard a great swish and watched as someone from inside shoved one of the big doors open. Then the two big drafts came charging out. The surprised man trying to break in screamed and went down, one of the horses hitting him and knocking him over.

Amos rushed forward. "*Was der schinner is letz?*"

His *daed* wanted to know what was wrong. So did Nathan.

They hurried toward the barn but when Nathan saw two caped figures emerging, he let out the breath he'd been holding.

"Daed, it's Mamm and Alisha!"

"Nathan!" Alisha tugged Martha with her as they hurried toward the two men. "Nathan, are you okay?"

He took her in his arms while his father did the same with his mother. The sight and feel of her alive made him want to never let go. "We're fine. What happened?"

She quickly caught him up. "We had to find a way to escape. We were hiding but he kept trying to get in."

"Stay here." Nathan went over to where the man lay unconscious, bending to check his pulse.

Alisha joined him while Martha stayed close to Amos. "Is he alive?"

"Yes. But he's probably going to be in a lot of pain when he wakes up." The two drafts circled back around and together his parents guided them back to the barn. "I need to call this in and get an ambulance out here."

"So now we'll have two suspects in the hospital."

"Yes, and behind bars after that. If we can hold them long enough to make them talk."

When he stood, Alisha touched his arm. "Nathan, this ends now. Hiding out isn't going to stop this. Tonight was another close call."

Nathan nodded and pointed to the ground. "Yes, too close."

Alisha gasped as she spotted the silencer on the gun the man had been carrying. "I knew he had a silencer. He tried to shoot out the barn door."

"A professional," Nathan said. "He's been watching for days and today, I gave him the perfect opportunity."

"Enough," Alisha said. "I'm leaving here with or without you and I'm going straight to the Philadelphia police and I'm calling the FBI field office to tell them I'm alive and well and ready to tell them what I know. We need to stop running and since that was our next plan and our best plan, I have to cooperate."

Pulling out his phone, Nathan realized he'd failed her yet again. He'd tried to protect her but she'd been close to death several times now. When would he learn he couldn't save anyone on his own? Not his sister and not even Alisha.

He hit numbers, but his heart cried out to God.

As the deer pants for water, so my soul longs for you, O God.

Nathan couldn't do this alone. He needed God with him.

And he needed Alisha with him, too. He'd been denying that for years now.

After calling the authorities, he turned to where Alisha stood shivering in the cold. "The police are on their way with an ambulance. Let's get you inside."

"What about him?" she said, staring over at the man on the ground.

"I'll stay here until they arrive. We shouldn't move him." Then he checked the road. "We need to keep this low-key."

"You might need this," she said, her voice stronger now.

Nathan looked down to where she held his gun against her cloak.

"I didn't fire it," she said. "But I would have."

"I know," he replied. "It's time to get you somewhere safe."

"Yes, a place that won't bring anyone else we love to harm."

Chapter Eighteen

Why was going away so hard?

Alisha looked into Martha Schrock's sweet eyes and saw the pain of a mother watching her son leave yet again.

"I don't know how to thank you," she whispered to Martha as they huddled near the door watching for the unmarked car to arrive.

It was early and dawn would be here soon. The whole world glowed white, the snow covering everything like a chenille blanket. The white houses and barns in the distance hulked like weary giants against the sky. The wind held a piercing chill that caused Alisha's tears to slip silently down her cold cheeks.

"No thanks needed or expected," Martha replied, taking Alisha's hands in hers. "No matter what, we have our Nathan back and that is a gift that can't be taken from us." Then she leaned close. "I know you will protect him with all of your heart."

Alisha nodded, unable to speak. Her grandmother and Mrs. Campton had explained this kind of love to her. Men were born protectors but women protected their men with a love that came from the heart—the fiercest kind of love.

Alisha had never truly known that concept until now. Even when they were young and so in love, she'd been selfish. She'd given up on Nathan too quickly and gone off to do what she thought she needed to do. But she'd become jaded and critical of love, had fought against it and closed off her heart.

She wouldn't do that this time, even if she and Nathan couldn't make it work. But she wanted it to work. "I'll try my best," she managed to say.

Martha hugged her close. "Send word."

Amos didn't hug Alisha but he patted her arm. "*Gott* will watch over you both."

Nathan stood nearby, awkward and clearly shaken. "We'll let you know how things progress."

His mother rushed to hug him. "Take care and Nathan, *kumm* home to see us soon."

"I'll do that, Mamm," he said, his eyes searching Alisha's face while he hugged his mother.

Amos cleared his throat and nodded. Nathan shook his father's hand. "*Denki,* Daed."

Amos didn't speak for a moment but his eyes were gentle on his oldest son. He had not condoned them arriving here but he'd held his thoughts and allowed them to stay. Alisha appreciated that for Nathan's sake. "Better get on."

Carson pulled up close to the house in a plain older-model car.

"Time to go," Nathan said, taking Alisha by the hand. Giving his parents a brief smile, he guided her to the waiting car.

Soon they were huddled in the back seat, warm air

taking away the morning chill. Alisha took one last look at the two people standing on the porch.

"Carson?" Nathan asked.

"They put undercover state police all around the property," Carson replied. "You two have kept the town and state police departments busy this Christmas season."

"Thank you," Nathan said.

Carson lifted something from the front seat. "I thought you might want this, Alisha."

"My briefcase," she said with glee. "You got it back."

"After they cleared the cabin, I asked permission to bring it to you. Nathan, your stuff is in there, too."

"Now we have the files we've saved," Alisha said. "Those men were in such a hurry to capture me, they didn't find this."

"We can all rest when this is over," Nathan said, his arm across Alisha's back.

She turned to face him and he gave her a wry little smile. "We'll get through this. I promise."

But that would be a hard promise to keep. If Nathan failed this time, it would be so much worse for him to get over. In saving Alisha, he'd find that redemption he so needed.

She had to work hard to make sure they both stayed alive. After that, she'd figure out the rest. Would he want to stay this close? Or would he go back to being a lonely nomad?

Since they'd left in the middle of the night, Alisha didn't object when Nathan tugged her close. "Sleep," he whispered in her ear. "Rest."

She didn't argue. She might not sleep but she could

rest in the safety of his arms. And she said a prayer of thanks for that at least.

When she later woke with a start, Alisha lifted up and stared out at the landscape. "Are we almost there?"

"Hey, sleepy-head," Nathan said, lifting her hair away from her eyes. "Do you feel better?"

"I don't know," she answered, slipping away from his warm embrace so she could get her bearings. "I've forgotten what better feels like." Then she noticed they were off the main interstate highway into the city. "Where are we?"

"Carson's taking the side roads in a zigzag fashion," Nathan explained. "Better to be safe."

"Not much longer," Carson said over his shoulder. "We're almost to the city."

Sitting back, she watched the buildings and began to recognize the area and then she glanced at Nathan. Since they'd kept on their Amish clothes, he'd put on a dark hat. He was handsome either way, she decided.

To take the edge off the pain that shot through her each time she thought of losing him again, she looked into the rearview mirror. "Deputy Benton, you've gone beyond the duties of a sheriff's deputy. Does Nathan have something on you?"

When both men saw the teasing light in her eyes, they glanced at each other. "He has a lot on me, yes. But I also have a lot on him. We've known each other a long time."

"I've known him for a while myself," she replied, thinking she knew Nathan better now, but she wondered if Nathan ever actually opened up to anyone.

"Is this let's-pick-on-Nathan-time?" he asked, grinning at her.

"Just trying to lighten things," Carson shot back. "Like playing a game of going down memory lane."

"Let's not," Nathan suggested. "We need to be alert."

"Has anyone tried to follow us?" Alisha asked, wishing she didn't have to come back to reality. Delving into Nathan's psyche would be so much more fun.

"So far, so good," Carson said. "I didn't inform anyone outside of the investigating officers about where I'm taking you."

Nathan checked the traffic. "No cars staying on us," he said. "I'll be glad when we're sitting in the police station in the middle of the city."

"So will I," Alisha said. "I'd like to mark running for my life off my bucket list."

Nathan took her hand in his, his eyes moving over her. He didn't speak but she knew he had to feel the same way.

Where would things end when they did stop running? What then? They hadn't had time to examine or explore this new kind of normal. Would the adrenaline go away and leave them wishing they hadn't grown so close? Would he regret getting involved with her again?

Nathan's eyes met hers, as if he was having second thoughts, too. "Are you ready for what's next?"

She wanted to tell him she was ready to come out of hiding, not only from these killers, but she wanted to stop hiding her heart and spend the rest of her life with a man she couldn't stop loving.

Instead, she said, "I need to do this so I can get on with my life and feel safe again. So yes, I'm ready."

His expression changed, just a slight shift that went dark for a moment as if a cloud had covered the sun.

And then it was gone to be replaced with a blank concern. "Same here. Getting on with my life sounds good."

So he wasn't ready to go all in on their renewed attraction?

Alisha should feel relieved, but all she felt was a deep ache in her heart. He was just biding his time until he could do his duty, find justice and be away from her again.

So she wanted to get on with her life? Nathan wondered if that life would now include him. They'd come a long way in a short time and he wasn't imagining the closeness they'd developed. But he knew being on the run and constantly on guard could mess with a person's head. Going back to normal might cause her to revert back to her old way of wanting to avoid him at all costs.

While he wanted to be with her even more.

"Take us to the station first. We can check into the place I rented later," he told Carson, giving him the directions. "They know me there, but the owner is always discreet and won't give out any information. We can change clothes and freshen up once we've talked to the police."

His phone buzzed as Carson maneuvered through traffic. "The state police." He answered, hoping for good news. "Nathan Craig."

Nathan watched as Carson took another side street toward Belmont Avenue and turned off toward the Philadelphia police department.

"I hate to be the bearer of bad news, Craig," the officer on the other end of the line said. "But the man who was trespassing on your family's property died during surgery this morning. Joe Watson—career criminal with ties to several alleged drug traffickers in the state of Pennsylvania. Mostly opioids, but he's pretty low on the ladder of drug runners."

Nathan inhaled a breath. "So we didn't get anything out of him?"

"He never woke up."

Nathan thanked the officer for the report then told Alisha and Carson. "One tight-lipped and one dead."

Alisha shuddered. "Those draft horses saved our lives but I wish we could have questioned him."

"Yeah, well, onward," he replied after Carson parked the car. "We're about to go into a whole new realm. I know you can hold your own with any LEO. But I'll be there with you."

She nodded. "And Mitchell Henderson should meet us here if all goes as planned."

"So let's do what needs to be done," he said, wishing he knew how she really felt. But like him, Alisha was used to holding her deepest thoughts close.

They walked into the station, Carson acting as body-guard, still dressed in their Amish clothes.

Nathan just hoped the ruse had worked. He now had something more important to take care of other than searching for missing people. Protecting the women he'd loved for most of his life. He only hoped she'd agree to that plan.

Once they'd been put in a conference room, they were given coffee and told to wait. Carson offered to stay, but Nathan shook his head. "You've done enough." Shaking his friend's hand, he said, "Go home and watch over our folks. And watch your back."

"Always," Carson said with a grin. "I'll check in with you later."

"Thank you, Deputy Benton," Alisha said, ever the professional.

She'd removed her *kapp* and shook out her upswept hair. Now her tresses flowed around her shoulders in golden-brown ripples. She looked so young and pretty but her green eyes still held that edge of steel.

Carson bobbed his head. "Anything else you need— just let me know."

After Carson left, they both sat down and went silent.

When had he become so tongue-tied? Nathan wondered.

Looking over at her, he felt the fatigue of the last few days weighing on him like a heavy mantle. "I think I could sleep for a week."

"I had a nap," she replied, her tone tense. "Now I'm wired and ready to get on with this."

"So you'll be done with me?"

Her eyes met his, a silent message that he couldn't read held there in a green forest of doubt.

Before he could answer, a man and woman came in and stood over them.

The man held out his hand. "I'm Detective Jack Mathers and this is Agent Sandy Fenwick from our field office here in Philadelphia."

After handshakes and the usual law enforcement scans and scowls to intimidate them, they all sat down and did another quick back and forth stare session.

Finally, Detective Mathers spoke. "Miss Braxton, you've come face-to-face with some very dangerous people. I'm sorry you had to see that and sorry you felt the need to go into hiding."

"I was running for my life," Alisha said, her voice

clear and sharp-edged. "I didn't think things through but I'm here now."

Then the agent leaned forward, her black bob sliding across her cheekbone with a precise swish. "You also got yourself involved in a sting we've been planning for over a year now."

"I didn't get myself involved," Alisha retorted in a touchy tone Nathan knew only too well. "I was in the wrong place at the wrong time and I've been chased, shot at and assaulted since that night."

The detective tapped his pen on the table. "We understand. You should have come in sooner though. This thing goes beyond what you witnessed. Way beyond."

"So you both do understand that she was in a lot of danger?" Nathan replied.

The door opened and a tall man with thick grayish-white hair entered the room, an air of authority about him.

"Alisha," he said, his eyes on her. "I'm sorry I'm late."

"Who are you?" the detective asked, glancing over at the FBI agent and then back to the man.

"I'm Mitchell Henderson, Alisha's boss. Just here to help guide her through the process."

"From Henderson and Perry?" Detective Mathers asked, his expression almost bored.

"The very same," the older man said with a smile that showed practiced grace. "We have firms all over the state and Alisha is a part of our family, so I wanted to check on her. We're all very concerned for her safety."

"Why do you need a lawyer?" Agent Fenwick asked, clearly suspicious.

"Why do you think?" Alisha retorted. "I've got some

dangerous people after me and I'm a lawyer for his firm. He's here to protect me and make sure I'm not vulnerable. I might not have made the right decision by running but I'm here now and I know the law."

"But you're not under arrest and we don't suspect you of anything," Detective Mathers pointed out. "Your only crime was not coming back to Philadelphia the night this happened."

"She'd be dead now if she'd done that," Nathan interjected.

"There is no harm in me listening in," Mitchell Henderson replied, his tone firm and polite. "Alisha witnessed a double homicide and she's the only eyewitness. She's here to cooperate and bring these people to justice. I'm here to guide her and advise her."

"Okay then," Agent Fenwick said. "Let's get on with this. Since our two best witnesses are dead now and you witnessed them being assassinated, I'd say we all want the same thing, Miss Braxton. To keep you alive."

"I'd appreciate that," Alisha replied. "PI Craig and I have come up with some notes based on our own investigation. The name Deke Garrison keeps popping up in conjunction with Dr. West. He's high on our list as a possible suspect. We also noted a woman named Andrea Sumter, a patient of Dr. West." Then she told them about the photographer who'd trespassed at the Campton Center. Would you like to compare notes?"

"We don't need to compare notes," Agent Fenwick replied. "We have a solid case but we can't name the suspect yet. We're waiting on more evidence."

Nathan glanced at Alisha and then back to the officials. "You said your two best witnesses are dead now. Are you telling us that this hit was on two people who'd turned state's evidence? The West couple was about to tell all?"

"Yes," Agent Fenwick said, her dark eyes full of aggravation. "They wanted out and we offered them a plea bargain. They agreed but they had to keep playing the part until we could get more evidence. They were scheduled to leave for a holiday trip once they told us everything. They were about to make a fresh start in a new place, under a new name."

Alisha shook her head. "So they *were* involved in criminal activity but they were killed for cooperating with the FBI?"

"That about sums it up," Detective Mathers replied. "We're talking a whole cartel made of several prominent members of society and fueled by low-life criminals who'll do anything for money."

"Why didn't you protect the Wests?" Nathan asked, radars going off in his head.

Agent Fenwick leaned in. "We told them to lie low and we had men on them but they elected to sneak out and do some shopping. So we're glad you decided to share things with us. Because believe me, you're next on the kill list. They don't want you to identify any of their hit men or any of them, and they won't stop until they can silence you permanently."

Chapter Nineteen

Once they'd given their statements, Alisha described the men she'd seen to a sketch artist. When the artist was finished, Alisha nodded her head. "That's definitely the shooter. They called him Ace but he also used the name Adam Baker."

Detective Mathers nodded. "That matches what we have on the official report from the Campton Creek town police." He handed the sketch to one of the lab techs, obviously leaning toward believing Alisha's story. "See if we get a match."

Agent Fenwick grabbed her notes to go off and work her side of the case—mainly trying to figure out if they had enough evidence to bring these criminals to trial. But she stopped at the open door, "All of these details will help and we'll keep after the man we've moved to a nearby hospital. He doesn't have a record other than an outstanding parking ticket. Does a lot of odd jobs here and there so we don't have an accurate work history. Scott Kemp is an alias. He also goes by Scott Kincaid."

Alisha's head came up. "Did you say Kincaid?"

The agent shut the door and came back to the table. "Yes. Ring a bell?"

"It sounds familiar," Alisha said, her gaze hitting on Nathan. "I don't know. Maybe a client?"

Mitchell Henderson had already left for another appointment so they couldn't ask him. Her boss was good at remembering names. "Scott Kincaid," she said, shaking her head. "I know I've heard that name before."

Agent Fenwick waited. "Do you know this man, Miss Braxton?"

Alisha gave her a perplexed stare. "If I knew him, I'd say so. Why do I get the impression that I'm being treated like the criminal here?"

Nathan held up a hand. "Because you ran away, Alisha. You know how this works. You stumbled onto their case and things got blown apart. The agent wants to find closure, so she's leaning on you since you didn't come straight here and put yourself in even more danger. But she's not willing to let us in on exactly who might be targeting us. Probably isn't too happy about the Philly police taking the lead on this, either."

"We can protect witnesses the same as you, PI Craig. Probably better from what we've heard. It is, after all, part of what we do."

Nathan's eyes flared with anger. "Oh, I'm counting on it."

Alisha stood up, putting a hand between them. "I won't have you two trying to one-up each other on my behalf. I ran because I was scared and confused and I wanted to make sure my grandmother was safe. I take full responsibility for not being rational but I gave a complete statement to the officers on the scene and I stand by that. They told me I could go and even offered me an escort."

"They didn't exactly clear that with the FBI," the agent pointed out, her eyes as dark as her hair while she shot a hostile glance toward Detective Mathers. "This whole thing could have been handled differently."

"Beginning with you taking responsibility for keeping your clients from getting shot," Nathan pointed out.

The agent pinned her stern frown back on him. "I have work to do. Since you came in so *we* could help protect you, I suggest you let us take you to our safe house instead of the place Mr. Craig has booked."

Alisha looked at Nathan. "What do you think?"

Nathan studied the detective and then lifted his gaze to the agent. "You *do* have more man power and you *do* want to keep tabs on us, right?"

"That's right. No more taking matters into your own hands."

"I'll consider that," Alisha said. "Right now, I want a hot shower, some food and some clean clothes. That is, if I'm free to go."

Detective Mathers stood up. "Yes, you can go but we'll take you to our safe house in an unmarked car and we'll station officers all around. I suggest you don't try to go it alone anymore, understood?"

"Got it," Nathan said, taking Alisha by the arm. "Let's go and get some rest. I'll keep the reservation at the other place. Just in case."

Both the detective and the agent gave him a bland lift of their eyebrows. "Don't move her again," Detective Mathers said.

After they'd been shoved into the unmarked car, Alisha turned to Nathan. "They have you figured out, I see."

"I don't know what you mean."

"They know you'll go all rogue if things aren't to your liking."

"Well, if I don't agree with how they handle this, yes, I'll do what I have to do."

"I trust you," she admitted. "In fact, I'd say you're the only person I can trust right now."

She wanted to say more but she wouldn't go that far until they had this behind them and could have a fresh start.

That is, if Nathan wanted a fresh start with her.

Late afternoon sunshine moved over what was left of the snow, painting the powdery white trees and sidewalks in shades of vanilla and cream. A leftover wreath on a street lamp hung in limbo, its faded red bows beating helplessly against the wind.

"It's strange being back here," Alisha said as they watched the skyscrapers change into row houses and condos.

Nathan grunted. "I try to avoid cities. Don't like the crowds."

"You could go home," she said, her tone quiet. "You've done more than enough for me."

"Trying to get rid of me now that you have the cavalry behind you?"

"No, just giving you an out."

"I can't turn back now," he replied. Glancing over at Alisha, he looked doubtful. "I don't like relinquishing things to the authorities."

Alisha saw him in a yet another glaringly new light. "Even God?" she asked.

"Even so," he replied, his expression telling her he'd move heaven and earth to protect anyone he loved. "But because of you and God, my parents, your grandmother and Mrs C, I'm learning to trust in Him again, too."

Alisha smiled at that, unshed tears pricking at her eyes. "That's something, I think. Something very important. You've realized the value of family and faith."

His gaze moved over her, a calm in his eyes that told her he'd changed over the last few days. He'd put himself on the line for her and in doing so, he'd come full circle in his faith.

The car pulled up to a quiet street of row houses in a modest part of town. "I'll escort you two to the front door," the patrol officer said. "Then you'll be in the capable hands of one of our best. I'll let her introduce herself."

They were met at the door of the townhouse by a female patrol officer who looked like she'd be able to wrestle a criminal with one arm.

"I'm Officer Milly Sanders," the redhead said with a tight smile. "I'll be with you for the duration."

"The duration?" Nathan asked, clearly not happy.

"Until further notice," Milly explained in slow terms, as if she were talking to a toddler. "Two bedrooms with bullet proof windows. Don't go near them, however. Two baths and this small living area. I'll take the couch to grab some shut-eye but mostly, I'll be sitting out in the vestibule where I have a clear view of the street."

"Thank you, Officer Sanders," Alisha said, watching as the tall woman lifted her chin and headed to her post.

"Don't try to leave," Milly said over her shoulder.

"There's also a guard at the back door into the alley and we've got patrols circling every half hour."

After Milly closed the glass door to the vestibule and took up her position in a folding chair sitting in the small hallway, Nathan turned to Alisha. "It's like they're holding us hostage."

"They're trying to save our lives," she reminded him, her fatigue mirroring what she saw in his expression. "Don't be so grumpy about it."

"They had you in the hot seat back there," he replied while he paced. "But you did a great job." Finally, he opened the refrigerator and found cold chicken and a fruit salad. "You need to eat."

"And you need to relax," she told him. "I feel better about things now. We were just drifting in the wind out there on our own."

"I guess so," he said, dragging the food out to put on the small counter. Then he located bread and cheese. "I haven't been a very good protector."

"It's a thankless job," Alisha replied as she tore off some chicken and nibbled at the grapes and blueberries. A slow fatigue took over, making her want to curl up and sleep for a long time. But she didn't think a good sleep would ever come to her again.

Nathan handed her some crackers and water then turned to make coffee. "I don't trust anyone here either," he admitted. "The agent perked up when she thought you might know Scott Kincaid."

"I don't know him. I just know the name," Alisha said, grabbing her briefcase. "I'm so glad Carson was able to bring this back to me. Now we can at least have something to do while we stay hidden."

She looked up in time to see the awareness in Nathan's eyes. Did he have other things in mind—holding her close again and maybe kissing her? Officer Milly would frown on that, no doubt.

The moment passed and he said, "Let's see what we can find—after we eat and change clothes."

Alisha looked down at her outfit. "I guess we don't really look Amish anymore."

For a brief moment, she wished she was back at Nathan's childhood home, enjoying the quiet of a cold winter evening, his hand in hers.

But that was just a dream. A silly dream that she could never have even here in the *Englisch* world.

Nathan was tired and so was she. They had to end this horrible nightmare. But ending this could also mean the end of them, too.

After food and a shower, Alisha changed into the jeans and sweatshirt she'd left in her briefcase and Nathan put on some clothes Carson had brought along with the briefcase.

"Our wardrobes are seriously lacking," he said as he padded in socks across the small sparse den, the muted light from one lamp allowing them to see each other.

"But I could get used to living in jeans," she replied. "Feel better after your shower?"

He sure smelled good—clean and fresh with damp hair that couldn't be tamed. She could get used to him, too.

To take her mind away from that, she stared at her laptop screen. "I can't find anything on Scott Kincaid. The name comes up but it's usually someone in another area of the country. No one in Philly as far as I can find."

"It could be another alias…or he's been wiped clean."

"You mean scrubbed from the internet?"

"Yep. It happened. Gone to ground."

"Why?" she asked. "I know he's a criminal but what is it about him?"

"Do you think he could have been the driver that night? Did you hear either of them speak, call out a name?"

"No. They didn't speak. Just pulled up and shot and then left immediately."

"But they watched you so that means they had to be nearby."

"Yes, but the police would have found them on the security tapes by now. I'm sure they hid in plain sight."

Putting down her laptop, Alisha yawned. "I think I'm actually sleepy."

"Then you should rest," he said, his eyes deep-ocean blue. "I'll stay up a while. Give Milly a break."

"Just remember, she called dibs on the couch."

He grinned at that. "Okay, Sugar-bear, go to bed."

Alisha made a face. "You won't let me forget that, will you?"

"I'll never forget it, no."

The silence stretched like an unbreakable wire between them. Alisha wanted to take him in her arms and tell him to rest but she knew that would be crossing the line that pulled at them like a tug-of-war rope.

"Well, good night, Nathan."

He stood and walked her to the door of her room. "How are you, really?"

"What does that mean?"

"I worry about you."

"I'm okay. I'm alive and I'm not giving up."

He held one hand on the door jamb while he kept his eyes fixed on her. "Okay."

Did he want to say more?

"Nathan?"

Touching a hand to her hair, he said, "Get some rest. We don't know what tomorrow will bring."

Alisha certainly understood that concept. So why couldn't he open up to her today?

Nathan heard a thump and then a sharp bang.

Jumping out of bed, he grabbed his gun and went into the den, the moonlight allowing him to do a quick search. Alisha stepped out of the bedroom, still wearing her jeans and sweatshirt.

"Stay behind me," he whispered. "I think we have company."

Alisha nodded and grabbed at his T-shirt, holding tight to the worn fabric.

Nathan moved around corners until he could see into the vestibule. "I don't see Milly."

Alisha shook her head. "I don't either. This isn't good."

Then they heard footsteps and the back door banged open and a dark figure stood looming.

"Run," Nathan said to Alisha. "Toward the front."

He pushed her ahead and fired a shot to give them time to get away, not sure if he'd hit the target or not. Alisha crashed the front door open and let out a gasp. Office Milly lay on unconscious on the floor.

"Nathan?"

"No time. We'll call it in. Right now, we need to get out of here."

They made it out into the yard, the cold snow wetting Nathan's socks as soon as he hit the ground near some shrubs. "Let's follow close to the houses and we'll hide until help arrives."

Alisha did as he said, staying with him as they moved through shrubbery and small entryway gardens until they were at the end of the street. Nathan called 911 and gave the dispatcher their location. Soon, they could hear the sirens off in the distance.

Pulling Alisha close while they waited in a closed storefront doorway, he could feel her shivering. "How did they find us this time?"

"Someone is always watching," she said, her voice shaky. "And we're running out of options."

Chapter Twenty

"I'll take care of everything."

Alisha gave her boss an appreciative smile. "Thank you, Mr. Henderson," she said, too tired to focus on the whirl of the precinct around her.

Dawn had greeted them by the time they'd arrived back at the downtown police headquarters. She should be warm by now since someone had provided her with a blanket and boots. But she couldn't stop shivering. Right now, going to Mitchell Henderson's house seemed like the right thing to do. Warmth and protection and someone else she could trust.

Except Nathan wasn't so keen on the idea.

"Look, we've tried everything," he said. "Something just isn't right. I think you need to be surrounded by a security team day and night and hidden away here at the station."

"I'd have to sleep in a jail cell."

"You'd be safe."

Mitchell Henderson sat down beside them. "I guarantee Alisha's safety, Mr. Craig. My home is gated. No one can get in or out without knowing the code."

"I'm coming with her."

Mitchell didn't even blink. "I'd expect no less."

Detective Mathers came in and slumped into a chair. "Milly has a concussion but she'll be fine. The guard on the back door is still in surgery." Shrugging, he added, "And the intruder got away. No prints. Nothing. I think you're being pursued by some kind of ghost who knows how to shadow people 24/7."

"You think?" Nathan asked, full of fire. "Do you want to tell us who your main suspect is so we can be more aware?"

"I can't do that," the detective replied, his face as blank as the old white blinds on both sides of the room hiding them from the buzz of the precinct and the outside world.

Mitchell stood up. "Look, my staff will take care of Alisha and provide everything she and Mr. Craig need. I've got my own experienced investigators on this, too. None of you have managed to stop this assault. It's time for me to step in and protect my employee. Alisha is a valued member of my law team."

Agent Fenwick came into the room. "Nothing on the intruder. I'm sorry, Miss Braxton."

Nathan looked from her to the detective. "All out of ideas?"

"We're pulling things together," Agent Fenwick replied. "I think I have to agree with Mr. Henderson. But on one condition."

"What's that?" Alisha asked.

"I'm going with you," the female agent said, her dark eyes daring anyone to protest. "I can't let a star witness out of my sight. Last night proved that."

"I agree with her," Detective Mathers said on a

drawn-out note full of grudge. "We'll do what we can to help, too. The opioid epidemic is going strong in the state of Pennsylvania but we're so close to nabbing these drug runners. We all want these pill mills gone."

"So, we agree?" Agent Fenwick asked the room in general.

"I'm in," Nathan said. "Where Alisha goes, I go."

"I feel the same, PI Craig," Agent Fenwick replied, her expression closed to discussion.

Mitchell Henderson looked around the room. "Seems I'm going to have a full house for the New Year."

After everyone had left to make arrangements, Nathan glanced at Alisha. "I don't like this. They agreed too readily. I think they know something they aren't telling us."

"Such as?"

"Such as—they know who's after us but they can't say it out loud. They're setting us up as part of a sting. If they mess this up, they'll have me to deal with."

"Why would they let us go to Mitchell's place if they're setting us up?" Alisha asked.

"Maybe he's in on it," Nathan replied. "He seems to keep his cards close to his vest."

"Nathan, we've got to trust someone."

"Like we did last night?"

"These people are relentless," she replied, her tone beyond weary. "If they find us at Mitchell's house, well, then I'll be ready to discuss moving permanently to an undisclosed location."

"Not if they kill you, Alisha."

Later, Alisha stood in the middle of the big bedroom where Mitchell's maid had placed her. "Mrs. Henderson suggested some clothes for you," the dark-haired maid explained with a practiced smile. "Dinner is at six."

"You'll have to thank Mrs. Henderson for me," Alisha said, thinking that had to mean dressing for dinner. But why? She wasn't here to socialize. Remembering Nathan's chilling words to her earlier, Alisha wondered where she'd go from here.

Her silent prayers held her in place. *Lord, let this end in a good way, with justice for those who have died and punishment for those who are evil.*

"Mrs. Henderson is out of town," the maid replied, bringing her out of her prayers. "She sends her regrets but she did instruct me to loan you some clothes."

Funny, Mitchell hadn't mentioned that but Alisha was glad she wouldn't have to indulge Miriam Henderson with idle chit-chat. Miriam was a kind, caring person who lived in her own little bubble of luxury and extravagance. But she'd always been polite to Alisha the few times they'd been at social events.

After the prim maid indicated the closet, Alisha checked and found a couple of wool dresses and some pants and sweaters. She and Miriam were close to the same size. Still, it felt strange to wear these obviously expensive clothes while hiding out.

No matter, she was here now and Nathan was down the hallway. Agent Fenwick had been put in a room between them. Strategy, or to keep her eye on both of them?

Alisha didn't want to delve into that. Nathan was safe and they had an experienced FBI agent on the premises. The Henderson estate had Campton House beat on state-of-the-art security. Gated and back off the street, the big house loomed dark and ominous in the middle of a huge acreage of snow-covered woods.

After going over her notes again, she left her room to go down to dinner. But her appetite disappeared underneath the weight of this stress. Soon it would be a new year. What did that year hold for her?

Nathan called after her. "Alisha?"

She whirled at the top of the spiraling staircase. "Do you have a tracker on me?"

He shook his head. "I heard a door opening."

"Have you seen Fenwick?"

"I'm right behind you," came the edgy feminine voice.

"Do *you* have a tracker on us?" Nathan asked, repeating Alisha's question.

"Should I?" the agent asked, still wearing her dark suit.

"Is it just me, or is this weird?" Alisha asked. "I've been here many times but this feels different. The house is so empty."

Fenwick lifted her eyebrows. "Yes, your boss seems to be thriving here alone and with a skeleton staff. I'm sure he figures the fewer people involved, the better for you."

"He's very dedicated to his associates," Alisha said in Mitchell's defense. "His wife Miriam is out of town. She tends to travel a lot."

"I tend to agree with you there," Agent Fenwick said, her tone and expression neutral. "I did my research on both of them. He's insistent, I'll give him that. His concern for you is touching."

"Why did you agree to this?" Nathan asked, obviously still suspicious.

"I have my reasons, one being I don't want you two out there on some vigilante mission," Fenwick replied, her expression completely blank.

"And you aren't going to share any other reasons with us?" Alisha asked, her gaze meeting Nathan's.

"Need-to-know basis," the agent said as they came to the bottom of the stairs. "Which way is dinner?"

Nathan gave Alisha a warning glance while she led the way to the huge formal dining room. Mitchell was waiting before the roaring fire near the long table. Four places had been set at the end near the fire. Cozy in spite of the opulent scale of the room. Alisha couldn't stop the shivers going down her spine, however. She wanted things to be normal again.

"Sorry we can't open the curtains," he said in greeting. "Best to keep the house closed up."

Nathan did his own sweep of the room and then pulled out Alisha's chair. "How long do you think we'll need to stay here?" he asked Agent Fenwick, who took care of her own chair across the way.

"As long as you're safe and Mr. Henderson doesn't mind us hiding out here, I'd say a while." She glanced from them to Mitchell. "But we're close thanks to your cooperation. We have a man in custody and we've taken Corey Cooper's statement. He's beginning to see the wisdom of telling us what he knows."

"Who is Corey Cooper?" Mitchell asked as he placed prime rib on each plate and passed them around.

Agent Fenwick's gaze hit on Nathan and Alisha. The photographer who'd showed at the Campton Center early on might help them break this case, after all. "Sir, I can't really discuss all of the details of this case with you, you understand. I shouldn't have mentioned that."

"I see," Mitchell replied with a knowing smile. "But *you* should understand that Alisha has given me most of the details already. I just don't recall that particular name."

Nathan took over. "This is an amazing house. What year was it built?"

"Nineteen-forty-five," Mitchell answered as he served the rest of the meal. "It's been in my family for well over seventy years."

The dinner went quickly after that, with stilted small talk. No one lingered over dessert and coffee.

"We should find a place to talk," Agent Fenwick said as they headed upstairs. "I saw a small den just past your suite, Miss Braxton. Meet there?"

"We'll be waiting," Nathan said.

After she went into her room, he added to Alisha, "I'll check the place for bugs."

"Nathan, stop being so paranoid," Alisha said, her own doubts nagging at her. "We have one of the men who attacked us at the cabin in custody at a hospital nearby and we have Corey Cooper's cooperation now. If he can verify my identification of any of these men, then that's something, right?"

"Right." Nathan guided her into the small den where circular windows highlighted the hills and valleys down past the pool and backyard. But the heavy blinds were shut tonight, the yellow glow of security lights shining against them.

After checking underneath lamps and feeling under the furniture and across the mantle of the small fireplace, he turned back to Alisha. "I've got a bad feeling, Alisha. I don't like this."

"Nathan, stop scaring me," she said, aggravation and exhaustion making her snap. "We're safe here."

"Don't you find it strange that your boss insisted on bringing us here? That he knows a lot about this case?"

"He knows me," she replied. "He's doing the same as you, trying to keep me alive. Do I need to remind you he's had a team on this since the night this all happened?"

"No, I'm well aware of that." Nathan plopped down in a cushioned chair. "I think we need to get out of here."

Agent Fenwick walked in and shut the door. "You aren't going anywhere. It's too dangerous."

"Thank you for being the voice of reason," Alisha said. "Nathan doesn't trust anyone."

"Well, PI Craig, you need to listen to what I'm about to share with you," Sandy Fenwick said, "and you need to understand that no one else can know this."

"We're listening," Nathan said.

"Alisha, you stumbled onto two of the major players in one of the biggest pill mills in the state of Pennsylvania. All of the people you've found in your searches—the Wests, Deke Garrison and Andrea Sumter—are a part of this highly efficient network. They have mules and runners and spies everywhere. They hire drifters, people who do odd jobs, criminals, you name it. They push Medicare fraud by soliciting legitimate doctors to write fake prescriptions and they give them a cut. That's how the Wests got involved—their greed finally did them in. This pill mill pushes fentanyl like candy and they specialize in everything from oxycodone to heroin."

She took a breath. "We were about to reel them in when this happened. Someone got word and hired this hit. Now they're all scattered to the wind."

"And one of them wants Alisha dead because of what she saw," Nathan said, his expression grim.

"I think they all want her dead," the agent replied. "And I think someone close to Alisha has been tipping them off."

"Do you believe her?" Nathan asked Alisha later after Agent Fenwick had gone to her room. She hadn't told them who she suspected but Nathan had a pretty good idea.

"I can't imagine who would do such a thing. I called you and then Carson got involved. I don't believe the Campton Creek town police would tip anyone off."

"Your grandmother and Mrs. Campton wouldn't knowingly tell anyone your whereabouts."

"No, and neither would your family."

"That leaves one person," Nathan said, hating to voice what his gut had been shouting.

"You can't be serious," Alisha replied. "Mitchell? He's been my mentor for years, Nathan. He promised me a job right out of law school and he's been working night and day to help us."

"I asked you before if you trust him and I can see that you do, but maybe we need to rethink this."

"What does that mean?" she asked, her expression stubborn, her eyes moving toward the big hallway outside the sitting room.

"Scott Kincaid knows something," Nathan replied. "But he won't talk unless we push him."

"Are you suggesting we try to question the man?"

"They did move him closer in to the city so they could watch him."

"I don't know how we can make that possible. We're supposed to stay here."

"Just consider what I'm saying," Nathan replied. "Let me walk you to your door." He stood there wishing he could pull her close and protect her forever. "I'm worried, Alisha. This is all too neat."

Alisha shook her head. "We're both just tired. Get some rest and we'll get back at this tomorrow. Maybe the FBI will get something out of this man."

Nathan could tell she thought he was either imagining things or he was just too suspicious.

But Nathan knew he was on the right track. And that meant he had to get her out of this creepy house.

Chapter Twenty-One

Once she was in her room, Alisha pulled out her laptop and did another search of the names Scott Kemp and Scott Kincaid. She'd always been good with retaining information but the constant running for her life had her brain muddled.

So if Scott Kincaid was in the system, why hadn't his name popped up when she'd done her first search? Surely, the firm's investigators had found something other than a speeding ticket on him. Wondering if Mitchell might still be up, she decided she'd go down and ask him.

But she stopped at the door. Nathan didn't trust Mitchell. Could he be right? Alisha didn't want to panic and she didn't want to jump to the wrong conclusion. For as long as she could remember, Mitchell Henderson had been on her side. Why would that change because of this case?

Could he be somehow involved? Agent Fenwick said this pill mill went far and wide, but Mitchell? He and his wife rarely drank anything stronger than wine. She couldn't see him being involved in moving illegal drugs.

They went to church, supported local causes and worked hard to fight for their clients. This didn't add up.

Deciding she'd go and talk to him and try to see if any warning bells went off, Alisha slipped out of her room and headed downstairs, her socks padding against the upstairs hardwood floors.

When she hit the marble floor near the stairs she saw a light on down the hallway to the right where Mitchell's study was located. The door was partially open but Mitchell wasn't in the study. Glancing around, Alisha decided she'd take a peek at his desk. What could it hurt?

Slipping past the partially open door, she checked the powder room attached to the study. No one there. Mitchell had to be across the house in the master suite. She'd just look around and see what she could find.

After searching the files on the massive desk, she only discovered legitimate cases. Nothing in the drawers or in the credenza. Nathan had to be grasping at straws.

She was about to go back upstairs when she heard Mitchell's voice coming from the kitchen.

"I don't care what it takes. Keep Kincaid quiet," Mitchell said into the phone, his back turned away from the arched doorway leading from the hallway to the kitchen and breakfast room. "We have to contain this mess."

Kincaid? Alisha gasped and turned to run away but in her haste, she knocked her leg against a hallway table, causing the spindly leg to scrape across the floor.

Sprinting toward the stairs, Alisha dredged up a distant memory. A man had been here at the estate once a few years ago, doing odd jobs. The entire office had been invited here for a picnic. Alisha had walked inside to use the powder room and she'd heard Mitchell talking to the man—right there in the kitchen. And he'd said almost the same thing that day.

"Get it done, Kincaid. We can't let anyone see this mess."

Who had Mitchell been talking about? At the time, she'd figured someone had spilled some food or drink in the immaculate house and Mitchell needed the handyman to clean it up.

But what if it had been something more sinister?

She was halfway up the stairs when she heard him behind her. "Alisha, we need to talk."

Nathan woke with a start. Sleeping wherever he landed tended to make him do that. But this time, he was up and searching for his gun. He'd heard a noise. A door slamming, footsteps moving through the house.

Grabbing his clothes, he hit his knee on the nightstand and moaned. You'd think he'd become less clumsy since this tended to be a normal thing. Hopping on one foot, he managed to get his shoes on. A door downstairs slammed. Then he heard an engine revving.

Rushing out of his room, he saw the cracked door to Agent Fenwick's room. Nathan moved fast and pressed open the door. No one there.

Hurrying toward the stairs, he saw a woman lying at the bottom. Not moving.

Nathan skidded to a stop and went on his knees.

The agent lay on the floor, blood seeping from her head. "Agent Fenwick, can you hear me? What happened?"

The woman on the floor moaned. "He took her. He took Alisha. I tried to stop him but…"

Nathan didn't have to ask who. He knew. "I'm going after them," he said. "I'll call for backup."

"Careful. He's going to kill her. Should have warned you."

Nathan stood up and shouted into his cell, his heart hitting against his chest with such a crushing beat, he almost passed out.

Why had he let her stay in this house? The FBI had used Alisha as bait to capture the real killer.

Why hadn't he put a chair in front of her bedroom door and sat there all night?

How had this happened?

You failed again. It's your fault.

The voice in his head screamed at him. But the voice in his heart told Nathan to be calm, to trust in the Lord, to pray with all his might. He couldn't lose Alisha now.

He wouldn't let that happen.

So he asked God to please be with him and to guard Alisha until he could find her.

"Scott has aged since I first hired him," Mitchell said in a controlled voice. Shoving Alisha through the snowy woods ahead of him, he kept talking. "You always did have a knack for details. I knew you'd remember sooner or later."

"I didn't recognize him that night at the cabin," Alisha said, hoping to get to the truth at last while she tried to figure out how to escape. Mitchell had hit Fenwick over the head after she'd spotted him dragging Alisha down the stairs. She wasn't sure if Nathan had heard anything.

"You and your PI are tenacious," Mitchell said, jamming the gun against her ribs. "Pity that you decided to stop at the Christmas market that night. What are the odds? My men didn't know who you were."

"Mitchell, help me to understand," she said, her breath coming in gasps as he shoved her down the hillside toward a stream below his property. "Why are you involved in this?"

"Miriam," he said, his tone shaky now. "She has a problem with prescription pain pills. An old injury from her show horse days. She found Dr. Joshua West and… that was that. Addicted to opioids."

Alisha's shock caused her to stop and turn to face him. "Miriam? That's hard to believe."

"Hard to cover up, too," he added, his expression bordering on frantic. "She learned to hide it from everyone, including me."

"But why are you involved in this shooting?" Alisha had to know the truth even if she never lived to tell anyone.

"That's simple, Alisha. I hired this hit. I wanted my wife safe and well but Dr. West kept plying her with the drugs and charging her exorbitant amounts of money. When I heard he and his uppity wife had decided to turn, I was furious."

Alisha's sympathy didn't stop her anger. "So you knew from the beginning? You're the one who's been trying to kill me?"

"No," he said, shoving her forward. "I didn't want to kill you, tried to help protect you but if Kincaid talks, he'll name me as the one who hired him. And…you saw the men. They took it upon themselves to try and find you. Too late, I realized they were trying to silence you to save their own necks. They failed and now they're going to turn on me, too."

Shivering, her socks wet and cold, her feet bruised as they moved over brush and rocks, Alisha shook her head. "Mitchell, why are you doing this now?"

"I don't have any choice," he said, his words chopped and rushed. "Kincaid has been blackmailing me for years and now you know who he is. He'll turn, too, and then with your testimony, everyone will know. The others didn't have anything to do with this hit. They'll kill me if they find out what I did."

The others meaning Deke Garrison and Andrea Sumter and a long line of criminals. "Because they'll see that you know too much."

"Yes. I had to send Miriam away for treatment. I'm so sorry, Alisha, but if I don't do this, they will. I'll make it quick."

"And what about Nathan and Agent Fenwick?"

"They'll be taken care of, sooner or later." Glancing behind him, he said, "They can't know, either. Everyone will believe the hit men found all of you."

Sick to her stomach, Alisha moved forward, too numb to wonder what would happen next. He'd shoot her and dump her in the water while someone else killed Nathan and Agent Fenwick. Probably blame it on an attack from outside, spin it to make people feel for him and his family. If he survived, Nathan would have to watch over his shoulder for the rest of his life.

She wouldn't let that happen. She had to find a way to end this.

Nathan found Mitchell's car near the gates leading to the road, the passenger side door open. Using his cell light, he found footprints in the melting snow headed into the woods.

Soon he was on a path that meandered down, the soft gurgle of flowing water telling him that Henderson was taking Alisha down to a mountain stream. To kill her and leave her.

The whine of sirens up on the road gave him hope. But he couldn't wait for backup. He had to hurry before it was too late. Stumbling in the slush and mud, Nathan kept moving down the hillside, the heavy brush and cold snow blocking him.

When he heard voices a few yards down, he stopped and readied his weapon. Before he could take a step, shots rang out.

Nathan's nerves hummed with a lightning fear. He took off running, sliding in the wet until he righted himself. Then he ran at breakneck speed toward the water.

Alisha had managed to distract Mitchell. "My foot. I think something's cutting my foot." She'd leaned down, moaning and waiting for the man holding her to let go for just a moment.

He did. "Sit if you must," Mitchell said, shoving her onto a jutting rock.

Biding her time, Alisha moved her hand over the icy snow until she felt a firm piece of a broken limb. Then with all the force she could muster, she lifted up and brought the heavy piece of frozen wood down on Mitchell Henderson's head.

He moaned and lifted his gun, shooting into the air. That gave her time to kick him and shove him, forcing him to drop the gun. Scrambling, she dived for it and found it then turned as he lunged toward her.

"Stop, Mitchell! Please stop."

With a roar, he kept coming. So she shot at him.

He fell over at her feet, his hands flailing in the cold creek bed's glistening water. Then he didn't move again.

Nathan came on the scene, the dim light from his phone shining over the woods and stream. "Alisha?"

He prayed, the silent screams inside his head holding him frozen.

"Down here."

Alisha!

"I'm coming." He slipped against the rocks, his knee jamming against a jagged branch. But he made it to the stream and called out her name. "Alisha."

"Here."

Nathan saw her then, sitting on a rock, her head down, her arms close to her chest. She was holding a pistol and staring at the man lying on the water's edge.

"Alisha," he said, falling down on his knees in front of her. "Are you all right?"

She nodded, sniffed. "I shot Mitchell."

Nathan pulled her into his arms. "It's okay. It will be okay."

"See if he's alive."

Nathan let her go and pulled the older man away from the water. "He has a weak pulse but he's alive."

Alisha gulped in a sob. "He's the one, Nathan. He hired the hit men."

"We'll talk about that later," Nathan said, sirens wailing back at the house. "I have to call for help now."

She nodded again, her hand reaching for him. "Where do we go from here?"

Nathan turned and lifted her into his arms and held her tight. "We go home, Alisha. We go home."

New Year's Eve

"How are you feeling, Sugar-bear?"

Alisha tugged at the warm quilt her grandmother had covered her with earlier. "I'm okay, Granny. Really."

"You had a nice nap," Bettye said, concern in her eyes. "No more nightmares."

Alisha thought about the last couple of days. "No. I'm sleeping better."

True to his word, once they'd given their statements and all of the law enforcement people were satisfied that they now had enough evidence to bring down the pill mill for good, Nathan had taken her out of the hospital and brought her here to Campton Creek.

Home. He'd brought her home.

And then he'd left while she was sleeping. That had been two days ago. She didn't know if he was ever coming back.

"We have more food than we'll ever eat," Miss Judy said from her chair in the corner. "Are you hungry, Alisha?"

"No," Alisha replied. "Not right now."

"We can watch the festivities on television tonight if you want," Granny suggested, her gaze meeting Mrs. Campton's.

"Whatever you two want to do."

"You've been through quite an ordeal," Mrs C said. "I'm sure Nathan is out there helping the authorities to wrap up this case."

"Maybe."

There would be a lot more to deal with but for now, Alisha was safe and warm and clean after enjoying a long, hot shower earlier. But still, she shivered.

Granny checked her watch. "Supper time."

"You two eat," Alisha said. "I'll just lie here and snooze."

"Okay then." Granny moved with swift agility toward the kitchen. Mrs C heaved herself into her wheelchair and did the same.

Those two, always conspiring.

The bell dinged, meaning someone was downstairs.

"Alisha, do you mind getting that?"

"Uh, okay." Alisha forced herself up and tugged at the black wool tunic that covered thick plaid leggings.

She went down the stairs and opened the door and stared at the man standing there. The man holding a bouquet of roses and a box of candy.

"It's not Valentine's Day," she said, her heart bursting with joy and fear.

Nathan filled the doorway with fresh air and spice. "No, but it is a good day to celebrate."

She glanced behind her. "If you say so."

"I do," he said. "Can you come with me?"

"I'm not sure. I mean, you left without saying goodbye."

"I had some things to take care of."

She had a feeling the two extremely quiet women in the kitchen were in on this surprise, so she didn't bother telling them where she was going. But she had to ask. "Where are you taking me, Nathan?"

"You'll see."

He guided her across the breezeway and into the

main house. When they reached the big sunroom, he stopped. "Happy New Year, Alisha."

Alisha stared in fascination at the twinkling lights someone had strung across the room. A bistro table complete with candles and china sat ready, covered dishes of food centered on a nearby cabinet. Outside, the backyard looked like a fairytale, all white and pristine and glistening.

"Who did all of this?"

"I know people," he said, sitting her down in one of the chairs. After he handed her the flowers, he placed the candy nearby and sat down across from her. "We've never actually had a real date, you know."

Alisha put the flowers on the sideboard and gave him her full attention. "This after you just walked away two days ago."

Taking her hand, he said, "Yes, this, after I walked away all those years ago. Because now I'm free and clear and so are you. We can finally have a fresh start."

"No, Nathan, we can't."

He looked so crestfallen, her heart regretted her words.

"Why not?"

"You know why. You're out there, putting your life on the line every day and this time, it was because of me."

"We survived and we've help put some nasty people away for a long time." Then he said, "But you're the one with courage here. You saved yourself, over and over."

"You saved me," she said. "Over and over. But how do we get past that and go back to normal? I can't work at Henderson and Perry anymore, even if Mr. Perry is begging me to stay."

"You don't have to," he said, lifting her out of the chair, his hands on her arms. "We can work here, together, Alisha. Put out our own shingle and…live the kind of simple life we both love."

Alisha's pulse quickened. "What are you saying?"

Nathan touched his hand to her chin, his fingers warm. "I'm trying in my clumsy way to ask you to stay here with me and…to marry me. Alisha, please. It took near-death to show me how much I still love you."

"You love me?"

"I do. And… I believe you love me. Don't you?"

She couldn't speak so she just bobbed her head, tears piercing her eyes. "So much."

He pulled her close and kissed her. "So want to partner up? Like forever?"

Alisha thought of so many reasons to say no. But then she thought of the one reason to say yes. She loved this man. Always. And it was her job to protect his heart. Always.

"I can live with forever," she said, tugging his head down so she could kiss him again. "And working here with you would be amazing and challenging and so perfect."

Clapping sounded through the old house.

Alisha looked inside and saw her grandmother guiding Mrs. Campton's wheelchair toward them. They must have taken the elevator.

"I see you do know people," she said, laughing and crying at the same time. "Special people."

Her grandmother and Mrs. C both laughed and started immediately planning a spring wedding. "We'll invite everyone!"

"We will invite everyone," Nathan said. "My family and yours."

"Together," Alisha replied, her heart healed at last. "Thank you, Nathan, for bringing me home."

"Don't ever leave me," he said, holding her close.

"I'm here to stay."

Alisha knew that in her heart. They were both here to stay.

* * * * *

WE HOPE YOU ENJOYED
THIS BOOK FROM

LOVE INSPIRED
INSPIRATIONAL ROMANCE

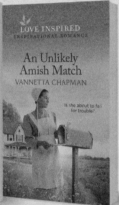

Uplifting stories of faith, forgiveness and hope.

Fall in love with stories where faith helps
guide you through life's challenges, and discover
the promise of a new beginning.

6 NEW BOOKS AVAILABLE EVERY MONTH!

SPECIAL EXCERPT FROM

LOVE INSPIRED
INSPIRATIONAL ROMANCE

*When Mennonite midwife Beth Ann Overholt went to
Evergreen Corners to help rebuild after a flood, she
never expected to take in three abandoned children—
especially with an Amish bachelor by her side. But this
temporary family with Robert Yoder might just turn out
to be the perfect Christmas gift…*

Read on for a sneak preview of
An Amish Holiday Family
by Jo Ann Brown,
available November 2020 from Love Inspired!

"You don't ever complain. You take care of someone
else's *kinder* without hesitation, and you're giving them a
home they haven't had in who knows how long."

"Trust me. There was plenty of hesitation on my part."

"I do trust you."

Beth Ann's breath caught at the undercurrent of
emotion in his simple answer. "I'm glad to hear that. I got
a message from their social worker this afternoon. She
was supposed to come tomorrow, which is why I stayed
home today to make sure everything was as perfect as
possible before her visit."

"I wondered why you didn't come to the project house
today."

"That's why, but now her visit is going to be the day after tomorrow. What if she decides to take the children and place them in other homes? What if they can't be together?"

Robert paused and faced her. "Why are you looking for trouble? God brought you to the *kinder*. He knows what lies before them and before you. Trust *Him*."

"I try to." She gave him a wry grin. "It's just…just…"

"They've become important to you?"

She nodded, not trusting her voice to speak. The idea of the three youngsters being separated in the foster care system frightened her, because she wasn't sure what they might do to get back together.

"Don't forget," Robert murmured, "as important as they are to you, they're even more important to God." His smile returned. "How about getting some Christmas pie before we have to fish three *kinder* out of the brook?"

With a yelp, she rushed forward to keep Crystal from hoisting Tommy to see over the rail. Robert was right. She needed to enjoy the children while she could.

Don't miss
An Amish Holiday Family *by Jo Ann Brown,*
available November 2020 wherever
Love Inspired books and ebooks are sold.

LoveInspired.com

Love Harlequin romance?

DISCOVER.

Be the first to find out about promotions, news and exclusive content!

- **f** Facebook.com/HarlequinBooks
- Twitter.com/HarlequinBooks
- Instagram.com/HarlequinBooks
- Pinterest.com/HarlequinBooks

ReaderService.com

EXPLORE.

Sign up for the Harlequin e-newsletter and download a free book from any series at **TryHarlequin.com**

CONNECT.

Join our Harlequin community to share your thoughts and connect with other romance readers! **Facebook.com/groups/HarlequinConnection**